HIGH PRAISE I ✐ P9-CQZ-218

HOPE'S CAPTIVE

"If you love a Wild West adventure, filled with gritty evil villains and scarred characters that need each other to survive, then *Hope's Captive* will be one story you won't soon forget."
—Romance Junkies (Top Pick)

"Kate Lyon proves that she is worthy of standing up with the greats like Cassie Edwards and Johanna Lindsey with *Hope's Captive*. She is a wonderful author who knows how to tell a story and makes every moment worthwhile."
—Romance Readers at Heart

TIME'S CAPTIVE

"*Time's Captive* is one of those rare books that will grab you and not let go until you finish the last page."
—Romance Junkies

"Lyon weaves well-known history into a new legend."
—*RT BOOKclub*

"The author has done a fabulous job of research into this time in history. Her vivid descriptions pull the reader right into the scenes."
—A Romance Review

"*Time's Captive* captured my interest on page one and kept me riveted until the final, satisfying scene."
—*Romance Reviews Today*

"*Time's Captive* is sure to please all time-travel and Native American fans…. This is a dazzling start to Kate Lyon's career."
—Roundtable Reviews

"A well-written story that uses these tragedies to tell a wonderful tale of love and hope. Highly recommended."
—*The Historical Novels Review*

A LITTLE PROBLEM

"Ma'am, you're not plannin' to wear *that,* are you?" He tried to keep his voice neutral, but felt his lip curl as he looked her over. Her tight lips and annoyed glance would have warned him, even if he hadn't just seen the knife strapped to her thigh through the slit in the skirt.

"I am," Caroline said, and shoved an armful of blankets at him. "Is that a problem?"

"Yes, it is. We're not in Indian country yet, and until we are, the locals and other travelers will like us much better if you're not dressed like a heathen."

She turned on him with a look that would have fried hardtack. Her eyes burned an unholy midnight blue, her cheeks flushed a becoming pink and her lips, pressed into a tight frown, turned cherry red. She was already a beautiful woman, but her beauty flared in anger, hitting him like an axe handle across the chest, leaving him breathless.

Damnation, he thought, finally inhaling a steady breath. *I'm in big trouble.*

Too late he remembered that she was rumored to have been the wife of a Cheyenne chief, and he knew she was very good with a knife. Perhaps *heathen* hadn't been the best word to use.

Other books by Kate Lyon:

TIME'S CAPTIVE

HOPE'S CAPTIVE

KATE LYON

LEISURE BOOKS NEW YORK CITY

Dedicated to Vern.
For his patience and support,
his faith and love.
Blyxxe, baby.

A LEISURE BOOK®

January 2006

Published by

Dorchester Publishing Co., Inc.
200 Madison Avenue
New York, NY 10016

ISBN 0-8439-5626-7

The name "Leisure Books" and the stylized "L" with design are trademarks of Dorchester Publishing Co., Inc.

Printed in the United States of America.

Visit us on the web at www.dorchesterpub.com.

HOPE'S CAPTIVE

Prologue

Virginia
July, 1878

"Wake up, thief!"

A sharp jab to his ribs jarred Zach McCallister from the first sound sleep he'd enjoyed in weeks. His eyes snapped open and he tensed to spring, but not before he got another jab.

"Wake up, dammit, and get your stinkin' carcass out of my barn."

Zach launched himself out of the hay and slammed his attacker against the wall of the stall. His knife glinted dully against the man's neck.

How did this happen? No man had ever caught him off guard before. He had never allowed himself to sleep that deeply. Had he compromised his assignment? The consequences did not bear thinking about. The man had to die. So, why was he still breathing?

Some instinct, gut-deep, told him to wait. Something wasn't right.

"Zachariah?"

His gaze snapped to the man's face, breaking another cardinal rule: *Never look them in the eye.* The face glaring back at him was very nearly the same one he saw in the mirror every day.

Josh! Home! He was home. Sweet relief flowed through him, headier than the scent of fresh-cut hay that filled the barn. He hadn't lost his edge. Somehow, even sleeping like the dead, he had known he was home, and safe.

"You goin' to put that knife away or have you taken to killin' kin?"

Zach stared into his brother's face and his stomach clenched. He jerked the knife off the pulsing vein in Josh's neck. What kind of animal had he become?

"Hello, Josh." Zach turned away and slid the knife into its sheath.

"Hell. Some greetin' for the brother you haven't seen in two years." Josh shoved past him, jerking his shirt straight. "Sorry 'bout the pitchfork. Didn't recognize you." He cocked his head at the steel gray stallion devouring a pile of hay in the next stall. "Should have known it was you when I saw the lines on that horse. He's eatin' like he's never seen hay before."

"That's Demon. Thought he'd make a fine stud." Zach crouched and grabbed his bedroll, anything to keep Josh from noticing his reaction. He was lucky it was Josh who had found him sleeping so soundly. Under different circumstances, that stupid mistake could have cost him his life. He was expendable. He knew it and lived with the knowledge every day. If he failed, his senior officers would assign another man, someone more concerned about the assignment than finding Luke. He couldn't let that happen.

"How's Abby?" Zach asked, feeling Josh's gaze burning into his back.

Josh snorted and shoved his hands into his pockets. "Cranky woman. Don't know why she's still married to me."

"It isn't your charmin' personality." Zach tossed his bedroll onto a stack of hay bales in the corner, faced his brother and braced himself. Josh wasn't one to sidestep problems.

"What took you so long to get here?" Fists clenched, Josh glared at him.

Zach stood firm under the accusing glare. "They had to find me."

He shoved past Josh and headed for the open barn door, where the rosy glow of a clear summer dawn beckoned. He planted his hands on his hips and sucked in a deep breath of home. It burned all the way down. The old place looked good, despite the ravaging of both Union and Confederate troops. The house could use a coat of paint and he had never seen the pastures so naked. Still, it hadn't been razed and Josh had managed to keep the thieving carpetbaggers from stealing it for back taxes.

"The place is lookin' good." Zach kept his gaze focused outside the barn as Josh pivoted on his crutch and stumped up to stand beside him.

"Easy for you to say, not havin' to be here tendin' half-empty paddocks," Josh grumbled, shifting his weight onto the crutch.

"The leg botherin' you?" Zach asked, resisting the urge to kneel and examine the thigh-length stump.

"What's left of it?" Josh snorted. "Nah."

"You're lucky. Many men have been left a lot worse off."

"Probably left a few that way yourself."

Zach eyed his brother. "You got somethin' stuck in your craw, spit it out."

"Where you been?"

"Can't say."

"Can't or won't?"

"Both."

"Fine. Keep your damn secrets," Josh said, "but don't be surprised if you're too late."

Zach ignored the familiar rush of anger. He hated wasting precious time arguing with Josh over things they couldn't change, like the faces of the men he had killed for his country. The scent of the blood he had spilled clung to him like a dark cloud of shame.

He scraped his hands down his legs, then shoved them into his pockets. The war had been over for years now, as far as most folks knew, but it continued in every rill and hollow big enough to hide the monsters who fed off the country's strife. He would not burden his brother with the horrors he had known and the fear that dogged his every step. Nor could he share the names of the men, in high and low places, who risked their lives daily to protect Josh's freedom. He would not trust Josh with knowledge of the new organization the government had created but had yet to acknowledge, the organization that controlled Zach's movements.

Zach knew Josh suspected most of this and resented his silence. His brother hated being tied to the home place, despised himself for his injury, said the bullet that took his leg might as well have taken his life; it had left him less than a man.

The two of them could argue all day and end up just as convinced of their own opinions at the end of it. Zach suspected Josh argued for the love of it. Small wonder Abby was ornery. Ah, but she loved the stubborn cuss, almost as much as she loved Luke. Not for the first time, Zach realized that his son was more theirs than his.

His feelings for Josh were such a mishmash of love and guilt, there was no sorting them out. But the guilt had brought Zach riding hellbent for home the minute he got Josh's message. The assignment came second, although he was expected to put it first.

He picked up a rock, tossed it hard. Daylight was wasting. "When did Patricia run off?"

Josh snorted. "I'll never understand why you married that woman."

"When?" he asked, refusing to be goaded. If his

brother hadn't yet figured out why he had married Patricia, Zach wasn't about to enlighten him now.

"Same day I sent for you. Two months ago."

The words hit Zach like a blow to the chest. Two months! The trail was dead cold.

"You're sure they headed west?" His mind raced, recalling the maps of the West in his saddlebags. How could he ever find the boy now?

"Yup. All that no-good drifter could talk about was how he was goin' to make it big, homestead a thousand acres, raise cattle, get rich. Hell, all he did was talk and make eyes at your woman. Right quick, he convinced her to run off with him, not too difficult since she probably can't remember your face. We woke up one mornin' and they were gone. Luke and the two best horses with 'em."

"McCallister horseflesh will be easy to trace," Zach muttered. As would Patricia, whose lines were probably better than the horses'. When he caught up with that woman, she would regret stealing his son and putting this pain in Josh's eyes.

Josh scuffed his feet and squinted at the darkening sky. "I got word last week."

"What?" Zach's chest felt tight and his breath hung on his brother's answer. He waited, watching Josh choke back his emotions enough to speak in a raspy whisper.

"Indians got 'em. Soldiers found the drifter dead, staked out naked and shot full of arrows. Said it looked like he tried to save Patricia, but she was dead, too." He swallowed hard and squinted at the horizon.

"What about Luke?"

Josh's big shoulders lifted, then settled. "No sign of him." He cleared his throat, but Zach heard the tremor in his voice.

The boy might still be alive! Zach's jaw clenched and his fists tightened. He would not give up hope. Not until he had kicked over every rock in his path.

He squeezed Josh's shoulder. "I swear, if it's the last thing I do in this life, I'll find Luke and bring him home."

Chapter One

Dodge City, Kansas
September, 1878

Caroline Whitley hurried across town without hesitating at the invisible boundary that divided the decent citizens of Dodge City from the drunks, whores and gunmen who populated the other half of town. She paused outside the light streaming through the Alhambra Saloon's half-doors. She clutched the pouch hidden in the secret pocket of her full skirt and drew a deep breath. She could do this. After the hell of life as a Kiowa captive, this would be easy as catching a lame horse. She had to do it. The Cheyenne needed her help.

Face your enemy with pride. The words of Little Wolf rang in her ears. She raised her chin and stood tall, as he had taught her. *Never let them smell your fear.*

She took a deep breath, then pushed through the swinging doors and stood blinking in the sudden brightness. The tinny patter of a piano off to her left combined with the long, slow beats of her heart, muffling the shouts and curses of the men seated around small round tables playing cards or standing along the high, wooden counter straight ahead. A gray, smoky haze hung over the place, making her eyes tear, and the acrid stench of unwashed bodies nearly gagged her.

A half-naked woman wrapped around a scrawny man at the counter turned and stared. Instinctively, Caroline patted the hair over her left ear. The woman nudged her companion and whispered something that made him whip around. Caroline stared as his hand dipped into the woman's corset, which was cinched so tight that her sagging breasts spilled out the top like over-ripe bread dough. Her black stockings revealed more of her flabby legs than they covered. Her face, with its harshly rouged cheeks and lips, seemed garish in the bright light of the chandelier overhead.

Ah, Caroline thought, *this is a whore.* Her own dress covered her from neck to toe and she had never painted her face. So why did the townspeople call her by the same name they gave this woman, a woman who let men use her body for money?

The noise from the piano stopped and Caroline suddenly felt the men's silent stares like hands upon her flesh. Panic rippled through her, stealing her strength.

"Stinkin' squaw," someone growled from her right. The title echoed across the room.

Don't show your fear. Realizing she should not have let the painted woman distract her, Caroline raised her chin and ignored their stares. She searched the room, seeking a man she could trust, but found only hatred and suspicion in each face. Her gaze slid over three men seated at a poker table at the back of the room, and paused on the fourth.

Though his low hat brim shadowed his features, his gaze caught hers. His eyes and face kept his secrets. He sat with his back to the wall. Smart. Cautious. From there he could see the entire room. No one could get the drop on him. He wore faded black, no bright colors, nothing to mark his appearance or draw attention, yet she would have noticed him anywhere.

"Cheyenne whore," the man closest to her snarled. Then he spat. His spittle hit the skirt of her new blue dimity dress, leaving a dark, spreading stain.

She pressed her hand over the knife strapped to her thigh, and fought down the urge to strike out at him. So he'd ruined her new dress; he hadn't drawn blood. It didn't matter. All that mattered was getting the wagon full of blankets and medicine to Little Wolf and his people before more of them died.

"Whatcha want, squaw?" the scrawny runt at the high

counter bellowed as he fondled the whore's breast. "You fixin' to join up with the other whores?" His gaze slid to her own chest, then lower. He licked his lips and grinned, revealing rotting teeth. Caroline's stomach pitched.

She waited for the laughter to die down. "I need a guide."

"I kin take ya where ya wanna go, squaw," a deep voice drawled. "I'll ride ya better than ole Little Wolf ever did."

Guffaws and more filthy comments followed. Caroline shot the ugly brute a knowing glance. She recognized his type by the look in his squinty, wide-set eyes—mean-spirited and cruel to anyone weaker than himself, but a sniveling coward when faced with a man like Little Wolf.

Foolishly, she had expected better. She had hoped to find an honest man. She had no choice now. There was only one way she was going to find someone to help her.

"I can pay," she cried, and held the pouch of gold over her head.

Every voice fell silent. Greedy eyes fixed on the pouch. Caroline turned, seeking the man in the corner. A wary stillness had come over him. One hand below the table, he met her questioning gaze straight on, then something in his eyes changed. He looked away.

Disappointment stabbed through her, but she turned back to the other men. Their hungry expressions made her tense, wary.

Have I overplayed my hand? she asked herself. Too late to change her mind now.

"Why, I'd be right proud to help you, ma'am," the scrawny man piped up, and shoved the whore away. He jabbed an elbow into the man beside him and started across the saloon. "Me and my two compadres here would be right happy to take you wherever you wanna go."

She ignored the snickers that followed his offer, well aware of the double meaning in his words. The rest of the men turned their backs, resuming their card play. There were no other takers.

"Fine." She tucked the pouch back into the secret

pocket, aware that the scrawny one followed her movements closely. "Come with me." She glanced once more at the man in the corner.

He stared back, a warning in his gaze that she intended to heed.

Damn! Zach took a long swig of his watered-down beer and picked up his cards. He hadn't expected her to be beautiful. Her blond hair had blazed like a beacon among the dirt browns and faded grays of the saloon. He frowned. For the first time, he questioned his plan to use her to get into Little Wolf's camp where a young, blond boy had been seen. He scowled at his cards. He was close. He felt it in his bones, but he had to move fast. Sick, dying, the Cheyenne were desperate and bound to flee the reservation any day now, and then all hell would break loose. He'd fought in the war, and knew that in the heat of battle soldiers didn't always shoot straight. And some of them didn't try. He had to find Luke soon. This woman was his best chance to get into the camp. He'd work this group for a little more information, then decide whether to take a chance on her.

"Who was that fool woman?" he asked, throwing out his losing cards and taking three more from the dealer.

"Didn't you listen, mister? She's Little Wolf's squaw."

"Little Wolf?" Zach hated to play dumb, but he needed more information.

The talker, a drifter on Zach's right, shook his head. "Where you been hidin'?"

"Just arrived from back east," Zach said. A half-truth, but as much as the man needed to know. "Is this Little Wolf one of those Sioux they write about in the dime novels?"

"Sioux?" The quiet man on Zach's left, probably a farmer, shook his head and added his money to the pile in the middle of the table. "He's a no-good, murderin' Cheyenne. Old Man Chief, they call him."

"I thought they were captured, put on the reservation."

The big, sullen man across from Zach joined in. "They don't like the place, but the guvermint won' let 'em go back north. Don' want 'em too close to ole Red Cloud and Sittin' Bull. But the Panther, he ain' likely to stay on the reservation much longer."

"The Panther?" Zach wasn't pretending the surprise in his voice. He'd been investigating Little Wolf's band for months and had never heard the nickname. Was it something new? Had desperation turned the man brutal? "You mean they could break from the reservation, head this way?"

"Why d'ya think his squaw wants a guide? I'm bettin' they got a ron-day-voo planned."

Zach looked from man to man. "You don't think . . . ?" The pretense stuck in his craw, but he didn't want any suspicious followers when he left. They waited for him to play. He saw, then raised. Two damned kings. Why did Lady Luck choose tonight to smile on him?

"Shi-it," the big man sneered. "You better pay closer attention to the goin's on, mister. Out here ignerance kin cost a man his life."

Well said, Zach thought. "What's her name?"

"Whudda ya wanna know that fer?" the drifter asked. "Her name's 'Squaw' or 'Whore,' whichever one ya like." He threw down his money with a smug grin.

"Caroline Whitley," the farmer said quietly.

"You know her?" Zach pushed. He'd been told the man knew Caroline Whitley, and he'd waited several days for him to come to town.

"We traveled in the same wagon train. Her folks' wagon broke down. We had to leave 'em behind." He squirmed in his seat as he studied his cards. "Couldn't hold up the whole train fer one broken axle. When they didn't catch up after three days, we went lookin' fer 'em."

"What happened?" Zach prodded.

"We found her father and brother tied to the wheels. Their eyelids were cut off so's they had to watch. Afterward, they'd been shot full of burning arrows." The man gulped his beer.

"Watch what?" Zach felt no remorse for pushing the man. He'd roast him alive if it would help find his son.

"Caroline's mother died under them ruttin' heathens, then they mutilated her body. There warn't no sign o' Caroline, just a torn-up place in the grass where they'd used her, and bits and pieces of her clothes."

Greasy bile rose in Zach's throat. The man's words reminded him of another, similar site. He hated what Patricia had done, but he would not have wished the death she had suffered—the same as Caroline's mother—on anyone. When he had found the place where she died, for the first time in his life, despite the horrors he had witnessed in the war, he had been physically ill. He drew a deep breath, hating the empty hole the experience had left inside him. The fear that had dogged him every day since hit him again. If those animals could do that to a woman as beautiful as Patricia, what would they do to a child?

The last man at the table called. Silently, they all began throwing down their cards.

"How did she end up back here?" Zach persisted, pulling his thoughts back to the present. He needed more. Something he could use to get close to her.

"White Bear, the Kiowa chief what killed her folks, musta liked her. He kep' her fer himself. Then one day he purt near beat her to death in front of some Comanch' medicine woman, a friend of Little Wolf's. White Bear woulda beat the medicine woman too fer stoppin' him, but her man, a Comanch' war chief, wouldn't let him. The way I heerd it, Little Wolf stopped a fight 'tween White Bear and the war chief by buyin' Caroline from White Bear."

Zach's fingers tightened around his cards. His heart started pounding. He was close. Very close. His plan would work. He'd play on Caroline's vulnerability, get close to her, make her trust him. She'd take him right to

Little Wolf, and vouch for him, too. But before he put his life in her hands, he needed an answer to one more question. "Why did Little Wolf give her up?"

"Caroline says he wouldn't let her stay with 'em on the reservation. Sent her here to her uncle. Wanted her to be safe. Her uncle owns the hardware store down the street. Heard tell she owns part, too. Her pa's part."

All the pieces of the puzzle that was Caroline Whitley slid into place in Zach's head. The last few days he'd watched the townspeople trample her pride. Only desperation could have made her walk into this saloon tonight. The sheriff, Bat Masterson, a hard-nosed ex-soldier, wouldn't have lifted a finger to help her. She'd probably begged everything she could get from that hardware store, but she couldn't take it to Little Wolf without help. Desperate people made mistakes, sure as the cards smiling up at him.

"Two kings." He threw down his cards and let the men figure out that he'd won. Again. He raked in his winnings and pushed away from the table. "Thank you for your generosity. Deal me out."

"The hell you say," growled the big man. His eyes narrowed on Zach's cards. "You been sittin' here takin' our money real regular-like. Seems to me you owe us a chance to git sum o' our own back."

Damn. He should have folded. He'd been so busy prying information out of the farmer, he'd missed the threat in the other man. He eased away from the table, his hand hovering over his pistol butt.

"Mebbe you oughta think this over," the drifter stammered. " 'Pears to me he won fair an' square."

Caroline's "friend" shoved away from the table. "Don't want no part of this."

Zach stared into his opponent's eyes, shutting out everything else. "I didn't come in here lookin' for trouble, but I never run from it when I find it."

"Well, run from this if you can." The man reached for his gun. His fingers never touched metal. Zach's Colt barked once. The man jerked. His eyes opened wide. Then he slumped in his chair as blood oozed from a small hole in his chest.

"Damn!"

"Taaar-nation."

"You see that?" Excited whispers ricocheted around him. Zach ignored the men's admiring, yet slightly fearful stares. Keeping his back to the wall, he edged toward the rear door, a thin line of smoke rising from the business end of his pistol.

Sheriff Masterson pushed through the saloon doors and stood, his hands hovering over two ivory-handled revolvers in a heavy belt, staring around the room. Zach swore under his breath. He'd kept a low profile since coming to town, not wanting to draw the attention of the infamous lawman.

"Self-defense, sheriff!" Zach recognized the voice of Caroline's friend. The man had a knack for cowering in the bushes, then telling tales afterward. All talk, no substance. Zach holstered his pistol and met the sheriff's keen stare calmly, not surprised that the man's cold, gray-blue eyes narrowed, seeing what most men missed.

"You leaving town tonight?"

Zach knew Masterson wasn't asking. "This minute."

"Don't take too long packing."

"Not planning to," Zach promised. He left by the front door, moving slowly and keeping an eye on the other two men at his table, feeling every stare like a spider scrambling up his spine. After shoving through the swinging front doors, he paused to let his eyes adjust to the dark, then searched both sides of the street.

Where could she have gone?

He started toward the hardware store, but a woman's scream, muffled, spun him toward the alley.

Damn, he muttered. Was she in trouble already?

Caroline screamed in fury as the scrawny runt slammed her wrist against the wall behind her. Her knife flew from her numb fingers. More concerned with watching to see where the knife landed, she let him knee her legs apart, then she rammed her own knee into his groin.

"Gawd damn!" he cursed, and stumbled away from her. Before she could get away, his friends jumped in to replace him. She fought them, kicking, scratching, biting, but she was losing. Their hands were everywhere, but mostly they pawed up and down her legs. What would they do to her when they found the gold?

"Get off me, you filthy scavengers." She couldn't let them have it. She bucked and twisted, but they stuck to her like ticks.

"Hold . . . her . . . still," the runt panted. He pulled his knife, twisting it from side to side in front of her face as he glared at her through pain-glazed eyes. "I've got a present for her."

"The lady isn't interested." A deep voice rang through the alley.

The men holding her froze. Caroline broke loose and threw herself toward her knife. She came up in a crouch, knife in hand.

"You fools!" the runt shouted. "Don't let her git away."

"But, Zeke. . . . Ah cain't handle that hellcat alone."

"Don't you sass me. Git her."

"You think that hellcat's a handful of trouble?" The newcomer asked, then paused, as if giving each man time to consider his question. "You don't want the kind of trouble I can give you."

Caroline kept her attention on her attackers, her knife arm swinging loosely. "I can handle this, mister."

"Yes, ma'am. You were handlin' things very well," the stranger mocked. "So well that these *gentlemen* were about to give you more than you bargained for in there." He jerked his head toward the saloon.

The man's smooth drawl gave him away. What was a southern gentleman doing in the alleys of Dodge City? "What do you want, mister?"

"We're the ones what dun accepted her offer, mister." Zeke had caught his breath. "Butt out."

"I've reconsidered her offer," came the smooth, untroubled answer.

"Git! Or I'll make you sorry! We got here first and we ain't sharin'."

The stranger strode closer to Zeke.

"Go away!" Caroline shouted. "You're either the craziest fool I've ever met or greedier than all three of these idiots lumped together." Either way, she didn't need his help. She could handle things now.

"Look out!" His warning came just in time. Caroline ducked and whirled aside as one of Zeke's friends leaped at her back. She swung her knife at him as she turned and felt the blade sink deep. When she yanked it free, he screamed. Breathing hard, she put her back to the wall of the saloon and watched the third man, her knife poised.

Zeke had made the most of the confusion and attacked the stranger. The two men were locked together, straining for control of Zeke's knife. She should run, but they blocked the mouth of the alley. The third man stood between her and the other end. She couldn't get out.

There was a loud crack. Zeke screamed and fell to his knees, clutching his arm to his chest, his wrist dangling at an odd angle. The third man bolted out the back of the alley, abandoning his injured friends.

The stranger stepped around Zeke, placing his big body between her and danger. "You all right, ma'am?"

Still wary, Caroline stiffened, knife poised. "I'm fine." She nodded to the man in the dirt. "He's not."

"No more than he deserves." The stranger knelt and poked at the man's chest. "Flesh wound." He looked up at her and smiled. She caught the gleam of sparkling white teeth and the flash of a deep dimple in his cheek and her breath hitched. The devil had less charm. "Next time, don't bend your wrist and thrust harder."

"I will." She wiped her blade on the injured man's shirt, then yanked up the far side of her skirt and sheathed the knife. She caught the stranger's raised eyebrow and yanked the skirt down. "Well? What are you waiting for? They're gone. If you think I'm going to thank you. . . ."

"What will you do now?"

"Hire another guide," she bluffed, praying her voice wouldn't crack and betray her. She'd been a fool to seek an honest man in a saloon, but time and circumstance had limited her options.

"May I offer my services?"

"What?" She barely noticed Zeke shuffling out of the alley behind the stranger. "If you were interested, why didn't you speak up in there? You would have saved us both a lot of trouble."

"You're right, and I feel responsible for your present predicament."

"And what might that be?" He was too smooth. She didn't trust him, but she had to admit, she'd trade him for those other three rats any day. She stepped closer and squinted to see his face better.

"If I'd spoken up, you wouldn't have been in this alley defending your honor."

"Do you have trouble hearing, mister? I don't have any honor to defend."

"I hear very well, ma'am, but facts are facts. I put you in jeopardy. I must make amends."

"Mister, you talk like your mouth's full of shaving soap. What do you think you can do to help me? I need a guide, not a preacher. Do you even know what direction you're facing right now?"

The stranger stepped closer, close enough that she saw a dangerous glint in his cool gray eyes. Most considered her tall for a woman, but her nose barely came to his collarbone. This close she had to tip her head clear back to get a good look underneath that black hat brim, and with a day's bristle on his jaw, his face was mostly shadow. He didn't radiate menace, like some men who were just plain mean for the fun of it, but his penetrating gaze and the width of his chest would give most men pause, along with every woman.

Without a doubt, this man could handle himself, and most anything he came afoul of. She felt herself begin to relax and jerked up short. Just because she liked what she saw didn't mean she could trust him.

"I've scouted the trails in this area recently and I did a lot of trackin' in the war. And, yes, I know that Little Wolf is your husband. The Cheyenne are unhappy on the reservation; they're dyin' of malaria and dysentery by the hundreds. The agency doctor has run out of quinine and there are so many sick that he can't treat them anymore. Little Wolf's been pleadin' to be allowed to return north with the ones who're still alive, but Agent Miles won't let him. The Army's called in a special unit of cavalry to keep the Cheyenne on the reservation, but Little Wolf is expected to break out any day now, on foot, with almost two hundred women and children and less than a hundred men to defend them. So if you plan to get to him before he does somethin' stupid, you'd better make up your mind. We could leave tonight."

Caroline's heart sank. He made it sound so hopeless, but Little Wolf was a dedicated, determined man, devoted to his people. He would do what he must to protect the Cheyenne, even if it meant making a run for it. After rescuing her from White Bear, he'd taken the people out on the range for the summer hunt and they'd missed the Custer fight. But he'd led his Elks and the Dog Soldiers into the fighting afterward. He'd taken six bullets in that fight but even that had not slowed him down. He'd led the survivors, eluding the pursuing Army, and only stopped to parlay when his people could go no farther. His mistake was letting Morning Star—Dull Knife to the whites—talk him into surrendering at Red Cloud. But first, he'd sent her back to her family in Dodge City where she'd be safe. Hah! She hadn't felt safe since. Even so, if there was a man alive who could accomplish the impossible, it was Little Wolf.

"How do you know so much about my husband's doings?" She hated lying to this man, but he'd no doubt already heard from someone in town that she was Little Wolf's wife. Maintaining the pretext made her feel safer, and would keep him from accosting her once they were alone on the prairie, miles from any town. She hoped.

"The whole town is talkin' about it."

"And not one person has offered to help. Why you?"

"Why not me?" He pulled off his hat and raked his fingers through dark hair that he wore short on the sides, longer and waving on the top. "You don't have much choice, ma'am. You want to get to the Cheyenne and I can get you there. What more do you need to know?"

He wasn't telling her everything. Was he after the Cheyenne for his own reasons? His drawl labeled him a southerner. A rebel. Just like Little Wolf. He stood with his hands pressed against his thighs while she considered. Why was he so tense? What was he hiding? Could she find someone else? Did she want to? She liked the way he'd handled Zeke and his friends. And, having been in the war, he was accustomed to hardship. He wouldn't fold on her halfway to Oklahoma.

"Ma'am," he said earnestly, "I mean you no harm."

No, he didn't. That much she knew—though she couldn't say how—but she didn't want to bring more trouble to the Cheyenne. She sighed and smoothed her rumpled dress. She didn't have a choice. It was him or nothing. She'd never be able to drive the wagon a full day. A woman wasn't safe alone on the trail—even one who could shoot most anything, use a knife as well as most warriors, and ride a mule sideways. He'd show his hand sooner or later, she reasoned, and she felt safer with him than with those other three sidewinders.

"Fine." She pushed past him, heading for the street. "We leave in one hour. Meet me at the livery stable at the west end of town." She pulled the heavy pouch from her skirt pocket as she walked. "I'll pay you half now. . . ."

"No need, ma'am. I trust you."

She dropped the pouch back into its pocket and faced

him, eyes narrowed, hands on her hips. "Half pay up-front is customary. Yet you don't want my money. Why not?"

He'd tensed, but he wasn't offering her an explanation. She cocked her head, remembering that he'd been playing poker. Hadn't she heard a gunshot just before those three oafs jumped her? "Ah," she said. "You won, but your friends questioned your integrity?"

"A sore loser," he admitted with a shrug. "I promised the sheriff I would be leavin' town tonight."

"All right," she said, "I'll pay you what I think is fair when you get me to the reservation. But I promise you, if any harm comes to the Cheyenne because of you, Little Wolf will not rest until your hair flies from his scalp pole."

His gaze burned her back as she walked away.

She reached up, patted her hair into place over her left ear, and smiled. At last, she'd found the right man for the job.

Chapter Two

Soft chanting rose to the tipi's smoke hole, lifted on the breath of sweet sage smoke. From where he sat behind the small altar, Little Wolf watched it rise from the fire. He smoothed it over his face, then blew it upward, letting the sage clear his mind and strengthen his soul. He puffed the waiting pipe alight and offered it upward.

"Great *Heammawihio*, Wise One Above, your people are poor and in need. Watch over us this night. Make our footsteps silent and sure, and hide us from the eyes of our enemies.

"*Aktuno'wihio*, Great Power Below," he prayed, offering smoke to the earth, "swallow the sound of our passing and make the ground beneath our feet firm and smooth."

He offered the pipe to the four winds—first to the

south, then east, north and west. "Carry news of our journey to our brothers, that they may help us if they are able, and keep our way secret from those who will seek to stop us."

Finally, Little Wolf drew deeply on the pipe and held the smoke inside until it burned in his chest like the anger that burned in his heart. Long before his people started dying on this hated land, they had lived free and roamed the land at will. No more. Forced to surrender, they had struggled to find their place, their hearts always longing for the sweet grass and singing waters of the Powder River. But the white man, too, saw the land's beauty and reached out to take it in his greed, forcing the Cheyenne to wander and to beg for shelter in strange lands among people who did not welcome them. His anger burned brighter as he thought of the lying *veho*, the white men his people called spiders, men who broke their word like a woman breaks a stick.

Here at the Darlington agency, among their southern relatives, his people had begun to die—slowly at first, then with frightening speed. The *veho* doctor had no medicine to give them; so many became sick with the fainting sickness, malaria, that the doctor stopped coming. So many voices stilled; so many hearts on the ground.

But these deaths were not enough for the *veho*. When Little Wolf begged to take his people away from this sickness and trouble, Agent Miles, the Little Father, refused. To punish Little Wolf, who would not promise to stay, he starved the people, giving only one scrawny cow at each passing of the moon to feed a whole family. On the promised buffalo hunt, Cheyenne warriors found only dry grass, for the buffalo were gone, destroyed by *veho* hunters greedy for the money men paid for hides and tongues. Worse, *veho* soldiers brought their enemies, the Crow, onto Cheyenne hunting grounds, a thing unheard of in many lifetimes.

For too many moons, Little Wolf had ignored the an-

gry voice in his head and told his people to do the same.
But no more would he listen to *veho* lies. Tonight, he let
the voice rage inside him while he added more grass to
the fire. The cloud of smoke surrounded him where he
sat behind the altar with the pipe resting across his bent
legs. He let his head fall back and closed his eyes. The
chanting grew louder and smoke from the fire joined the
pipe smoke to dance around his body, warming his chest,
arms, face and legs, drawing his spirit upward through
the smoke hole and into the night air.

Silently he glided on the wings of the breeze toward his
enemies, whose big guns squatted on the hills around the
camp like so many fat black toads. His anger raged as he
circled each *veho*, stinging his enemy's eyes and fogging
his brain, leaving a shadow that dimmed his sight.

As he rode the wind around the camp from south to
east, Little Wolf saw shadows slip from each tipi below,
one by one, as he had told them, running north. The familiar shapes of his wives and daughter melted into the
darkness. The moon's face smiled only on tipis glowing
soft in the dark. The wide eyes of the soldiers looked but
saw nothing.

With a weary sigh, Little Wolf settled back at his altar,
picked up his pipe and smoked. In the smoke he
searched for his memory of *Heammawihio*'s messenger.
Again, he watched her face as he asked her what lay
ahead for his people. As always, the pain in her eyes as
she spoke ripped through him. But her hard words,
though they promised much pain and sorrow, made his
heart soar.

"*What would you like to know?* she had asked him in a
sorrow-filled voice. "*How many of your people will die, how
much you will suffer, or simply that—in the end—you will be allowed to live where you wish?*"

She had said no more, but her sorrow had told much.
And her words had been true. His people had died—in
battle at the Washita, on the march south from their
beloved Powder River country, and in the bogs of the

hated reservation where the Little Father would have them make their homes. More Cheyenne would die before the end came, but because of her words, hope lived at the end of their journey. Because of her words, his people, the *Tsitsitas*, ran tonight with nothing but the little they could carry on their backs. They ran, hoping that before the end came, they would see their beloved homeland once more.

The anguished face of the messenger faded into the yellow hair and smiling blue eyes of another woman, the *veho* woman whom he loved like a sister. Caroline. Little Wolf frowned at the image. He had sent her back to her white family so that she would be safe. Why did her thoughts turn to him now? Was she unhappy? Had she been unable to find a man to love her? He had taken her to his tipi to keep her safe from his people, but he feared her own would despise her, thinking she had shared his furs. They would not believe her if she told them the truth. Had she heard of the Cheyenne's troubles? He pulled his blanket closer around him as his concern for her grew.

Suddenly, a man appeared in the smoke behind Caroline's image—a man whose piercing gray eyes tried to penetrate the smoke. The man stood close, but did not touch her, and Caroline did not shy away from him.

Little Wolf's eyes narrowed. Could this be the man he had seen standing beside her in the mist of days to come? He stared into the man's eyes and sensed his strength and purpose. This man sought the *Tsitsitas* and would use Caroline to find them. Little Wolf whispered a quick prayer for her safety and stood, shaking the blanket off his shoulders, driven by a sudden need for action. He could not guide Caroline now, but when trouble came, if she needed him, he would be there.

These thoughts were for another time, ahead in the troubled days to come. He must keep his thoughts on this night, stay calm and move swift and silent as the snake in the grass. He knelt and banked the fire, tossed more sweet grass on it. Again, he wrapped himself in smoke and slipped out of the tipi.

Beneath the unseeing eyes of the soldiers on the ridge above, he strode from the camp. The *veho* could eat their empty promises. He was taking the *Tsitsitas* home.

"What's wrong?" Zach stopped in the act of swinging his saddle onto the wagon. Caroline had straightened abruptly and stood staring into the dark street beyond the stable door.

She remained alert, searching the street. "I thought . . . it feels like we're being watched."

Zach stepped up behind her and followed her gaze. Still and tense, they stared into the darkness. He knew why she'd frozen like a rabbit scenting a fox. He smelled smoke and burning sage, but he saw nothing nearby and none of the nearby chimneys were smoking. The street was deserted, the town quiet. The hair on the back of his neck stood on end, then suddenly, the smell faded, leaving the two of them alone.

Caroline stepped away from him. "Whatever it was, it's gone now."

"And that's where we need to be, before the sheriff backs up his suggestion with buckshot."

"Oh, he doesn't use buckshot." Caroline glanced over her shoulder, smiling innocently. "He carries a Winchester."

"I hadn't noticed," Zach said, rubbing an old wound with a grimace as memories of battle threatened. He found himself staring at Caroline's buckskins. When he'd arrived at the livery stable, he'd been surprised by her attire. A white woman in buckskins was sure to draw attention everywhere they went, and the last thing they needed was attention. He'd been so preoccupied deciding how to initiate a discussion about it, that he hadn't looked at her getup closely. Now he wished he hadn't. The more he saw, the less he liked it.

The top, a kind of tunic, tied at her shoulders and fell

to her hips, with slits in the bottom at the sides, fringed seams and wide sleeves, also fringed. The skirt, cut off at mid-calf, fit loose everywhere but across the hips, where it strained whenever she bent or knelt or breathed heavily. Long fringe adorned the hem, apparently to make up for its lack in length. On her feet, she wore a pair of nicely beaded, calf-high moccasins—the only part of the outfit he liked. It was the perfect thing to wear to dinner with a Cheyenne chief, but on the trail they were sure to run into cowboys, ranchers, even soldiers. One look at her and they'd have a hand on their pistols and a leer on their faces.

"Ma'am, you're not plannin' to wear *that*, are you?" He tried to keep his voice neutral, but felt his lip curl as he looked her over. Her tight lips and annoyed glance would have warned him, even if he hadn't just seen the knife strapped to her thigh through the slit in the skirt.

"I am," Caroline said, and shoved an armful of blankets at him. "Is that a problem?"

"Yes, it is." Zach dropped the blankets to the side. Until they finished "discussing" her choice of clothing, he wanted to be able to duck if she took a swing at him, or dodge a kick if she didn't like what he was about to say. She looked like a woman who punctuated her conversation.

"My buckskins are more comfortable when I'm driving a wagon." She frowned at him, then picked up the blankets he'd dropped.

"*I* will be drivin' the wagon." Zach refused the blankets she again shoved at him.

"And how will you do that and scout at the same time?" She pushed past him and put the blankets on the wagon herself, while he frowned at her back.

"We're not in Indian country yet, and until we are, the locals and other travelers will like us much better if you're not dressed like a heathen."

She turned on him with a look that would have fried hardtack. Her eyes burned an unholy midnight blue, her cheeks flushed a becoming pink and her lips, pressed into a tight frown, turned cherry red. She was already a beautiful woman, but her beauty flared in anger, hitting him like an ax handle across the chest, leaving him breathless.

Damnation, he thought, finally inhaling a steady breath. *I'm in big trouble.*

Too late he remembered that she was rumored to be the wife of a Cheyenne chief, and he knew she was very good with a knife. Perhaps *heathen* hadn't been the best word to use. "I mean, we don't want to draw attention."

She stepped close, hands on her hips. "Let's get something straight right now, mister. I'm running this outfit. You do what I tell you and we'll get along fine."

Zach took a quick step backward. "You've hired me to protect you, ma'am. How can I do that if you won't follow my advice?"

Caroline again closed the distance between them. She leaned forward, her nose pointing upward into his face. "We haven't even hit the trail yet, and already I'm sick of listening to you talk, talk, talk. Didn't you hear the men in the saloon earlier? I am not a lady," she said, emphasizing each word. "You do not have to 'ma'am' me. Don't sashay around me like you're escorting me to afternoon tea. Don't assist me, unless it's to provide cover if we come upon trouble or maybe share your ammunition. Do I make myself clear?"

Zach glared down his nose at her, insulted to the toes of his boots, but determined not to lose control. He forced a smile. "I never sashay, ma'am. I'm sorry my manners offend you, but my father beat them into me so you'd best get used to them. Despite your unfortunate circumstances, I am a gentleman and you will always be a lady to me. Now, if you will step into one of these stalls, I promise to remain a gentleman and not look while you change into somethin' more appropriate."

"Mister—"

"Zach," he inserted, trying hard not to shout.

"—you can stand there with your back turned until the cock crows, but I plan to climb onto that wagon—by myself—and get out of this town." She grabbed hold of the wagon and prepared to do exactly that, but turned back to him, this time shaking a finger in his face. "Cut your silly speeches short. Keep it simple and we'll get along fine."

Zach slapped her finger out of his face. By God, he'd give her short. "Take off the buckskins."

"You'll have to cut them off me."

"Fine."

"You wouldn't dare!" Blue eyes narrowed, she jutted her stubborn chin at him again.

No one, not even his brother, who was bigger by at least twenty pounds and had arms like a gorilla, had ever dared to defy him. Blood boiling, Zach fought the urge to throw her over his knee and paddle her buckskin-clad bottom. He took off his jacket, unbuttoned his shirt cuffs and rolled up the sleeves. Once she saw he was serious, she'd back down. He didn't want to cut off her buckskins and had no idea why he'd challenged her, but he wouldn't back down now.

"I warn you," he said, "there won't be much left when I'm done." He reached for the knife at his waist.

Caroline backed away, her eyes growing wider. "Touch one corner and you'll come away bloody," she warned and reached behind her back.

Damnation! Zach swore, remembering the knife he'd spotted tied to her thigh. Did she have one hidden at her back, too? Steel flashed in her hand and he reacted by pushing her into a pile of hay before she could use it. He grabbed her arm and pulled it to the side, then trapped her underneath him until he could disarm her. The air in her chest whooshed out as he shoved her knife hand into the hay above her head and squeezed her wrist until she released the weapon. He flipped the knife into the air, caught it by the blade and threw it at the wall above their heads, where it stuck, quivering.

He stared into Caroline's stunned face. "I prefer to do things the easy way, but I'm up for hard."

"Get off me, you sidewinder!" She shoved at his shoulders, but he didn't budge.

"Take them off." He pretended to reach for his knife.

"All right!"

Savoring his victory, he stayed where he was, admiring the close view of Caroline mad, with golden sparks in her deep blue eyes, cheeks stained pink, and lips ripe and moist as fresh-picked berries.

Something sharp pricked his side. Startled, his gaze flew back to her eyes, which had cooled to ice-blue shards. She'd gone pale and her lips barely moved as she whispered, "Get off. Now."

Moving only his head, Zach glanced down his body and found the source of the pain. She held the knife, its tip sunk into his side. Fresh blood trickled from the wound. If he moved too fast or in the wrong direction, he'd be gutted. He turned back, prepared to offer an apology and realized she was terrified. Of him. His gut clenched.

"I may be wrong," he said, glaring down at her, "but isn't it a little extreme to stab someone for thinking about stealin' a kiss?" He winced as the knife slid deeper. "You're right. I forgot that you're a married woman. I apologize."

Blood rushed into his face. He'd never treated a woman so badly. Back home, he was renowned for his cool control with women. He'd never let lust overcome his common sense. Stupid, stupid move.

"Remove it." He smiled at her in what he hoped was a conciliatory manner. "Please."

She jerked the knife tip out of his side. He winced, feeling blood ooze in its wake. Quickly, he rose and extended a hand to help her up.

She slapped his knife into his palm and got to her feet while he stared at the blood on the blade. His blood. He felt suddenly cold.

"I told you," she said, "I don't need your help." She shoved past him, swiping hay off her backside.

He stared after her, dumbstruck. His circumstances couldn't be worse. He was about to leave the only town within hundreds of miles with a woman he couldn't control. He must be insane.

Suddenly, Luke's face rose in his mind and he cursed himself all over again. How could he have forgotten? He needed this woman to find his son; he had to win her trust. He bunched his shirt and pressed it over his wound to stop the bleeding. He'd known her less than two hours and had already annoyed her enough to stab him. He grimaced. It was not a promising start.

"We'd better get moving," Caroline said, as she stuffed the last blanket into the wagon. "It'll be daylight soon." Still wearing the buckskins, she climbed onto the high seat and snapped the reins.

Zach blinked at the flash of bare thigh and sighed. He'd better get used to her buckskins. He hoped there was no one but Indians where they were headed.

Caroline gripped the reins tight, struggling to stop the tremors wracking her body. *It's not fear,* she told herself. *No, it's panic.* The man had tossed her in the hay and stared at her lips. So what if he'd looked like he wanted to eat her? He hadn't torn off her clothes, whipped her until she bled, then rammed himself into her from behind like she was a bitch in heat. He was not White Bear.

He *said* he was a gentleman from Virginia, and his soft drawl and polite ways bore that out. But anyone could fake an accent and put on fancy airs. Until she knew more about him, she'd have to stay alert and be wary.

His behavior shouldn't have surprised her. She'd told him herself that she was no lady, and if he'd been in Dodge City long he'd have heard the gossip about her. Still, she'd hoped he was a better sort of man. After his timely rescue in the alley, she'd expected better from him than a sloppy kiss and a fumble in the hay. He'd said he knew how to treat a lady, and she'd translated that to mean that he knew enough to keep his hands to himself.

She should have trusted her instincts and been on her guard. Although his speech and manners labeled him a gentleman, he had a ruthless edge to him, a dangerous, dark side that she shouldn't have ignored. Behind those cool gray eyes, a predator lurked. That edge assured her that he had the skills to protect her. But could she protect herself from him?

Their argument hadn't been solely his fault, but he shouldn't have threatened to strip her, or thrown her down in the hay. Her darned stubborn pride, that damnable need to always be in charge, had gotten her in trouble again. Why couldn't she learn to compromise a little, discuss problems instead of jumping to conclusions and overreacting? Sticking his knife in his side had really been too much.

Her knife! She'd forgotten her knife. She hauled back on the reins, feeling suddenly bereft, naked. She had to get her knife.

He rode up beside the wagon, reined his horse close and extended his hand. He was holding her knife.

Relief washed over her and she snatched it from him, but waited until he'd ridden on before sliding it into the sheath at the small of her back. The warm blade touched her back as it slid home, reminding her of the heat of his body pressing hers into the hay. She'd only been that close to one other man, and the result had always been painful. Her heart raced and her fingers tightened, making the reins bite into her hands. She'd been lucky to walk away from this encounter unscathed, but would her luck hold?

It wasn't too late. She could turn the wagon around and return to town, to safety—and the hatred of the townspeople, even her own family. Or she could take a chance and trust this man.

Did she dare? She snapped the reins over the fidgety mules, eyeing Zach's straight, strong back.

She had no choice. The Cheyenne were dying. She owed them her life. If she had to risk it to help them, so be it.

* * *

Little Wolf paced beside the small fire they had risked when they reached the young braves and their horses. Were no others coming to join them? Finally, a runner approached, but he stopped a few feet away. Bad news.

"The *veho*, the white soldiers, have found the empty tipis?" Little Wolf asked, impatient with old traditions in this time of urgent need. "Tell me all."

"It is so, my chief," the runner said, his chest heaving as he walked closer. He sank onto his haunches and gave Little Wolf the rest of the bad news.

"*Hou*," Little Wolf muttered and sent the man to tell the people to prepare to ride west. So, American Horse and his family had chosen to stay. Anger flashed inside him, like lightning on a bare hill. Could the Horse not have waited until morning to carry the news of their going to the *veho* chief? Did he have to ride to the agency chief in the dead of night to tell his news? Little Wolf clenched the butt of his whip, wishing American Horse stood before him.

It could not be changed. And he would not whip the Horse even if he were here. He had given up anger when he became Sweet Medicine Chief and accepted the Sacred Bundle. He touched the token that lay beneath his arm, beside his heart. It was all that remained of the bundle Sweet Medicine, their ancient lawgiver, had brought with him when he returned from their sacred place, Bear Butte. As the bearer of this burden, Little Wolf had forsworn anger for himself and vowed to think of the people only.

Black Coyote stood and crossed his arms, waiting to be acknowledged. Little Wolf nodded permission for Black Coyote to speak, glad that at last the long, troubled silence around the council fire would be broken. Better that the Coyote speak freely here than whisper behind the backs of the chiefs where they could not answer.

"We have decided to take the north road. There are more *veho* homesteads, more guns and horses to take." Other young warriors shouted, "*Hou!*" and Black Coyote motioned them to follow him. Morning Star stopped them with a withered, upraised hand.

"You know that the trail has long been decided. We go west to avoid the *veho*. The hunters and horse tenders are already down that trail, working, as you should have been. Were you not asked to hunt meat for the young ones? Do you make this noise to keep from hearing their hungry cries?"

"There must be no trouble with the whites," Little Wolf said in support of his brother. "We do not go to war."

"We will take the other road," Black Coyote said, waving toward the northern trail. He started to leave again, but Little Wolf stepped in front of him. He would have to let his medicine speak or the Cheyenne would fall apart before they began this journey.

"You have heard our brother, your chief, speak. He is tired of your loud noise and of the trouble you are always making. I, too, am tired and will not hear it from you now. We need less talk and more work or we will all fail."

"We take the north road," another man shouted, and the rest of the warriors took up his cry.

"No!" Little Wolf said, low and flat, letting the dark anger build inside him. He dropped his blanket from his shoulders. "Do you now question the wisdom of your Old Man Chief? Many of you are young. You have never seen battle. Do you forget the guns of the *veho* soldiers? I do not."

He pulled his shirt tight over his chest. He did not need to bare his chest for all to remember his many scars. He pointed to each, especially the six new scars that he had earned in the last battle in their homeland, before their surrender. He searched the faces around the fire. Some turned away, ashamed that their stubbornness had forced their chief to remind them why they had made him chief.

The anger rose inside Little Wolf and his voice deepened with each word. "*Heammawihio* protected me that time, but many good men died because of the noise of a few like you." He jerked his whip free and sent it snapping around his head, letting the blackness of the anger inside him follow its stinging tip. "No more *Tsitsitas* will die because of your noise. We take the west road, as Morning Star has said."

Sullen, but silent, the warriors left the fire circle, heads hanging in shame. All but Black Coyote. The pistol he had taken at the big fight after Custer was killed rode heavy on his hip, and his courage there had puffed up his chest so that he could not see his feet beyond it. Since that fight, he had been loud and angry, fighting against his chiefs, chafing at the restraints of life on the reservation. He counted the personal loss of glory in battle higher than the good of his people.

Little Wolf returned the Coyote's angry stare as he coiled his whip, holding the anger ready in case Black Coyote should move against him. Black Coyote made no move, but Little Wolf saw the hatred seething. The Coyote left without speaking and they heard him tell the men who waited beyond the fire's light, "We go west."

Little Wolf shared a long look with his brother as he kicked dirt over the fire.

"There will be trouble with him." Morning Star sighed as he rose to leave.

"But not tonight, my brother."

"No." Morning Star rested a hand on Little Wolf's shoulder. "Let us hope the fire burning inside him burns only him."

"*Hou!*" Little Wolf agreed, and pressed his hand over the Sacred Bundle under his arm. He would make it so.

Chapter Three

Zach dismounted, jerked off his gloves and slapped them against his thigh. He forced himself to take a deep breath and let his shoulders relax before he started unsaddling his horse. No sense taking his frustration out on the animal. It wasn't Demon's fault they hadn't traveled farther, but he couldn't help feeling that time was getting short. He had to find Luke soon. He felt it gut deep.

"What's got you so riled up?"

Zach looked up as Caroline swung down from the wagon. He took a quick step forward to assist her, then remembered her demand that he *not* assist her, or touch her. *Damn,* he didn't know if he could even look at her without getting his head snapped off.

"Long day," he said with a shrug, forcing a smile. "I expected to make better time."

Caroline rubbed her back and nodded. "How many miles do you think we made today?"

"Not enough." Zach knew he should keep his mouth shut, not reveal his anxiety, but his nerves had taken control of his common sense. "Either your mules are the slowest in history, or that wagon is too heavily loaded. What have you got in there?" A sudden suspicion made him pause and study the wagon, then Caroline. Surely, she wasn't crazy enough to take guns and ammunition to the Cheyenne.

"Mostly food and blankets, clothing, shoes . . . things like that."

"Those are all soft goods. They shouldn't be that heavy," Zach said and pulled a pile of blankets aside to check the load beneath them.

"Most of the food is canned or bottled," Caroline explained and started unharnessing the mules. "Pretty heavy. And everything's in wooden cases."

He poked around in the wagon a little more, but saw only crates of canned food and boxes of clothing, as she'd said. Her indifference to his snooping eased his concern more than her words. If she'd had anything to hide, she would have tried to stop him.

"While you're in there, pull out the cooking gear, would you?" she asked, and kept working on the mules.

He found a crate of assorted cookware, including a coffee pot, and hoisted it out of the wagon, biting back a groan when his back protested. If his back was protesting after only driving half the day, hers must be screaming. Any woman he knew would have fainted at the mere thought of driving a six-span of mules half a day and most of the night, as she had. Her easy, graceful movements as she moved around the camp told him she'd suffered no ill effects.

Pleased, but also annoyed, he investigated the contents of the box more closely and was relieved to see real pots and pans inside. He'd been afraid she expected him to survive on the tough jerky she'd shared at their noon break. But could she cook? Nothing was worse after a long day in the saddle than his own cooking. Mostly he ate cold beans and stale bread or biscuits bought from farms he passed during the day. A hot meal at the end of the day could be a blessing or a curse, depending on her skill.

He looked up from hobbling his horse to find her scraping brush away from the wagon with a heavy branch.

"What are you doing?" he demanded, snatching the branch out of her hands.

"What does it look like I'm doing?" She tried to take the branch back, but he jerked it out of her reach. "I'm clearing so I can start a fire and so I don't have to sleep on rocks tonight. Is that all right with you?"

"I'll do that," he said and started awkwardly mimicking her efforts. "This branch must weigh more than you do."

"I've told you before, I don't need your help. I'm not some hothouse flower that has to be pampered. Now give me that stick."

"Stick!" he shouted. "Lady, you've been out in the sun too long." He took her by the arm, led her to a large rock and helped her ease down on it. "Sit there quietly and sip this water." He handed her his canteen. "You'll feel better in no time."

Instead of drinking, she burst out laughing. Tears ran down her cheeks and she pressed her hands to her thighs to keep from falling off her rock.

Zach straightened, insulted right down to his boot heels. But the more he watched her laugh, the less annoyed he felt, until finally his own lips turned upward.

"Feel better?" he asked when she slowed to giggles. Feeling sheepish, he swatted his thigh with his hat. A cloud of dust arose and swept straight up his nose, making him choke and cough, which set her to braying like one of her mules. Disgusted, he left her to sort herself out while he took care of the other dumb animals.

He had all the mules picketed and fed before she hiccupped to a stop.

"Oh, lordy," she gasped, holding her side. "I needed that."

"So happy to help out in your time of need," he said, knowing he was being mulish, but still stinging from her rudeness.

"I apologize," she said simply.

Certain she'd found another way to antagonize him, he searched her face, but found only sincerity in her eyes and a wry grin on her lips. "I've been pretty hard on you today," she said. "I'm anxious to get there and the mules are so slow, it's hard to bear."

Zach started to slap his thigh with his hat again, but stopped himself and glanced up to find her grinning at him. "Apology accepted. How about taking your frustration out on the mules tomorrow?"

"Done," she said, and climbed onto the wagon, where she started unloading food and bedding. "Now why don't you go down to that stream and fetch me a bucket of water?" An empty bucket slapped him in the chest. "Then you can wash off the day's dust while I fix dinner."

He started for the stream, but turned back. "Do you need some help with the cookin'?"

"Nope," came the muffled reply.

"You're sure?" When she ignored him, he gathered up soap and a razor and a clean shirt. So far, she'd taken him on faith. He couldn't do any less.

* * *

From the far side of the wagon, Caroline watched until Zach disappeared through the bushes lining the stream.

So, she mused, *he doesn't trust me, or my cooking.* She snorted. She ought to burn everything to spite him. Truth to tell, she wasn't sure she wouldn't do just that without trying. She hoped her newly acquired cooking skills would stand the test of a campfire. Once she'd moved into her uncle's home, never expecting to have to cook over a fire again, she'd focused on mastering the basics—biscuits, gravy, roasting meat—and learning how to manage her aunt's cantankerous stove. Surely, a campfire couldn't be much more difficult.

Caroline set about preparing her redemption, refusing to examine her reasons too closely. She couldn't say why she cared what he thought of her, just knew that she did. By the time Zach returned from the stream, she had a nice fire going, their bedrolls spread out on either side, and dinner teasing the air with scents of roasting rabbit, potatoes fried with salt pork, fresh biscuits and her specialty: tinned apple crisp. Not bad, if she had to say so herself.

Zach approached the fire warily. "What's all this?"

"Dinner," she answered with studied nonchalance. "Aren't you hungry?"

"Yeah, I'm hungry." He tossed his dirty clothes near his bedroll and eyed the meal as if it might bite first. "But I prefer to know what it's goin' to cost *before* I eat."

"I figured you're as tired as I am, and a good, hot meal will help us both get the rest we need. I'll wash those clothes for you after dinner," she offered, and swallowed a laugh at his alarmed glance. Did he think she was going to steal his clothes? The thought of him relaxing by the fire in red flannels, or the altogether, stopped her cold. Had her casual offer led him to think she might welcome his advances? Startled by that possibility, her throat tightened and she went cold all over.

"No thanks. I take care of my own belongings." He set about dishing up a plate, further surprising Caroline when he turned and offered it to her. "Smells delicious. Every drifter in the county will be headin' this way."

"Thank you," she said, beginning to relax when he didn't react further to her suggestion. She decided not to begrudge him his manners this time. Indulging herself a little wouldn't hurt, but she could not become accustomed to his kindness. Western men were not kind, let alone mannerly, and his easy friendliness was disarming. She'd do well to keep up her guard and not let him worm his way into her confidence. She couldn't trust him. She still didn't know why he'd agreed to escort her, but she knew he'd lied about wanting to meet Little Wolf.

The meal passed in silence. Zach ate with relish, but Caroline found the food tasteless. However, she welcomed the time to reinforce her barriers. He was about to devour the last biscuit when the sound of an approaching horse, ridden hard, brought him to his feet, pistol drawn.

"Under the wagon," he told her, his voice low and urgent.

She didn't pause to argue; she was, in fact, already on her way, with a swift detour to snatch a rifle and a box of ammo from under the wagon seat. Her heartbeat pounding in her ears, she scooted under the wagon, where she quickly loaded the rifle and tried to breathe quietly as she waited for the stranger to ride into camp.

"Hello, the camp!"

"I hear you," Zach replied from the shadow behind the wagon. "Come in slow and easy. We've got you in our sights."

As if to prove his words, Caroline cocked her rifle and snapped it to her shoulder. The mechanical snick sounded like cannon fire in the quiet camp.

From across the camp, Zach watched the stranger approach on a weary, lathered horse. Caroline kept her finger on the trigger, noting Zach's tension as he stared at the stranger's face.

"Take off your hat," he told the man, who hastily complied.

"No harm, no harm," the rider assured him. "I only need yer spare horse."

"It's not for sale," Zach said, still tense. "If that's what you came for, ride out the way you rode in."

"Well, I didn' have in mind to buy him frum ya," the rider said, then started talking faster when Zach stepped closer. "I wuz thinkin' more in the way of a trade fer this un."

"Not a chance. That nag's dyin' where it stands." Zach kept his gaze on the rider, but Caroline looked the horse over and wrinkled her nose. Its head hung low, its sides were still heaving, and its tongue hung out of its mouth. The poor horse looked like it might fall over before the rider could dismount. She was careful not to reveal her presence or give away her location by even a sniff of disdain. She knew Zach would shoot the stranger if the man tried to take his horse, which looked to her to be a thoroughbred. And she'd have to be hog-tied before she'd let him take hers, although it wasn't nearly as fine a mount as Zach's. If the fool tried to touch one of her mules, she'd shoot him first and chew him out later.

"Now look here, mister," the rider said, his voice rising, "I have orders from Bat Masterson hisself, the Dodge City sheriff, to round up the settlers an' bring 'em all to safety afore them savages git here."

Caroline barely silenced a gasp. *No! It can't be. He's mistaken.*

"Have the Cheyenne broken from the reservation?" Zach demanded.

"Hell, yes!" the stranger exclaimed. "What rock you bin hidin' under? Happen'd las' night, and they're headed this way right fast. So, you kin see why I rode this horse plumb to death. Now, you gonna give me that horse or not?" He licked his lips and nodded at the fire. "An' some of them vittles'd go down easy, too." Apparently confident of his welcome now that he'd explained his mission, the rider moved to dismount.

Zach cocked his pistol. "Not so fast, mister." He motioned with the gun for the rider to stay mounted. "How do I know you're tellin' the truth? Do you have proof?"

"Why shur, I have proof," the rider exclaimed and started to reach into his vest.

"Whitley!" Zach shouted, and Caroline placed a shot over the rider's head.

He yelped and his arms shot into the air. "Now why do ya wanna go shootin' at me? I got a letter in my vest from the sheriff hisself."

"Two fingers only," Zach warned and watched the rider ease a paper out of his vest. "Toss it to me." The rider complied, moving carefully. Before Zach bent to pick it up, he said, "Whitley?"

In answer, Caroline cocked her rifle. The rider gulped and searched the shadows while Zach read the letter. "All right, I believe you. Now dismount and start walkin' back the way you came."

"Walkin'?" the rider demanded, his color rising and his fingers tightening on the reins. The weary horse's head lifted. "Whudda you mean?"

"Just what I said. That horse is spent. Give it a rest by walkin' a while. If you think I'd give you any animal I own after seein' how you abuse yours, you're a bigger fool than you look. Now get out of here!"

The rider's lips thinned, but he swung out of the saddle and flipped the horse's reins over its head. He tried to lead it in a circle, but the horse balked. He jerked on the reins, adding more blood to the animal's already blood-flecked muzzle. With an oath, Zach stepped forward. His pistol wavered, and the rider jumped him, kicking the pistol away and landing a solid right against Zach's jaw.

Zach staggered back, but the rider didn't give him time to recover. He followed and delivered a solid blow to Zach's abdomen, but the blow didn't affect him. Surprised, the rider hesitated and Zach punched him in the nose, hard. The rider's head snapped backward and blood spurted out of his nose. His eyes teared up and he fell to his knees holding his face as blood gushed through his fingers.

Shocked by the rider's sudden move, Caroline had struggled to get a clear shot, but couldn't shoot without possibly hitting Zach. She scrambled out from under the wagon seeking a better vantage point.

Zach grabbed the man's hair and yanked his head back. "Finished?"

When he tried to nod, Zach let him go, then disarmed him, also taking the knife he found in the man's boot.

"Is that all you've got? A pistol and a knife?" Zach demanded. "You're either very confident or very stupid."

The rider glared at him.

"Whitley!" Zach called.

"Here!" Caroline shouted back. She bit back a smile when Zach jumped, but she kept her rifle steady on the rider. "My vote's on stupid," she said, recognizing the man as one of the bullies from town who'd made her life hell.

The rider ogled her buckskins and sneered. "Shoulda figured you'd be hot-footin' it to catch up with ole Little Wolf. You hankerin' fer a *ride* afore your man gits shot or locked up? Where you s'posed to meet up with him, whore?"

Zach's fist cut off any further filthy observations. "Keep it shut."

"One shot. That's all I need," Caroline promised, her finger already on her trigger.

"Not a bad idea," Zach said with a chilling smile. The rider moaned and leaned away from them. "But you might regret it if you had to return to Dodge City sometime in the future."

"Not a chance," she said firmly as she lowered her gun. "I'm not patching him up."

"Can't blame you," Zach said and pointed at the rider. "You. Stream's that way. Clean up."

Caroline watched the rider hustle toward the stream. "See there? You can be very brief when it suits you."

Zach ignored her jibe and set about unsaddling the exhausted horse. "Better fix him a plate of food so we can get rid of him. I don't want to have to stand guard all night."

"You're giving him your horse?"

"Of course not. I'm givin' him yours."

"What!" Caroline cried, almost dropping the plate she'd started filling. "You can't give away my horse without even asking me."

"I would never do such a dastardly thing. You'll give your permission, of course." Cool as an icicle in January, he flipped the rider's saddle onto her mare's back.

"Why would I do such a stupid thing?" Caroline asked. She left the partially filled plate on a rock and stomped over to her horse with her fists clenched.

"For three reasons," Zach said, continuing his task and not sparing her a glance, although she could tell he was enjoying his moment. "You bought this horse at the town livery?"

"Yes!" she said, then cocked her head and considered the animal. "Why?"

"Because it's knock-kneed, has no chest to speak of, and I think it has worms. In short, you got taken," he whispered. He nodded toward the other horse. "Now that animal, though exhausted, will rally. When it does, you'll be much happier with it."

"You have a point," Caroline agreed, grudgingly. "You mentioned other reasons?"

"His 'proof' was a letter from the Dodge City sheriff, empowerin' our friend to act as deputy, exactly as he stated. It also verifies his allegation: the Cheyenne fled the reservation last night and are believed to be headin' north. The Army is in pursuit."

Caroline's heart plopped into her boots. She couldn't speak. She knew the situation on the reservation was unspeakable. Hundreds of Cheyenne had already died from malaria and starvation, yet the government's agent had been withholding promised rations for months to force cooperation. The authorities in the North had promised that the Cheyenne could return if they didn't like the southern reservation. They hated it, but according to the newspapers, Agent Miles didn't feel obliged by someone else's promise.

She hated to think of the fear and misery her dear friends must have endured, and were now suffering as they fled the reservation. Did they at least have horses to ride, or were they on foot? Cheyenne women were a sturdy lot, but no woman should have to endure such hardship.

Caroline sighed. What would happen to the Cheyenne now? Why had Little Wolf taken this drastic step? His people would be killed, imprisoned at the very least or returned to the reservation. Worse, if cornered, they would fight and die to the last woman and child.

"Do you want to be responsible for the deaths of the settlers this man couldn't reach?" Zach asked. "You know the Cheyenne will have to forage on their way north. Could you live with yourself if you prevented him from warnin' the settlers in time for them to escape to safety?"

"No," she replied softly, tears starting in her eyes. She dearly loved Little Wolf and the *Tsitsitas*, but she couldn't ignore the needs of the settlers. "Let him take the mare."

"Good decision," Zach said.

"What's the third reason?" she asked, as she helped him finish saddling the mare.

"I had hoped we wouldn't get to that."

"Why?" she asked, startled into dropping the horse's halter.

"If you'd disagreed with my first two reasons, I was prepared to buy this bag of bones from you and give it to him myself." He grinned at her over the horse's back.

"You're a gambling man?" she asked, cocking an eyebrow at him. She wasn't fooled by his charming smile, flashing dimple and sparkling silver eyes.

"Yes, ma'am. Would I be here if I wasn't?"

She eyed him over the saddle, determined to wipe the

smug smile from his face. "Oh, you're here for a reason, Mr. McCallister, but I doubt it's something you'd ever gamble."

Zach watched the sheriff's deputy whip Caroline's mare out of camp. Despite the bloody nose and split lip Zach had given him, he seemed focused on his assignment, not retribution. Today. Zach shifted in the saddle. One more reason to watch his back.

His hand settled on his Colt. He had wanted to shoot the man where he stood for his hateful, obscene words to Caroline. In all the time he had spent hunting deserters, traitors, criminals and their ilk, he'd never wanted to kill a man in cold blood. Until today. The deputy would have been the first.

What was it about this woman? Though he'd only known her two days, he could see himself killing a man for insulting her. Yes, she was beautiful, but he had known many beautiful women. His mother had been stunning, but she'd had a heart of stone. His wife, too, had been beautiful, but more concerned about her own needs and wants than anything else in life, including her son. Zach knew she had only taken Luke with her when she ran away because she had known he would come after the boy, and pay well to get him back.

No, he had learned from sad experience that beautiful women could not be trusted. The beauty on the outside could not disguise the decay inside. He shivered, suddenly feeling a chill. Beautiful women had ice in their veins. They used their attractions to get what they wanted, and they never stopped wanting. He blessed this knowledge and his finely honed will for staying his hand this night. He had no desire to hang for a rotten beauty.

He resolved to watch Caroline as they got closer to the Cheyenne. The deputy's ugly questions had struck a chord. Was she planning to rendezvous with Little Wolf? Was her hiring of him as a guide some kind of ruse? He pondered the question, then shook his head. He had seen the suspicion on her face when she'd heard the news that the Cheyenne had broken from the reservation. Though she must have known it could happen, she had believed Little Wolf would honor the treaty.

Zach had hoped she could get them into the camp, where he could look for Luke and, if he didn't find him, ask questions that would lead to his recovery. Now that the Cheyenne were on the run, what should he do? If he left Caroline and caught up with them on the trail, he'd be at a disadvantage. If he found the Cheyenne, they'd shoot him on sight. He could be killed before he had a chance to look for Luke. Then what would happen to the boy? If he stayed with Caroline, they could change course and attempt to rendezvous with the Cheyenne, but he didn't like the idea of a hundred angry Cheyenne warriors surrounding them so far from any settlements. If he and Caroline must catch up with them as they ran, he preferred to do it closer to a fort. The threat of nearby soldiers might keep his scalp intact longer.

His best option was to turn north and head for Fort Dodge, and on the way to continue trying to charm Caroline. He must earn her trust.

Might as well try to saddle a twister. But Luke's life depended on his success. As a father, he had failed the boy so far; this time he must succeed.

Seeing no sign that the deputy planned to circle back, Zach turned toward camp and Caroline. She was bent over, banking the fire, her buckskins stretched tight over her buttocks. His jaw tightened as his body jerked in reaction, heat filling his groin as his body swelled. He muttered a curse and forced thoughts of those revealing, bottom-hugging buckskins from his mind.

Foolish, stubborn, bossy . . . intriguing woman. He groaned, and again asked himself why he was so intrigued by an Indian's wife.

What the hell had he gotten himself into?

He kicked off his boots and lay down across the fire from her, throwing his blanket over his lower body. His annoyance made him less tactful than he'd intended. "We're going to have to turn north tomorrow."

"What?" She slid to her knees and stared at him over the fire. "Why?"

He sighed. So much for a quiet night. "We have no idea which trail the Cheyenne will take, but I'm guessing they'll try to avoid the more settled areas. I think they'll take the old Kansas stock trail to the northwest and avoid Dodge City."

"That makes sense," she said, "but I still don't understand why you think we need to head north."

"Think about it. The Cheyenne will be moving fast and traveling light to outrun the soldiers. They won't have enough horses for everyone, and certainly none to spare to carry supplies. Even if we met up with them on the trail between here and Dodge City, they wouldn't be able to take the wagon; it would slow them down too much. And they'll be too tired to carry much more."

"You're right," she said, frowning. "What do you recommend we do?"

He grabbed a stick of kindling Caroline had stacked beside the fire and smoothed the ground in front of him, then beckoned her closer. "Here's Dodge City, us, and the western trail," he said, using the stick to draw a map in the dirt. "Here's the most dangerous place for them." He made an X west of Dodge City. "They'll have to cross the Arkansas River, then the railroad. If the Army doesn't catch them in the next few days, they'll try to stop them there."

"How can you be sure?"

"I can't," he admitted, "but it's what I'd do if I was on the run. If we head for Fort Dodge, only a couple days' journey, I'll find out for sure. If I'm wrong, we'll be close to the northern trail and can easily change our plans."

"Fort Dodge?" Caroline stood and crossed her arms over her stomach. "What if the soldiers find out what I'm planning to do and try to take my wagon?"

"Trust me," Zach said. "I won't let that happen. We'll camp outside the fort and I'll go in to reconnoiter."

She eyed him, clearly suspicious. "And how will you do that? Do you have a military uniform rolled up in your saddlebags?"

"Of course not," he said, averting his gaze. He hated lying to her, but if she knew his military status, he'd never earn her trust. "Saddle bums ride in and out of the forts all the time lookin' for odd jobs as scouts and hostlers."

"Gunmen, too?" Her gaze was questioning, speculative. He wished he could tell her the truth, but he had too much at stake. "I'm not a gunman," he said and turned back to his map. "If I'm right, we'll take the Dodge Road west to the Cimarron station and try to get there ahead of the Cheyenne." He made the corresponding marks in the dirt, then drew another X a half inch north of the Arkansas River. "We'll camp near here and try to rendezvous with them. If they make it that far, they'll be in need of supplies."

"How long do you think it will take them to get there?" Caroline asked, studying the map intently, as if she could see the Cheyenne struggling along the trails in the dirt.

"They left the reservation on the ninth." Zach doodled toward the south, estimating the Cheyenne's departure point, and dragged the stick north and west. "I'd say twelve days, two weeks, thereabouts, depending on how many times they have to stop and fight."

"How can you be so sure? What if we miss them?"

"Remember, they're on foot and there are women and children and old folks, not just warriors. It will take time."

"They'll never make it." Caroline knelt and followed the trail he'd outlined in the dirt with her finger, then looked up, her expression determined. "They saved my life. I'll do whatever I can to help them."

He helped her stand, impressed by her grit. "Not much we can do tonight. Get some sleep." He led her to her bed under the wagon. "Tomorrow will be another long day."

Zach crawled into his own blankets and pretended to close his eyes. Instead, he watched from behind the screen of his lashes as Caroline struggled to sleep. As she lay half asleep, watching the fire, she reached up and patted her hair into place over her left ear.

Zach's eyes flew open. This wasn't the first time he'd seen that gesture. Why was she so self-conscious about her ears? Now that he thought about it, he'd never seen her pat the other ear, only the left one. Why? As he slid into sleep, he pondered it and many other aspects of the intriguing Caroline.

Tomorrow he'd see about finding some answers.

Chapter Four

Little Wolf walked around the fire circle, talking to his exhausted people as they ate. For three days they had run, stopping only to water their horses and let the women and children running behind catch up. Now he whispered encouraging, heart-filling words and worried.

Where are the stragglers, the women and children on foot, the woman heavy with child?

Unable to eat, he motioned to Black Crane. Silent, watchful, they walked down the grassy meadow between the twin canyons leading to Turkey Springs, a good place to stand and fight the soldiers who were close behind them now. If they must. Where were the walkers? Had soldiers overtaken them? There had been no shots, no cries carrying on the wind, no runners bringing bad news. Only silence.

"It is too quiet," Black Crane said. "The soldiers could have come upon us three days ago, before we butchered the small herd of fat buffalo cows. We are stronger now, ready to fight."

"*Hou,*" Little Wolf nodded, not surprised that the Crane's thoughts followed his own. Always it was so between them. Black Crane's thoughts stayed always on the needs of the people, even before the needs of his family.

"They will hide from the soldiers and come to us when it is safe."

"They will need food, water." The Crane turned to make preparations.

"Wait." Little Wolf pointed to the scout riding hard toward them.

"Soldiers are coming," the scout called as he drew near, and pointed behind him where Little Wolf could see a cloud of dust rising. Little Wolf turned to the waiting warriors. "Bring up your horses and gather your guns, but do not shoot. Let them be the first to shoot."

He turned to Black Crane. "Send the women and children to hide in the bluffs beyond the creek."

Black Crane hurried away. "Do not be frightened, my children," he called to the women who had begun to run to the north, seeking holes in which to hide. "Your men are ready to fight."

Little Wolf watched them go, knowing they would soon come creeping back to sing the war songs and cry encouragement to their men. He glanced over the ground where those men would fight and nodded. It was a good place. Mounted now, his warriors whipped their horses back and forth on the high ground between the approaching soldiers and the creek, heating their blood for the approaching battle. Behind them, in the high banks before the creek, rifle pits had been dug. The soldiers' last water hole had been salty, brackish water. They would not have let the horses drink there. After riding hard under the punishing sun, men and horses would be thirsty, but his warriors would keep them from fresh water.

On both sides of the green meadow leading up to the creek, the deep ravines hid more warriors. Little Wolf frowned as he watched the tired, dusty column of soldiers ride closer. So few? Then he knew. These *veho* thought the Cheyenne were no longer men. They believed they could round up his people like so many sick cows and herd them back to that pest-hole of a reservation.

He stepped forward, making sure his medal, a gift

from the Great White Father in Washington, caught the sun. It would remind this soldier chief that he had been a friend to the white man, before their lies began killing his people. He sighed. The *veho* would want to talk first, then fight.

Behind him, his young warriors whooped and thumped their chests. The soldiers stared at them, their eyes wide and their shoulders slumped, their uniforms sweat-stained. Little Wolf's anger grew. These soldiers had not expected to fight at all. At a shouted order, the soldiers dismounted and their horses were removed to the rear, thirty men going with them.

The soldier chief makes it too easy. Little Wolf thought, but his heart swelled. *We will make a good fight this day. They will not take us back without bleeding first.*

A scout walked forward, a man Little Wolf knew, an Arapaho from the Blue Clouds. So, the Cheyenne must also fight old friends. *Pah!* In these dark years, they had even been forced to fight family. His people had no more friends.

The scout stopped several feet away, the coward. He greeted the men he knew—Little Wolf, Morning Star, Wild Hog and Tangle Hair—by name, then began speaking fast and loud. "They want you to give up and return to the reservation," he said, flapping his blanket in the sign of surrender. "They will give you your rations. You will be treated well."

Little Wolf said nothing. The scout repeated his message. *So,* Little Wolf thought, *the Little Father now wants to give us the food he withheld to force us to stay.* Miles had used his people's empty stomachs to force him, Old Man Chief of the Cheyenne, to agree to stay there, to do nothing and watch his people die. If they stayed, they died of empty stomachs or from the fainting sickness, but in the end, they would all die. He had heard enough *veho* promises. The *veho* fathers did not yet understand.

"Go back," he told the scout. "Tell them we do not want to fight, but we will if they try to force us to return."

The scout started to speak again, but Tangle Hair rode up beside Little Wolf. "Go back and tell them we are going home."

The scout spoke their message to the leader of the white soldiers and suddenly, from the back of the soldiers, shots were fired. At Little Wolf's shout, his warriors returned fire. Soldiers started falling. The soldier chief leaped off his horse and, with the scout and two other soldiers, ran up a small hill to their left. Quickly, Little Wolf sent mounted warriors after them, but their position on top of the hill was too strong. Little Wolf's hidden warriors rode out of the ravines and attacked the soldiers from the rear. The soldiers fell to the grass and began digging pits to hide from Cheyenne bullets. They returned fire, but their carbines didn't have the range of the Cheyenne's guns, and they weren't repeating rifles. The soldiers had to stop and load after each shot.

The Cheyenne again attacked the soldier chief's hill and were again pushed back. But this time, they killed the scout and whooped loud and long. Again, they rode up the hill and lost two more men before Little Wolf gave up on the hill. All day, his warriors kept the soldiers pinned down under the angry sun.

Toward dusk, Little Wolf and Morning Star met at the creek. "It cannot be long now." Morning Star shouted to be heard over the shots still being fired. "They are thirsty. Their guns will soon be empty."

"They will try to reach water after dark, my brother," Little Wolf said. He did not believe the soldiers would give up yet, but he did not want Morning Star to lose hope. The Cheyenne would win this first fight; but not tonight.

"Not a drop will pass their lips," Morning Star said. "I will tell the Dog Soldiers."

"*Hou!*" Little Wolf sat on his haunches and watched his brother crawl back into the fighting, his gun blazing. It was good to see the fire in his brother's eyes that for too long had been dulled by trouble and worry. He watched his warriors and his heart swelled with pride, but dark thoughts soon followed. The *veho* fathers had thought the Cheyenne were men no longer. Today they would learn they were wrong. They would send more soldiers. This would not be the last fight on the long road home.

Black Coyote wounded a soldier and gave a loud yip. From the tall grass beyond the creek, his wife, Buffalo Calf Woman, trilled her pleasure at her husband's prowess. The young warriors close around the Coyote yipped in approval.

Little Wolf scowled. It was good to defeat the soldiers, but their victory would fire the hot blood already stirring in the Coyote. The young braves looked to him too much, and Morning Star was becoming old and frail, losing control over the young men. If they started slipping away—raiding, killing, stealing horses—the white ranchers would band together and come after the Cheyenne, too.

Returning to the creek, Little Wolf found Morning Star urging his Dog Soldiers to make one last great charge over the soldiers in their shallow pits. "My brother, you have done many brave things in days past, and this would be a thing for the women to sing about. But we have done enough today. Our ammunition and the sun are low. If we do not shame the soldier chief too much, he will return to his fort when he gets thirsty."

"Our great Medicine Chief has grown soft on the reservation," a Dog Soldier taunted.

"No," Morning Star said. "Did you not see him walk through the soldier bullets at the start of this fight? He fought like the bear. Without fear. We·will rest and fight again with the new sun."

Black Crane pulled Little Wolf aside and pointed past the creek to where a small bunch of women and children were being tended and fed by the others. "They have come. And there is a new one. See there?"

Little Wolf saw the tiny bundle on the back of the woman being tended by his wife, Quiet Woman. The woman had been heavy with child the night they left and had been on his mind. He nodded but turned to the Crane with a troubled frown. "It is good, but the road ahead is long and many soldiers will stand across it."

"She is strong and knows her child will have a better life in that good country."

Little Wolf touched the Sacred Bundle under his left arm and prayed it would be so.

Fear has a singular stench, Caroline realized as she and Zach pulled into Fort Dodge. The fort and its parasite town, perched on the banks of the Arkansas River, was busier than she'd ever seen it. The hardware store had a line out the door as the local citizens, nervous and short-tempered, all tried to beat their neighbors to the last of the store's goods. Greedy eyes watched her and Zach as they moved down the street to the livery stable. Though she'd objected at first, she was very glad now that she'd given in to Zach's demand that she wear a dress to town instead of her buckskins.

"Look straight ahead," Zach cautioned, and snapped the reins over the mules' backs.

"The whole fort's gone crazy." Caroline patted her hair into place over her left ear, then let her hand settle over the hilt of the knife strapped to her leg. She'd have to yank up her skirt to get to it, but the feel of it reassured her.

"Scared spitless." Zach crooned to the mules, which had begun tossing their heads. "The Cheyenne must be headin' this way."

The windows of every building were being boarded up; she could hardly hear Zach over the hammering and shouting. Even the horses were whinnying. "There won't be any lodging available," Caroline said, noticing the NO MORE ROOM sign on the only boardinghouse. "They're living in tents in the alleys and on the streets. It was a mistake to bring the wagon here." She clutched his arm. "The soldiers will take it away from us."

"They won't even notice us," Zach assured her. "They

have their own problems." He nodded toward the fort's commissary, where wagons were being loaded. "I couldn't leave you out there alone, and we have to find out what's happenin'."

Caroline bit her lip. Her plan to help the Cheyenne was falling apart. She should pay Zach for his time and return the wagonload of goods to her uncle's store for safe-keeping. But he wouldn't be able to resist selling everything. Heavens! In this frenzy, he could get twice, possibly even three times what the goods would normally bring. How would that help the Cheyenne? If they were captured and returned to the reservation, they would still be sick and starving. She couldn't bear to imagine her friends sick, let alone hungry. Three of the women had patiently nursed her back to health, body and soul. She needed to find them, make sure they survived.

If anyone could elude the soldiers, it was Little Wolf. She bit her lip. There was little hope of that happening. Little Wolf couldn't have more than a hundred men left to protect twice that many women, children and old ones. She looked around her at the hundreds of soldiers preparing to march against the Cheyenne and shuddered. Abruptly she decided to keep her wagonload of goods, no matter how difficult that task proved to be. When the dust settled, the Cheyenne who survived would need it.

"Where are you going?" she asked Zach. "I think I'll stay with the wagon while you reconnoiter." That military-sounding word of his made her uneasy.

"I'll take you to the livery stable. We'll need more grain for the animals, if they have any left. We'll have the blacksmith take a look at that rear axle while we're here, too, and your new horse's shoes."

"There's nothing wrong with the axle."

Zach winked. "He doesn't know that."

"Very sneaky," Caroline said, cocking an eyebrow at him. The yawning abyss of the stable adjacent to the blacksmith's shop would hide the wagon from curious eyes and give her a place to lie low. Still, it bothered her that he hadn't told her where he was headed.

"If I'm not back by the time you finish, pull up outside the saloon there." He pointed to a nearby establishment that seemed to be overflowing with men engaged in animated conversation.

"There?" She winced. When had her voice become this tinny squeak? "I don't like the looks of it."

"Don't worry. They know you're with me." He sounded more confident than Caroline felt, seeing some of the men glaring their way. "No one will bother you."

Zach braked in front of the livery, gave the owner his instructions and ambled next door to the blacksmith shop. Caroline remained perched on the wagon seat and watched him talk to the blacksmith, never looking toward the group of men. All of them watched him with narrowed eyes. A few shot angry glances her way.

Heavens! she gulped and patted her hair, trying to look calm, though her fists were clenched in her skirt. *Why isn't he moving faster?*

As Zach stepped up on the boardwalk, he waited for the men to move out of his way, staring into each face as if memorizing it. One by one, the men dropped their gazes and eased out of his path, turning their backs on him, falling silent. None spoke above a whisper until he was a good fifty feet down the street, and even then their voices were hushed. None of them looked directly at her, but she felt their slippery glances slide over her.

She was safe, but must guard her actions. She drew a deep breath and eased her hand off her knife. Her gaze followed Zach's progress down the street. He walked like he owned the town, looking each person in the eye, his hat pulled low and his black duster flaring around him. Men shied out of his way and women paused to stare after him, but he kept walking, as if unaware of his effect. If she hadn't seen it, she would never have believed it. She smiled and shook her head. The man could intimidate a rattler.

Relieved, her guard down, she turned toward the

sound of an approaching horse, still smiling. Instantly, she realized her mistake.

"Sir!" Zach snapped a salute. "Major Zachary L. McCallister reporting."

"For duty?" Lieutenant Colonel William H. Lewis asked, leaning back in his chair. "At ease, Major. What brings you to this hellhole?"

Zach pulled a packet of papers out of his shirt and handed them over. Lewis took them and indicated the chair across from his desk. "Have a seat. Looks like this will take a while."

Zach had to hand it to him. The man seemed very relaxed for someone in the path of hundreds of rampaging Cheyenne. Without looking away from the papers in his hand, Lewis flipped open a box of cheroots and shoved it across the desk to Zach.

Zach lit one up and studied the bustling fort out the window while Lewis continued to read. Finally, Lewis looked up, lit his own cheroot and studied Zach through the smoke. "Says here I'm to give you any support you require and not impede your mission."

"Yes, sir." Zach returned Lewis's stare. "That's exactly what it says."

"You've been in the area for a while, Major," Lewis commented as he continued to scan the documents. "Why is it you haven't visited until today?"

"Until today, I had no reason to visit."

"Ah." Lewis glanced up, his eyes narrowed. "You're the man who rode in with Little Wolf's squaw."

"Caroline Whitley," Zach said, bristling. He didn't like the man's tone. "I'm hopin' she'll get me into the Cheyenne camp when the time comes."

"She'll get your scalp lifted." Lewis examined the glowing tip of his cheroot. "But she's so beautiful, it might be worth it."

"I beg your pardon?" Zach straightened and leveled a stare at Lewis.

The man returned his glare with a smug smirk. "That is, if you don't mind dipping your wick in the same hole ole Little Wolf's already watered."

"I don't appreciate your humor," Zach said and ground out his cheroot in the ashtray. "Miss Whitley is the victim of circumstances beyond her control."

"Yes." Lewis nodded in agreement and remained at his ease. "Very unfortunate that she spread her legs for a damned Injun."

Zach shot to his feet and leaned over the desk. "I'll thank you to take back that remark."

The legs of Lewis's chair hit the floor. "Who do you think you are, Mr. Special Agent of the U.S. Government? I don't care what your 'orders' say. You waltz in here with a whore on your arm when we're under siege and expect me to give you a key to my commissary?"

"Perhaps you didn't notice the signature on those orders."

"Sheridan's not the man you're dealing with today."

"If you oppose me, he's the man you'll be dealin' with tomorrow," Zach warned.

Lewis stood, anger radiating from him in waves. Zach straightened, but didn't back off. He'd hoped it wouldn't come to this, but if Lewis didn't agree to let him move through the territory unhampered by his troops, Zach might as well leave that wagonload of goods in the middle of the fort and let the frightened settlers help themselves. He relaxed his stance, raised his hands palm up.

"I have reason to believe my son is still alive. As long as there is any hope, I must continue my search."

"And your primary objective?" Lewis asked, settling back into his chair.

Zach hesitated. Luke was his primary objective, but here and now he had to put his military duty first. "I will do everythin' in my power to convince Little Wolf to surrender. But I have to catch up to the man first."

"Is Miss Whitley aware of your dilemma?" Lewis stressed Caroline's name.

Zach acknowledged the man's concession with a slight nod. "No, sir. She has no knowledge of my objectives. She's a very, uh, headstrong female. She would not have allowed me to accompany her if she knew my true purpose."

Lewis chuckled. "Well, you are in a tight spot, aren't you, Major? Far be it from me to make your position any more untenable." He rose and began pacing behind his desk, dropping the relaxed façade. "Little Wolf is headed this way with approximately one hundred mounted warriors and another hundred-and-seventy-five women and children, some mounted, most on foot."

"About what I estimated," Zach murmured, nodding agreement. "Conditions must have been very bad on the reservation. He doesn't stand a chance."

"Conditions, hah! He's insane. The citizens of Dodge City and the outlying ranchers and settlers are arming. Troops from as far away as Fort Sill are awaiting orders. He appears to be taking the old Kansas Stock Road rather than the Camp Supply trail, which would bring him directly here. His first mistake. There are fewer ranches and settlements in that direction; less forage. Captain Rendlebrock is in pursuit from Fort Reno; hot on his heels. He should have caught up with him before they reached Turkey Springs yesterday. We're expecting word any moment that the Cheyenne have been contained and are headed back to the Darlington Agency."

"I hope you're right. I would prefer visitin' the Cheyenne on the reservation over attemptin' a rendezvous on the open plains." Zach shook his head. "Matters could become very ugly if Rendlebrock fails. The Army must see that Little Wolf is a real threat. His scouts will be miles ahead foragin', and his Dog Soldiers will bring up the rear. No one has ever defeated this man in battle. He's a master strategist. Very intelligent."

Lewis laughed. "He's an Injun. The whole tribe's been starved and the men are all weak with untreated malaria. There isn't a healthy warrior in the bunch. I'm more concerned about these hysterical citizens. Already they're blaming rampaging Injuns for everything that goes wrong."

He threw up his hands. "Yesterday, a farmer and his family abandoned their farm, three miles from Dodge City. The fool left the stove lit and the house burned down. Of course, they're screaming Injuns did it and demanding restitution from the government that should have protected them. Now I'm getting frantic messages from Dodge City's mayor demanding arms and ammunition. As if I kept an arsenal out here in the middle of the prairie.

"No, major," he said, settling on a corner of his desk with a sigh. "I'm not worried about the injuns, but I'd recommend you get that squaw out of town as fast as possible. The blood's running too hot in this town. I'll advise my officers that you're not to be impeded in any way."

He offered his hand and Zach shook it. "She's not a squaw."

Lewis's hand tightened on his. "Wake up, Major. Don't let those beautiful blue eyes fool you. She is the *wife* of an Injun." He passed Zach his papers.

Zach saluted, pivoted and stuffed his orders back in his shirt. He found himself wishing Little Wolf was headed this way. Lewis needed to be taken down a peg.

Shouts and a woman's muffled scream jerked him out of his thoughts as he stepped onto the street. A crowd of men had gathered in front of the blacksmith shop. Through their legs he saw a tumble of petticoats on the ground, then a blue skirt and a pair of bare legs kicking.

Damnation! he cursed, as he started running. *Can't that woman stay out of trouble for five minutes?*

Zach caught the bridle of a passing horse, jerked the rider out of the saddle and leaped onto the horse's back. He galloped down the street and straight into the mob surrounding Caroline without pulling up. Launching himself from the saddle, he flew over the men's heads, reaching for the man kneeling over her. He managed to hit the man from the side, knocking him off her. As he flew past, he caught a glimpse of bare breasts, reddened by rough handling before he hit the ground and rolled into a crouch.

He let his Colt speak for him, firing into the air. The startled mob leaped backward.

"Nobody do anythin' stupid, now," Zach warned. "This gun's got a mean temper and so do I."

The fool he'd knocked off Caroline jerked to his feet with a growl. Caroline kicked him in the knee as she clutched her dress over her breasts. He yowled in pain and went down again, clutching his knee.

"You all right?" Metal gleamed in her right hand and Zach knew that she was fine—and armed.

"Shaken. But I'll live." She sounded winded, but very angry.

"You hear that, boys?" Zach asked, panning the group with the Colt. To a man, they blanched away as the bore of the gun swung over them. "Don't be foolish. She knows how to use that knife."

The fool moaned, writhing from the pain in his knee. A big man pushed to the front of the crowd, hands raised, gaze questioning. Zach nodded, and the man took a cautious step toward the injured man.

"Cum on, Igor, you stupid ox," the man said. "Yu'll git us all kilt."

"But she smiled at me," Igor cried, as the big man hefted him over his shoulder like a bag of oats.

"Nah, man," the big man said with a wry grin for Zach. "She whar smilin' cuz it's a pritty day, not cuz she like the cut of yur pants." A few reluctant chuckles followed him as he swung away, toting Igor as if he weighed no more than a sack of meal. The rest of the crowd followed, glaring at Zach and Caroline as they turned away.

Zach waited until they all moved off before holstering his Colt. Then he turned to Caroline. "You smiled at him?"

She gave him a cool glare, then turned away to yank down her skirt and sheath her knife. "It was an accident," she said, and stuck her nose in the air as she headed for the back of the wagon, where she grabbed the carpetbag containing her clothes.

"What did he do that made you smile?"

She spun to face him, almost losing her grip on her bodice. "So this is all my fault?" she sputtered, her eyes shooting sparks that made Zach thankful she'd already sheathed her knife.

"Of course not, but be more careful whom you direct that smile at. It's as dangerous as your knife." He stepped closer and reached out, catching hold of the torn bodice. "Are you hurt?"

"No, but you will be if you don't let go right now." Her eyes had gone wide and her fingers tightened.

Zach lifted both hands, palms out. "I forgot. You don't need my help." He cocked an eyebrow at her, expecting her to thank him for saving her from the mob, but she remained tight-lipped and furious. "You're sure you're all right?"

She nodded stiffly.

"Better change quickly," he said, as he left to return the horse he'd borrowed. "I want to get out of here before anyone else gets hurt."

Once his back was turned, his grin faded into a scowl that he turned on the men still loitering nearby. Some of the men met his glare, but most kept their backs to him. Igor might have acted out of ignorance, but he suspected that others had egged him on, wanting Caroline hurt.

He would have to make camp farther away from the fort than he'd originally planned. He'd ask Lewis for a couple of men to post a discreet watch.

He was getting too close to allow a bunch of hot-headed civilians to keep him from finding his son.

Chapter Five

Caroline grabbed her valise and stepped into an empty stall to change. She walked straight into the corner, braced her forehead against the wall and tried to stop the trembling. How could she have been so stupid? It had almost happened again.

She jerked her bodice open and stared in dismay at her reddened, tender breasts and shuddered. He had touched her, mauled and even sucked on her. His drool was on her skin. She had to wash it off. She dashed to the trough outside the stall and bent over it, splashing water onto her chest and frantically scrubbing at her skin. She couldn't get clean. The marks he'd made wouldn't come off.

Gentle hands pulled her away from the trough. A kind voice whispered soothing words as the hands pulled the torn, soiled dress off her shoulders and wrapped her in a blanket. She looked up, desperate to continue washing and found herself looking into Zach's face. What must he think of her? She was filth, dirty. Every man, woman and child in town had spit on her, called her names. The women wouldn't even allow their skirts to touch her as they passed her on the street.

But the men . . . ! Oh, the men thought they could touch her anywhere they wanted, whenever they wanted. And they frequently had.

Now this. Zach must have heard the men's comments in the saloon that first night, but now that he'd seen men treat her like a whore, he wouldn't want to have anything to do with her. So why was he holding her, trying to soothe her? Would he leave once she calmed down? That must be it. He wanted her to calm down so he could tell her he was leaving.

What would she do? She needed his help to get all that food and medicine to the Cheyenne. She pushed him away, wanting to be alone, needing to pull herself together, to think of another way to achieve her goal. Every bone in her body ached to be held, but she couldn't let herself be weak, couldn't let the tears come. If she let go, she might never be able to stop.

"It's over," he said, bending to look into her eyes. "You're safe now."

He tucked a stray lock of hair behind her ear and she flinched away from his hand. "Don't touch me. Please," she said, pulling the scratchy blanket tighter over her bare breasts.

"Do you need to talk about it? Will it help to tell me what happened?"

"I—I don't know how it happened," she began, meaning to fob him off, but she found herself suddenly frantic to explain. "He rode up after you passed the saloon. I was smiling at the way you handled those men and I turned when I heard him. I—I didn't mean to smile at him. It was an accident."

A muscle flexed in Zach's jaw and he scowled. "That's it? You smiled at him?"

"The next thing I knew, he had hold of my hand. I tried to pull it away, but he wouldn't let go, so I pushed against his chest, but he took it wrong and then he . . . he tried to kiss me." She knew she was babbling, barely coherent, but she couldn't seem to keep the words from tumbling out of her mouth. "He shoved his tongue in my mouth. I gagged, but he wouldn't quit. So I kicked him and that made him mad.

"Then the men at the saloon started coming over and shouting. I got loose long enough to slap him, but that only made him more determined." She paused and gulped a deep breath. "They started passing me around. I kicked and clawed, but they only laughed."

She shuddered. "Their hands were all over, touching me everywhere. Then someone tore my dress and it wasn't long before they ripped it open and I couldn't cover my . . ." She squeezed her eyes shut, but couldn't escape the leering faces and groping hands in her mind.

"Caroline," Zach said, gripping her shoulders and giving her a firm shake. "Don't do this to yourself. It's over now."

Startled, she stared up at him, not seeing him clearly at first, then focusing on his eyes, which had turned the shade of hoar frost. His features seemed brittle. A frown creased his forehead, and his lips had pulled into a thin, taut line. Of course he didn't want to hear her incoherent babbling. The whole incident probably disgusted him. How he must have hated defending her.

"You're right." She shrugged out of his hold, gathering her dignity along with her self-control. "I'm sorry," she said, and prayed for strength before continuing. "I understand if you feel you can't continue our . . . arrangement."

Zach stared at her. He took a long time answering and when he did, the words were sharp-edged, biting. "Why wouldn't I want to continue? You've done nothing wrong. What happened out there was not your fault."

"People think I'm a whore," she said, calmly but firmly, "because of what happened to me, and because I'm . . . because Little Wolf is my . . . husband." It was becoming more and more difficult to say the words. How much longer could she keep up the pretext?

"You are not to blame," Zach said, cutting her off abruptly and once again gripping her arms. "I shouldn't have left you here alone with them millin' around."

He wasn't listening to her. She took a deep breath, bracing herself to explain further. Her fingers tightened on the blanket, but she looked him in the eye and forced the words out. "You don't understand. Several years ago, I was captured by the Kiowa . . ."

"I know," Zach said, his gaze as steady as hers.

Her eyes widened. *He knew?* She returned his intent gaze, her eyes narrowing when his hands slid off her arms. "How long have you known?"

Zach hesitated, as if considering how much to reveal.
"A while."

She tipped her head. "How long?"

He flushed and his Adam's apple bobbed as he took a
noisy gulp of air, then glanced away. "A man from your
wagon train told me what happened."

"You knew *before* you accepted my offer?" she asked,
frowning. If he'd known her miserable history, why had
he agreed to take the job? Her stomach lurched as she
was forced to reconsider everything she knew about him.

"You knew those skunks who attacked me in the alley?"
She started pacing in front of him. "How much did you
pay them to let you play hero?"

"That's not true," he shouted, going all stiff and outraged. "I would never have done something so under-
handed."

"Oh, no?" She stopped in front of him and stuck her
nose in his face. "You would never take advantage of a
desperate woman? Never *use* a woman to serve your own
ends?"

Zach leaned closer. "I would never do anything to
hurt you."

"Who would you hurt, Mr. McCallister?" Caroline
asked, determined to get a straight answer from him.
"Why are you so determined to get to the Cheyenne that
you'd tolerate someone like me? Are you after revenge?
Did the Cheyenne hurt someone you cared about?"

He swung away from her, but not before she saw his
jaw clench and something like fear flash through his
eyes. "I can't talk about it," he said, propping both fists
on his hips.

"And you want me to trust you," she said and sighed.
"How can I trust you when you won't tell me why I
should?" She glared at his back and waited, hoping he'd
relent. She might as well wish for six new dresses. Whatever drove him must be a matter of life and death. He did
not seem to be a man who acted rashly.

"You're wrong, you know." He glanced at her over his

shoulder. "I don't tolerate you. You're one of the bravest women I've ever met."

Her mind went blank. His words and the expression on his face left her speechless. No one had ever said anything like that to her, and she didn't know what to say or how to react. She thought of herself as a survivor, not a victim, but the people around her, even the people she loved, found her sullied beyond redemption, a social pariah. Only among the Cheyenne had she been accepted and loved for herself.

He nodded at her torn, muddy skirt. "We need to get out of this hellhole. Do you want help getting out of that dress?"

"No!" she assured him with a little more heat than she'd intended. She hadn't meant to snap at him, but his return to the matter at hand seemed abrupt, especially when she was still reeling from his compliment. She drew a steadying breath, knowing she had no choice but to follow his lead, until she could ferret out his secrets.

"No, thank you," she said, in a more controlled tone, and made a show of studying the damage to her dress so that she wouldn't have to look him in the eye. "I can manage."

"I have some business to finish. I'll return shortly," he said, and slapped his hat onto his head. "I'd like to make camp before nightfall. Don't leave the stable until I return."

"You'd better talk fast," she said, wishing she had something handy to throw at him. "I won't cower in here like a scared rabbit in its hole."

She thought she heard him mutter, "Stubborn woman," as he stomped out of the stable. Her hands shook as she stripped off the ruined dress and dirty, torn petticoats. She shook her head at the waste. She didn't need to open her valise to realize the dilemma facing her. Her wardrobe was limited to her best buckskins, her Sunday dress and the patched muslin that she wore to do chores. And her everyday buckskins, of course.

Her fingers caressed the supple hide as she considered. Zach had urged her to wear a dress into town. With so many frightened settlers and ranchers seeking refuge at the fort, they had agreed that it wouldn't be wise to flaunt her affiliation with the Cheyenne.

She wadded the ruined dress into a ball. Fat lot of good that had done. She stuffed the dress and her petticoats into a corner of the wagon to be washed later. No sense wearing her fingers out trying to mend it. She'd wash it, then tear it into strips for bandages. No telling what would happen to them, alone out there on the prairie. She stripped off her torn camisole and slipped into her buckskins. As the cool hide settled against her skin, she sighed.

Much better, she decided with a pleased nod as she adjusted the knife sheath on her thigh and patted her hair into place over her ear. Now she felt normal.

Zach spurred Caroline's horse away from their new camp, pausing only briefly to make sure Lewis's men were on guard before he turned toward Fort Dodge. He finished the short ride at full gallop, pulling the horse up in a rearing slide before the last saloon on the street. Not because he wanted to announce his arrival. Well, not completely, he admitted with a wry grimace. The pace was a result of the anger that had been building inside him since he'd seen Caroline on the ground struggling while the mob cheered.

Forcing himself to a slower pace, he pulled off his riding gloves and secured them on the saddle, then looped the horse's reins over the hitching post. He would have to make this quick. He'd seen a couple of soldiers scurry toward Lewis's quarters when he arrived. It wouldn't be long before they returned with reinforcements.

As they had earlier, men filled the boardwalk, drinks in hand, watching his every move in wary silence. The raucous clamor from within grew as he mounted the steps, heading for the saloon's swinging half doors. The men parted, opening a narrow path to the door, which Zach took without hesitation, feeling the ranks close behind him. He pushed the door open and studied the crowd inside as his eyes adjusted to the sting of smoke. He spotted his quarry among a group of beefy, bearded giants. He recognized the huge men by their throaty accents and robust physiques as Russian Mennonites, recent arrivals whose plans to settle a large section of land near the Cimarron station must have been delayed by the escape of the Cheyenne.

Zach's eyes narrowed as he identified Igor, the man who had accosted Caroline. He pushed through the doors, barely aware that he left silence in his wake as he shoved through the crowd, sloshing beers on unsuspecting patrons as he passed. Many grumbled, but choked down any challenge after one glance at his face. His anger surged to the boiling point when he reached Igor and waited behind him to be noticed.

"Yah," Igor said and set his beer down on the nearest table, spilling most of it on the men nearby. "She have bee-yoo-ti-full titties." He gestured with both hands at chest height, palms open wide. He spun to show everyone. "And taste like straw . . ." He lurched to a halt facing Zach. His eyes popped wide and his mouth dropped open.

Zach heaved a mental sigh as he cocked his fist. This wasn't going to be nearly as satisfying as he'd hoped, still it had to be done. He threw his weight into the punch, aiming for Igor's nose and watched with satisfaction as he reeled backward, shattering a table behind him and landing in the lap of the huge man who'd carried him away earlier in the day. Silence reigned as the man eyed Zach, then propped up Igor, who was blowing bloody bubbles and whining about his nose.

"Yu touch, yu taste, yu pay," the big man growled and tossed Igor aside. He stood, holding his arms out to his side, palms up. "No!" he shouted at several younger men who'd begun rolling up their sleeves and spitting into their fists. "This Igor's fight. Yu watch or yu leaf."

"Outside," the barkeep shouted, firing his rifle over the crowd. "No fighting in here." He leveled the gun at Zach. "I mean what I say."

Zach nodded and backed toward the door. Men shoved away tables and chairs and followed him to the street where they circled Zach and Igor, quickly placing bets. A few grabbed lanterns off neighboring buildings and held them high.

Zach studied his opponent in the wavering light. Although staggering drunk, Igor had him by at least forty pounds and several inches' reach. Zach figured his agility and speed, not to mention his anger, would give him the advantage.

He glanced around him at the angry faces in the crowd and realized he might be fighting more than Igor before he finished. Good, he thought. He needed to let off some steam. Lewis's men would stop the fight before things got out of hand, but first he needed to pound some meat.

With that, he threw his weight into a jab to Igor's jaw and watched him sprawl on his ass in the dirt. When he made no effort to rise, Zach kicked dirt over him. "Get up. The woman you put your dirty hands on has more fight in her little finger than you have in your whole body."

"No more," Igor moaned, to the obvious disgust of his comrades, who tried to yank him to his feet.

"What's all the fuss about, anyhow?" a voice from the crowd shouted. "The woman's a squaw to one of them heathen Cheyenne." A murmur of assent rose from the crowd.

"You an Injun lover, mister?" another voice taunted. Other voices chimed in and the mood of the crowd swung to ugly. "Mebbe someone needs to knock some sense into you." The circle around Zach tightened and suddenly, several men rushed him. He swung, connected with someone's nose, but caught a blow to the midsection himself as the crowd swarmed over him. The lantern light faded, then went out completely. Zach swung at the menacing shapes in the dark and blocked the blows he saw coming, but the ones he missed started taking a toll.

Shots sounded and the fighting stopped abruptly as Lt. Colonel Lewis and several soldiers waded into the center of the melee. "I should have known I'd find you in the middle of this," Lewis said as he helped Zach to his feet. His soldiers circled Zach and Lewis and started pushing outward, encouraging the mob to return to their drinks, using their fists or the butts of their guns when cajolery didn't work.

Zach didn't realize he was leaning against someone until the man moved and Zach staggered, struggling to stay upright. The huge Mennonite faced him. "Yu fight gud, but one against a hunnerd, not a fair fight." He shrugged. "I even odds."

Zach grinned and extended his hand. "Thank you. Zach McCallister."

"Peter Stanislovskya."

"Very pleased to meet you." Zach winced as Peter shook his right hand firmly.

"I put Igor to bed now," Peter said. With a nod to Lewis, he threw Igor over his shoulder and marched away.

"You've made a friend," Lewis said, and shoved one shoulder under Zach's, pulling Zach's arm around his shoulders. "I've got a little something that will take the sting out of those cuts, and some news that will cheer you up."

Zach stumbled to a stop. "What have you heard?"

"Not here," Lewis murmured. "Too many ears."

Once Lewis's medical officer finished patching him up, Zach settled back in his chair and took a long sip of surprisingly good whiskey. "Your news?"

Lewis took a long drag from a fat cigar and blew a neat circle into the air, then leaned forward, his elbows on his knees. "The reason for my tardy rescue? A messenger came. Ridiculous that the telegraph still has not been installed between these forts, isn't it? How do they expect us to maintain order when we have to rely on couriers for communication?" He shoved to his feet. "But you aren't interested in my paltry concerns, are you, Major?"

"Of course, I am, sir. Your limitations affect my ability to fulfill my orders."

"Then you will soon come to lament my 'limitations' as heartily as I," Lewis said, settling again in the chair behind his desk. "The Cheyenne have eluded the men sent to round them up. Little Wolf lured Rendlebrock into a trap at Turkey Springs and shot his command to pieces. He had the advantage of both position and firepower, being in possession of higher caliber repeating rifles and an entrenched line strategically positioned between Rendlebrock's outfit and the nearest water source. Rendlebrock is now limping to Camp Supply with his wounded."

"How bad was it?" Zach asked, not at all surprised that the Army had lost its first skirmish with the desperate Cheyenne.

"Little Wolf, husband of your charge, pinned them down for an entire day and night without water. The men were reduced to drinking horse piss."

Zach choked on his whiskey, mid-swallow. "Horse piss?"

"Mark my words," Lewis said, punctuating his comments with a fist to his desk. "Heads will roll. Rendlebrock will be court-martialed. No one will underestimate those savages again."

"Are you sending troops after them?" Zach asked, keeping his tone heated, his expression outraged, while he marveled at Little Wolf's guile.

"Eventually, all five forts in this area will have troops in the field chasing these Injuns," Lewis predicted, stubbing out his cigar in the overflowing ashtray. "Now that the Cheyenne have won the first engagement, their blood will be up, their confidence restored. We'll never round them up without a bloodbath."

He turned to Zach, as if beginning to resent his presence. "I won't be able to keep a lid on news this big. As everyone in town appears to knows about your woman, you'd better get her out of here," he advised. "I can't guarantee her safety, or yours. I'm afraid you're on your own. I'll advise my men that you're not to be hampered in any way, but your safety is your own concern."

Zach didn't bother correcting Lewis. Caroline Whitley might not be his woman, but for now, she was his responsibility. He finished his whiskey and headed for the door. "Thank you for the excellent refreshment and your able assistance." He raised his bandaged hand in salute.

Lewis acknowledged him with a nod. "Major."

Zach mounted his horse and pointed its nose out of the fort and the surrounding town. Only when he'd cleared the last makeshift shelter did he crouch over the animal's neck, hounded by thoughts flying through his head apace with the horse's drumming hooves.

Why had he been unable to wish Lewis success in his efforts to contain the Cheyenne? Where did his loyalties lie? Had his agreement to aid a certain beautiful woman diluted his sense of duty?

Duty was the least of his concerns, Zach reminded himself. Only Luke's safety mattered. Nothing—not even the luscious Caroline—was going to keep him from finding and rescuing his son.

Caroline heard Zach's signal, a series of whistles, and let her finger slide off the rifle's trigger. Muscles she hadn't realized were tense finally relaxed, leaving her neck and shoulders aching. She slid out from under the wagon, added a small log to the fire she'd already banked, and watched Zach materialize out of the shadows.

"You do that as well as a Cheyenne."

"Do what?" he asked, shrugging out of his duster and dropping it on his bedroll, which she'd spread beside the fire. He kept his hat on and pulled the brim low.

"Sneak up on people." His gaze slid over her buckskins and his jaw tightened, but he said nothing. "It's a gift."

Something in his glance made a shiver slide up her spine. He looked almost . . . predatory. "Hungry?" she asked, bending to slide the food she'd set aside for him onto a plate, knowing she wasn't fooling him, but unwilling to give him the satisfaction of seeing that he'd affected her.

"Oh, yeah," he said, his voice a deep purr that made her nerves leap and her hands shake. She'd heard men's voices go deep like that, moments before they lost control.

The rag she'd been using to hold the heavy iron skillet slipped and she burned her hand. She bit her lip to keep from crying out, but dropped the pan with a clatter, barely managing to keep the food from falling into the fire.

"Are you all right?" Instantly, Zach was beside her, his arm sliding around her waist to pull her away from the fire. She stiffened at the scent of alcohol on his breath.

"It's nothing." She eyed him warily. He didn't seem inebriated, but the fact that he'd been drinking while she was out here alone irritated her. She turned out of his arm and headed for the back of the wagon, seeking the crock of salve Old Bridge, Little Wolf's medicine man, had given her long ago, the salve that had healed the wounds on her back and saved her life. She knew Zach watched her go, felt his gaze sear her back. Her clumsiness wasn't his fault, but she had to convince him to keep his hands off her and stop looking at her that way. He reminded her of things she'd rather forget.

"What did you find out?" she asked, as she dabbed on salve and wrapped her hand.

"Humph," Zach mumbled around a mouthful of food. "The soldiers caught up with the Cheyenne at a place called Turkey Springs." He paused for another bite.

"And?" Caroline demanded, so impatient for news that she itched to snatch his plate away.

"The soldiers, what's left of them, are limpin' to Camp Supply."

"Yes!" Caroline cried, pressing her fingers to her lips. "Were many Cheyenne killed?"

"No," Zach told her, shaking his head. "Little Wolf kept the soldiers away from the only fresh water for miles.

They ended up drinking horse pi—uh, horse urine to survive."

"Oh, my," Caroline whispered and clutched her arms around her middle. "That was well done, but the soldiers will be incensed." She turned to Zach. "The Cheyenne will have to run even faster now."

Concern for her friends escalated. She imagined them on foot, running as fast as they could, casting frightened glances over their shoulders at mounted soldiers in hot pursuit. The vivid images made her nauseated and left her feeling helpless.

"Our best plan is still to rendezvous with Little Wolf at the Cimarron station." Zach looked into the dark surrounding their camp and Caroline shuddered at the steely glint in his eyes. Little Wolf's warriors would take one look into those eyes and shoot him down, or die trying. She pitied the men he sought. They didn't stand a chance.

He rose, empty plate in hand. "We'll camp near the river and wait for them to find us."

"But what about the soldiers?"

"We'll have to avoid them, won't we?"

"How? There's no cover near the river and it will be crawling with soldiers." She reached for Zach's dirty plate, but he shook his head.

"I'll wash it. You need to keep that bandage dry."

She reached for the plate again, but only succeeded in scraping her nails across Zach's knuckles. He bit off a curse and dropped the plate in the fire.

"Let me see your hand," Caroline said, and grabbed his hand, pulling him into a crouch beside the fire where she could see better. "Mercy!" she whispered, seeing the raw, scraped flesh revealed by the flames. She turned to berate him and saw the dark circle around his right eye.

"Drinking and fighting?" she asked. She sniffed his knuckles. Someone had poured whiskey over them and a few threads from a crude bandage had stuck in the raw spots. She frowned. "What was it again that you had to hurry back to town for? It wasn't to pound some sense into a certain fool, was it?"

She shoved his hat off and grabbed his chin, ignoring his indrawn breath, and turned his face to check for more bruises. "You should have left the bandage on. The eye's a dead giveaway. I did have a brother, you know."

"Quit fussin'," he growled. "I'll be fine in a couple of days." He flexed the fingers of his right hand and winced.

"Looks like you got the worst of it." She glared at him. "What were you thinking? You could have been seriously injured. Then what good would you be to me?" Her throat clenched. Fear, she told herself, from imagining herself alone on the prairie, not knowing where he was or if he was coming back.

"Sit," she said, and shoved him backward onto his bedroll. She retrieved her crock of salve and some clean rags for bandages from the wagon and dropped them in his lap. His flinch was very satisfying.

"I'm fine," Zach said, and tried to stand, but she shoved him back with a hand firmly pressed to his chest. He gasped and his whole body went still. She glared into his face, daring him to stop her as she unbuttoned his shirt. The sight that awaited her rocked her back on her heels.

His chest, all bulging muscle and rock-hard abdomen, bore a light covering of black, curling hair that spread across his upper chest, then narrowed into a thin line that shot down his rippled belly to disappear below his belt. Caroline's mouth went dry and her eyes widened. She'd seen plenty of bare male chests, but none that exuded such strength and power. She prayed she'd never have to defend herself against him.

She'd also never seen bruising like this. Carefully, she pressed a finger to the biggest bruise.

"Damn! Are you tryin' to kill me?" Zach growled, confirming her suspicions that the ribs beneath were broken.

She gently turned him and gasped at the damage she

found. His back was completely covered in bruises. "What on earth happened? Did Igor do this to you?"

"No," Zach growled and pushed her away. "I'll be fine. It's just a few bruises."

She snatched up the petticoat and pulled her knife. "You've got at least one broken rib. Does it hurt when you breathe?"

"Like the very devil," Zach muttered, giving her an ungracious scowl.

"Men," Caroline grumbled. "You're all such babies when you're hurt. You'd think I was going to stick pins in you, or rub you all over with chili peppers."

"I've already been bitten by that blade, so you'll have to forgive me if I'm not very trustin'." He shoved her crock into her hand and started to get up, but the quick movements caused him so much pain, he subsided with a deep groan. "Make it quick, all right?"

"Might as well get it over with," she said, feeling pretty grim. She didn't like being this close to his bare chest, but he'd gotten hurt defending her tattered honor. She'd have to suppress her nervousness long enough to help him.

Caroline opened the crock and the smell of bear grease filled the air between them. Zach recoiled and she grinned. "Good medicine. Sit still."

Quickly, she spread a thin layer of the precious salve over the worst of the bruises, then helped Zach stand while she bound his chest with long strips cut from her ruined dress.

"I smell like a dead grizzly," he complained as she tied off the last strip below his rib cage. "How long do I have to wear this stuff?"

"Oh, a couple of weeks should do it," she said, and busied herself re-bandaging her burned hand. She didn't want him to see that her hands were shaking. Surprisingly, the warmth of his body, the texture of his skin and the hair-roughened planes of his chest and back had raised feelings in her that she couldn't identify. She felt breathless, and her body tingled in places that had never known a tingle, but had suffered many brutalities. It was reacting in ways she'd never have dreamed it could. And that frightened her.

She had no illusions where this man was concerned. He'd take what he needed from her and leave. Abruptly, the long path of her life loomed before her and she gazed down the barren stretch with wrenching hopelessness. She'd had such dreams once, back in Maryland, before her father had bundled up the family and torn them from everything dear and familiar. She'd been so young then, just a girl enjoying her first parties, dances, beaus. She remembered how it felt to have a man take her arm, open doors for her, fetch her a glass of punch after a rousing dance.

She gave herself a mental shake. Life had changed. She would never again be that young woman. She wouldn't want to be that naive, that innocent again. Better to understand what she was up against.

She glanced up to find Zach watching her, his face tense, his eyes storm dark. Could he read her feelings in her face? Did he see her confusion, her uncertainty? She saw her own reluctance mirrored in his eyes, along with the heat that had stirred something deep inside her to life. Something she didn't welcome.

"Caroline," he said, and his voice had again become that low, deep growl. This time her fear was curbed. She trusted him to control his raw power, as she now realized he'd done in past encounters. Her heart pounded hard in her chest, but she ignored it and rose on tiptoe, let her hands settle on his broad chest and met his lips as he leaned toward her.

She tensed, expecting the screaming to start in her head, but it never came and she let herself sink against him. His lips were firm and warm, and his whiskers rasped the tender skin around her mouth. His breath fanned her face and she inhaled deeply, holding it tight, holding part of him inside her. She returned the pressure of his lips, and when it wasn't enough, slid her fingers up through the soft curls at his nape to pull him closer. He groaned against her lips, then turned her so that her head fell back against his arm.

She lost her balance, clutched his arm for support, but it was no use. She felt swallowed by him, overwhelmed by his body over hers and the rising passion she felt in him. She ripped her mouth from his, her heart pounding a staccato beat. She staggered away from him, the back of her hand pressed over her throbbing lips, as fear stole the warmth from her body.

"I-I'm sorry," she whispered. "I can't." She hurried out of the circle of firelight, letting the darkness swallow her. She ran toward the small stream nearby and leaned against a tree while she caught her breath. The rough bark dug into her fingers, reminding her that she was a living, breathing, feeling woman.

So why was she huddled here in the dark with tears streaming down her cheeks, gasping for breath? She let go of the tree and swiped at the tears. Tonight she had chosen to let herself feel, to try to understand what her body was telling her about this man. But it was no good. The fear would rule her life forever.

She might as well accept that she was ruined. Sobbing in the woods wasn't going to make it better. She slid down the bank to the stream and splashed her face with the cool water until her cheeks cooled.

Then she sat on the bank and watched the moon pass from cloud to cloud on its journey across the night sky. She sighed. Her fear might have spoiled the kiss, but . . . she sighed.

For a few minutes, it had been splendid. And she could live with that. Stolen moments of incredible splendor. She smiled and pressed her fingers to her lips, reliving the heat, the pleasure. Many women lived their entire lives with much less. For a long time, she'd been one of them.

She'd hoard this moment. She wasn't likely to steal many more.

Chapter Six

Zach started to follow Caroline, but after a few quick steps, he began to black out. His ears were ringing, too. He tried to remember if he'd been kicked in the head, and realized he might have blacked out when several men fell on top of him. He'd be lucky if he could ride to-morrow, let alone chase a frightened female through the woods tonight.

He'd give her some time to herself, but if she didn't return soon, he would find her. Somehow.

If he hadn't already been black and blue, he would have kicked himself for scaring her. Again. What was it about this woman that made him lose control? He had known hundreds—well, perhaps not hundreds, but many—beautiful women in his life. He had been married to a beautiful woman and knew from personal experi-ence that, generally speaking, they were highly overrated. Patricia, though shallow as a drought-plagued stream, had been exceptionally beautiful, with platinum-blonde hair, large brown eyes, full lips and a perfect nose. Odd, he noted with surprise, her image didn't come to him readily. He'd had to concentrate to remember her face.

That face—along with Patricia's voluptuous body— had overcome his objections to marriage. Still, his pri-mary purpose in marrying had been to provide an heir to please his ailing father. Then there had been Josh and Abby to consider. Josh's injury had left him unable to fa-ther a child. Abby had been grief-stricken, but stoic, and hungry for a child of her own. Marrying Patricia had been the least Zach could do for his family.

All would have been well if Patricia hadn't been such a shrew. Zach had told her that once they married, he would not relocate to Richmond to work in her daddy's bank. She'd ignored him, certain that her charms would sway him. If he'd known how badly her disappointment would sour her disposition, he might have reconsidered.

When she finally became pregnant, she gave full rein to her petulant nature. She'd refused to lift a dainty finger to help run the family's thoroughbred farm or maintain the family home. Her pregnancy, she was quick to explain, rendered her nigh unto an invalid who must be waited upon hand and foot. Her only departure from this languor was shopping. She had begun spending money in the nearby town of Lexington as if it was so much sand sifting through her fingers.

When Zach put an end to her spending spree, a tearful plea to her daddy had brought the man running. But when Daddy arrived and discovered what his darling daughter had been up to and learned she was also pregnant, he'd refused to take her home and, probably for the first time in Patricia's overindulged life, he'd given her a stern lecture about her responsibilities as a wife and a member of the McCallister family.

Zach snorted. Then the old man had left him to deal with the aftermath. Fortunately, another call to duty had conveniently arrived and he'd answered with embarrassing alacrity. He had been home only rarely in the past six years, and his visits had become fewer and further between due to Patricia's vitriol. Luke had been the only bright spot in his visits—a healthy, active little towheaded toddler, thanks to the love of Zach's family, not the child's mother. But Patricia had done her best to keep him away from his son, and when the boy started shying away from him, Zach had begun limiting his time with him.

No, Zach acknowledged, his experience with beautiful women had not been pleasant. He preferred short, mutually satisfactory liaisons with experienced women who had no expectation but a night's pleasure, and whose perfumed skin was soft and lush. Despite her natural beauty, Caroline's sun-browned skin, rough hands and chipped, broken nails did not inspire thoughts of intimacy. Let alone her preference for buckskin, though he had to admit her attire wasn't a total hardship on his part.

So, why couldn't he keep his hands—and lips—off her? The woman recoiled from his touch and the only time he'd dared a taste of those cherry-red lips, she had run from him in tears. And she kissed like a virgin, as timid as a doe, not the kiss of a married woman.

He could hardly blame her for being wary. He had seen how she was treated by the townspeople, but he could understand their reasoning. Unlike them, he had stood at the place where Patricia had died and felt the horror of her passing. He knew that Caroline had been a victim, at least she had been while a captive of the Kiowa. He admired her for surviving that nightmare. What he could not understand was why she had married Little Wolf. Had she been forced there, too? Had the man bought her from White Bear and made her his personal slave?

Zach shook his head. No, the townspeople referred to her as Little Wolf's wife, or squaw, a term that made his blood boil. It implied she was of less worth than a whore, an object of open scorn with whom no decent woman would even speak, yet the same term implied that she was available, even willing, to satisfy the base needs of any man willing to stoop low enough to have her. He had learned that her uncle's business had fallen off so sharply after she returned and began working in the store that the man had been forced to keep her out of sight, never allowing her to come in contact with his customers. Still, his business had not recovered from the stigma she brought. Small wonder that he'd allowed her to buy out her share of the business and leave town with it.

Zach's fists clenched and his breathing became labored, increasing the pain in his ribs. He forced himself to relax. This outrage on her behalf surprised him, too. He knew who Caroline was, what had happened to her, but it didn't keep him from admiring her determination and her devotion to her husband's people. She shouldn't have risked her own safety to deliver relief to the Cheyenne, but her safety was his responsibility now. Although he felt the weight of that responsibility keenly, he could not let it overshadow his own goals.

With the Cheyenne on the run, he worried for Luke's safety. He feared that, if pressed, the Cheyenne would kill their captives to keep them from slowing the group. Everything he had learned about Little Wolf persuaded him that the man was honorable, but Cheyenne warriors were known to be rash, even emotional. How long would they tolerate a child that with every glance reminded them of their hated enemies? How was his son being treated in such desperate times? Was he being forced to run, or was he being carried or allowed to ride? His nerves jangling, Zach forced his fingers to unclench, his jaw to relax, his mind to turn from the horrors he could imagine all too well, but could do nothing to prevent at present.

Also, he had his orders to consider, and keep secret from Caroline. If she learned he was a soldier, he could not predict her reaction. Would she turn him over to the Cheyenne, let them kill or torture him? He couldn't let that happen. Without him, Luke had no one, and no hope.

He must tame this unwanted fascination with Caroline and strive to keep his distance. Yes, her kiss tonight had nearly brought him to his knees. Her sweet surrender had instantly turned him hard as a fence post in a January blizzard, but he could not let lust cloud his reason. He shifted as his erection once again strained against his pants. What was he thinking? The woman was the *wife* of a Cheyenne chief. He'd heard that some Indians burned off the noses of unfaithful wives, so that everyone who looked at them knew what kind of woman they were.

Damnation! What did they do to the man involved? Where did he get burned? Zach's knees jerked upward instinctively and he went soft faster than if he'd been tossed in an icy river. He was crazy to take chances. If he wanted to earn her trust and eventually convince her to help him find his son, he'd better apologize and make sure he never kissed her again.

Hearing her light tread approaching the fire, he struggled to stand. She stopped before him, making no effort to conceal her tear-streaked face. Her eyes were puffy, the tip of her nose was bright red, and her lashes were wet and spiky. She might as well have punched him in the gut. He felt like a heel.

"I'm sorry, Caroline," he said, itching to hold her and console her, but suspecting she'd knee him in the groin if he tried. "I never should have touched you. It won't happen again. In the future, I'll keep my distance."

"Don't worry about it," she said, turning away. "I'll live. Get some rest."

He lay still with his hat tipped over his face, forcing himself to feign sleep when she stopped beside him. She knelt beside the wagon to pull the pins from her hair, being careful not to lose a single pin, then she dragged her fingers through the tangles. His fingers itched to sift through the soft, shining curls that tumbled halfway down her back as she separated and neatly braided them again. The hair over her left ear shifted and, before she patted it back into place, he glimpsed a knot of mangled skin at the base of her ear. His breath caught, but he covered the gaff with a snore and shifted to his other side.

What could have caused such an injury? What was she hiding beneath that carefully placed swath of hair? He completely lost his train of thought, and nearly his mind, as he watched her crawl under the wagon, her derriere wiggling. He bit his sore lip to keep from groaning.

Who was he kidding? No matter how hard he tried, he couldn't keep his eyes off her. Something about her pulled at him. She made him want her as he had never wanted a woman before.

Distance? Hah! He wanted nothing between his skin and hers.

He decided he *had* blacked out during the fight. It had left him delusional.

* * *

Little Wolf settled beside Feather On Head's tiny fire and breathed deeply of the fragrant smoke and the scent of the meat his wife was cooking. After two days of running fights, he had allowed small fires, carefully tended, to cook the cattle Little Finger Nail and his young warriors had brought.

Feather stepped close, singing a song about him, her husband, and the people who looked to him for guidance. He smiled at her and speared a chunk of meat from the great horn spoon that she had filled with stew. He offered it to the sky, the earth and the four directions before eating and nodded, "*Napeheve'ahta.*"

While he finished eating, he watched the rest of the camp settle into blankets. Some, who had no blankets, buried themselves in leaves and twigs to find warmth. There was much singing, and many gave thanks that none had died in the fighting at Turkey Springs. The injured slept, including Lame Girl, whose ankle had been shattered by a stray bullet during the fighting.

The hurting of this child, here in their own country, angered Little Wolf more than any other injury. No word of this harm would be carried on the talking wires, but the story of the three soldiers and one scout killed would bring the *veho* soldiers swarming like a cloud of locusts. Tomorrow the people must run hard.

This first fight had given the *Tsitsitas* new hope. Little Wolf's few good men had held off the soldiers for two days, and the young warriors who had never known battle were satisfied at last. He stared into the dancing flames, listening to the soft music of Little Finger Nail's flute and let his spirit travel the long road ahead of them. Beyond the rolling bluffs and canyons ahead lay the tracks of the iron horse and the great, flooding river. Ahead of that stretched much open ground with no trees to hide their passing.

The *Isitsitas* now drew near places where many of their people had died—Sand Creek, Sappa, Washita—places where much blood had been spilled, blood that had not yet been avenged. Many hearts would be filled with sorrow. Many eyes would burn as they followed Yellow Swallow, the son of the Yellow Hair, Custer, and their own Monahseta, who had become Custer's wife after the deaths at Washita. Little Wolf had hoped that this child of the enemy would soften the hearts of the soldiers toward his people. But nothing had changed and his people had grown to hate the daily reminder of their enemy living among them.

It was good that the boy had not brought bad luck in the fighting, as some had said he would. Little Wolf watched him now, chasing a rabbit with the other boys. Many times he had found Yellow Swallow hiding, his eyes troubled because the people whispered against him. The whispering would grow louder as they moved north. How could he protect the boy?

His gaze returned to the flames and he blew on them, searching out Caroline, whose yellow hair made her look so much like Yellow Swallow. He found her sleeping beneath a wagon that Little Wolf knew held food and blankets for his people, if they could only reach her. The man that Little Wolf had seen with her before slept beside the fire.

No, he did not sleep. The man watched Caroline, his body stiff, hungry for her. Alert, Little Wolf watched the man, but when the man only closed his eyes and slept, Little Wolf turned from the fire and searched out Yellow Swallow, who was settling down to sleep with his friends.

Little Wolf pulled his blanket tighter around his shoulders as the fire dwindled and his new plan for the Swallow took shape in his head. Tomorrow would come soon enough with its sorrows, but tonight was a good night.

Caroline pulled the wagon to a stop on a bluff above the Arkansas River and set the brake with a weary sigh.

Heavens! She was bone-weary and sick of the trail. She longed for a hot bath and a feather bed, but knew she'd get nothing like that here. She pulled out her spyglass and pointed it north to where Zach's horse was tethered outside the Cimarron Station of the Santa Fe Railroad, the first of three railroads the Cheyenne must cross on their journey home.

The Cimarron Station was not much of a train station. If they hadn't been desperate for news, she and Zach wouldn't have stopped here. She would have preferred to travel farther north, not bring attention to themselves and their wagonload of goods. Zach had pointed out that they'd be hard to miss on the broad, sparsely wooded prairie. Better to step right up and shake people's hands than leave them to imagine the worst.

At least it was a fine day and the rain that had caused them so much misery during the past two days had finally stopped. She'd begun to fear she'd never be dry again. She must remember to thank Uncle James for the fine tarp he had included in the load of supplies; otherwise, her attempt to aid the Cheyenne would have ended with the goods being ruined by the deluge.

Her arms and shoulders had finally rebelled at the constant abuse of driving the wagon, especially in the sucking mud. Zach had cheerfully taken over the task, but she couldn't help wondering how long even his rock-hard body could bear the constant jerk and strain of the reins.

She climbed wearily off the wagon and began unharnessing the mules. With the Arkansas River running at flood stage due to the recent rains, Zach didn't want to try fording it without at least one more man to help. They had planned to camp near the station their first night here, then scout for a better camp the next day—somewhere less noticeable, preferably with a few trees. Caroline snorted as she scanned the horizon. There was so little natural cover here, tending to her personal needs had required a scouting expedition. If Zach wanted better cover for the rendezvous with the Cheyenne, they'd have to backtrack to the southwest. Assuming the Cheyenne made it this far.

Rumors, whispers, suspicion, fear—the country they'd passed through was rife with it. Hundreds of settlers, ranchers, cowboys and drifters had been reported missing. The citizens were near hysteria. The Cheyenne must be having difficulty waddling north, given all the beef and sheep they'd been reported to have stolen and consumed. If it wasn't so frightening, it would have been funny.

But there was nothing amusing about the stories of running battles with soldiers, of Cheyenne men, women and children dead and wounded. She couldn't bear to think what her friends were going through. She'd hold her breath every time she saw a rider approaching. She couldn't help it. Her fear that each stranger brought news of the death of someone she loved had her sweating through the long nights, wishing the Cheyenne's journey would end.

She jumped at the sound of approaching hoofbeats and ran to the wagon for Zach's rifle. She'd barely settled it against her shoulder when Zach rode up.

"I could have shot you six times before you got to that gun," he shouted, as he swung out of the saddle and stomped over to her. Obviously, he wasn't satisfied with merely yelling at her. He wanted to make certain she knew he was angry. "Were you sleeping?"

"I'm not that lucky." Too weary to argue, she let him take the rifle and returned to picketing the mules. "How do cold beans sound for dinner?"

"Tired?" he asked, and cocked an eyebrow at her answering snort. "So ladylike today."

She gave another snort. "Any news?"

"Some good, some bad," Zach said, but avoided looking at her. "You'll be happy to hear that your Cheyenne friends are still at large and mainly well and whole."

"Honestly?" Caroline dropped to the ground and gazed up at him, weak with relief. "What about all the reports we've heard of battles and such?"

"Some skirmishes. The reports were exaggerated," he

told her. He pulled the saddle off his horse and carried it back to where she had parked the wagon before setting it down. "Shall we build the campfire here?" He indicated an area largely free of brush and glanced up at her.

She nodded and couldn't help smiling. Over the past week, they'd settled into a civilized nightly routine. Luckily, they shared similar philosophies concerning life on the trail and what entailed a satisfactory camp. She wouldn't say they'd become friends, but after that one explosive kiss, they'd become allies. They skirted each other beautifully, keeping a safe distance, never touching, and rarely making eye contact. She appreciated the distance, but his politeness was driving her crazy.

"What about the reports of dead Cheyenne?" She rose slowly, pausing once she gained her feet to rub the small of her back, which always ached now that she'd traded sweeping floors for driving mules.

He paused in the process of hauling her box of cooking supplies out of the wagon to look at her. "One death. A man. The papers didn't have a name, but it wasn't Little Wolf."

"Oh, my." She froze and pressed her hand over her heart, which had screeched to a halt and resumed an unsteady beat. "Thank God." She sat on his saddle and watched him pull her box of pots and pans out of the wagon. "Soldiers?"

"Several dead," he said, and set the box beside her, looked directly at her. "You do understand what this means?"

"More troops," she said with a solemn nod. "How will the Cheyenne make it? They're not even across the first railroad and already there have been, what, three battles?"

"Not battles. Skirmishes. Although the one at Big Sandy last night involved several hundred soldiers and civilians."

She gasped. "Several hundred? How are the Cheyenne doing this?" She scrubbed her hands over her face, elated by the news, but alarmed by its consequences. "They're running as fast as they can go, most of them on foot or on worn-out horses. They're all carrying supplies, food, even children. Where are they finding the strength?"

Zach shook his head. "The newspapers claim the soldiers are at a disadvantage—unfamiliar terrain, single-shot rifles and faulty ammunition versus the Cheyennes' Winchester repeating rifles—but the truth is Little Wolf is outmaneuverin' them. Every time the soldiers have approached them, the Cheyenne have had the advantage of terrain, position, water—everythin'. They've built fortifications, dug rifle pits. He's out-soldierin' the soldiers." Zach marched off to put his horse on a picket line, giving him plenty of lead to graze on the sparse grass, then returned to lean on the wagon. He braced his shoulders against the wagon bed behind him and crossed his ankles.

Caroline had cleared a small circle and was arranging kindling. "We're low on wood. We'll have to start gathering buffalo and cattle chips for fuel. I'll keep the fire small tonight. Even a small one can be seen for miles on the plains."

"The smell of your biscuits will get their attention long before they see a fire," Zach said with a dry chuckle.

"Is that a complaint or a compliment?"

"A compliment, which could quickly become a complaint if I have to share."

She smiled as she struck the flint, then bent to blow the tiny sparks to life in the kindling and began adding larger sticks. She'd make a cobbler tonight, she decided, pleased by his compliment. "When do you plan to tell me the bad news?"

His continued silence told her she wouldn't like his news. She settled on the ground, knees bent and legs to one side, and waited. The turmoil of emotion on his face surprised her. Why did he seem so torn?

Over the past few days she'd begun to suspect that he had a military background—a very recent military background, given the packet of official-looking papers she'd glimpsed one day when he'd been rummaging in his saddlebag. She suspected he might be using her to infiltrate Little Wolf's camp. But why? Until a few days ago, he could have walked into Little Wolf's camp, escorted by an agency official, although it would have been difficult to get to Little Wolf himself. Why had he sought her out? The only thing she could do for him that he couldn't accomplish himself was assure Little Wolf that he could be trusted. That would enable him to move freely among the Cheyenne, which meant that he was searching for something or someone among them.

Why did he dodge her questions? Whenever she tried to make conversation, asked about his family, his work, his life before this, he changed the subject. Several times he either left or ignored her completely.

And why had he been acting so strange lately? His behavior had become more erratic with each day that passed. He questioned every stranger they encountered, demanding to know what they knew, how they'd come to know it, from whom they'd learned it. She'd awakened several times in the night to find him sitting up, staring into the fire. Keeping watch, he'd told her. She hoped he'd soon learn to trust her enough to confide in her.

"Until now, the military action has been led by a couple of idiots. They've failed so miserably that the commander of Fort Dodge, Lieutenant Colonel Lewis, has taken over." Zach started pacing, his hands shoved into the pockets of his pants. "Lewis is more experienced. He's even said that the only way he'll leave the field without capturing the Cheyenne is to be carried off."

"Oh," Caroline murmured and watched him stalk back and forth. Although that wasn't good news, it didn't warrant this much agitation. His pacing made her tense, but she hadn't missed his informed assessment of the situation. She'd been right about his military background, past and present. He must have been in communication with the Army to be so well informed. Soldiers weren't likely to reveal so much information to anyone other than another soldier. And his information seemed detailed, things only an officer would know. "Do you believe Lewis is capable of fulfilling that threat?"

Zach finally stopped pacing and looked at her. "Yes, and if he does, I'm afraid your efforts will have been in vain."

Caroline added several larger sticks to the fire and watched it flare higher. She rose and carefully dusted off her buckskins, giving herself time to absorb all that he'd said, and not said. Assuming her observations were correct, did he plan to turn in the Cheyenne, take Little Wolf captive? Zach estimated that they should rendezvous with the Cheyenne any day now. Hardly long enough for her to find out what he was planning and try to stop him, without letting him know she suspected him.

"Your information can be trusted?" she asked, careful to keep her voice neutral.

He nodded, looking miserable. "Yes, but I don't know if I can stand by and let that happen."

Caroline blinked, completely taken off guard. "I don't understand." She searched his face. Did he realize she suspected him? Was this a ruse to confuse her?

"I believed Rendlebrock would fail and he has," he said, gripping her arms and staring into her eyes. "But Lewis won't." He released her and ran his hand through his hair as he turned away. "It's killin' me, hearin' about battles, about children and innocent bystanders bein' shot." He stood with his back to her, hands on his hips.

"Don't worry about the children," she said. He shot her a disgruntled look over his shoulder and she raised her hands, palms out. Why was he so concerned with the safety of the women and children? "The Cheyenne cherish their families. Believe me, they will do everything in their power to keep them safe."

She placed her hand on his shoulder. When he didn't shrug it off, she stroked his arm and leaned forward to peer into his face. "Perhaps I could help, if you told me what's bothering you."

He turned to face her. "You're certain the children will be protected?"

"Little Wolf would surrender before allowing them to be harmed," she assured him. "It's the soldiers you should be worrying about."

"I am," he assured her. "I am." He said nothing further on the subject the rest of the night. In fact, he hardly spoke at all. But Caroline found herself watching him, her curiosity aroused.

Could he be searching for a child? The possibility seemed far-fetched, but not impossible. She couldn't recall a white child being adopted by anyone while she'd lived among the Cheyenne. The only child the whites might possibly be interested in was Yellow Swallow. Had Custer's white wife had a change of heart and decided to acknowledge his half-Cheyenne son? Was Zach here to claim him?

She doubted it. Libby Custer had too much pride in her husband's name to allow it to be tarnished by a half-breed child. She had refused even to meet the boy.

However, another child could have been adopted since the Cheyenne had moved onto the reservation. If time allowed when Little Wolf caught up with them, she would ask his wives. If anyone knew, it would be Quiet Woman and Feather On Head.

Chapter Seven

Zach woke to the sun on his face and the smell of fresh coffee. He sat up and ran a hand over his eyes, sloughing off the deepest sleep he'd had since hitting the trail with Caroline. He glanced around the quiet camp, but found no sign of her. He listened, but heard no rustling in the bushes. He jumped to his feet and searched the terrain surrounding the camp, but there was no sign of her, and he could see for miles.

Hell, the sun was barely up. Where could she be? Then

he spotted the trail of footprints in the dew-covered grass. She'd headed toward the river. How many times did he have to tell her not to try to carry the heavy water barrel by herself? He shook his head and started after her. The crazy woman thought she was still living with the Cheyenne. Well, he'd remind her again. Her refusal to allow him to help with the heavy chores was wearing thin. He was not some lazy brave, to sit by and watch his woman work.

His woman? Zach scoffed. He'd better watch himself and not utter those words aloud.

Busy imagining the result of a confrontation with Caroline, Zach's feet shot out from under him and he slid partway down the grassy slope to the river below. There, only a few feet away, Caroline stood naked in the river shallows. Bending away from him, she was busy rinsing soap from her hair. Zach stood, rooted to the spot. Where he should have seen beauty, he beheld horror. Her back was a hideous mass of raised scars. From her shoulders to her buttocks, her beautiful, alabaster skin had been torn to shreds and left to heal in gaping, gray slashes.

Rage rose in him in a wave of red. All he could see was her back, bathed in blood as she writhed beneath a whip. He wanted to kill, to maim, to torture the monster who had done this to her. Pain stabbed him in the chest, stealing his breath. An inhuman growl was shoved out of his chest and he shot forward, startling her.

She struggled to toss her streaming hair out of her face, but lost her balance on the slippery rocks and started to fall. He caught her, amazed that he had the presence of mind to be gentle while trying to control his reaction. She'd obviously seen his expression; he didn't want her to think he found her scars disgusting.

"Who did this to you?" He held her steady until she found sure footing again, then turned her so that he could see her back. He wanted to lash out, to hurt the person who had wounded her. "Is he dead?"

"Go away!" Caroline shrieked, her voice high and shrill, laced with panic. She clutched one arm over her breasts and the other over the apex of her thighs. Her eyes darted from her exposed body up to his face. She swung her hair to fall over her left ear. "Leave me alone!"

Zach had been about to oblige her, not sure he could control his anger at the realization of her injuries, but the sight of her wet hair plastered over her ear stopped him. Here she stood, completely naked, vulnerable, all her secrets exposed, and she still made certain that ear was covered.

"What else are you hiding, Caroline?" he asked and quickly stepped to her left side.

"No!" she cried and she tried to swing away from him, but he had a tight grip on her arms. He anchored her slippery body against him and reached for the hair lying over her ear. His heart hammered in his chest and his vision seemed to sharpen and narrow as he lifted the hair.

Screams filled the air as he stared in horror at the mutilated stump that should have been a delicate shell. Nothing remained of the structure that had obviously been burned off and left to heal without treatment. His stomach pitched and he forced himself to draw a deep, steadying breath. He could not lose his gorge here where she would see and know that she had caused it. Sickened by his invasion of her privacy, he carefully replaced the hair over her scarred ear. Only then did the screaming register.

Caroline had gone rigid and stood leaning back against him. Mouth wide, eyes rolled back in her head, she screamed continuously. The sound scraped up his backbone, reaching into his very soul. How could he help her? She was obviously reliving the horror, which was more than she could bear, more than he could bear.

Determined to relieve her suffering—caused by his stupidity—he turned her to face him and wrapped his arms around her.

"It's all right," he crooned into her right ear. He

squeezed his eyes shut as he thought of the other, mangled stump. "Stop, Caroline. It's over, sweetheart. No one's ever going to hurt you again." Automatically, he started to stroke a hand down her back to soothe her. He encountered a scarred ridge and jerked his fingers off her back, raising his shaking hand to her bright hair. Again and again, he stroked her head while whispering words of comfort. He kissed her cheeks, her temples, holding her close to keep her warm, praying that she'd recover from the shock, afraid her screams would never end. Suddenly, she stopped, leaving his ears ringing.

"That's good, sweetheart," he said, and pressed one last kiss to her cheek. If she'd been lucid, she would have berated him, but he was so relieved that she'd stopped screaming, he was willing to take that chance. "It's over now. You're safe."

She sucked in a deep, shuddering breath and her body slumped against him. He held her, supporting but not confining her. A few breaths later, she pushed herself away and blinked up at him, her face pale but with bright spots of color blooming on her cheeks.

"Let go of me," she said, her voice low and shaky, her eyes curiously flat, her face still.

"Can you stand?" He didn't want to add to her emotional trauma by allowing her to fall and injure herself.

She took a step back, her chin coming up in that damn-it-all gesture that usually infuriated him. Now he was relieved to see it. He wasn't feeling too steady himself. His stomach rolled, confirming his suspicions.

"Do you mind?" she asked, and he relished the glint in her eye, welcomed her haughty dignity. "I'd like to finish bathing."

He blinked, amazed at her swift transformation from emotional wreck to spitfire, and marveled at the strength of her facade. Someday, he would penetrate it to the woman beneath, but not today. Today, he had caused her untold pain and humiliation. Today, he needed to retreat and allow her some privacy.

He stumbled back up the bank to camp, haltered his horse, slung himself on its bare back and tore out of camp as if a thousand Confederate gorillas were hot on his heels. In truth, nothing but his own conscience rode in pursuit, but today it goaded him.

When he finally felt distant enough from the camp, he pulled the horse to a walk and slid off, retching into an unlucky bush until his insides felt hollow and scarified. Then he staggered away to a deep clump of grass and fell onto his back. He dragged his sleeve over his mouth and stared unseeing at the cloudless sky.

Until today, he'd thought he was strong. He'd thought he could handle any conflict, any challenge that came his way. But today, as he'd stared at Caroline's mutilated ear, he'd known she was stronger than he could ever be.

He had heard the horrible stories told of the Indians' mutilation and torture of white captives, but he'd thought they were just exaggerations. Today he had seen the results, and he suspected that he could not have survived such treatment.

He remembered the women of Dodge City who had sneered at Caroline and his temper seethed. How could people shun someone who had survived such horrors? Of course, she didn't prance around town displaying her scars, but if people knew . . .

What? They'd fall at her feet and beg her forgiveness? They'd put her on a pedestal and sing her praises? Hah! He had no illusions where society was concerned. He had survived the war, been a patient in the hospitals, he'd even been imprisoned for a short time. He'd thought he understood the ugly side of war. He knew that the average citizen, those privileged few who had been untouched by the war, could not begin to comprehend war's life-altering capabilities. They had no understanding of the heights man's inhumanity to his fellow man could reach. When faced with bits of the truth, they recoiled in horror, as he had done today. They recoiled from the sufferers, many even blaming them for their experiences. God had punished them, they often said. He'd even heard one old crone observe that women captured and raped by the Cheyenne had "wanted it."

How could those people look at themselves in a mirror, let alone speak such atrocities aloud, and still attend weekly church services?

He thought about his wife, Patricia, and the horrible death she had suffered because of his neglect, and his soul shuddered. Who was he to point an accusing finger at others when so much blame lay at his own door?

He sighed and pressed his forearm over his eyes. He must return to camp soon. How could he face Caroline? She would see any compassion on his part as pity and scorn it—and him. It would tear his guts out, but he must treat her as he had always treated her—no better, no worse. He couldn't reveal his admiration of her courage, her determination, though he feared it might burst out of him in some unguarded moment.

She hadn't survived with the intent of impressing anyone. She'd survived because her will to live was so strong, she couldn't accept less.

He surged to his feet, eager to face the new challenge, to prove to Caroline that he was made of equally stern stuff. He looked forward to the rendezvous with the Cheyenne with new determination. He would find a way to question Little Wolf, he vowed, and the man who was responsible for Caroline's pain would die.

Caroline finished her bath, being careful not to think about the morning's events, and not allowing herself to worry or wonder what Zach had thought. It was obvious. He'd reacted exactly as she'd expected any man would. He'd run. So fast it had been funny. He couldn't stand being around her now that he'd seen her scars. She'd been right to keep them hidden.

But it hurt! Oh, how it hurt to watch him scramble away from her, to hear his horse's hoofbeats pounding out of camp. She'd suspected that her scars were ugly, but now she knew they were truly hideous, more than a grown man could bear.

Well, she could bear them. She had survived them, and that was all that counted. She'd been wrong about Zach. He was no different from the rest of the men who'd thought that because she had been with an *Injun,* she would spread her legs for any man. Fools!

No, she reminded herself, *that's not true in Zach's case.* He had defended her at every turn. He hadn't taken advantage of her, even though he'd had ample opportunity and knew that no one would have blamed him for it. Well, except for Little Wolf.

Her reaction to the incident disturbed her more than Zach's. It worried her. She still couldn't look back on her capture and that first rape; the memory was too raw. But she'd thought she had forced the memory of the burning to the deepest recesses of her mind. Zach's sudden appearance during her bath had caught her unprepared, vulnerable. Her normal defenses had been down or she would never have allowed him close enough to see how ugly the Kiowa had made her. And her burned ear was only a small part of what they'd done—what *he* had done.

She bent over the fire, brushing out her hair. The comforting routine reassured her, as she listened for the hoofbeats announcing Zach's return. She wanted her hair dry and back in place before he returned. Then she could handle his rejection. She'd pay him for helping her travel this far, and wish him well when he left. Surely, someone would come along who could be persuaded to help get the supplies to Little Wolf and his people. Then she'd return to her life in Dodge City.

The thought left her sick at heart. She'd originally hoped to convince Little Wolf to take her along, but with emotions running high among the younger braves, especially now that Little Wolf had formally set her aside, she wouldn't be safe among the Cheyenne. The simple divorce ceremony, performed after she'd returned to Dodge City, was to ensure that no one thought she belonged to Little Wolf. All it had done was confirm the rumor that she'd been his third wife. Even Little Wolf's denial and that of Feather and Quiet Woman hadn't changed anyone's mind. People had shunned her. The Cheyenne because she'd been set aside by their Old Man Chief and was, therefore, unworthy—and poor to boot! The whites had shunned her because she'd been Little Wolf's wife, and a Kiowa captive.

She remembered daydreaming as a girl of the home she would have someday. Now all she wanted was a man who could love her in spite of the mess her life had become, but no man would take an Indian's leavings. She couldn't even turn to prostitution—not that she ever would—no man would pay to have her.

She could not expect Little Wolf to go on providing for her, protecting her without claiming a husband's rights. Not that he'd ever tried. He had understood that she couldn't bear for a man to touch her, and had never approached her as a husband. But Zach had snuck past her defenses on more than one occasion and surprised her. Whenever she was close to him, she could almost imagine what a normal woman would feel when attracted to a man—a little breathless, and queasy inside. And when he kissed her, her whole body had gone limp and warm, which had scared her. How could she defend herself, if she was limp as an overcooked noodle?

Quiet Woman and Feather On Head had tried to explain that being with a man was not painful, unless it was a woman's first time. Living in the same tipi with them, she had seen them leave Little Wolf's furs with smiles on their faces—after many sighs, deep groans, loud cries and sometimes even laughter. They were always eager to return. But Little Wolf never forced them. She was thankful White Bear had never lain with her as Little Wolf lay with his wives. If White Bear had tried to kiss her, she would have been tempted to bite him. Her body went cold, for she knew how White Bear would have reacted. She would have been lucky to survive his punishment.

Often during the night, as she lay trying not to listen to Little Wolf and his wives during their love play, she had envied them their happiness. She had known she would never experience the joy they shared. Her highest expectation of life was to grow old sweeping up for Uncle James. She would have liked to have a friend. If only Zach hadn't been disgusted by her, she might eventually have been able to count him as one.

As she placed the last pin in her hair, Caroline heard approaching hoofbeats. She nervously patted the hair over her scarred ear and began rolling up her blankets.

"There's a plate of food for you by the fire," she told Zach as he tied his horse to the back of the wagon. She tried to sound normal, but her voice seemed thin, lifeless. She cleared her raw throat and rubbed her arms, bracing herself.

"Thanks," he said and sat on his saddle to devour the food. "I'm hollow as a stump."

She risked a quick glance and found him glancing away from her. She waited, holding her breath, for him to tell her he was leaving.

"I've found a good camp for us tonight, close to the best place to ford the river. Little Wolf would have to be blind to miss us." He rinsed off his plate and wiped it dry, then saddled his horse and tied his bedroll behind the saddle. His movements seemed stiff and awkward, and he avoided looking at her, but he was preparing for the day's travel as he always did.

He's not leaving! she thought, finally allowing herself to believe her eyes. She braced herself on the wagon as relief and disbelief washed over her, leaving her weak-kneed and wobbly. She tried to answer him, but though her throat worked, nothing came out. She swallowed hard and moved to climb into the wagon. He stepped up, as always, to assist her. Stunned, she froze, staring at his hand beneath her arm, touching her. She had thought he'd be too disgusted once he'd seen what had been done to her. As if he read her thoughts, he released her.

"You're staying?" she asked, looking over her shoulder into his face, still struggling to believe it. She waited for him to answer. Would she know if he was lying?

"Of course," he said, his eyes narrowing to slits in the shadow of his hat. "What kind of man do you take me for?"

She saw no lie in his face, but her uncertainty must have shown, for his jaw twitched and his lips thinned. He held her gaze, his eyes flint-hard, his expression determined.

"You're not getting rid of me yet." He helped her climb onto the high wagon seat, his grip firm on her arm. "It's not far," he said, as he handed her the reins. "Then you can rest."

She wrapped the reins around her hands and snapped them over the mules' backs. "I'm not in need of a rest, but if you're feeling poorly, I'll find something to keep me busy." His unusual consideration smacked of pity, and she didn't need anyone's pity. She kept the mules moving, shouting at them like a regular muleskinner, but with a little more delicacy, she hoped.

Zach rode closer than usual and she felt the searing touch of his gaze frequently as they traveled the few miles to the new camp. What was he thinking as he looked at her today? Was he remembering her deformities, her disfigurement? She stiffened, offended by the mere thought.

Rest! she snorted. She appreciated his consideration about as much as she'd appreciated the disgust of the fine ladies of Dodge City. Yes, her body had been damaged, but no one had ever touched her soul. She had never let anyone close enough.

She hoped the rendezvous with the Cheyenne happened soon. She was beginning to care too much what Zach thought of her. That way loomed excruciating pain. Thankfully, he'd never find out the rest of her secrets.

Zach struggled to free himself from a frightening dream. Luke was being whipped and he couldn't stop it. Something sharp bound his throat and someone kept punching him in the ribs. He could barely breathe, let alone fight off his attackers and rescue his son.

"Stop!" a voice cried. A woman's voice. Zach's eyes flew open and he reached for his rifle, but it was gone. He tried to rise, but the sharp prick he'd been dreaming was a real knife pressed to his throat, and the face looming above him had come straight from his nightmare, including the black paint and smiling white teeth. He lay very still, hands out, palms up. Zach had faced death many times in his life, and learned something each time. This time he'd discovered its eyes were as dark and fathomless as the pits it inhabited.

A deep male voice issued a command, which had no effect on the devil whatsoever. Zach remained prone, eyes locked on the man who hadn't yet decided he would live. A whip snapped in the air above him. The devil didn't even blink, but his eyes went flat, empty, and Zach knew those black holes mirrored the man's soul. He didn't fear death; neither giving nor receiving it. That indifference made him the most dangerous man Zach had ever faced. It made him a worthy opponent. Zach took careful note of the man's features.

Surprise flashed across the devil's face as he noted Zach's expression, the emotion barely recognizable under the heavy paint. He jerked the knife off Zach's throat and walked away without a second glance.

Zach sprang into a crouch, reaching for the knife hidden in his boot, only to find it gone, too. The bitter taste of fear annoyed him. He'd only been caught flat once before and he hadn't liked it then either. This time it could have cost three lives: his, Caroline's and Luke's. The last two weren't his to risk. He straightened slowly, keeping his hands loose at his sides.

An older man stood before him wearing ragged buckskins, with a moth-eaten blanket tied around his waist and a large, silver cross on his chest. He was thin, but wiry. Seasoned, Zach realized, a man who had weathered many battles. And he wasn't done yet. He waved a hand

and the warriors surrounding them slipped into the night. Caroline stepped up beside the man.

"Little Wolf, this is Zach McCallister." She gestured to Zach and smiled. "I wouldn't have been able to get here without his help."

Little Wolf nodded, still studying Zach's face. "I have seen him."

The hair on the back of Zach's neck stood straight up. A sudden breeze blew past him, carrying the scent of sage, leaving no question in Zach's mind that the man before him was much more than a chief and warrior. Zach studied the man's lean, almost regal face, noting his many scars, marks of honor and character—hard-won and respected. Little Wolf's broad face was deeply seamed by time and weather, his black eyes keen as a hawk's, yet mysterious. No detail escaped that gaze, but it revealed nothing. Zach resolved never to underestimate him.

Little Wolf nodded and turned to Caroline. "*Nepevomotahehe?*"

Caroline nodded and held her arms out at her sides. "Tired, but well."

Zach watched their interaction intently. They didn't act like a husband and wife who'd been separated for a long time. They hadn't even touched.

Little Wolf glanced between Zach and Caroline, and Zach flinched. Had Little Wolf noticed him studying the two of them? How much had the man seen? Did he know or sense what had happened this morning?

Little Wolf held his gaze. Zach felt like a moth pinned to a wax board as the penetrating gaze searched out his secrets, even poking into the dark places he avoided. There was knowledge and experience in those eyes, and so much more: canniness, wisdom and understanding. Long and deep they probed, until Zach felt the need to squirm. Odd to be on the receiving end of the tactic he often used on others. At last Little Wolf nodded. "It is good."

Caroline shot Zach a questioning glance. He

shrugged, but felt himself relaxing under the other man's stare. Enough to reply with certainty, "Yes, it is good."

Little Wolf clapped him on the back, then took Caroline by the arm. "Come, bring your medicines. Many are sick, and Bridge is tired."

Caroline hurried to the wagon and Little Wolf turned to Zach. "Watch for walkers. They come soon." Then he led Caroline away.

Zach stared into the darkness. "Walkers?" He counted about sixty men and boys in the vicinity, all armed and some painted, but none as heavily as the devil Little Wolf had called off. None of the others looked as fierce or left him feeling cold inside. Of course, none of the others had held a knife to his throat. Had any of them hurt Caroline? Was the man who had murdered Patricia and stolen his son among them? If he was going to learn anything from them, he had to earn their trust. But how?

Carefully, Zach studied them and was surprised to find several middle-aged women among the men, also bearing rifles. Some of the group had followed Little Wolf and Caroline, but most had settled cross-legged on the ground. Many of them wore strips of green hide wrapped around their worn moccasins. The less fortunate made do with tattered moccasins that were more hole than hide. The feet showing beneath them were tough and blood-stained. He felt their weariness like a weight around his neck, dragging him downward. But when their gazes met his, that weariness became the sting of distrust, the burn of determination.

Some of them gnawed strips of jerky, some sipped water from strange-looking containers—animal bladders, he realized with a shudder. With a start, he remembered the extra biscuits Caroline had cooked that night, anticipating the Cheyennes' arrival. He pulled out the first of two boxes and offered it to the nearest man.

The man stared at it for a second, then nodded to Zach

and took the box. He chose one biscuit and passed the box to the next man, then ate slowly. His eyes fell closed and Zach was sure he heard him sigh. He looked up at Zach and smiled. "*Nia'ish*," he said, and rubbed his stomach. Zach grinned back and nodded.

Zach bent to add a log to the fire, but the man stopped him. He replaced the large log Zach held with a much smaller one, and a tamping gesture.

Ah, Zach realized, with a nod. *Keep the fire low.* He brought out some supplies and soon had a kettle of beans warming and a fresh pot of coffee perking. The man had come to investigate the supplies and had discovered the bag of sugar. With an exclamation of delight, he carefully poured some into his hand, then licked his finger, dipped it in the sugar and sucked off the sweetness. Several others exclaimed over his find and tried to dip their own fingers into his sugar, but he jerked his hand away, refusing to share.

Zach laughed and doled out the sugar, then the coffee and the beans. The people's enjoyment of the simple food, and their gratitude, touched him deeply. Conditions on the reservation must have been brutal, he realized, for them to risk their lives in this desperate gamble with so little hope of success.

He wanted to hate these men, for one among them might have killed his wife and taken his son captive, but he found it difficult. He studied them as they ate. Occasionally, they nodded their thanks, their eyes no longer wary and distrustful. Zach realized his own hatred didn't rise as quickly as it had before he'd seen their sorry condition. They couldn't all be guilty, he reasoned, but he would find the man who was.

Someone pointed into the dark beyond the firelight and Zach blinked as small figures began to materialize, heading for the tiny fire. As if he'd called him, a young blond boy stumbled into the light and collapsed beside the fire, out of breath and clearly exhausted.

"Luke?" Zach asked, reaching for the boy as his heart

rose into his throat. The boy looked up, startled, and Zach jerked upright. The boy's waving blonde hair and facial features were vividly reminiscent of the only man who could be his father: Custer.

Disappointment left a bitter taste in Zach's mouth. This must be the blond boy he'd heard about. Not his own son, his kidnapped boy, but George Custer's half-breed son.

Though he felt like he'd been gut-punched, he couldn't succumb to the wrenching emotions tearing through him. More and more children stumbled into the camp, their condition sorrier than the men's. Women followed, some with babies strapped to their backs. Instantly, the men began passing them food and water. Zach retrieved the second box of biscuits from the wagon, then counted heads as the "walkers" ate in absolute silence. Over a hundred and fifty women and children crowded around the tiny fire, but every one got at least a bite of biscuit and several sips of syrupy coffee before they curled up where they sat and slept.

He noted that several people talked about the blond boy while he slept by the fire and the looks they gave him were suspicious, distrustful. The boy must be a constant reminder of Custer, one of their most hated enemies after his attack on Dull Knife's camp at the Washita. Zach resisted the urge to pick up the sleeping child and take him somewhere private, somewhere safe. He hadn't known Custer well, but whether the stories he'd heard were true or false, the boy deserved better.

Though Zach examined the group of children as closely as he could in the flickering light, he saw no more children with light-colored or even brown hair, and Luke's eyes had always been as dark as Patricia's. His hope was dwindling as fast as the fire, but he refused to give up. There were still the Sioux to investigate if his search among the Cheyenne proved fruitless. He would not give up hope.

He would find Luke.

Chapter Eight

Caroline straightened with a groan, pressing a hand to the small of her back. She'd done all she could to help the sick and wounded, which wasn't much. Every person she'd seen—not just the sick, who desperately needed a doctor's care—was a shadow of the person she remembered. She'd like to have five minutes alone with that agent at Darlington. She heard a low growl and jerked, realizing she'd made the sound. She relaxed her jaw, unclenched her fists and took a deep breath. The Cheyenne were a proud people. They would not want to be reminded of their sorry condition. She gathered her medicines and went looking for Little Wolf's wives and Old Bridge, their exhausted medicine man.

She didn't have to look far. Bridge listened carefully as she told him how to administer the quinine. He accepted the box of medicine and supplies with a solemn, *"Nia'ish"*

"You're welcome," she told him. "I wish I could do more."

"You have done much," he said and looked up with a smile as Quiet Woman and Feather On Head joined them. Smiling, nodding politely, they pulled Caroline away.

"Hena'háane," Feather said, and Quiet Woman agreed. "That's enough. We need to talk. Come, sit and eat." They pulled Caroline away from the group and offered her one of her own biscuits.

Caroline refused it with laugh. "I can't talk if my mouth is full. How are you? Are you feeling well? Tired?" She turned each woman about, looked closely at their faces, then gave each one a hug. "I've missed you."

They returned her hugs, then settled on the ground and spread their blankets over her back, shutting out the cold and creating some privacy. Caroline grimaced, guessing what was on their minds by their secrecy and the occasional, mischievous grin.

"He is very handsome, your new *hetan*," Quiet Woman said. She caught Caroline's hands and squeezed hard.

"Does he keep you long in his furs?" Feather asked with a delicate shiver, sticking her head above the encircling blanket to glance at Zach. "He looks very strong."

"He's not my man," Caroline said, reluctant to tell her well-meaning friends that she and Zach weren't intimate. They were sure to chastise her and demand to know why she hadn't snatched him up, as any smart Cheyenne woman without a man would do. "That is, we're not . . . Uh, we're just friends."

As she'd expected, both women frowned at her. Before they could respond, however, Short One, Morning Star's wife, joined the huddle. "Does he make you happy?" she asked Caroline with a pat on the knee and a sideways hug. "He will keep you very warm when the snows come."

When no one spoke, Short One glanced at the faces around her, and Caroline winced at the dismay on Short One's face. "You do not share his furs?"

Quiet Woman and Feather shook their heads, their expressions sad. Short One took Caroline's hand and squeezed it. Quiet Woman and Feather grabbed hold, too, and no one spoke for several heartbeats. Nothing would be said, but each of her friends understood Caroline's reluctance to be with a man. Seeing her with Zach, they had leaped to a hopeful conclusion, only to learn she was no better, no closer to trusting a man again than she'd been when they'd last seen her, almost two years before. Sensing their disappointment Caroline fought the tears she felt gathering, burning her eyelids, but one escaped and rolled down her cheek.

"I have missed you all so much," she whispered, "and I've been worried about you. I'm glad you're safe and well. That's all that matters right now."

Short One gave a very uncharacteristic snort. "*Nápévomóta.* I am well, we are all well, and we do not fear the road ahead." She turned Caroline's face to hers and ·searched her eyes. "You must let go of your fear, *navés'é*. You cannot continue to live half a life. I have watched this man. His eyes follow you and I see hunger in them."

"He must be a good man," Feather added, her head bobbing earnestly. "He would not have brought you to us if he were bad."

"I'm paying him," Caroline told them, at last swallowing the lump in her throat, anxious to help them understand her feelings for Zach. "I don't know very much about him and I don't trust him. He's keeping secrets from me. He's been anxious to catch up with you, but he won't tell me why." She leaned closer and asked, "Have any children been taken captive recently?"

The women gave a low hum of understanding, but shook their heads. "None," Short One said. Feather and Quiet Woman nodded. "Perhaps he does not trust you with his secrets," Short One said, looking to the other two women for agreement.

"Men give much away to the woman who shares their furs." Quiet Woman nodded sagely.

Feather and Short One burst out laughing and Quiet Woman blushed. "It is true," she said and turned to Caroline. "Once you're in his furs, you must stroke his chest and let your hand move lower, down to his penis. Then take it in your hand and do this." She took Caroline's hand, curled her fingers just so and showed her the motion to use. "And while you're doing this, ask him what you want to know. He will tell you everything and not even remember doing it. To make sure, you must then throw your leg over him and take him inside you."

Feather and Short One had stopped laughing and were staring at her, their mouths hanging slack and their eyes wide. Caroline jerked her hand free, which seemed to release Feather and Short One, who again burst out laughing. Caroline shook her head at her friends, but their laughter was so infectious she couldn't help grinning.

"Throw your leg over him?" she said to Quiet Woman, who nodded, got up on all fours and demonstrated.

"Your face!" Short One choked out, laughing so hard she collapsed on Caroline's shoulder, gulping air and wiping tears off her cheeks.

"No more! I cannot listen!" Feather cried. She threw off the blanket, jumped to her feet and hurried away, keeping her knees pressed together tightly.

Short One recovered first, catching a glance from Morning Star, her husband. Caroline saw the exchange, and the warm look Short One gave him in return. It was a look she'd seen the couple share often, filled with understanding and need. It never failed to make Morning Star's chest lift and his eyes smolder as they lingered on Short One. The flush on her cheeks and the glow in her eyes was apparent even in the dim light from the small fire. Caroline felt she had intruded on a very private moment, but Short One noticed Caroline watching and smiled. "Do you see something to fear? You have been hurt in the past, but not every man is an animal."

"Hou!" Quiet Woman agreed, nodding. "Let this new *hetan* teach you the joy. Ask him to . . ."

"Woman!" Little Wolf's voice stopped her cold, something no one else could do. *"Nehetéa'a.* That is enough. We go now."

Quiet Woman rose and went to her husband. "What did I do wrong? She must learn . . ."

Little Wolf hushed her with a finger to her lips, then put an arm around her and whispered in her ear. Caroline smiled, knowing what would follow. She'd also seen this moment many times in the past. As she expected, Little Wolf spoke to Quiet Woman briefly, then kissed her cheek, slapped her fanny and smiled at her over his shoulder as he walked away. In the past, she had found their actions amusing, but tonight, for the first time, she envied her friends' loving relationships with their husbands.

Caroline glanced up and found Zach watching her. He caught her gaze and let his slip to her lips then back to her face. She caught her breath at the hunger in his eyes and Short One gave a low exclamation and sighed beside her.

Short One watched Zach for several long moments, then turned back to Caroline. She kissed each cheek and gave Caroline a hug. "Do not be afraid to share yourself with this man, my friend. Cast away your sorrow and embrace life."

"Not with him. Not until I know more about him. For all I know he could be married." Caroline returned Short One's hug and took a shaky breath. "I wish I could take you with me. It hurts to say good-bye so soon, when we've only just found each other again."

Feather and Quiet Woman returned to add their hugs and good wishes. Quiet Woman opened her mouth to say something, but Feather shushed her and nodded behind them to where Little Wolf stood waiting. "Careful, *navés'é*, or I will be trying your tricks on him this night."

Short One chuckled. "*Nia'ish*, Caroline, but here are my strong sons with a horse to carry these old bones." One son knelt and she stepped onto his thigh, then swung her leg over the horse's back as he boosted her up. Caroline stroked the horse's spotted neck as Short One settled herself, then leaned down to whisper, "Quiet Woman would be proud."

Turning the horse, she called out softly, "Woman! Did you see?"

Morning Star stopped beside Caroline, shaking his head. "What does she speak of?"

Caroline choked and pressed her hands to her cheeks as heat flooded her face. "Short One will tell you," she said with a weak smile. "Later."

Morning Star noticed her blush and smiled. "Ah!" he said. "I will enjoy hearing of this?"

Caroline nodded.

"*Hou,*" he said, returning her smile. "It is well." He watched until Short One disappeared into the darkness. "She is my sun."

"I will see you again," Caroline whispered past the lump rising in her throat.

Morning Star repeated the familiar sentiment and mounted the horse his son held ready for him. "*Ma'heo'o*, take pity on us!" he whispered, staring into the canopy of stars, then he followed Short One into the darkness.

Caroline watched him go, wishing she were once again riding alongside her friends. She sent a fervent prayer for their safety and protection in their wake.

Zach estimated that less than an hour had passed since he'd first awakened, when Little Wolf began sending the Cheyenne to the river in small groups. Caroline had helped the women add supplies from the wagon to their packs and once again strap them onto the ponies or their own backs.

Two strong young braves passed Zach, headed for the river, leading a black-and-white paint pony that carried one of Caroline's friends.

"My sons," a gruff voice said, and Zach found himself facing another old warrior. He must be Dull Knife, the other chief and Little Wolf's brother, whom the Cheyenne called Morning Star. His almost regal face was deeply lined, his eyes deep wells of worry. "They will keep their mother safe as she crosses the river."

Zach struggled for a response, then said simply, "She has given you strong, brave sons."

"*Na'ish.*" The old man smiled and placed a gnarled hand on Zach's shoulder. "Thank you for the help you have given my people, even though you are a soldier. For this reason, my Dog Soldiers not take your weapons or your fine horse. But we help ourselves to your ammunition. Do not worry. We leave you enough to keep our loved ones safe." He nodded to where Caroline and Yellow Swallow were helping the women.

Zach stilled. How had Dull Knife known he was a soldier? Who else knew? The old man's grip tightened and he leaned close to whisper, "My brother and I see many faces in the wind and the smoke."

"I mean you no harm," Zach said, surprised that he could even speak.

"This we know," Dull Knife said, and shrugged. "For this reason, you still breathe." He gathered his worn blanket around his shoulders and turned to leave. "Remember the Cheyenne kindly when you again speak to our father, Sheridan."

"I-I will." Zach stammered, and nodded.

"May you soon find the one you seek," the old man said, and with a last smile, he turned to Caroline and her friends. Zach stared after him, wanting to stop him, to ask him what he knew of his search, but Dull Knife was gone.

A couple of braves drove several horses toward the river and as they passed, the shoulder of a horse bumped Zach. He stepped out of the way, but not before two of the horses caught his eye. They looked like McCallister stock—especially in their lines and gait—despite their sorry condition. They were also bigger than the rest of the horses, which were mostly Indian ponies. He started to follow, wanting a closer look, but Little Wolf stepped into his path.

"Yellow Swallow," he said and spoke a sharp command. Instantly, the young blond boy appeared beside him, his eyes downcast. "You know his father? You have seen the distrust of my people toward the Swallow?"

Zach nodded, surprised by Little Wolf's bluntness.

"You will follow the *Tsitsitas* with the woman and boy. Meet us at winter camp, here." He crouched and drew a crude map in the dirt.

Zach nodded, committing the map to memory. The small valley not far off the intersection of trails to the north and east would be easy to find. "I can find the place, but . . ."

"*Hou.* It is good." Little Wolf destroyed the map with a quick swipe of his moccasin. "Do not follow closely. I do not want Swallow or Caroline hurt in fighting." He turned to leave.

"Wait," Zach said, catching Little Wolf's arm and leaning close. "The man who hurt her. Where can I find him?"

Little Wolf's arm tensed beneath Zach's hand and he saw that the man's fist had clenched around the small quirt he carried.

"He died," Little Wolf said, his gaze feral as it settled on Caroline. "Too easily." He looked into Zach's eyes and Zach saw his own thirst for revenge reflected there, but Little Wolf pressed a hand to his left side and the ferocity disappeared, leaving only a weary chieftain.

"Why didn't you avenge her? She's your *wife*, for God's sake!"

Little Wolf stared into Zach's eyes, once again struggling to control his anger, and once again Zach watched him succeed. This time he was very relieved, for that anger had been directed at him. "Caroline never shared my furs," Little Wolf said curtly, then left.

"Damn." Zach stared into the dark, his thoughts in turmoil. Why was he behaving so rashly? Yes, he wanted to know that the bastard who had hurt Caroline had paid for his abuse of her, but she was not his to avenge. He should be glad the bastard was dead and could no longer harm her, not be wishing he'd been the one to put a bullet in him, or cut off his balls, or any of the other very painful means of death he'd contemplated meting out if he ever met up with the vicious bastard. He'd pushed too hard with Little Wolf. Luckily, the chief had better control of his emotions than Zach seemed to have lately. He reminded himself to keep his goal of finding Luke foremost in his mind and not let concern for Caroline distract him.

What had Little Wolf meant by his cryptic comment about his furs? Had she been his wife, but never allowed him to bed her? Given what he'd seen of her physical scars, he felt sure she probably carried matching emotional wounds. If he wanted to understand, he'd have to ask Caroline. But how could he do that without sounding as if he was accusing her of lying to him?

As the last group of walkers prepared to leave, a small boy yanked away from the woman holding his hand and ran to Zach. With tears streaming down his face, he clung to Zach's leg, but he said nothing. Abruptly, the devil who had threatened Zach earlier stepped in and pulled the boy away. He shouted at the child, cuffed him hard, then kicked him when he turned back toward Zach.

"Stop that!" Zach shouted, horrified by the man's actions. Little Wolf appeared and stepped between the man and boy and with a few sharp words stopped the beating. He spoke with the man as the woman tugged the boy toward the river.

Little Wolf turned to Zach. "You look like a man the boy knew, a friend of his Sioux father," he explained. "His mother was Cheyenne, a cousin of Black Coyote's wife, but she died and Black Coyote brought the boy here to his wife to raise. Tempers run high. Many of my people do not like having a *veho* among them, but Black Coyote has said he will stop kicking the boy."

Zach still didn't like the situation, but knew it wasn't his place to interfere. Once he caught up with the Cheyenne at their winter camp—if they made it that far—he'd keep an eye on this Black Coyote and the child.

As they watched the last of the Cheyenne disappear, Custer's boy made some small sound of distress and moved closer to Caroline. Unsure of his new role, Zach tried to remember what he knew of Custer, mostly stories about his early days in the war. His son might like to hear them. How much did the boy know about his famous father? In return, the boy might know something that could help in his search for Luke—such as who owned those two horses.

"I'm Zach." He bent and stuck out his hand. His reward was a hesitant smile and the warm clasp of a small but strong hand. "Pleased to meet you."

Damn, but he's skinny. Zach frowned and examined the boy's hand, then his arm. *Custer would have skinned the polecat who hasn't been feedin' him.* "What do you say we rustle up some grub?" he asked.

At the boy's perplexed frown, Caroline mimed eating.

The boy nodded eagerly and together, Zach and Caroline prepared a pot of oatmeal, then smiled as they watched him devour it. Zach settled the boy in a nest of blankets across the fire before joining Caroline at the wagon.

"Are you okay with this?" she asked, keeping her voice low. "A boy can be a big responsibility. Especially this one."

"Custer's son," Zach said, shaking his head. "He's what, six years old?"

"Nine," Caroline said. "Little Wolf says that after the Washita fight, Custer lined up the Cheyenne maidens and picked Swallow's mother out of the line. He made her his woman for the summer. When his wife joined them, he sent her back to the people, knowing she was pregnant. He's never seen the boy. She didn't take a new husband until he died."

"Did you see the way some of the warriors looked at him?" Zach asked. "Little Wolf was right to leave him with us. It wouldn't have been safe for him to travel with them any farther."

"They're afraid he'll bring bad luck, especially in the fighting ahead, and they've had plenty of that already." She straightened a pile of blankets and shook her head at the wagon, which he noticed was still full. "They didn't take much, mostly food, a little medicine and one or two blankets." Her voice shook. "So many have died, and many are still sick with malaria. The medicine I brought won't help them much. They've been weakened by the disease and aren't strong enough for the trip, but they didn't want to be left behind."

Zach decided to confront Caroline with Little Wolf's cryptic comment now, before he lost his nerve. "Caroline, Little Wolf said something that puzzles me."

"What?" She stopped fussing with the blankets and looked up at him, simple curiosity in her direct gaze.

"He said you had never shared his furs."

Her eyes flared wider and her mouth opened, but she said nothing.

"What did he mean by that?" Zach asked, knowing he really had no right to an answer.

"It means we've never made love." She blinked and shrugged, looking away as she re-folded the top blanket.

"But you were married, weren't you?"

"No," she said, sighing as if the admission was a relief. "He bought me from White Bear to stop a fight between him and a Comanche war chief. White Bear had tried to strike a Comanche shaman who helped me. Little Wolf took me to his wives, Feather On Head and Quiet Woman, who cared for me and saved my life. I lived with them after that and everyone assumed I was his wife, but he never . . . I guess he could tell I couldn't bear to be touched. He never even tried."

"You lived with him and his wives, but he never touched you?"

She nodded. "My body healed, but the fear White Bear taught me has never diminished, as you discovered yesterday morning."

Yes, he'd seen her scars, so he could understand her reserve, but Little Wolf's generosity amazed him. Not many men would have accepted the responsibility without some sort of compensation. His respect for the chief soared, even as pleasure swept through him. She wasn't married, had never been married. The emotion overwhelmed him, leaving him short of breath and wondering what to do now, what to say to her. He no longer had to keep a respectful distance for fear of antagonizing her husband, whom he hoped would eventually help him find his son. He leaned against the wagon, trying to appear casual, but he was grinning inside.

She stepped away from him, working her way up the side of the wagon, adjusting, reorganizing and folding as she went. He followed her—not so close that he'd make her nervous, but close enough that he could hear her low voice clearly.

"But you were ridiculed and harassed once you returned to Dodge City because everyone thought you were Little Wolf's wife. Why didn't you tell the truth?"

She whirled to face him, her eyes narrowed. "Do you think it would have made my life easier if everyone knew I'd never been the wife of a well-known Cheyenne chief, just the slave of a brutish Kiowa chief?"

"Not really, no," he admitted. She had been enslaved against her will and had the scars to prove it. Many white captives took their lives when returned to white society. The shame and disdain of friends and family was often more than they could bear. Caroline's tenacity, her determination to survive, amazed him.

"My life was ruined either way, so I chose to hide behind the myth, rather than answer rude questions about a period of my life that I'd rather forget." She folded her arms over her waist. "I've answered your questions, now I have a couple to ask you.

"First . . ." She didn't wait for him to agree to answer, just pushed forward, even though he'd already started backing away.

He held up a hand to stop her. "I appreciate your candid answers, but I may not be able to answer all your questions."

"Why not?" she demanded, her blue eyes wide and puzzled. "Don't I deserve the same consideration I gave you?"

"Ask your questions," he said with a sigh, knowing she was right. "I'll answer if I can." He knew where this was headed, but he'd try to distract her before she could ask something he'd have to refuse to answer, which would only make her determined to know what he was hiding.

"All right, is Zach McCallister your real name?"

He laughed, startled by the simple question when he'd anticipated having to dodge much tougher ones. "Yes."

"Are you married?" She couldn't look him in the eye when she asked that one.

He grinned, very pleased that she wanted to know.

"My friends were asking," she said, bursting his prideful bubble.

Ah, but they're not here now, are they? he thought. "I'm a . . . widower," he answered, using the term to describe his status for the first time and finding it an awkward fit. He was distracted by her surprised glance.

"How long has your wife been dead?"

"Several months."

"My sympathies," she whispered, searching his face.

"We were estranged," he explained, then realized that told her very little about his relationship with Patricia. Perhaps if he expanded on the subject, without mentioning Luke, he could divert her attention from the questions he figured she really wanted to ask, such as: *Why were you so determined to meet the Cheyenne? What, or who, are you looking for?*

"Beautiful woman, Patricia, on the outside. But not inside. She used her charms to manipulate people, to obtain her heart's desire at any given moment. I didn't discover her deception until it was too late."

"Are you glad she died?" Caroline's gaze had narrowed on him, and she searched his face as she awaited his answer.

The question surprised him. He stilled, considering his feelings. Was he glad she had died? She had been selfish and demanding, petulant and shrewish when she didn't get her way, but she'd also been young. If he had stayed, instead of abandoning her and their infant son, he might have been able to help her overcome some of those faults. Her only saving grace had been that she was Luke's mother, but he realized that was enough. "I'm sorry that she died, but not sorry to no longer have to share my life with her."

Caroline looked shocked, and he realized his answer had been too curt.

"I apologize." He took off his hat and dragged his fingers through his hair. "I hadn't realized that the subject would still be difficult for me to discuss. If you'll excuse me, I'll turn in."

Zach flopped onto his back in his bedroll and threw an arm over his face. Even her simple questions were tough, and her last had probed a sensitive spot. He was finding he didn't bear introspection well. Until now, he hadn't realized he held himself entirely to blame for Patricia's death and Luke's disappearance. And the only way he could redeem himself was by finding his son.

Chapter Nine

Caroline watched Zach and Yellow Swallow sleep, unable to do the same. So many thoughts chased through her brain that she knew she'd lie awake all night.

The brief visit with the Cheyenne had left her restless and uneasy. Many familiar faces were gone and her grief over their deaths surprised Caroline. She hadn't realized how much she loved the Cheyenne people—all the Cheyenne people. Now she understood what had driven them to leave the reservation. They had died there, not one by one as people normally died, but in handfuls, often whole families one right after another. The sudden, gaping holes left by their deaths had shredded the fabric of the Cheyenne's daily existence. They'd had no choice but to run to save what was left of that fabric, of their culture and beliefs.

She had been shocked to learn that the Sacred Arrows, one of their most powerful medicine bundles, had remained in the south with the man who carried it. Their only protection was the Sacred Bundle that Little Wolf bore, the last remnants of the medicine bundle given to them by their ancient culture hero, Sweet Medicine. This—more than disease, starvation or death—told Caroline how desperate their situation had become.

Also puzzling was Little Wolf's interaction with Zach. The two men had sized each other up within moments of meeting, and afterward Little Wolf had treated Zach as a trusted ally. He'd also entrusted Zach with the care of a Cheyenne child, something she'd never known any Cheyenne to do. She'd been surprised, too, by Little Wolf's revelation that he'd never made love with her. In the past, he'd allowed the myth to stand, even perpetuated it. Why had he revealed something so personal to a complete stranger? It troubled her that Zach knew the truth about her relationship with Little Wolf. She felt vulnerable without the protection the myth had provided, especially while traveling with him, essentially alone.

Even believing she was married, he'd tumbled her in the hay and would have tried to kiss her if she hadn't stopped him. Who knew what would have happened if she hadn't been armed? Since then, he'd more or less kept his distance, but how would his knowing that she'd lied, that she'd never been Little Wolf's wife, alter their relationship? Would she have to be on her guard against him from now on?

For that matter, how would her knowing that he was a recent widower change things? She'd been surprised by his admission, and taken aback by his lack of grief, his utter dislike of his wife. Her question had surprised him, but she was right to have asked it. His indifference when he revealed his marital status had given her the impression that he was shallow, unfeeling, but his response to her last question showed that he'd had deep feelings for his wife, though she couldn't guess exactly what they might have been. Perhaps he felt regret or remorse only.

He'd mentioned that his wife had been beautiful. Did he believe that all beautiful women were like his wife? Caroline smiled. For once she was glad she wasn't beautiful; he couldn't apply the stereotype to her. She knew she'd been pretty as a girl and might someday have become a beauty like her mother and grandmother, but her experiences, her scars, had destroyed any hopes she'd had in that regard. And now her plainness would keep Zach from thinking she was shallow, and keep him from pursuing her.

If not for Yellow Swallow, who would provide a buffer between them, she'd be nervous about traveling with Zach now that he knew the truth about her. She glanced again at the boy, curled into a snug ball within the blankets. He'd surely eaten more tonight than in a week of meals put together. Even his position close beside the fire was a luxury due to his half-blood status. The aunt he lived with had no husband and Caroline knew Swallow must have spent his time watching the other boys' lessons, learning by imitation, without the benefit of personal instruction. Zach's friendship could benefit him tremendously, if it lasted.

And why wouldn't it? she asked herself. Zach had agreed to take her and Yellow Swallow to the Cheyenne's winter camp. Thus far he had stuck to their agreement, even when other men would have cut and run. So, why did she expect him to abandon them now? And why did his agreement to take them north seem so right, instead of threatening? She'd vowed to avoid the man before he knew her secrets; now that he knew, she was stuck with him for several more months. Those months would give her time to learn what drove him. She knew any concern he might have for her hadn't made him agree to Little Wolf's request. So why had he agreed?

Frustrated by the ceaseless cycle of questions to which she had no answers, she closed her eyes, determined to quiet her thoughts long enough to doze off. She woke with surprise to the sun on her face and the smell of fresh coffee heating on the fire.

Yellow Swallow sat beside the wagon, waiting for her to awaken. She suspected he'd helped her along a bit with the long blade of grass he tossed away with a guilty grin.

"New sun," he said, speaking the Cheyenne tongue. "Your man and I have already bathed." He shook his head at her, looking very somber despite his slicked back hair and shining cheeks. "Come. Get out of bed. He will not keep you if you are lazy."

Caroline glanced at Zach, wondering what he'd

thought of the Cheyenne custom of early-morning bathing. The vision of him naked, walking into the river, shot her upright with an alarmed gasp. Her head hit the wagon bottom with a dull clunk and she fell back with a groan.

Yellow Swallow nodded sagely. "It is good that you worry. Many Cheyenne women gave him looks last night, but he had eyes for no one but you. Why do you not share his blankets?"

Startled by Swallow's questions, Caroline jerked upright again and again bumped her head. She crawled reluctantly out of her cozy bed and checked her head for blood. "That's none of your concern, young man. And speak English when you talk to me. Have you been practicing since I left?"

"*Veho* words taste like dirt," he objected, helping her to fold her blankets into a neat roll.

"Better to eat dirt than go hungry." She nodded at Zach, who was dropping biscuit dough into a hot skillet. "He might decide not to feed you. And you're too skinny already." She tweaked a fold of skin at his waist.

"He say call him Zach," Yellow Swallow said in halting English.

"That's right," Zach said, continuing with his biscuits.

"He *said* I *could* call him Zach," Caroline corrected with a sigh. Swallow's English needed work.

"He did?" The boy gave her a big grin and a nudge with his elbow, then leaned close to whisper, "Maybe he keep you long time."

"Oh, you . . ." Caroline reached for him, but he dodged her and ran to the fire, laughing. He sat on a large stone beside Zach and looked toward the river, sobering quickly.

Zach reached out and tousled his hair. "That's a pretty gloomy face for such a beautiful morning."

Yellow Swallow blinked hard and nodded toward the river. "We see them again?"

"I'm sure we will," Zach said, and glanced up at Caroline, who read the doubt in his eyes. "We're to meet them where Little Wolf plans to camp for the winter."

"When?" the boy asked, still staring to the north.

"Not long," Caroline assured him. "In the meantime, I think we need to get you some new clothes. And maybe a hat?" she asked, raising an eyebrow at Zach, who nodded. The boy's uncanny resemblance to his father would draw too much attention. They had to minimize it.

Zach handed Yellow Swallow a plate of eggs and gestured to Caroline to follow him to the back of the wagon. "A haircut, too?" he asked.

"He'll probably be spending the winter with the Cheyenne and he already reminds them of Custer. We shouldn't do anything to make him look more like a white boy. He has enough trouble fitting in as it is. Maybe we could trim it, tie it back?" She pulled her gaze from the hungry boy to look up at Zach. "We're lucky he's too young to grow a mustache."

Zach grinned. "You're right. I don't want to change him, just make his life a little easier."

"What do you propose we do now?" Caroline asked.

"We need to get away from here as soon as possible," he said, glancing about the camp. "Too many signs here—unshod hoofprints, clear moccasin prints, travois trails." He pointed out the marks in the soil. "Too much to clear away and very obvious to a trained eye."

"What do you say to crossing the river? The stationmaster knows a man who lives nearby who would be willing to drive the wagon."

She turned a wary look on the river and the strong wind from the southwest blew her hair about her face. She quickly pressed the hair down over her left ear.

He scowled at the goose egg on her forehead. "What did you do to your forehead?"

Caroline smoothed her hair. "Yellow Swallow's impertinent questions."

"Ah," Zach said with a commiserating grimace. "I understand completely." He pointed to a nick on his jaw.

"Oh, no," she groaned. "What did he ask you?"

"Let's see—" Zach ticked off the questions on his fingers. "How long have you been my woman? Why don't I like sleepin' with you? How can we have children if we don't sleep together? Am I plannin' to give you up soon? Did I see a Cheyenne maiden last night that I might like better? Do I prefer the bow or the lance? Oh, and could he shoot my rifle?"

"He should have been named Magpie, not Swallow," Caroline observed wryly. "I'll talk to him."

"Don't bother," Zach said, with a chuckle. "He's harmless. At least he will be if we can disguise his parentage. We'll also have to come up with a white name for him."

"George is out," Caroline said, and smiled at Zach when he chuckled. "How about my brother's name—Samuel, or Sam for short?"

"That would work well. His blond hair will be an obvious tie to you, but won't your brother mind?"

"Sam died," Caroline said, surprised that the reminder of Samuel's brutal murder by the Kiowa was less painful than usual. "He would have liked Yellow Swallow. Perhaps I'll be able to replace some of the ugly memories of his death with happier ones."

Zach reached out and ran a finger down her left cheek, drawing her gaze to his. His finger traced her bottom lip.

She shivered at the soft stroke, and her breath froze in her throat. She remembered Short One's advice and tried to relax as he pulled her closer, but she could feel tension coiling inside her. His eyes had turned storm dark, but the lightning bolts to match were shooting through her. His breath fanned her cheeks and she read the question in his eyes.

Would she let him kiss her again? Zach was moving slow, letting her see his intent, giving her time to choose whether to allow it. Her heart drummed so loudly in her ears that she could barely think, but her body answered by settling closer to his. Her gaze slipped to his lips, then back to his eyes, and the tip of her tongue swept her upper lip.

He drew in a sharp breath and reached for her.

"I go. Hunt rabbits. Leave you alone."

Caroline froze, blinking up at Zach, who pulled her against him when he turned to answer Yellow Swallow. She should stop this now, but her body seemed to be making all the decisions—a good thing, too, since her mind had stopped functioning.

"Why do you want to hunt rabbits?"

Yellow Swallow whispered loudly, "Rabbits fast. Hard to catch. Give you plenty time."

Caroline let her forehead settle against Zach's chest, hoping to hide her vivid blush from the too-knowing eyes of Yellow Swallow. She could feel Zach's heart pounding under her fingers as his arm tightened around her waist. She drew in a sharp breath, but forced down the panic, challenging herself to relax and see where he would take this moment. He responded by pulling her hips against his.

Her eyes widened as she came in contact with the hard ridge below his waist, and she jerked back. She'd thought he wanted a kiss, not *that*. She gripped his forearms tight and braced herself. Her tension increased when she heard Zach give Yellow Swallow a task that would keep him busy for several minutes.

"Caroline?" Zach murmured and searched her face.

"What?" she asked. She glanced up quickly, then let her gaze fasten on the top button of his shirt. His brows drew together and he pressed a kiss to her forehead.

"I'd like to kiss you." He kissed her cheek, the tip of her nose, then her lips, but he didn't try to pull her close again. Her heartbeat slowed and her grip on his forearms relaxed.

"That's better," he said, and nibbled at the corner of her mouth. Then he kissed her bottom lip and sort of sucked on it, letting it go with a tiny pop. She glanced up and found him grinning at her. He pulled her closer and she went, but kept her hips well away from his erection. Her chest met his and he lifted her arms onto his shoulders, which forced her to go up on tiptoe. Then his lips settled on her mouth, pressing her closed lips firmly against her teeth. He ran his tongue along her lips and she wondered if they were too dry.

When he finally stopped kissing her, she pressed her lips together and he chuckled. She felt the vibration in her chest and smiled at him.

"That wasn't too bad, was it?" he asked.

"Not bad," she said. "A little strange, though."

"Strange?" He sounded outraged, but he was grinning. "I'll have you know, no other woman's ever complained about my kisses, but then I really haven't kissed you yet."

"You haven't?" she asked, surprised. "If that wasn't a kiss, what is?"

He gave her a lopsided smile that was more of a leer and said, "Open for me."

"Open? Open what?"

"Your mouth, darlin'." His voice had gone deep and vibrated in his chest.

She opened her mouth and said, "Li' thith?"

He threw back his head, gave a sharp bark of a laugh and said, "No! When I run my tongue over your lips, then open your mouth. Not so much. Just a little."

She nodded, adjusted her arms on his shoulders and lifted higher onto her toes, then realized that while they'd been talking, her hips had come to rest against his. But she couldn't feel the hard ridge anymore and she was curious to know what he was going to do once she opened her mouth, just a little.

She closed her eyes, said, "I'm ready," and waited. But nothing happened. She opened her eyes and found him watching her, grinning. She stomped her foot. "Well?"

"You're adorable. You do know that, don't you?" His arms tightened around her and she opened her mouth to protest, but he swept in, catching her open mouth with his.

At first, it felt funny; then she felt his tongue slide along her bottom teeth and he turned his head and that clever tongue slipped past her teeth into her mouth. The rogue was *tasting* her. And she tasted him, and liked what she tasted. His arms tightened around her and he lifted her off her feet, high against his chest and he began to thrust his tongue into her mouth. Thrust, withdraw. Thrust again, deeper. Withdraw. Her heartbeat suddenly raced and a cold chill washed over her as she recognized the motion and its resemblance to the sexual act. She pulled away from him.

"No," she said, her voice firm. She shoved against his chest until he finally set her on her feet and let her step away. Her heartbeat gradually slowed, but the chill remained. "What's the point in kissing? To prepare a woman for violation?"

She pressed a hand over her chest to still her pounding heart. Old memories raced through her mind, stealing her breath. "It's a waste of effort. I already know what comes next, and kissing isn't going to lull me into forgetting it."

He grimaced and drew a deep breath, squeezing his eyes shut. "When it's done right, kissing can be very stimulating. I keep forgettin' that you don't know the joy of makin' love, only the pain. It doesn't have to be a 'violation.'" He rubbed her arms and gave her a wry smile. "I get carried away when I get close to you. It's my fault you didn't enjoy the kiss. You know I would never hurt you." When she didn't respond, his eyes widened. The storm in his eyes had intensified, blurring the line between iris and pupil. "Don't you?"

God help her, but she hated her fear. She wanted to throw caution to the winds and stride into the storm beside him, but fear once again had her by the throat. "Yes," she whispered.

"I can show you the joy and the pleasure, Caroline, but you have to want it. I would never force you." He stopped, took another deep breath. "Earlier you talked about replacing bad memories with happier ones. Do you want your memories of the brutality you suffered to be all you ever know? Don't you want to know how it can be between a man and a woman who—"

She bristled. "Who what?" she shot back. "Love each other?"

"No." He stared at her, his eyes returning to their normal light gray as he talked. "We both know that's not the case here. I was goin' to say, between a man and a woman who want to pleasure each other."

At his words, she drew a sharp breath. "That's all I would ever be to you, isn't it? Someone who once gave you pleasure."

"That's nothin' to disdain. If you only understood how rare it is . . ." He reached for her, but she avoided him.

"I'd rather keep my memories," she told him with a sniff. "They may be brutal, but at least they're honest."

"Honest?" he scoffed, and before she could stop him, she was in his arms and his head was descending, his eyes blazing into hers before they locked on her lips and closed. Beneath her hand, his chest rose as he took a deep breath, then his lips settled whisper-soft over hers.

Because she'd expected violence, his gentleness overwhelmed her. His lips were warm and firm, and when his tongue slid along the seam of her lips, she clutched his shoulders and moaned. Tenderly, he coaxed a response out of her, and to her amazement, she clutched the back of his head and opened for him, welcoming his invading tongue and pressing closer to him.

She couldn't get close enough! God help her, she wanted to rip open his shirt and feel his bare skin beneath her fingers. Tentatively, she responded to his teasing tongue and returned his thrust and parry, becoming so absorbed in the play that she barely noticed his hand sliding down her side to her hip.

He turned her, laying her back across his arm while his hand roamed upward and closed over her breast, lightly stroking at first, then urgently kneading. She cupped his jaw, her tongue tangling with his for dominance, relishing the scrape of his beard against her palm and face.

Every breath she drew was his first, every thump of her heart was an echo of his and still, it wasn't enough. What madness had possessed her?

She struggled upright again and braced herself away from him, her arms rigid. They were both breathing hard, fighting for control. She forced her eyes to focus, her breathing to slow, her legs to support her.

He gave her a tiny shake. "Tell me you don't want me inside you right now."

Violent images ricocheted through her mind, conjured by his words. "I don't!" she cried.

"You're lyin'," he said softly, releasing her and leaning against the wagon, leaving her shivering without his heat to warm her. "Someday, I'll prove it to you."

"I couldn't bear it. I could never let you do those things to me." A shudder silenced her.

The fierceness slowly left his expression and he looked away from her, raking his hand through his hair. "I'll leave you alone."

She cringed when he left, circling wide around her. She straightened her buckskins, splashed some water on her face, then finished loading the wagon. She had tried, as she'd promised Short One. What more could a woman do?

She could live without love, she told herself. Many women did—nuns and spinsters lived long, productive lives. So could she.

Then why did the prospect of all those years alone leave her feeling hollow and empty?

"Run! Faster!" Little Wolf called to the last of the walkers hurrying past him in the dark. "There is no place to hide. Watch for soldiers. They will come soon."

The women picked up their feet and pushed forward, silent and strong. The short rest and good food had strengthened their legs. The fight the day before at Sand Creek had strengthened their hearts.

Little Wolf shook his head. All day he had braced him-

self for a full charge by the soldiers, but dark came first
and with it, the cover he needed to get his people away.
The Cheyenne had shown the soldiers that they were
men and ready to fight. But he did not understand these
soldiers who shot from a distance all day long, accomp-
lishing nothing. Did they not want to fight? Or did they
wait for more soldiers to come? The soldiers still did not
fear the Cheyenne, not as they once had, so he had
pushed his people fast and hard to the Arkansas River.

Finding Caroline there, well and protected, had lifted
a weight off his heart. He had looked inside the man who
rode with her and had seen many things, and some troubled him. But the time to deal with that lay ahead, beyond the prairies and the fight to come. The man would
keep Caroline—and the Swallow—safe. That must be
enough for now.

Little Wolf let his concern for Caroline slip from his
mind. He must think only of his people and their safety.
He felt soldiers gathering, like a rope tightening
around the people. The soldiers were tired of chasing
them. The Cheyenne had made them look foolish. They
no longer cared so much about taking the *Tsitsitas* back
to the reservation.

The long, flat prairies stretched ahead of the
Cheyenne now with no hills or canyons and very few trees
to hide their passing. But he knew a place, three days' fast
running from here, a place where two rivers came together. This place had strong medicine for the people,
who called it Punished Woman's Fork. Hard things had
been done there, things the people did not discuss but all
remembered. There the husband of an unfaithful
woman had given his wife to the men of his tribe, then
turned his back and walked away. At this place of judg-
ment, the Cheyenne would turn and fight.

But the people needed time to reach the hidden
ravines and secret cave with its passageway to the north.
Many farms and small towns stood in their way. Now the
buffalo were gone, they had sprung up on the face of the

land, like mushrooms in the shade of a tree. His people would need to run around these places and try not to be seen. Only with his medicine could he hide their passing.

He began a chant, singing low but strong, holding the song inside, letting it fill him. He closed his eyes and felt the air stretch his chest, pushing outward, struggling to be free. He held it in, letting it build until the air brought him pain. Then he opened his mouth wide and let the air escape—a small breeze that grew bigger and blew harder and faster, snatching up the dirt on the ground and throwing it into the lightening sky. The dirt-filled wind shoved the people forward and wrapped around them, hiding their passing from staring eyes, giving new hope to faint hearts.

Little Wolf pulled his blanket up over his head and urged his pony into the wind. It was not much, but it would keep the cowboys in their log huts and the farmers in their sod houses. None would see the people pass, but all would remember the keening wind that stung their eyes and filled their hearts with sorrow as the Cheyenne ran by.

As he rode, he prayed that his wolves, the men sent ahead to scout and forage, were riding hard, too, that none had stepped aside to harm the innocent.

"Well, there goes the day," Zach muttered from the makeshift tent he and Caroline had struggled to erect in the lee of the wagon. They'd forded the Arkansas River without any problems, but only miles down the trail the strong wind and low visibility had forced them to stop.

"This is an odd wind," he said, peering out at another swirling dust devil. "There isn't a cloud in the sky. Don't you think it's strange?"

"The Cheyenne needed a break," Caroline replied with a shrug and continued measuring Yellow Swallow's back. She'd decided to make use of the delay to begin a shirt for the boy. "Put your shirt back on," she told him when she finished measuring. It hurt to look at the bones poking through his skin. "Have another biscuit," she told him.

"I no want white man's shirt," he told her with a sniff as he picked at his biscuit. "Buckskins plenty fine."

"We've already talked about this," Caroline said, transferring her measurements to the fabric in her hands. "In order to keep you safe, you need to look more like a white boy."

"You wear buckskins," he said and ran his hand through the fringe from her elbow to her wrist.

"Not after today," she told him with a firm shake of her head. "We'll be seeing more white people as we travel north, and we don't want to make them nervous." Her answer seemed to satisfy the boy.

Zach reclined against his saddle, propped on an elbow, legs crossed at the ankles as he watched her. His nonchalant pose didn't fool Caroline. He'd already occupied himself cleaning his guns with meticulous attention, and he poked his head out to check the weather at least four times an hour. Clearly, he preferred being outdoors to being cooped up under a tarp with a woman and a small boy. She found it hard to believe he had ever been married. It must have been complete misery for him.

She'd been afraid that their encounter earlier in the day would strain their relationship and make him irritable, difficult to deal with, but he acted like nothing had happened. It annoyed her. Was he biding his time, thinking she'd eventually fall into his arms out of sheer need? She caught back a haughty sniff. She hoped he didn't wait in the rain; he'd get awfully wet waiting for her to need *that*.

"You don't think this wind is odd?" he asked, sitting forward and dangling his arms between his upraised knees as he fixed her with that intent gray gaze that made her so nervous.

"What are you saying?" she asked, stabbing her needle into the fabric with more vigor than it required.

"Well, it seems pretty convenient, comin' hard on the heels of the Cheyenne as they move into open territory."

"Surely you don't think Little Wolf caused this wind."

She shot him a disbelieving look. "Oh, come on." She shook her head. "Little Wolf isn't . . . He can't . . ." She looked at Yellow Swallow. "Can he?"

The boy shrugged, then mumbled around a mouthful of leftover bacon, "He Sweet Medicine Chief. Strong medicine."

"I don't believe it." Caroline shook her head. "No one can control the weather. It's a lucky coincidence."

Zach pulled back a corner of the tarp and peered north, the direction the Cheyenne were heading. "Can't see your own feet out there, let alone a column of runnin' people wearin' dirt-colored buckskins."

"Coincidence," Caroline repeated. She caught Zach's attention and gave a significant nod in Yellow Swallow's direction. "Let's talk about something different, shall we?"

"Such as?" His gaze drifted to her lips and Caroline's breath caught in her chest. If not for Yellow Swallow's presence between them, she knew exactly what the two of them would be discussing.

"Where were you raised?" She gave Zach an arch look. *Dodge that bullet,* she thought.

"Borin' subject," he said with a smile. "Tell us about your family. I'll bet there's a family mansion back home, surrounded by a garden."

"My white father's family very rich," Yellow Swallow said in a low voice, "but they not want me in Mun-row, Mish-a-gun."

"Oh, Swallow—" Caroline put her arm around his shoulders. "I'm happy that you're here with us."

"I no care," the boy looked up, his eyes blazing, his chin firm. "My aunt say my white father a fool. When Sioux kill him at big fight, their women poke holes in his ears with their sewing awls." He nodded as if he both understood and approved of their action. "He hear better in next life."

Caroline stared at the boy, not knowing what to say to comfort him. She didn't want to undermine his aunt's influence, and he had no reason not to believe her, but there was so much he didn't understand.

Zach lay back against his saddle. "I'm sure that's the way your aunt sees things." He settled his hat low over his eyes, as if he were about to take a nap, and crossed his arms over his stomach. "Your father was a great warrior in the white man's war. He started out as a private." He tipped his hat up to explain, "That's like an untried brave to your people."

"You mean like a brave before the Sun Dance?" Yellow Swallow twiddled with a twig, stripping the bark and trying not to look interested, but Caroline saw the tremor in his fingers. She guessed where Zach was heading, but kept quiet. She might learn something useful—about Zach.

"Exactly," Zach said, and yawned. "He was a good soldier. Very brave. He fought hard and it wasn't long before he became a captain—like a chief. By the end of the war, he was a big chief, in charge of many men, the whole Seventh Cavalry."

"A soldier chief," Yellow Swallow whispered, his face bleak. "He killed many *Tsitsitas*. Morning Star said it, and he does not lie."

Zach tipped up his hat and pinned the boy with a steady stare. "Your father did what he was told to do by the President, the Great Father in the east. He died doin' his duty. That's all any man can do. He was not a man to be ashamed of."

Yellow Swallow nodded and sat quietly ripping the twig to shreds. Then he turned and watched Caroline sew. Finally he asked, very quietly, after shooting a lowered glance toward Zach, "Me get boots, too?"

Caroline nodded. "Why don't you get some rest?" She glanced at Zach, merely to suggest the boy follow his example. To her surprise, Zach extended an arm for the boy. Yellow Swallow crawled up beside him and settled his head on Zach's shoulder.

Only firm concentration kept her needle moving. It surprised her that Zach had a soft spot for children. Was it just sympathy for this boy, who would never know his famous father—a man cut down in battle a short time ago, or was there more to Zach than his tough facade?

She reminded herself that he hadn't run yesterday after discovering her disfigurement. She'd assumed that was because he wanted something from the Cheyenne, something that was very important to him. Now that he'd met Little Wolf, had his purpose changed? What was he after? Her gaze narrowed and settled on the two males. Had he been searching for this boy all along? As she pondered, Zach shifted, pulling the sleeping boy closer to his side.

Not likely, she thought. If so, he'd never have agreed to meet Little Wolf at the Cheyennes' winter camp. He'd have taken the boy and returned to wherever he came from. He was searching for something else, Caroline decided, something that he hadn't yet found and Swallow was connected.

Caroline ignored the screeching wind, its voice muffled by the soft breathing beside her, and vowed to keep a close eye on both Zach and Yellow Swallow. The boy had never been strong, and he had suffered too much in his short life.

She would make sure he wasn't hurt more.

Chapter Ten

A large, black bird circled lazily on the horizon, then was joined by another and another.

Damnation! Zach cursed as he spurred his horse. Buzzards. He hated buzzards. He could have happily lived the rest of his life without seeing another one, but whatever lay dead or dying out there had drawn a whole flock. Dread made his stomach clench as he rode closer.

He noticed a broad, careless trail and slowed to study it. The trail told an ominous tale, with its few unshod

pony tracks, along with a few travois trails and many moccasin prints, almost obliterated by the hoofprints of shod
horses and wagon ruts. He eyed the buzzards, a regular
black cloud now, and kneed his horse again, his sense of
dread increasing. He didn't like the looks of this at all.

He slowed as the trail narrowed. The broad plain on either side rose into high bluffs that led into a deepening,
stream-fed canyon. Several smaller canyons branched off
to either side as the floor of the canyon rose, then leveled
off facing a high bulwark that appeared to have been bar-
ricaded. The signs of recent battle were unmistakable. A
briny hint of gunsmoke lingered in the air, muted only by
the coppery overbite of decaying blood. The hair on the
back of Zach's neck rose straight up and stayed that way
as he passed hastily dug rifle pits, pitted with bullet holes
and decorated with the blood of unlucky occupants. Up
against the bluffs, several shallow graves had been covered with rocks to keep scavengers away from the bodies.

Though he looked closely, Zach saw no sign of the
Cheyenne. He spotted bits and pieces of soldiers' gear—
gloves, hats, buttons, even a lone bugle—but not a trace
of buckskin or fringe or even an arrow or club. The
stench of decay deepened as he approached a small
canyon on his right where the buzzards circled. His horse
balked when he turned its nose toward the canyon.

"Come on, Demon," he said, patting the stallion's
neck. "What's the problem, boy? I've seen you take lesser
hills than this at a trot." The stallion's ears were laid back,
his eyes rolling, but when Zach dug in with heels, Demon
took the hill in three bounds. When he reached the top,
his sides were heaving and the white of his eyes showing
as he tossed his head. Zach kept a tight grip on the reins,
letting the horse dance under him as he stared in relief
and horror into the canyon. In a small canyon below, lay
a smoking mound of dead horses.

Must be almost a thousand ponies, Zach estimated
quickly, holding his breath as he yanked his kerchief up
over his nose and mouth. Stunned, he stared at the stink-

ing mound, sickened not by the smell or the carnage, but by his own fear. Were the two McCallister horses he'd spotted among the Cheyenne part of the mound below? If they'd been burned, how could he find out if they were the horses Patricia had taken? How would he find Luke?

The soldiers had done their work well. The horses' bodies were so badly charred, it would be impossible to distinguish individual animals. Feeling like his soul had been ripped out of his chest, Zach looked for human remains, but saw no signs of human bodies.

Demon didn't balk when he kneed him back down the slope. Once in the main canyon, Zach yanked his kerchief away and sucked in a deep breath, finding even the fetid, battle-fouled air refreshing after the canyon's stench.

Anxious to finish here and be on his way, he forced his worry aside and kneed his horse toward the breastworks at the end of the canyon and the deeply dug rifle pits above it. He dismounted and checked the vantage point from within one of the pits and shook his head. Little Wolf's strategy had been brilliant and well executed, but obviously, something had gone wrong. Although it was clear by the boot prints overlapping moccasin imprints that soldiers had taken the breastworks, he saw no boot prints in the rifle pits, which meant that Little Wolf's final position hadn't been overrun by the soldiers. Little Wolf's ingenious trap must have been sprung before the mouse got to the cheese. Zach shook his head. If he'd been in charge, he would have been tempted to shoot the idiot who'd fouled the plan. And if he'd been leading the soldiers, he would never have followed the trail into the canyon without first scouting from the ridges above.

Remounting, Zach followed the Cheyenne's trail out of the lethal canyon and frowned. His horse shook its head and mane, obviously glad to be out on the open plains again. Zach turned Demon's head into the wind and let the fresh wind blow over them both. Little Wolf had foiled the soldiers again, but at tremendous cost. Without the ponies, the Cheyenne were almost all on foot now, and the soldiers, embarrassed at being defeated again, would be hot on their trail.

Zach scouted the ridge above the canyon and found confirmation of his observations—the trail of mounted soldiers, only a day or two older than the moccasin trails, paralleling the Cheyenne. Using his eyeglass, Zach searched to the south and spotted Caroline and the wagon.

His horse jerked at the bit. Zach forced himself to relax his grip on the reins as he stared down the soldiers' trail. If they caught up with the Cheyenne, there could be another massacre. Then how would he find out if those horses were McCallister horseflesh, especially if they'd been destroyed? If all the Cheyenne were killed, who could tell him what had happened to his son? How would he ever find him?

Every muscle in his body screamed at him to race after the Cheyenne, force the information he needed out of Little Wolf and get on with finding Luke before it was too late. But he couldn't do that. He'd accepted responsibility for two people, Caroline and Yellow Swallow, and they were depending on him. He couldn't abandon them out here on the prairie with vigilante mobs chasing every shadow, hungry for blood.

Despair filled Zach, stabbing through him as if he were being stretched on a rack. A vivid image of Caroline's scarred back and mangled ear filled his mind, and he shuddered. If the savages could treat a woman as beautiful as Caroline so heinously, what chance did a small, blond boy have? Where was Luke now? Was he being tortured? Zach forced himself to stop imagining the worst. He'd never been a praying man, but he'd never before felt this desperate and helpless. He threw his head back and silently sent a short, intense prayer skyward.

God, protect my son. Keep him safe until I can get to him. And God? Help me find him soon.

He scouted the ridge for a safe detour, then, using a

small mirror, he signaled Caroline to change direction, leading her safely past the horror. He knew she'd see the buzzards, and unfortunately, the wind was blowing south to east, so she'd be sure to catch a whiff of the ponies' remains as she passed by. He kneed his horse and rode to meet her, battling his anxiety and trying to see her and Swallow not as an unwelcome burden, but as two innocents caught in the middle of another government mess. Just like him and Luke.

He appended his earlier prayer:

God, get us all out of this alive.

"Look!" Yellow Swallow cried, pointing out Zach's mirror signal. "That way." They soon saw Zach cantering toward them. He wasn't pushing his horse, Caroline realized with relief, so the change in direction wasn't due to danger ahead.

She urged the stubborn mules off the well-worn trail, biting back a groan as their head-tossing jerked her arms and shoulders. After driving all day, her body was protesting. At the beginning of this journey, she'd been confident she wouldn't have any problems handling the daily rigors of the trail. After all, she'd done a lot of heavy lifting alongside Uncle James. She'd even done some tanning, making moccasins, belts and a parfleche or two because they sold so well. Now, almost three weeks later, she would gladly have traded her most-prized possession for a long, hot bath. And a week to enjoy it. Hefting crates, sweeping floors and packing supplies for Uncle James seemed like child's play compared to this. Heavens! She'd even be willing to smile at Aunt Abigail's parsimonious pucker. At least once.

She giggled, imagining her persnickety aunt's horror if she could see her now—her hair a flyaway mess and her skin toast-brown from riding or driving all day. And the rest of her . . . well, Aunt Abigail would be the first to agree that she needed a bath.

Caroline glanced over at her companion and

grinned. If Swallow were to join them "at table," as her aunt liked to refer to dinner, Aunt Abigail's delicate heart would seize up completely. As always, Caroline caught herself thinking she'd have to remember to share the laugh with her mother. As always, the wave of grief that assailed her when she remembered she'd never do so again, left her eyes burning and her chest tight.

How she missed her parents, her mother especially. What splendid plans they'd had for their new home. Apple-pie dreams, Caroline realized now. Unrealistic expectations, brightly illuminated by high hopes. Never to be realized.

She shook off the debilitating grief. If she let herself dwell on it, it would haunt her for days. She must present a cheerful face for Yellow Swallow. She knew now that her mother had done the same for her on that long, fateful wagon ride to hell. Swallow deserved no less.

"So, what sounds good for dinner?" she asked the boy. "Beans, or beans?"

He laughed. "Beans very good." He licked his lips. "Better with biscuits."

"You're so right. Biscuits, too, then."

"You make this many pans?" Swallow raised two fingers. "Mr. Zach like biscuits too good."

Caroline grinned at the boy, who looked very different wearing his new "duds," as Zach had taken to calling the boy's shirts and dungarees. Swallow's straw cowboy hat would keep distant observers from noting his resemblance to his famous father, but everyone who'd gotten within five feet had noticed it right away. They'd also noticed that the boy was half Indian. Their reactions had ranged from polite surprise to outright ridicule—but not so much of the latter if Zach was around. Custer had cut a wide swath through this territory. Although most civilians regarded him as a hero of biblical proportions since the battle at the Little Big Horn in June the year before, local folks remembered and resented his arrogance and high-handed attitude. This half-breed son proved their longtime contention that Custer was human, too.

The people who didn't get close enough to see Swallow's resemblance to Custer, merely saw a blonde woman with a child and didn't look further. And that's the way she liked it. She had no problem pretending the boy was her son. Determined to strengthen the illusion, she'd started teaching Swallow—she had to remember to call him Sam—to speak better English. She'd even purchased a slate and primer for him at their last stop and begun teaching him to read and write.

"After dinner, we'll work on the alphabet some more," she told Sam. Ignoring his muttered complaint, she continued cheerily. "One day you'll be able to read newspapers and books all by yourself. Won't that be grand?"

"What good newspapers and books?" he demanded. "They no teach me to catch rabbit for dinner, or tell me where turkey hide. No good." He turned his face away, kicking at the wagon. He stopped, scowling at the scuffs he'd made on the toes of his new boots. He rubbed each toe on the back of his pant legs, and sighed when the marks remained. "No good being white. Always do wrong." He raised a foot, pointing at his scuffed boots.

"Zach has something that will take off those marks," Caroline assured him. "You're doing fine, Sam. You didn't get a turkey the first time you went hunting, did you?"

"No," he said, crossing his arms over his chest and flashing her a look of challenge. "Hunting not like reading. Hunting put food on table. Reading good for nothing."

She had to admit, the boy had a point. How could she convince him that he'd benefit from learning the skill? What could he read that would help him, add to his present life? She smiled as the perfect answer came to her.

"Well, I guess you won't be able to read about your father, then, will you?" She snapped the reins over the mules' heads and hollered encouragement to keep them moving up the rising ground as they approached Zach. Ahead and to her left she noted the beginnings of a canyon. Why hadn't he directed her into it? It was already mid-afternoon; they needed to be on the lookout for a safe place to camp for the night.

"My father in books?" the boy asked, his face eager and surprised.

"Oh, yes," Caroline told him and waved at Zach. "Lots of people have written about him, and I'm sure many more will."

Swallow gave a high, yipping call to welcome Zach. Caroline jerked upright at the sudden, piercing sound. The boy grinned at her, apparently pleased that he'd surprised her. "I read, but no write. Me *Tsitsita*, not white."

"You're a scamp," she told him and yanked on one of the curls dangling behind his ear. In truth, she envied the boy his ringlets. "Next time just tell me and spare my ears." She gave him a hug and laughed when he pushed her away and straightened his clothes indignantly. The familiar motion made her grin. How many times had she seen her father and brother do the very same thing after being hugged?

Men, she thought. *They're all just little boys.* Every day she spent with Swallow made him dearer to her. She dreaded having to return him to his aunt, which would certainly happen if the Cheyenne were forced to return to the reservation.

Zach pulled his horse alongside the wagon, took off his hat and whacked it against his thigh. Dust flew, rising straight up at Caroline. She coughed and sneezed, while Swallow laughed. "So nice to see you again," she finally managed between wheezes. "Could you do your house-keeping somewhere else, please? Behind the wagon? And what is that horrible smell?"

"Sorry," Zach said, and tried to hide his chagrin behind his careful re-situation of his hat.

"You don't fool me, mister," Caroline told him, keeping her tone light, although she recognized Zach's hat-slapping ritual as an indication of tension. Since he didn't seem to be in a hurry to tell her what was bothering him, she realized it must be bad. She turned to Swallow. "Only one pan of biscuits tonight, and they're all yours and mine."

"Now wait just a minute," Zach objected, flashing her an understanding glance before he scowled at Swallow. "Are you two in cahoots against me?"

"You better believe it." Caroline winked at Swallow, who giggled and pulled his hat brim lower, mimicking Zach. "The mules aren't liking this any better than I am." As if to corroborate her complaint, one wheel hit a large rock and the whole wagon bounced and the mules danced nervously in their harness. Caroline groaned as the reins went taut, straining her arms and shoulders. "I'm ready for a break. Let's stop at the top of this rise."

"Not a good idea," Zach said. "I just scouted that canyon and didn't like the feel of it."

"Is that where you picked up that smell?" Caroline sniffed and frowned. "What did you find, a whole family of skunk? Or something worse?"

"What smell worse than skunks?" Swallow asked, his own nose wrinkled.

"Can you handle a few more miles?" Zach's gaze was as direct as his question.

"Sure," she replied, sensing his unease. "Do I need to get out the whip and move them along faster?"

"No," he said and kneed his horse closer to the wagon. "Swing the wagon farther to the right, though."

Caroline obliged him, noting with mounting curiosity that he stayed directly to her left as if he was protecting them from the canyon, and whatever he'd found in it. He cast frequent glances toward the dark crease in the land, his edginess increasing until her nerves began to fray. He didn't like whatever he'd found there.

When they'd settled Swallow into bed for the night, Zach beckoned her away from the fire.

"What did you find?" she demanded, too anxious to give him a chance to tell her.

"It's not what you think," he said, and wiped his face with his damp kerchief.

"How do you know what I think?" she snapped. "I've been jumpy as a flea on a hot skillet ever since you caught up to us. Just tell me and quit acting like a nervous polecat. And why do you keep mopping your face?"

"To get the smell off!" he snarled. "It's stuck in my head." He sighed and stuffed his kerchief into his hip pocket, then led her farther away from camp before bending close to speak softly in her ear. "It looks like Little Wolf almost trapped a whole battalion of soldiers in that canyon. It's a box canyon, you know?"

Caroline's heart plunked into her shoes. "Is that what I've been smelling? Dead that need burying? How many Cheyenne?"

"No, no, the dead have been buried."

She gasped and clutched a hand over her heart. "Little Wolf?"

"Would you be quiet, woman, and let me tell you?" Zach tipped his hat brim up and glared down at her, bracing his hands on his hips.

"Mercy!" she growled back at him. "Quit dancing around and spit it out."

"Horses!" Zach said, and glanced toward Swallow, then leaned close again and lowered his voice. "Somehow the soldiers got between the Cheyenne and their horses. They shot them. All of them. Then they burned them." He stepped back, jerked his hat off and looked away from her. "There were a few left, some that must have been kept closer to the cave where the women were hiding. But not more than ten, a dozen. I trailed them for a couple miles."

"How long ago did it happen?" she asked, understanding what the loss would mean to the Cheyenne.

"Three, four days," he muttered. Then he gripped her shoulders. "They'll have to replace those horses, and the only place they can get them—"

"They'll have to steal them," Caroline said, feeling the

blood leave her face. "But this area's only recently been settled. It's all poor families, farmers with plow horses and old nags. They can't afford riding horses. The ranches would have some, but they're all south of here." She caught her breath. "What about the women's packs? Were they on the horses?"

"Not enough left to tell, but I'd bet they were. We're going to have to travel faster, stay away from the settlements," Zach said, nodding in decision as he released her. "If we keep our distance, we can avoid trouble and get these supplies to Little Wolf as quickly as possible."

Caroline shook her head. Feeling chilled suddenly, she crossed her arms over her waist and held tight. "It was inevitable that the Army would catch up with them, and better that they killed the horses than the people. But didn't they stop to think? Do they realize what they've done?"

"Better for whom?" Zach demanded. "The settlers will pay a steep price for the Army's success. More warriors will be raiding," he said. "Isolated farms won't have any warning. The soldiers were delayed in pursuing them, probably to bury their dead and tend to their wounded, so they won't be able to help. We've got to get the supplies to the Cheyenne quickly. It may already be too late."

Caroline nodded, rubbing her arms against the goose bumps his words had raised. She knew only too well what the settlers faced, but couldn't bear to recall her own family's fate at the hands of rampaging Indians. Until now, Little Wolf had told her, the Cheyenne had only fired when fired upon. Little Wolf said that he had told the soldiers himself that the Cheyenne didn't want to fight, but they would, if forced to defend themselves. By destroying the Cheyenne's horses, the soldiers had gained a strategic advantage, making it next to impossible for the warriors to protect the women and children. Zach was right. Little Wolf would be forced to send more men out to raid, and they would have to range farther from the main group in order to find enough horses to outrun the soldiers.

The soldiers couldn't have picked a worse time or place. The Cheyenne had reached familiar territory—Sand Creek, the Sappa and Washita Rivers—where the blood of unavenged loved ones cried out to them. She doubted even Little Wolf could stop his foraging warriors if they were determined to seek vengeance as well as horses.

She shuddered and Zach put an arm around her and led her back to the fire. For once she welcomed his touch and leaned into his side.

"I'm not sure we can help, but we'll leave early, before dawn." Zach waited for her to get settled under the wagon before he crawled into his bedroll near Swallow. The boy rolled close and snuggled up to him and Caroline smiled as Zach put his arm around him. Luckily, the night air was mild, but it was nearing the end of September. They'd soon need each other to stay warm at night if this journey dragged on any longer.

She dreaded what lay ahead and her heart ached for the Cheyenne's troubles. She thought of the sick and weak she'd tended only days before. Didn't the government know or care that they were dying? Before Dull Knife first convinced Little Wolf to surrender, their camp numbered over two hundred tipis and almost two thousand *Tsitsitas*. Now there were less than a hundred fighting men, but almost three times that many women and children and old ones.

Why couldn't the soldiers help them, instead of chasing them? For that matter, why couldn't the government have allowed them to stay on their home range in the north in the first place? There was no gold in the Powder River valley, just antelope and deer and maybe a few buffalo. Nothing white men coveted. Why did the Cheyenne have to pay with their lives for the opportunity to live there?

Caroline ached at the plight of these people she loved. What more could she do to help them? Should she try to talk Little Wolf into surrendering? Even if he succeeded in getting some of them to the Powder River, he had no guarantee that they'd be allowed to stay.

She knew he believed that the Northern Cheyenne would eventually live in the Powder River Valley; it had been foretold by the Comanche medicine woman who saved Caroline's life. She frowned, trying to remember Little Wolf's version of the events. The confrontation between Little Wolf and White Bear, she recalled clearly. She shuddered. The medicine woman had bumped into her, knocking her over. The leash White Bear had tied around her neck had been ripped from his hand, infuriating him. He'd been quick to punish her. She'd been on her knees, stunned and bleeding from White Bear's first blows, when the woman interfered. White Bear had turned on her and delivered a blow that would have ripped the woman's face open, if the Comanche war chief hadn't stopped the whip with his arm.

Little Wolf had offered to buy Caroline to allow White Bear to save face and avoid a fight. He'd acted to protect the alliance—the first between the Cheyenne, Kiowa and Comanche nations—but when he'd seen Caroline's injuries, he'd wanted to take his quirt to White Bear.

Whatever his reasons, she owed him her life. She'd been so weak from previous beatings that she wouldn't have survived another. When Little Wolf asked about the shaman, the war chief had told him she was a messenger from the Great Spirit, sent to help the Comanche overcome their enemies. Curious, Little Wolf had asked her what lay ahead for the Cheyenne. She had told him that they would suffer greatly, but that, in the end, the Cheyenne would be allowed to live where they wanted.

Caroline frowned. That had happened more than three years ago, and the Cheyenne had certainly done their share of suffering since. So had most of the other tribes—including the Comanche, who had *not* overcome their enemies. That alone brought the shaman's medicine powers into question. How could she have known what would happen in the future? If Little Wolf hadn't lost so many of his people on the hated reservation in Oklahoma, would he still cling to the hope the woman's prediction inspired?

She sighed and tucked her blankets closer around her, feeling a chill breeze. For the first time since the momentous day when she'd been rescued from White Bear, Caroline wished she'd never met the shaman. She would gladly have died to spare the Cheyenne this perilous journey.

Chapter Eleven

Little Wolf walked among his people, his right hand pressed against the Sweet Medicine bundle under his arm. He needed what strength it could give this day to keep them moving. His heart bled as he gazed upon them—exhausted, hungry, sick and frightened—and wished he could tell them to build a fire, offer them fresh buffalo meat to fill their empty, growling stomachs, give them good words to strengthen their confidence. But he had none of these things to give, only more long, hard days of running, always running, on little food and water, and even less hope.

Woodenthigh rode into camp with a string of six sorry-looking horses. "Fit only for the soup pot, Father," he said as he tossed Little Wolf the lead rope. "They may give us a day or two. The only good horse is green as grass." He pointed to a dirty brown animal at the end of the lead. "I will rest and try to ride out his meanness."

"*Hou,* my son," Little Wolf told him and squeezed his shoulder. "You have done well. Did you see the others? Have they found more horses?"

His son looked away. "Do not ask me, Father. Many things are being done, things that you would not like to know." He shrugged off Little Wolf's hand and left, calling softly for Feather and Quiet Woman. Little Wolf watched him go, saddened that the boy had become a man in such hard times. Would he ever again know the joy of hunting with him? Would he ever know the pride of looking on a grown man with a wife and fat babies of his own?

His son looked back at him and started to smile, but his face froze. *"Veho,"* he shouted, pointing to several white men on the ridge behind Little Wolf. "Get down!" he cried and pushed the people near him to the ground.

Bullets buzzed around them like angry bees as many of the men returned the white men's fire and others ran for their horses. Some of the women began wailing until Black Crane crawled among them, quieting them and urging them to crawl to one side where there were no bullets.

Woodenthigh leaped onto his horse and pulled his rifle, leading the men who had found horses to mount to chase the *vehos* away. If they couldn't be chased away, the men would charge them and try to get the *vehos* to chase them, leading them away from the women and children. But before the warriors got close enough to get off a certain shot, the *vehos* whipped their horses and ran away. The warriors chased them, but not far. Soon, Little Wolf heard the lowing of cattle and many shots.

Woodenthigh returned, wearing a wide smile and carrying a warm, dripping liver. He presented it to Little Wolf, who gave it to Feather. "Cattlemen, Father," he said and took a big bite of the meat before Feather walked away with it. "And a big herd. We will eat well this night." His dark eyes gleamed and the people hurried to find the herd and do a little butchering.

"Do not worry that the meat will be wasted," Quiet Woman told him breathlessly as she skipped to keep up. "We can smoke the meat as we walk. All we have to do is—"

Little Wolf cut her off with a sharp motion of his hand. The woman would tell him every cut and stroke she must make if he did not stop her. *"Pah!"* he said. "You would make it easier for the *veho* soldiers to find us? Our moccasin tracks are not enough? Must we now leave a smoke trail, too?"

Quiet Woman shook her head. "You will see, my husband, and then you will eat your words for I will not let

you have any of my smoked meat. See if you like that."
With a disgusted huff, she hurried to catch up with
Feather and Woodenthigh.

Little Wolf watched her go, her hips swaying with her
fast walking. Her tongue was becoming too sharp. He
would take her to his blankets this night after she was well
fed and rested. His body stirred as it had not for many
suns. He smiled. When he finished with her, Quiet
Woman would be too tired to talk.

He saw Morning Star, with his two tall sons and his
wives, Short One and Pawnee Woman, already at the
butchering. Morning Star raised a full, bloody fist and
the people called in soft voices.

After helping his wives pick out and gut a young cow,
Little Wolf went in search of his brother. "A good night,"
he said when he found him feasting on a fat, barely
roasted rib. "Our people will rest well and run fast with
the new sun."

Morning Star said nothing, only picked his rib clean of
meat, then rose to his feet and beckoned for Little Wolf
to follow. "We must stop here and let the women jerk this
meat, while our men search for horses."

Little Wolf shook his head. "Have your eyes grown dim,
brother, that you cannot see the danger riding fast on the
wide trail we left behind us?"

"You push them too hard." Morning Star stepped so
close that the toes of their moccasins touched and glared
down at him. Little Wolf stood his ground, but he hated
this old trick. Taller by two hands, Morning Star knew
that Little Wolf did not like to look up to see his face. He
had done this many times when they were younger men,
even though Little Wolf had never backed down. Once
Little Wolf knocked his legs out from under him. After
that, Morning Star did not try it again until Little Wolf
became an Old Man Chief, bearer of the Sacred Bundle,
a position that required him to swear never to act or
speak in anger. Now Morning Star did this again, in front
of all the people. Little Wolf heard their whispering like a

summer wind sighing through a stand of cottonwood trees.

"You push hard, too, Morning Star," Little Wolf said, reminding his brother of his Cheyenne name and his responsibility as leader of the Dog Soldiers to not provoke a fight.

Morning Star glared at him, but said nothing.

Little Wolf returned his hard look without anger, though his fists were clenched at his sides. His brother did nothing without much thinking before. "What makes you look at your brother with anger in your heart? Why do you show this anger for me to our people?"

Morning Star smiled and started walking, leaving Little Wolf no choice but to follow. "We have come far," he said in a mild voice that did not fool Little Wolf. His brother was smart as a fox when it came to controlling the will of their people.

Little Wolf stopped. He did not like the look in his brother's eyes. "Tell me what it is you want me to hear, brother."

"Now that we are away from the reservation and in our own country again, we should surrender."

Little Wolf kept his face still, letting no emotion show as he waited for his brother to finish.

"We will go to the Pine Ridge Agency and surrender. Red Cloud and our relatives there will welcome us." Morning Star turned back toward the people and started walking fast.

Little Wolf put out an arm and stopped him, his arm catching Morning Star across the stomach. He kept it there and spoke in a low voice. "That was not our plan, brother. We agreed that we would try to return to the Powder River, our home range. Some of our people are still there, waiting for us. You know this. Why do you try to change our plan now?"

Morning Star shoved Little Wolf's arm away. "Our people are exhausted. They are dying. We must surrender while some of us still live."

Little Wolf fought against the anger rising inside him in a red haze. "We have lost only one man. Yes, many are sick and will die before we reach our journey's end, but you knew this when we started. Everyone agreed and said that if they must die, they wanted to die in their old country, not on the reservation."

"It is too hard," Morning Star argued. "Now that we have no horses, too many must walk. We do not even have travois for the sickest. We must surrender."

"This meat will give the people strength until our men can find more horses. Until then we will put the youngest in sacks and tie them on the horses' backs."

"They need rest," Morning Star insisted, but with less force. "We can stay here for two or three days, until we can replace the travois."

"No! Too many soldiers follow behind us. Would you have the people butchered where they sit, like Black Kettle's people on Sand Creek?"

Morning Star swayed, and Little Wolf steadied him. "It will be as you say, brother," Morning Star said with a long sigh, but he stirred himself to glare at Little Wolf one last time. "But I have not given up."

Morning Star let Little Wolf support him until his sons came running up. Then he pushed himself upright and called to the people. "Eat your fill and sleep well. My brother says we must run, and run we will."

A low rumble ran through the people. Little Wolf listened, but could not see who complained. He would know soon enough.

Zach returned to the fire after picketing his horse and sat on a rock next to Caroline.

"Everything look good out there?" she asked, without looking up from the shirt she was mending for Swallow.

"Fine, quiet." He tapped his hat brim against his shinbone, raising puffs of dust with every tap.

"Then why are you so tense?"

He straightened indignantly. "I'm not tense."

She eyed his hat pointedly. "Your hat says otherwise."

He hated that she recognized his ticks, the subtle hints his body gave off instinctively. The woman was too canny for her own good, but he supposed her knack had been developed out of dire need. It must have helped to be able to tell when that Kiowa fiend had been irritated. And she was right. He was worried.

"Take a walk with me?" He rose and held out a hand to help her stand.

She glanced at Swallow, already sleeping.

"Not far," Zach said. "I don't want to wake him."

Out beyond the circle of firelight, past the picketed horses, the night was alive with the music of crickets, the call of an owl and the frantic scrambling of its wary prey, and glowed softly in the light of a sliver of moon. A cool breeze drifted around them, and Caroline pulled her shawl over her shoulders and tied it over her breasts, leaving her hands free to catch fireflies. From where they stood, they could turn in a circle and see for miles and miles across the great dark sea of grass that waved uninterrupted from horizon to horizon.

"Living back east, I would never have known such stark beauty existed," Caroline said. "It took me a long time to learn to appreciate it and not be frightened by the vast, lonely stretches. They make me feel . . ."

"Insignificant?" Zach offered. "Smaller than a flea in God's eyes?"

Caroline smiled. "You understand."

He reached a hand to her. "Can I hold you?"

She clutched the ends of her shawl and looked up at him warily.

He smiled. "I don't have a shawl and there's a cool breeze tonight."

"Huh," she sniffed. "Doesn't that great black duster you're wearing keep you warm?"

He took the few steps to stand in front of her. "Naw. It flaps about so much, it makes the breeze worse. See?"

As he spoke the breeze whipped around him and his

duster waved briskly, making them both chuckle. He stepped closer and she pushed his hat brim up. Her eyes were sapphire pools in the moonlight, deep and beckoning, as she smiled at him. Her hair shone cool and regal around her face, its sunny warmth softened by moonglow.

"What is it, Zach?" she asked, rubbing her arms briskly. "I know you didn't bring me out here to listen to the crickets chirp. They're doing that back by the fire, too."

"I found six small graves just off the Cheyenne's trail today. They were well hidden, but someone, possibly a mother, had left something on top of one of the graves and it drew my eye." He pulled her close and settled his arms around her shoulders to provide additional warmth.

"Children?" Caroline asked, surprised.

He nodded and glanced away, not wanting her to see how deeply the discovery troubled him. "I thought it was pretty strange, first that they were small children, and because there were so many together." He glanced back at her. "It's a mystery to me."

"I've heard of a very old practice the Cheyenne call 'bundling,' but they haven't done it for years."

"Bundling?" Zach frowned. "Wasn't that some kind of courting ritual back in colonial times?"

"It's the same principle. The person lies down and is sewn into a bag with only their head extending. The colonials used it to keep a couple chaste."

"Men let themselves be sewn into bags?" He shuddered.

"Back then, I suppose men had to travel long distances to court and sometimes they had to stay overnight, often sleeping alongside the woman they were courting. The bundling bag was intended to keep them from . . . well, you know."

Even in the moonlight, he could see her cheeks flush, which he found annoying tonight. He'd brought her out here for answers, not missish embarrassment. "That hardly explains this situation, or the six dead children."

"It's the same concept," she said, tensing at his curtness. "The children are sewn into bags and two bags are connected together by a piece of rope, then hung over the back of a horse, usually one that isn't completely trained yet. That way the children don't have to be carried by their mothers, and the untrained horses are put to use."

"Why can't they attach a travois and let the children ride on it?" Zach asked, horrified by the thought of the tiny bodies dangling on either side of a horse. "What if the horse got spooked and started bucking, or worse, ran off?"

"Young children can fall off a travois and get hurt. There's always a brave holding the horse's halter, watching over the children." She patted his arm. "The Cheyenne don't take chances with their children, but accidents happen."

"It makes sense. They're trying to get through this stretch fast." He looked past her at the prairie and frowned. "There isn't a tree for miles, and nowhere to hide if the soldiers, who will be better mounted now, start catching up. Little Wolf doesn't want to be run down in the open." Though Zach understood the man's methods, he couldn't agree with them. "You've said the Cheyenne cherish their children, but six are dead. It seems to me that the distance gained by risking them was lost in the time it took to bury them. They died for no reason."

Caroline shuddered and he rubbed her arms, mentally kicking himself for upsetting her. "I'm sorry," he said, wishing he could share his concern with her for his own child. "Those tiny graves hit me hard." He held her for several minutes, neither of them moving, holding one another for comfort. When she shivered again, he pulled her closer to share his body's heat, and steal a little of hers. His body's reaction made him groan softly. Instantly, he knew it was the wrong thing to do, as he felt her stiffen in his arms.

"Caroline, I . . ." he began, but she cut him off.

"You said you'd leave me alone, Zach." She braced her arms between them and glared up at him. "I can't give you what you want—a quick roll in your blankets followed by a friendly pat on the rump when you ride away. There's nothing but heartache for me in your arms. When you tire of me, or find whatever it is you're seeking, you'll walk away, move on to another woman. But for me, there's no hope of another man. It would hurt me more to know the pleasure and never have it again, than never to have known it at all."

"You're wrong," he whispered, holding her loosely with his arms about her waist. He couldn't bear to let her go. Not yet. He kissed her forehead, her eyelids, the tip of her nose.

"Zach, please stop," she said, but without heat, without emotion, without fear. Her soft sigh as he captured her bottom lip in his lips told him her head might be against a kiss in the moonlight, but her body was willing. He listened to her body's response and nibbled her lip again, then kissed his way up her jaw to her perfect right ear and nibbled on the earlobe.

She groaned and tipped her head. "You don't play fair."

"Oh, darlin'," he breathed into her ear, delighting in the shivers that made her tremble in his arms. "I'm a saint." He followed the line of her neck with nibbling kisses, punctuated by small licks. He loved the sweet, salty taste of her. Finally, he slid into the curve between her neck and shoulder and settled there to feast, smiling when she groaned and sagged against him. Her arms slid up his chest and over his shoulders and he returned to her mouth, nibbling at the corners, coaxing and persuading until she angled her head and captured his mouth.

A thrill chased through him at her aggressive move and he let her have her way with the kiss, until she tentatively thrust her tongue into his mouth. Then he was the one groaning. He lifted her higher, giving her better access and returned measure for measure, until his body turned rock-hard and became insistent. Then he eased her down his body, careful not to let his raging erection scare her, and reclaimed control. He'd lost control too many times in the past. He was determined not to let anything alarm her this time.

"Enough, darlin'," he gasped, letting his forehead settle against hers. "You don't want to take this farther, and I can't do any more of that unless we do." He hadn't meant to draw attention to his condition, but the pain had become unbearable. He pushed at his erection, trying to ease it into a more comfortable position, but there was none. At her gasp, he glanced up, saw her wide-eyed gaze and grimaced. "Don't worry," he said. "It's not getting near you."

To his surprise, she raised up on her toes, gave him a quick peck on the cheek, then, with a last wary glance at his erection, hurried back to camp.

Zach ripped off his belt, doubled it and stuck it in his mouth as he ripped open his pants and brought himself to release. The full-throated roar that blasted out of his chest a few seconds later sounded more like a gruff bark.

Once he recovered from the convulsions that had wracked him, he removed the belt and grimaced at the new tooth marks he'd cut into the fine leather. Belts and bundling, he thought with a shrug. When it came to keeping a woman happy, a man would do just about anything.

He didn't return to camp right away. Instead, he visited Demon and, after giving the animal a quick rubdown, he hung an arm over the horse's neck and relived the moment when Caroline took control of the kiss. His mind strayed to their conversation and he frowned at her comment that all he wanted from her was a "quick roll in his blankets."

No, he wanted much more than that from Caroline. He craved her kisses, any way she was willing to give them. He wanted to spread her on his bed and explore the full curves of her body. He wanted to ease himself deep inside her until his cock throbbed at the mouth of her womb. He wanted to make her forget the horrors that had come before. He wanted to be the man who healed her, who taught her that being with a man didn't have to be painful or debasing. He wanted to be the man, sunk to his hilt, to see those blue eyes widen in surprise the first time she experienced pleasure, just before he filled her with his seed.

And, he was beginning to fear, he wanted to be the only man who ever did.

The sun still slept behind the eastern hills when Little Wolf and his men began helping the women tie their children into sacks made from the green hides of the butchered beeves. They then tied the sacks together and hung the bags on either side of the green horses. A strong warrior held the horse's head until it quieted and accepted its burden. Many mothers shed tears as they watched their children led off into the gray shadows, dangling so near the horse's legs, not knowing if they would survive the dangerous trip.

Woodenthigh led the ugly brown horse up after he'd ridden it until foam flecked its dark hide. Little Wolf looked over the horse and shook his head. "Do not worry, Father. He is too tired to lift his head, let alone buck."

Little Wolf took the horse by the lower lip and stared into its eyes. The animal's eyelids drooped and his head sat heavy in Little Wolf's hand. He nodded to the warriors holding the next two bags of children.

Before they could be hung over the horse, Morning Star and his sons pushed Short One forward. "My wife will take this mount. It looks strong and quiet."

"It is only quiet now because . . ." Woodenthigh began, but Morning Star laid his hand flat over his lips, in the strong sign for silence. Woodenthigh obeyed, but looked to Little Wolf, who shrugged. "If the horse is calm enough to carry children, it can carry one small woman."

Woodenthigh took a good hold on the horse's rope

bridle as Morning Star's sons boosted Short One onto its back. She wrapped her fists in its mane and nodded. "All will be well, my husband. You worry overmuch about one old woman."

Little Wolf smiled and patted her arm. "Ah, but your beauty rivals the sun, Shorty. Without you to calm every argument and tend every hurt, the rest of us would be lost."

Woodenthigh chuckled, still holding tight to the lead rope. "No harm must come to you, *nha'i*. Who would help me choose the fairest maiden to wife, and keep Morning Star and my father in good spirits?"

"Do not think your sweet lies will earn you extra meat from my stewpot," Short One said with a laugh and a nod to Woodenthigh. "You will have to get along without me."

The horse stood quietly under its burden and everyone breathed a sigh. But when Woodenthigh turned to pass the reins to the mounted man who would lead it, the horse gave a sharp, high buck. Short One wound both hands into the horse's mane and her blanket slid off her shoulders and began snapping at the horse's flank. Woodenthigh tried to throw his arms around the horse's neck to keep it from rearing, but the horse sank onto its haunches and lashed out with its front hooves. Then it sprang back onto all four legs and began jumping and jerking, trying to shake off its burden. Short One's fingers had become tangled in the mane and she was thrown off, only to dangle at the horse's side. Again and again, the horse's hooves struck her as it bucked, until Woodenthigh clubbed it between the eyes. One of her sons sprang forward and cut her hand free, then pulled her away from the animal. The women in the camp were yipping and crying, the men and the remaining children stared in dismay at her broken, bleeding body.

Old Bridge crouched beside her, but he soon shook his head. "She is broken inside. I can do nothing."

Little Wolf stood nearby as Morning Star and his sons wept and Short One's spirit took the long walk home.

The long poles cut for a travois became a sturdy scaffold where they laid her body, along with her few possessions. No one could put her in a hole in the ground for all knew that Short One feared the dark. Morning Star forbid the people to cut themselves in sorrow for they were too weak and needed all their strength. Many cut their hair instead and rubbed dirt on their faces, and sang death songs to relieve their pain.

Little Wolf's heart bled as he looked back at the lone scaffold, and prayed that the soldiers who followed would leave her body alone. He turned back and walked behind his brother, wanting to be close in his time of sorrow. The people walked slowly, heads hanging, their hearts on the ground for Short One.

"Come, my friends," he cried to them. "Short One would not want her death to cause us to be caught by the soldiers. Run!" he cried. "Run for Short One, who would tell you the same if she were here. Run for her, for hope, for life. Run!"

Their heads came up and their tears flowed faster, but they ran as they had never run before. As if this was the only way they could grieve their lost one, they ran.

Little Wolf ran beside them, his heart bursting with love for his people and sorrow for the one they left behind.

Caroline stared at the scaffold in the distance with dread blooming in her heart. Who could it be? There hadn't been any reports of battles or skirmishes from people they'd passed on the trail recently. It must be one of the old ones, weakened by malaria, she reasoned, but that didn't explain this horrible feeling that something was wrong. Not just a little wrong, but dreadfully wrong.

"I've got to find out who it is," she told Zach again.

"No stop!" Swallow clutched the side of the wagon's high seat, easing himself to the edge as if about to jump.

"Stay put, boy," Zach told him with a stern glance. "I don't intend to chase you all over this prairie." He turned to Caroline. "We'll find out soon enough who it is. If they died of disease, you don't want to be touching those blankets."

"Oh, please." Caroline shrugged off his concerns. "I touched every one of the sick Cheyenne days ago and we're all still healthy. I have a very bad feeling about this. You don't need to do anything but pull the wagon close beside the scaffold so I can reach—"

"No," Zach said, but he sighed and Caroline relaxed, realizing he intended to climb up and find out who it was for her.

"But you won't know who it is," she said.

"I know who's important to you," he said and glanced at her.

"It's not Little Wolf," she said, then wondered at herself. "I don't know how I know that, but I do. It's someone else."

"Do you two have a spiritual connection?" Zach asked, the look he shot her challenging. "If you ask me, you barely know each other."

"No, we don't, and nobody asked you." Her gaze caught on the scaffold drawing nearer and her stomach pitched. She clenched her hands in her lap, unaware that she was wringing them until Zach put a hand over them.

"You can't help them now," he said, giving her hands a last pat. "No sense worrying yourself sick over something you can't change." He studied the scaffold in the distance, his head canted. "Is this how the Cheyenne typically bury their dead? I didn't see any scaffolds in that canyon, but there was blood in one of the rifle pits."

Caroline clutched his arm as the blood drained from her head, leaving her suddenly dizzy. "Hold on there, darlin'," he said and put his arm around her shoulders.

He clutched all the reins in one hand, while bracing her against his side. "I apologize for givin' you a fright. I'm sure nobody was killed, probably only wounded."

"Oh, thank you," Caroline said sarcastically, pushing off his arm and bracing herself against the seat. "That's so comforting."

"I aim to please," he told her with a wink and a smile.

She rolled her eyes, but her gaze once again slid over the scaffold looming ever nearer and her stomach pitched. "Could you hurry, please?"

Instead of snapping the reins over the mules' heads, Zach hauled back on the reins. "Here," he said and handed them to her. "I'll ride down there. By the time you get there with the wagon, I'll have climbed it."

"No," Swallow said, clutching Caroline's arm. "No let him wake the dead." The boy's eyes were wide and frightened, his grip on her arm punishing.

"Don't worry, Swallow," she said, gently removing his hand from her arm and putting it around his shoulders. "We won't wake him, or her. We'll look at their blankets and belongings. That should tell us who it is. Or was."

"Be careful," Swallow said, nodding to Zach, but his whole body had begun trembling.

Zach didn't bother saddling his horse. He untied him and leaped on the animal's bare back, then dug in his heels.

Caroline urged the mules on and when she pulled them to a halt near the scaffold, Zach had already climbed it, examined the corpse and shimmied back down again. His face grim, he again tied his horse to the back of the wagon and took the reins from Caroline's hands. Giving the reins a firm snap, he drove the wagon several yards past the scaffold, then handed the reins to Swallow.

"Who is it?" Caroline demanded. Why hadn't he told her? "Do you know?"

"Step down," he said and reached up to help her.

She refused his help and scrambled down without aid. "Tell me," she said, her voice low and tight. "I've told you I'm not some hothouse flower you have to pamper. Give it to me straight."

"It's Short One," he said, and watched her carefully. "I'm sorry."

"How do you know?" she asked, startled, her gaze flying to the scaffold. Her brain shouted, *No! Not Short One.*

"I recognized her blanket. It's not like any of the others."

"You're right," Caroline whispered. "It was a gift from Pawnee Woman, Dull Knife's other wife. She gave it to Short One to celebrate her marriage to Dull Knife." She looked up at Zach, wanting him to understand, to appreciate her friend. "Dull Knife's first wife hated Pawnee Woman and made everyone miserable. But Short One brought laughter and peace to that tipi. Everyone loved her." Caroline choked and tears came in a flood. "Would you excuse me, please? I need a little time."

Zach nodded and watched her walk away. She wasn't wandering, and she didn't appear to be wracked with grief. Where was she headed? If she didn't stop soon, he'd have to go after her. Moments later, she knelt near a clump of wildflowers and began gathering them. Zach turned his attention to Swallow and wasn't surprised to find fat tears streaming down the boy's cheeks.

"Hand me the reins." He reached for them and tied them to the brake handle, then climbed up and sat beside Swallow on the driver's bench, high above the mules' rumps. He put an arm around the boy's skinny shoulders, glad that someone needed him to comfort them. "I'm sorry, Swallow."

"What happen?" the boy asked, seeming dazed. "She well, happy when we saw her. No sick."

"I don't think she died because she was sick, son," Zach said, and took a deep breath, praying he'd find the right words to tell the boy what he needed to know. "I think she got hurt very bad. One arm didn't feel right and one of her legs wasn't laid out straight."

"How she get hurt?" Swallow's lower lip quivered and Zach could tell the boy was struggling to be stoic.

Zach sighed and pulled him closer, wishing he knew more, but knowing details wouldn't bring comfort. "It's not important how she got hurt, only that she's not hurtin' anymore. Right?"

Swallow gulped and nodded. After a few seconds, he handed Zach his flute. "I want to give her this, to remind her of me. Will you put it by her side?"

Zach nodded, too moved to speak.

Swallow bent and pulled a knife from his boot. Zach started, surprised. "Where'd you get that?" he asked.

Swallow shot him a speaking glance, then flipped the knife into the air and caught the blade in his hand. He extended the handle to Zach. "I give you this to cut my hair for flute. So she know it comes from me. You give it back, right?"

"If you promise that you won't use it to cut your arms or legs." Zach had seen the damage wrought by a blade in the hands of a grieving Indian.

"I promise."

Zach took the blade, snipped off a long curl and handed the knife back. He watched uneasily as the boy slid it into his boot with far too much surety for a child, but refrained from comment. The boy obviously knew how to use it. Another time, Zach promised himself, he'd test the boy's ability, but not today.

"You hold here," Swallow asked and Zach held onto one end of the curl so that Swallow could braid it, secure it with a couple of strings pulled out of a ragged petticoat Caroline kept for bandages, and tie it to the flute. Zach shimmied up the scaffold and placed the flute under the corpse's blanket-wrapped hand, where Swallow said she was certain to find it.

"*Hou,*" Swallow said and nodded in satisfaction. "It is good." Then he returned to the wagon and began clearing a circle for a fire. Between the two of them, they had a hot lunch ready by the time Caroline returned with her flowers. After securing the bouquet with a strip cut from her ruined blue dress, Caroline handed them to Zach, who again shimmied up the scaffold and placed the flowers beside Swallow's flute.

"Hungry?" he asked as they turned to walk back to the wagon where Swallow waited.

"No," she said. "I need to do something first, if you don't mind."

"Fine," he said. "I'll keep an eye on Swallow."

"It involves you," she said, and looked up at him for the first time since she'd returned from gathering wildflowers. Her eyes were red, her face tear-streaked and flushed, but her gaze was steady. "I made a promise to Short One and it's about time I kept it. Would you hold me? I find I'm in need of comforting after all."

"Certainly," he said, feeling suddenly awkward. He stood still as stone and waited for her to come to him. She walked to him without hesitation, laid her cheek against his chest and wrapped her arms around his waist. Her chest lifted on a sigh. For the first time since he'd known her, their proximity didn't produce the hot, lusty reaction he'd grown to expect. Instead, he felt a deep connection and sympathy for her loss, and was glad he was here to comfort her. He laid his cheek against her head and let her lean on him.

A breeze stirred her hair, playfully lifting the swath that lay over her left ear, but she didn't move to pat it down. The air circled them and by the time it reached his nose, it smelled of sunshine, woman and fresh flowers. It wove itself higher, stirring his hair, then lifted upward and he heard the flowers rustle, smelled their sweet perfume.

Softly, in the distance, he heard the single trilling note of a flute.

Chapter Twelve

"Hi-yah!" Caroline hollered at the mules to get them moving faster. Since discovering Short One's body, she'd been tense and anxious, short-tempered and irritable. She'd even had words with Swallow this morning when he didn't roll out of bed fast enough to suit her. Zach had taken to scouting farther afield, more than likely because she hadn't had a kind word for him in three days. She'd better get control of herself or she'd end up alone on the prairie. Not a happy prospect.

She tore her gaze away from the six brown-and-black rumps in front of her and lifted her head. For miles and miles in every direction, all she could see was waving grass baked gold by the long, hot summer and dried by the whistling wind. Out here, where there were few trees, the wind had a different voice. It took on the rustle of dry grass blades rubbing in a raspy chorus, and it moaned for lack of something substantial to wrap its arms around. Here and there clumps of wildflowers dotted the grassy vistas, like tiny boats bobbing on an undulating sea of gold.

The stark beauty of the plains awed Caroline and left her longing for the solid warmth of wood and plaster walls, the hush of carpeted floors, the scent of roses in crystal and bread baking in the oven. She'd happily settle for a willow backrest and a length of tanned hide shaping itself into some useful item in her hands, the scent of venison roasting over the fire, a column of smoke winding up and out through the blackened hole at the tipi's top, and the cheery laugh of a friend come to visit. A steady diet of the vast plains left her feeling like an ant on God's giant's picnic blanket, in danger of being squashed at any moment, as Short One had been.

Zach had told her what he believed caused Short One's death. He'd explained the damage he'd noticed even through the blankets wrapping her friend's body. Before leaving Dodge City, Caroline had known the journey was dangerous, that the Cheyenne were dying before she'd undertaken this venture, but until Short One's death, it had always been a vague notion, something that was happening to someone else. Now death had stolen someone she loved, forcing her to face her own mortality and remember the deaths of others she had lost. She'd spent three days dwelling on life's fragility. Enough! It was past time to put her fears aside and celebrate survival.

She tipped her head back and stared up into the clear blue sky, watching a few lonely clouds scudding along before the wind. "Look, Swallow!" she said, and pointed upward. "A horse."

Swallow followed her finger and snorted. "That no horse, it's a skunk. Legs too short. See? Two skunks and a bear."

"Hah!" she said. "Looks more like a bunny to me."

"What is bunny?"

Caroline shot him a teasing glance, even as she registered his unfamiliarity with the childish term. "It's a rabbit you don't eat. A pet." When he still looked puzzled, she added, "You play with it."

"Play with food?" He shot her a disgusted look, then squinted at the cloud. "Now it looks like chicken."

"What do you know about chickens?" she asked, eyeing him suspiciously. The Cheyenne didn't keep chickens. He wouldn't know a chicken from a hippopotamus, unless some of the warriors had been raiding.

"Taste like rabbit," he told her. "There! You!"

She let him distract her for the moment, promising herself she'd revive the subject later and get to the bottom of it. "My face isn't that round," she said, and jabbed him in the ribs, noting with satisfaction that her elbow no longer connected with bone. He'd put on some weight and was so full of energy, it was difficult for him to ride beside her on the wagon all day. He'd taken to frequently nagging Zach into letting him ride for short distances, and proved to be a skilled rider. Zach was also instructing him in knife fighting and throwing, which Caroline also enjoyed.

The evenings spent watching Zach and Swallow horse around had helped her to relax and feel more at ease around Zach. He seemed to genuinely care for the boy and Swallow worshipped him. She dreaded the day the two would have to part, but knew it would arrive soon. She noticed Zach's tension, his habit of gazing at the horizon, especially after spending time with Swallow. He

was more anxious than ever to catch up with the
Cheyenne, but he kept her and Swallow away from the
Kansas settlements, except when they needed corn for
the mules. He minimized even that need by occasionally
bringing two or three bags, bought from some obliging
farmer, strapped over his horse's hindquarters.

Come to think of it, his habit of avoiding the farms and
settlements was making this trip longer than it needed to
be due to his continual detours. Given his anxiety, why
would he do that? Was he trying to protect her and Swallow? If so, from what? She snapped the reins over the
mules' backs and searched the surrounding plains suspiciously. He was hiding something, she realized, and it was
about time she found out what.

Topping a large hill a few hours later, she pulled back
on the reins and used the brake to stop the wagon.

"Ah! Pretty," Swallow said, clearly awed by the idyllic
scene spread in the small valley before them.

"Very pretty," Caroline agreed, admiring the neat, tidy
sod farmhouses laid out in a row, flanked by large barns
overstuffed with hay. Well-kept, thoroughly harvested gar-
dens sat beside rows of young, staked fruit trees. Smoke
wafted gently from the chimneys and sheep grazed in the
fields, but something was wrong. She saw no one at work
in the fields, baskets of clothes sat waiting to be hung but
there were no women in sight, no children playing.

"Where people?" Swallow asked. He pointed toward
the last house in the row. "Zach here."

"Hi-yah!" Caroline cried and snapped the reins sharply
over the mules, who jumped into motion. She released
the brake, but kept a hand on it to control their steep de-
scent into the small, green oasis. As she passed each sod-
walled home, she noticed details that increased her
unease: wide-open doors; an overturned butter churn
oozing soft clumps partially melted into the dirt; clothing
strewn in the dirt, as if dropped by a careless hand. The
stench of fire rose strong from one sod house and smoke
drifted out the door as she drove by.

In a field between two of the houses lay a large pile of long pine logs beside a neat stack of firewood. She realized they were lodge poles, their bark long ago scraped off by Cheyenne women before being used to support their tipis. These had probably been scavenged from the abandoned Cheyenne village on the nearby Washita River after the village was attacked by soldiers, a wrong that the Cheyenne still muttered about whenever they traveled in this area. Her stomach clenched as she approached the last house, where Zach waited beside a battered, dangling front door.

"What's happened here?" Caroline asked, keeping a tight hold on the reins. The mules had picked up on her nervousness and were tossing their heads and jigging in their harnesses.

"Easy," Zach said, and stroked the noses of the two lead mules before taking the reins from her. He set the brake and tied the reins to it, then helped her down. "Swallow," he said, lifting the boy down beside him. "I need you to talk to the mules, give them some corn and water. Get them settled down. Can you do that?"

Swallow nodded and hurried to get a bucket of corn and the nosebags from the back of the wagon.

"All right," Caroline said, in a low whisper, "now you've really got me worried. What's going on?"

"I think you might be able to help these folks," he said, holding her by the shoulders, "but if you don't think you can, it's all right."

"What kind of help?" Caroline hated the tight, tinny whisper her voice had become. There was nothing she couldn't face, hadn't already faced. These people couldn't surprise her.

"You'll know what to do," he said, and pulled her into his arms and held her tight for only a second. Then he took her arm and led her into the sod house.

She blinked, letting her eyes adjust to the dim light, and kept a tight grip on Zach's forearm until she got her bearings. The poverty of the place struck her first. The floor was hard-packed dirt and though there were several narrow slits cut in the sod walls for air and light, the dank, musty interior smelled like moldy mushrooms. A small stove was set in a corner, its crooked stovepipe shoved through the low, thatched ceiling. Beside the stove a leaking bucket set on the floor held a few cups and plates in soapy water. The only furniture was a rickety shelf made of hand-planed lumber with cross-cut logs set between the planks for support; a rough plank table and a few stumps for chairs; and a rope-and-pole bed. A fresh straw tick was spread over the bed and over that a colorful patchwork quilt provided a bright spot of color in the otherwise drab room.

Caroline turned to Zach, who nodded to the corner opposite the stove. She looked closely, but light from one of the windows cut into the dim room, leaving the corner dark as night. Only when she stepped through the light did Caroline see the women huddled together in the corner: a middle-aged woman and a girl of about seventeen.

Why were they standing in the corner? Caroline stepped closer and then she saw their eyes. Her knees locked and a breath of cold swept up her spine as she realized why Zach had thought she could help them. She stood for a moment, gathering her strength, debating how to proceed.

She turned to Zach. "I'll be a while here, but I need a bucket of fresh water and some soap and towels."

He nodded. "I'll set it outside. If you need me, I'll be out back."

She watched him leave, propping what remained of the door over the doorway to ensure their privacy. Caroline took a deep breath and stepped forward.

"I'm Caroline Whitley," she said, slowly approaching the women, who had relaxed some now that Zach had left the room. "I was captured by the Kiowa, and . . ." She tried to finish, but couldn't say the words. "Can I help you?"

* * *

Hours later, Caroline stepped out of the house with a sigh and found Zach watching for her. He'd parked the wagon in a field across from the house, where he'd set up camp. A weary group of farmers, women and small children huddled around the campfire, bent over their plates as if the effort of lifting a fork was more than they could manage. Swallow had settled near the mules and was busy tending his own tiny fire.

"Water?" she asked, in a scratchy whisper.

"Have you been talkin' all this time?" Zach asked, as he handed her a full dipper. "Your voice sounds like sandpaper."

"I've done everything I can for them. The rest will take time. How many dead?" She dragged the back of her hand over her mouth and leaned against the wagon, letting the cool water revive her body and spirit.

"Five, six, maybe more," he said, shaking his head. "We can't be sure. Some haven't come in from the fields and one man is overdue from a trip to town."

"When did it happen? How many were there?" She kept her voice low, not wanting to disturb the survivors.

"It was definitely Cheyenne. They'd only been gone a few hours when I got here." He yanked his hat off and slapped it on his thigh. "Where are the blasted soldiers?" he growled, and stuck the hat back on his head. "They destroyed the Cheyenne's horses, burned their provisions and now they're takin' their time chasin' them down? They could have had them cornered by now, but they're too busy escortin' Lewis's body back to Fort Dodge. And who pays for it? Innocent civilians."

"Lewis is dead?" Caroline asked, stunned. "When? The Cheyenne killed him?"

"In the last battle." Zach turned away to hide his dismay. He hadn't agreed with Lewis, but the man had saved him from being stomped to death by an angry mob, and shared his excellent whiskey. "I've known for several days now. He was shot in the leg. Bled to death."

"That's terrible news," Caroline said. "And it will

harden the Army's determination to catch the Cheyenne. This won't help their case either." She glanced around her. "I hope the Army will remember that this country used to be the Cheyenne's hunting grounds. Did you see that pile of poles? They're lodge poles, taken from the tipis abandoned at the Washita battle."

Zach stuck his fists on his hips and glared at her. "Are you sayin' these folks *deserved* what they got?"

"For heaven's sake," she whispered, glancing at the men by the fire. "Keep your voice down."

He took her arm and pulled her along behind him, away from the fire and listening ears.

"I'm merely pointing out that there are two sides to this situation." She yanked free, wincing as she rubbed her arm above the elbow. "As you said, the soldiers created the problem by destroying the Cheyenne's provisions, leaving them no choice but to raid."

He tipped his hat up and stared at her. "How can you defend them? You've experienced the horror yourself. Today, you treated their victims."

Caroline sighed. "You don't understand."

"You've got that right, at least," he said, his lip curled. "A bunch of Cheyenne rode up to one of these men in the field. One of them offered a hand in friendship, and when the man reached to take it, the Indian shot him in the face. The man who was with him hid in a ditch and got away when they gave up and quit huntin' for him."

Caroline slapped her hands on her hips and stuck her nose in his face. "Do you think I haven't been listening for the last few hours? I know what's been done here, and I abhor it. All I'm saying is that the raiders probably saw those lodge poles and were harder on these folks than they would have been otherwise."

"You're wrong," Zach told her, so tempted to shake some sense into her that his fingers were twitching. "Why do you think I've been sendin' you circlin' around these settlements? This isn't the only place *your friends* have visited. They've left a trail of rape, murder and destruction all the way from the Kansas border. These people are armin' themselves and they'll be after *your friends* as soon as they finish buryin' their dead."

Caroline stared at Zach, her mouth hanging open in shock. "That can't be true," she whispered. "Little Wolf wouldn't have allowed this. He'll fight if he has to, but only when he's shot at first. This isn't like him at all."

"Well, it may not be like him, but it sure fits a few of the others. Several people have described Black Coyote as the man leading the raids. And the group hurtin' the women are all young braves—hot and randy young bucks. The kind who . . ." He broke off, snapped his mouth shut and looked away from her, his jaw clenched tight against his anger.

"Who what?" She searched his suddenly closed expression, hating the blank stare, the wall that he'd thrown up between them. "Is that what you're hunting, Zach? A bunch of 'hot and randy young bucks'? Who did they hurt? Your sister? Your niece? Your father and brother, your *mother*?" Her voice had risen with each question until she nearly shouted the last. "Who are you hunting?"

"My son!" he shouted, full in her face. "Those bastards raped and murdered *my wife* and stole my son." He grasped her arms and leaned close, his eyes alive with pain, his features drawn tight with fear and anguish. "They have my son." He shoved away from her, strode to his horse and leaped on to its bare back.

She watched him ride away, sick at heart. Dear God, how could she help him?

Zach didn't ride far. He couldn't leave Caroline and the boy alone with those folks. If they learned who she was to the Cheyenne, there was no telling how they would react, what they'd do to her. He pulled up his horse and slid to the ground. He needed to regain control over his emotions. The last week had been hell. The destruction the Cheyenne raiders left in their wake reminded him daily what had been done to Patricia, what might still be happening to Luke, and ate at his gut. At times, he'd barely been able to breathe, the fear for his son had become so overwhelming. If he hadn't been afraid the same thing would happen to Caroline and the boy at the hands of vigilantes, he would have chased down the raiders days ago.

And now he'd slipped and revealed his purpose to the one person who never should have known, at least not until he'd accomplished his goal and found his son or learned what happened to him. He had compromised Luke's life. Guilt and fear spurred him. *Damnation!* He stomped to the nearest tree and smashed a fist into it. Ignoring the searing pain in his knuckles, he hit it again. A raw, snarling cry broke out of him with the third blow. It echoed back to him, reminding him of an animal— enraged, frustrated, deprived. He was no animal, damn it all. He was a man, capable of controlling his destiny, rising to any challenge he faced.

Or so he'd thought. He despised his inability to overcome, to conquer, to find Luke. He hated the beasts who had raped and murdered Patricia. Like the people he'd tried to help over the last week, she'd been innocent. She hadn't been at the battles where Cheyenne women and children had been cut down under a flag of truce, where their children had been thrown on fires alive. But she had paid the price, and Luke was paying it still. He had to make it stop.

But how? How did he proceed from here? What path should he take? How could he protect Caroline and Swallow, convince the Cheyenne to surrender, and find Luke?

He examined the damage he'd done to his hand. The knuckles were raw, bleeding freely. He pulled off his bandanna and wrapped his hand tight, then leaped back onto his horse and pointed its nose back to camp.

He may not be able to do it all, let alone do it all tonight, but somehow he'd find a way to make it happen. All of it.

Foolish! Caroline thought to herself as she washed and bandaged Zach's battered hand. "How could you do this to yourself?" she asked, giving voice to her thoughts despite her resolve to keep her opinion to herself. "Your hand will be stiff, sore and swollen for days, maybe even longer, *if* it doesn't get infected."

When he didn't answer, just stared into the darkness over her head, she felt her simmering anger flash to boiling. "What set you off? Were you annoyed at yourself for slipping and revealing your secret to the enemy? Or were you annoyed at me for defending the 'bastards'?"

His eyes, when they snapped to her face, burned like live coals in their sockets. "Every day, every victim I see, every body I bury reminds me that my son is still out there somewhere. I don't know whether to pray that he's alive or hope that he's dead and thus spared the misery of captivity. You're a daily reminder of the horrors he could be experiencing, and being tied to this wagon and its team of plodding mules tests my patience daily."

She recoiled from the frustration and anger seething inside him. "I'm sorry," she whispered and tied off the bandage. She looked away to repack her medicines. "I understand you're anxious to find your son, although I resent being used in pursuit of that goal."

She stood, then turned back. "How old is your son?"

"He would be five now, much younger than Swallow."

"And he's blond?" She glanced at Zach's hair, gleaming in the firelight, the color of coal. "What color was your wife's hair?"

"Pale blond, both of them," Zach said and glanced aside to where the top of Swallow's head could be seen poking out from under a blanket that rose and fell quietly as he slept. "Not yellow; more of a silver blond."

"When was the last time you saw him? And when was he taken?"

Zach looked up at her, his eyes narrowed. "Why?"

"Just curious," she said, but her mind had begun scanning the faces she remembered seeing the last time she'd been among the Cheyenne. If only she'd known then; she would have been looking more closely. "Lots of kids are towheaded when they're young, but their hair darkens as they get older. Were you a towhead?"

"No." Zach's tone was quick, decisive. "Don't you think I've considered that Luke's hair might have gone dark? I'm not a fool."

Caroline's gaze lifted from his bandaged hand. She raised an eyebrow in question.

He sighed. "My brother and I have the same color hair. Neither one of us was a towhead."

"What color was your mother's hair?" When Zach rolled his eyes, she added, "Humor me."

"My parents both had dark hair. Mother's was a reddish-brown, Father's like mine." He followed her to the wagon, snapping his hat against his thigh with every step.

"But Patricia was very fair. Isn't it possible that your son—Luke?—could have been different? His hair could have darkened considerably by now. It might even be as dark as yours. Had you heard that there was a blond child among Little Wolf's band?"

He nodded. "Several people mentioned seein' one, but no one had ever seen him up close."

"Was that your only reason for seeking Luke among the Cheyenne?"

"No. A company of soldiers examined the site where they found"—he swallowed hard, then continued—"the bodies. The arrows in the, uh, man she'd run away with were identified as Cheyenne. Also, a Cheyenne raidin' party struck a ranch not far from there the same day. The soldiers determined from the survivors' descriptions that the raiders were Cheyenne."

Caroline busied herself settling her medicine box where it would be cushioned from the jostling wagon while she considered Zach's dilemma. "You must have been pretty disappointed when you met Swallow and realized who he really is."

"Huh," Zach said on a heavy sigh. "You have no idea."

"But you're still pursuing the Cheyenne?" She gazed up at him, watching his face change from defensive to alert and intense. His brows came together and his eyes narrowed. "I was ready to leave, follow up some clues that led to the Lakota Sioux, when a horse bumped into me. Come to think of it," he said with a frown, "that was no accident. The man leadin' the horses wanted them to hit me." He described the man to Caroline, who identified him as Woodenthigh, Little Wolf's son.

"He's a tease," Caroline said with a smile. "He was probably frustrated that he couldn't take a whack at you because of me, so he tried to knock you on your—uh, you get the idea. His way of counting coup."

"Well, he did me a favor," Zach said, shaking his head. "Those horses looked familiar. I think they're the ones stolen from Patricia when she was killed. They can lead me to Luke, if they weren't burned in that canyon."

"Were they very good horses? Like Demon?"

He nodded. "Broodmares, if they're the ones I think they are. Good stock."

"Then the Cheyenne would have kept them tethered close for the chiefs to ride, just in case the battle didn't go the way they planned," Caroline told him, shaking her head. "But the Cheyenne are gift-givers and their favorite gift, suitable for all occasions, is a horse. Tracing those horses may be harder than you think."

"Well, I won't know until I get to their camp," Zach said, looking very determined. He turned to face her, and stepped closer.

Caroline backed into the wagon, her pulse kicking up at the look on Zach's face. His features seemed hard and angular in the flickering light and when he braced an arm on either side of her, effectively trapping her between him and the wagon, she gulped. "So what will it be?" he asked, his voice much too low and controlled for her tastes. "Are you goin' to help me, or run to Little Wolf with my story?"

She bristled. "I'm no tattler."

"But this isn't about tattlin,' is it?" He stepped closer. "It's a matter of life and death. My son's life and death."

"You know I'll help you," Caroline told him and ducked under his arm, then turned to face him. "And not because you're trying to intimidate me, either."

"I'm not tryin' to scare you." He chuckled and his breath caressed her hair. He reached up and smoothed it back into place, his fingertips leaving a trail of fire along her cheek, her chin. "Do you still want me to leave you alone, Caroline? I've been tryin' to honor your wishes, but it's very hard. I can't forget that moonlight kiss you gave me."

His change of subject threw her off guard, but she assumed he didn't want to discuss it further, just wanted her to know how he felt. She drew a shallow breath, sensing the edge beneath his control. She'd had a hard time forgetting that night herself.

She straightened to move away, only to collide with Zach, who'd angled into her path. She tried to jerk back, but his arm came around her waist and held her to him.

"Zach, this is hardly the time or the place." She glanced over his shoulder at the farmers nearby.

"Does that mean that at a better time, in a better place, you'd welcome me?" He searched her face, waiting for her answer.

She could see that she'd have to give him a satisfactory answer, not fob him off with an excuse. She let the memory of their moonlight embrace envelop her and blushed. She *had* kissed him, and she'd reveled in it. She'd never imagined kissing, just kissing, could be so thrilling. To her dismay, she found she could only nod in answer.

"Tell me, Caroline," Zach insisted, catching her chin in his fingers and lifting her face, still searching her eyes.

"Yes! I would let you kiss me again," she whispered, hating the hot blood rushing to her cheeks, surely setting her cheeks aglow. She looked up at him. "But that's all. I couldn't . . . I can't . . ."

"Hush, darlin', it's all right." He kissed her cheek and backed away from her, smiling.

Caroline blinked. She'd seen him smile at Swallow, but he'd never smiled at her until now. It was like standing in a gleaming ray of sunlight streaming between two storm clouds. It warmed her body and soul. "Just, please don't get carried away? And not in front of Swallow? He gets too . . . inquisitive."

As Zach backed away, he nodded, then said, "Tomorrow, I think we need to pick up the pace. We'll travel faster because the wagon's lighter now that we've given some of the goods to the settlers. Agreed?"

Caroline watched him go with her arms wrapped tight around her middle. She felt as if she teetered on the edge of an abyss, not knowing how deep it might be or what she would find at the bottom. Though Zach promised to catch her if she took that leap, she couldn't trust him to cushion her fall. He might be the only man she'd ever trust intimately, but her fear of the sexual act was no longer her sole reason for holding back. Now, she feared that if she let herself go to him, she'd be left with debilitating regrets.

She distracted herself by adjusting the wagon's load, knowing she was too nervous and shaky to retire for the night. Their heavily diminished supplies brought the day's horrors firmly back to mind, along with Zach's plan to push ahead quickly tomorrow. She agreed with his plan wholeheartedly, knowing her safety and Swallow's could be at risk from the vigilante patrols being raised. If the soldiers were busy dealing with the death of their commander, the Cheyenne could make it into the sand hills of Nebraska where they could hide.

Winter loomed ahead. It wouldn't be long before the blizzards came. She shuddered, feeling the bitter edge to the evening breeze, remembering the sting of windblown snow, the bite of hoarfrost on unprotected flesh. She wanted to be settled somewhere safe and warm before winter's icy breath blasted across the plains, even if that was only a brush shelter in the lee of a sand hill.

But the thought of living in the same camp as the men

who had raped the women she'd treated today and pillaged their way from Kansas to Nebraska, men who might have killed Zach's wife and stolen his son, left her shivering harder than thoughts of winter's breath.

How could Little Wolf allow it? Had he lost control of the young braves, or had he become so desperate that he'd had to look the other way and not allow himself to see his men's depredations? If that were true, she didn't have much hope for the Cheyenne's reception when, *if*, they reached the Powder River country they loved.

Even more troubling was the realization that, by agreeing to help Zach find his son, she had aligned herself against the Cheyenne.

Chapter Thirteen

"Little Wolf! Little Wolf!" The Crane's voice carried clearly on the still morning air, urging Little Wolf to cut short his morning bath. Only bad news would have sent Black Crane crying through the woods, forgetting the need for quiet. Little Wolf dressed fast, but his mind moved faster. Had his wolves spotted soldiers? How far away were they? Could the *Tsitsitas* run and hide in the sand hills, or must his men dig in and get ready to fight? Where would be the best place to stand and fight? Where should he hide the women and children?

He answered Crane with a birdcall to remind him of the need for quiet. The Crane found him while he was tying his moccasins.

"Come quickly," he said, his breath short, his eyes wide and worried.

"How many are there?" Little Wolf asked as he gathered the rest of his clothing.

"How many what?" the Crane asked, looking confused.

"Soldiers," Little Wolf said, impatient to find out what

he faced and decide what he must do, what plans to put into action. "What direction do they come from?"

"No soldiers. Much worse than soldiers," the Crane said and turned back toward the camp, motioning for Little Wolf to follow. "Your brother has gone *loco*." He rolled his eyes and wagged his head.

Little Wolf started to run. Morning Star could make trouble—big trouble. He had grown sick of his noise. Every day they argued—his brother talked of nothing but surrendering once they reached the Laughing Waters, and now they were here. Little Wolf could guess what Morning Star was saying and doing while he was out of the camp.

"*Ahatóneste!*" he heard Morning Star shout as he ran back to camp with the Crane puffing beside him. "Listen to me! Pack your belongings, my sisters. We must surrender, quickly, before the soldiers come. We will run to the Pine Ridge Agency where we will be safe. Our friends and relatives there will feed us, care for us. We will be happy again. Hurry!" he added, seeing Little Wolf run into the camp. He gave the Crane a hard look before facing Little Wolf.

"*Hena'hánehe,*" he said to Morning Star, keeping his voice low. "That is enough. Do not blame Black Crane for warning me, brother. He thinks only of the safety of our people, though you do not." Little Wolf motioned for the Crane to move among the people, to quiet them.

"Be at peace, my friends," he called to them. "We have no word of soldiers coming. We are safe here in the sand hills. There is no need to run and hide. Our brother, Morning Star, is mistaken. *Hámestoo'e!* Sit down and be quiet while I talk to him." He motioned for Morning Star to walk ahead of him, out of the hearing of the people in camp.

"Why do you try to frighten the people, brother? There is no threat. We are safe here, as I have told you."

Morning Star glared at him. "I am tired of you always choosing the way the *Tsitsitas* should go. Now it is time for me to choose and I choose to surrender at the agency. Do you think the soldier chiefs will listen to you after what you have allowed your men to do to the innocent and helpless settlers?"

"My men?" Little Wolf asked, struggling to stay calm. He could not let his brother's accusations make him angry, though he knew that was Morning Star's intent. "Your men, your Dog Soldiers, led the raiding, brother, crying for the blood of their loved ones. Your men hang their heads when they see me, for they know that if they told me what they had done, I would whip them out of camp, not praise them. Do you think the agency chief will welcome you with open arms, feed you, give you clothes, make you tipis for shelter against the winter winds?"

"Yes!" Morning Star cried, his eyes burning with his wrath. "I am sick of running. I have lost one wife and do not wish to lose another. How many babies have died in bags on the backs of green horses? Do you know? You do not care! Our people are dying in their moccasins. Many cannot stand."

"It is true that we have lost many loved ones," Little Wolf said, feeling their loss as a heavy weight upon his shoulders. "My heart bleeds for them. But we are safe here by the Laughing Waters. We could not stop to rest when you wanted, not with soldiers following behind and the farmers and ranchers angry over their innocent ones. The soldiers will not find us here in the sand hills. And there is plenty of game—antelope, elk, even a few buffalo if we are lucky." He placed a hand on his brother's shoulder. "We can hide here through the winter, under the soldiers' noses. When the ponies again eat the green grass, we will run to Fort Keogh. Our friends there, Two Moons and his people, our new friend the soldier chief, will speak for us when the time comes."

"Your words are poison." Morning Star threw off Little Wolf's hand and turned back to camp. Little Wolf sighed. If he talked until the sun lay down to sleep, his brother would not change his mind. He followed Morning Star, sick inside, fearing that the people who listened to his stubborn brother would suffer.

"My people!" Morning Star cried upon reaching the people who had waited to hear what their leaders decided they should do. "I leave for the agency when the sun climbs this high." Morning Star pointed to the sky. "Everyone who is sick and wants medicine, come with me. Everyone who is tired of running, be ready to leave. Everyone who no longer wishes to fight the soldiers, come with me." Morning Star continued shouting as he walked down the length of the camp.

In spite of his vow to forsake anger, Little Wolf could not let Morning Star take his loved ones without trying to help them understand that his brother's decision to surrender was wrong, even dangerous. So he followed, calling out against Morning Star. "My brother asks you to leave this place where you will be safe, where there is much game for you to hunt, where no soldier will touch you, and go with him to the agency. You have lived the agency life. You know that there you eat what is given to you and if you are given nothing, you go hungry. There you must ask to walk to the home of your friend for a smoke, and hunting is forbidden. That is the life of the white man, not the *Tsitsitas*. Stay here, my friends. Be safe with me and with my family. In the spring we will return to the Powder River and our home."

Black Coyote stood and Little Wolf watched him warily. The Coyote looked over the group of people, then spoke with a snarl in his voice. "We are warriors, not old men to be told where to go and who to follow. We make our own way and we spit on the agency." He spit on the ground and walked away, followed by most of the young braves, except for Morning Star's two sons and a few of their friends, including Little Finger Nail.

Little Wolf's son, Woodenthigh, laid a hand on his father's shoulder. Together they watched the young men huddle together, their angry faces and sharp gestures telling what lay in their hearts. Little Wolf shook his head. "Without Morning Star, they will be harder to control. This winter will be long and cold."

"Not if you keep them busy," Woodenthigh said with a smile. "As you said, there will be much hunting. The people must have meat, and the women need to replace the goods burned by the soldiers." He lifted a foot and pointed to the holes in the soles of his moccasins.

"*Hou!*" Little Wolf agreed, laughing. "It is so, my son. And a few warriors, seen riding fast here and there, far from here, will draw the eyes of the soldiers away."

He said no more to the people, but asked the Crane to watch and let him know how many left with Morning Star. Then Little Wolf looked for a place to be alone, a place where he could pray for the future of his people and the safety of his foolish brother.

"Now, remember," Zach cautioned Caroline and Swallow as he pulled his horse alongside the wagon as they entered Oberlin, Kansas, the last town before the Nebraska border. "Keep your heads down. Don't talk to people unless you have no choice, especially you, Swallow."

He glanced around, glaring at the curious townspeople who ogled them in spite of his scowl. *Damn!* Zach growled. He must be losing his touch. Why weren't these people backing away, heading indoors, down the street, anywhere to get away from him and the possibility of danger? It had to be the company he kept these days. People weren't as afraid of a man traveling with a woman and child as they were of a man alone. Whatever their reason, their curiosity made him all the more anxious to buy the supplies they'd need to get through the winter, get his horse's loose shoe fixed, and get out of town.

If Caroline kept that blanket over her head, she wouldn't attract the attention of every living, breathing male within twenty miles. As if to scoff at his plan, a brisk breeze snapped past him and he watched Caroline's blanket slip. Her golden hair shone past the dark blanket like the sun peeking from behind a storm cloud. So much for keeping a low profile. He shook his head. At least she wasn't smiling, but that couldn't last long. He'd better move quickly.

"Wait there." He motioned for her to pull up at the store beside the blacksmith shop where there was no boardwalk, only a steep wooden stair, and no loitering men, not even another horse.

Caroline watched Zach lead his horse into the yawning black abyss that was the blacksmith shop, and sighed. Despite a stiff, cold breeze, it was a glorious fall day. The sun shone brightly from a crystal-blue sky, making it very stuffy under the heavy wool blanket Zach had insisted she keep over her head. The darned thing was already slipping off and sweat was trickling down the back of her neck. She peeked out from under the blanket's edge. No one was looking at them, and what would they see if they did? The nearest person was twenty feet away.

Beside her, Swallow giggled. "You look like bad squaw hiding from husband."

"Thank you very much." Caroline yanked at the blanket, but the stubborn thing wouldn't sit where she wanted it.

"What that word?" He pointed at the shining glass window of the store beside them, his eyebrows pulling together as he tried to read the words painted there. "Li-co, lic-o-rihk?"

"Licorice," Caroline said slowly, pronouncing each syllable clearly for his benefit.

Swallow repeated the new word dutifully, then smiled. "What lick-o-rishh?"

"Don't you mean, 'What *is* licorice?'" Caroline corrected.

Swallow corrected and cocked his head, clearly expecting an answer.

Caroline stared at the precocious boy, feeling her mouth water and her lips lift. Why couldn't he have picked any one of a dozen other words off that gleaming window? Why did it have to be her one true weakness:

candy? How could she explain licorice? She shook her head and grinned, remembering her own first bite. Licorice couldn't be explained; it had to be experienced.

She let the blanket slide off her head and down her back and climbed off the high wagon seat. "Come with me," she said in a conspiratorial whisper and shot a cautious glance toward the blacksmith shop. "If we hurry, he'll never know. Keep your hat on tight."

Swallow pressed his hand to the top of his hat and jumped down from the wagon, landing beside her. She smoothed her hair and grabbed his hand. "Not a word, now." When he didn't respond, she tipped his chin up and gave him a stern look. "I mean it, Swallow. You've got to be quiet."

"Quiet," he said and nodded.

The mischievous gleam in his eyes made her hesitate, but the thought of licorice was too tempting. With a tight grip on his hand, Caroline climbed the narrow wooden steps and sashayed into the combination hardware and drugstore. She paused inside as a myriad of scents assaulted her with bittersweet memories. Many, many times she'd stepped into her grandparents' and her uncle's store, smelled all these wonderful aromas and never been affected. But today, the smells assailed her with memories of home and a busy, happy childhood from long-gone days when she was an accepted, even cherished member of the community. Her brightest hope had been to marry a handsome young man, establish a home of her own and raise at least six babies.

Swallow's nervous tug on her hand brought her tumbling back to reality. She smiled brightly at the storekeeper and approached the counter where several large glass jars of candy had been strategically placed to tempt shoppers both coming and going.

"And what can I do to help you this bright and shining morning?" the shopkeeper boomed, his confident smile telling her that he'd smelled her money the instant she walked in the door.

"How about a peppermint stick for you, young man, while your mother looks around?" Swallow's grip on her hand tightened when the shopkeeper's inquisitive stare settled on him. He scooted partially behind Caroline, who beamed at the shopkeeper and smiled wider. "He's shy."

The man scooped out a peppermint stick and handed it to Swallow with a flourish. "What might your name be, young fella?"

"Sw—" Swallow started to say.

"Sam," Caroline interjected and moved to block the man's view of Swallow. She leaned toward the shopkeeper and whispered, "He only stutters when he's feeling shy." She turned what she hoped was a tender, motherly look on Swallow. "Now eat your candy like a good boy while I pick out a few things." She nearly gagged on the syrup in her voice as she pushed Swallow farther behind her. "Let me have a nickel's worth of your licorice," she asked, and was relieved when the man hurried to do her bidding. "Is it fresh?"

The man nodded, eager to tout the virtues of his goods. "Just arrived by freight yesterday. Lucky it didn't come a few days earlier. Some no-good, thievin' Cheyenne would be enjoying it. They surely would have stolen the whole shipment when they tore through here."

Caroline let her eyes go wide, even as she squeezed Swallow's hand, hoping he'd remain quiet. "Did you have trouble here?" She glanced around as if to search for a Cheyenne hiding behind the yard goods.

"Oh, no, ma'am," the shopkeeper quickly assured her. "We have ways of dealing with varmints around here. See that there?" He pointed to the beam above him. "The local sheriff and his posse caught that old buzzard hiding out in a creek. But they took care of him. They hung this here to reassure the local citizens." He chuckled, very pleased with his trophy.

Caroline's mouth went dry as she gazed up at the fresh, barely dry scalp of an elderly Cheyenne man dangling over the counter. She recognized the crow feather still tied in the gray strands and realized the scalp had belonged to Big Crow, an old man from Dull Knife's band. The last time she'd seen him, at the crossing of the Arkansas River, he'd been so weak from malaria and dysentery, she'd given him something to ease his pain and warned Bridge that Big Crow probably wouldn't live to the end of their journey. Crow had been a quiet man, a storyteller, beloved by all the children. He would be sorely missed.

"Hiding out in a creek?" she asked the shopkeeper, finding it very hard to speak normally with the bloody scalp dangling over the counter.

"Uh-huh. Sitting there singing to beat the band. If you'd like, I can let you touch it," the shopkeeper offered. "Usually we charge folks ten cents, but seeing as you're so interested, I'll let you and your son touch it for free." He reached for a long pole with a hook at the end.

"Oh, no!" Caroline said, pressing her fingers to her cheeks to hide the blood flooding into them as her fury mounted. "That won't be necessary. Come along, Swa— uh, Sam."

She pushed Swallow ahead of her, shushing him as he began muttering in Cheyenne. She heard something about his knife and cutting and pushed him faster.

They arrived at the wagon just as Zach stepped out of the blacksmith shop. Caroline helped Swallow climb into the wagon and clambered up behind him. Swallow leaned over the side of the wagon, spit out the peppermint and threw down the remainder of the sweet clutched in his fist.

"What have you two been up to?" Zach demanded, tipping his hat up to glare at her. "I told you to stay put."

Swallow pointed at the window, but all he could manage was, "Lick-o-rish." Then he gulped and a fat tear slid down his cheek.

Caroline swallowed hard, too, feeling a telltale burning behind her own eyes. "We didn't like the selection," she said, hoping Zach would mount up and save the questions she saw burning in his eyes after they left town.

"Licorice?" he asked, cocking his head and speaking to Swallow. "You didn't get any?"

Swallow couldn't speak, but shook his head.

Caroline saw Zach's eyes narrow and tried to reassure him. "Zach, it's not what you're thinking. Let's leave. You don't need to go in there." He turned on his heel and marched toward the store, his jaw set, his eyes flinty. "We'll, uh, wait here then. Shall we?" she asked Swallow, who nodded glumly and grabbed her arm, his fingers digging into her muscles. She pried his fingers loose and patted his hand. "It's all right. Zach will be out in no time at all, you wait and—"

Zach stepped out of the store and slammed the door behind him. His face still, expression unrevealing, he took the stairs very decisively. On the last step, he stomped the dirt and dust off his boots, then quickly mounted his horse. Reining in beside the wagon, he glanced up at her and she flinched at the rage he held back. His lips were pressed into a thin line, his eyebrows drawn together in a deep frown, but a look of understanding warmed his eyes as he gazed at her, then Swallow. "You're right. Poor selection. Dirty store."

He glanced up at the sky. "I don't like the looks of that sky. The blacksmith says it's going to snow, and snow hard. His bunion's driving him crazy."

Caroline looked up then down the street, sizing up the hotels and rooming houses. None looked welcoming, let alone cozy. If this town relished the kind of grisly trophy they'd just seen, what would they think of Swallow? "I'd rather take my chances on the prairie," she told Zach. "Are there any hills or thickets up ahead where we could make some kind of shelter?"

"You're sure?" Zach asked. "It could be a blizzard. The blacksmith said they get these early winter storms sometimes, before people are ready for them."

She stared up at the sky, weighing her decision carefully. No clouds were visible, but the whole sky had taken on a whitish cast and the breeze had picked up and acquired a bitter edge. She shivered and pulled her blanket tight around her shoulders. Storms could blow up very quickly on the plains, but this one probably wouldn't hit until tomorrow afternoon. Was that enough time to find a safe place and build a shelter?

She turned to Zach, keeping her voice low. "If it was just you and me, I'd be driving out of this town already." She glanced around her at the blank windows, feeling the eyes she couldn't see watching them. Her fingers tightened in her blanket. "But do we have the right to risk Swallow's life because we're uncomfortable?"

"It's more than that," Zach assured her. "The blacksmith asked a lot of questions that I chose not to answer. He'll be suspicious."

"From what the shopkeeper said," she nodded toward the window and noticed uneasily that the man hovered just out of sight, watching them, "I believe Big Crow had gone off by himself to die and was singing his death song when the townspeople found him. The Cheyenne's raiding has stirred up too much bad blood. I don't think it's safe here for Swallow, or me."

"Agreed," Zach said. "I saw a draw a few miles north of town. We should be safe there. We'll string up that big tarp, use some brush . . ." He glanced at Swallow's frightened face and his turned grim. "We'll be fine. Let's ride."

"Where rest of Big Crow?" Swallow asked as Caroline whipped the mules and followed Zach out of town. He clutched the seat as if he was afraid he'd fall off and be left behind. His eyes were still luminous with unshed tears and his face pale.

"Buried near the creek, I'm sure," she told him, though she doubted the probability herself. She too felt like crying over the old man's sad end, but she had to hold herself together for Swallow. "You mustn't worry that it hurt him when they—uh, when his hair was cut off." She gave Swallow a hug. "I'm sure he must have been dead already. You remember that he was very sick, don't you? He lived a long and happy life, Swallow, and now he's with his loved ones. He's not hurting anymore."

"He happy dead, without hair?" Swallow mumbled, eyeing her as if she'd told him to play with a skunk.

"Once you die, you no longer feel any pain," she explained, feeling her way and hoping she didn't bungle this. "Your body stays here, buried in the earth or up on a scaffold, but your spirit goes to heaven, to live with *Heammawihio*, the Wise One Above."

Swallow nodded. "He take away Big Crow's pain before white man steal his scalp?"

"Yes," Caroline said, but couldn't muster a smile at Swallow's simple translation of her explanation. She only hoped it eased his grief.

"Who take away my pain?" Swallow asked, looking to her for an answer. "I love Big Crow. Make me hurt, here," he pressed his hand over his heart.

"I'm sorry, Swallow. In time, your pain will ease and you will be able to think about Big Crow, remember the happy times, without feeling the pain."

"How you know this?" Swallow asked, looking at her chest, then her face. "You feel pain, too?"

"Yes, I felt a lot of pain when my mother and father and my brother, Sam, died." She focused on Swallow's inquisitive face, shutting out the brutal images that always accompanied her painful memories.

"You give me name of dead brother?" Swallow gave her a surprised look. "Why? He do great things?"

"I loved him very much," Caroline said. "Giving you his name helps me to remember him. I look at you and remember when he was your age and the fun times we had."

"Hmmph," Swallow said and let go of the wagon seat to cross his arms over his chest. "I think on your words." He stared into the distance, saying nothing more.

Caroline patted him on the back, then concentrated on driving the mules and keeping up with Zach, thankful that Swallow had focused on her explanation of life versus death without asking why the white men had killed and scalped a harmless old man.

How could she possibly have explained bigotry, racial prejudice, hate for the sake of hating? Was he old enough to understand that his people were struggling to survive, as were these white people? No one understood the situation completely, not the white men—soldiers or civilians—and certainly not the Cheyenne.

How could she possibly explain it to a child with a foot in both worlds?

Zach shuddered as he tossed more cold water over his face and upper body, washing away the dust of the day's ride. He'd had to break the ice at the river's edge to wash up tonight. Though he knew Caroline kept a pot of water heating at the fire, he preferred the cold, bracing water.

He had another reason for choosing the brisk ablutions: Caroline. Now that they were deep into Nebraska, away from towns and settlements, she'd taken to wearing her buckskins again. The woman was wreaking havoc on his nerves.

He expected to rendezvous with Little Wolf any day now. He wondered how Little Wolf would get the wagon's supplies to his hidden camp without leaving a telltale trail for the soldiers and vigilante civilian posses to follow. If they didn't strike Little Wolf's camp soon, he wouldn't be able to keep his promise to leave Caroline alone. He suspected she knew what he was going through, because he'd caught her giving him long, considering glances, even saw her drag her tongue across her bottom lip one night. He'd stomped out of camp and walked straight into the nearest water, which was barely a puddle and no help at all. The woman was driving him crazy. She needed distracting. Maybe being with the Cheyenne again would give her something else to think about, someone else to watch.

At the thought, Zach kicked the nearest rock and heard a loud crack, then felt a sharp pain. *Damnation!*

Could this day get any worse? First, he'd had a messenger from Camp Sheridan, bearing a message that was over a week old. A band of Cheyenne had been captured, led by Dull Knife, Little Wolf's brother, called Morning Star by the Cheyenne. The two brothers had argued and the Cheyenne had split up, with Dull Knife and his followers choosing to surrender at Red Cloud's agency. But they had no way of knowing that the agency, along with Red Cloud and all his Sioux, had been moved northeast. The old agency was now Camp Robinson. Dull Knife's group had been captured by soldiers, who had stumbled upon them while out on patrol. They were being held at Camp Robinson until the government decided what to do with them.

According to Dull Knife, Little Wolf and his band were hiding out somewhere in the sand hills. Once winter passed, Little Wolf planned to make a run for Fort Keogh in Powder River country and throw himself on the mercy of the officers there, one of whom was a man the Cheyenne called White Hat Clark. Zach had met Clark during the war, but hadn't followed his career since. From what he'd heard, though, Clark had been a friend to the Cheyenne in their dealings with government bureaucrats in the past. Little Wolf apparently hoped to prevail on him one more time. Zach had a feeling he might be prevailed on, too.

Zach doubted Clark would have much pull with Sheridan, the commander of the Department of the Missouri, into whose jurisdiction the Cheyenne had passed as they moved into Nebraska. Sheridan would be looking to Zach for recommendations when the time came to decide where to put the Cheyenne. How could he convince Little Wolf to surrender peacefully if he couldn't even talk to the man? And how could he find those McCallister horses if he was stuck out here with a woman and child to protect? His frustration increased daily, until Zach felt like he was dangling from an unraveling rope.

With winter nipping at their heels, his concerns for his

missing son weighed on him. He couldn't be sure the boy was still alive, but he couldn't bring himself to even think that he might be dead. He had to keep hoping and searching. He scooped up another handful of ice-flecked water and held it to his face, telling himself to get control of his emotions, trying to believe that everything would work out well in the end.

A twig snapped behind him. He spun, drawing both guns. "Swallow," he cried, re-holstering his guns. "You know better than to sneak up behind a man."

Swallow glared at him. "No sneak. Step on twig, like you say. Next time I tell Caroline get water. Woman's work," the boy said with a sniff and pushed past Zach. "Dinner ready. She say you come eat."

"Bossy, infuriating . . ." Zach muttered.

"What this word, bossy? In-furr-ee-ate-ing?"

"Never mind, mister," Zach said as he pulled on a clean shirt. The last thing he needed was Swallow tossing those two words into his ever-expanding vocabulary. He took the full water barrel from the boy and swung it onto his shoulder. "What are we eating tonight? Did you do any hunting today?" The boy had a talent for snares, and rabbit was beginning to taste even better than chicken.

"Pheasant," the boy said with a boastful swagger. "Two big ones. Plenty for you, too."

"Why, you little rooster," Zach said, tousling the boy's hair. "What about that buck I shot last week?"

"Very big," Swallow said. "Easy to hit. Pheasant hide, fly up in face. You find arrow, they gone. Very hard."

Zach couldn't argue with him; he'd done his share of hunting the elusive birds himself. The boy deserved to boast. "But very tasty. Well done, Swallow."

"Yes, Swallow," another voice echoed. "Well done."

With a glad cry, Swallow ran to embrace the man who stepped out of the shadows ahead of them. Zach waited, then nodded and extended his hand. "Little Wolf." Zach tried not to stare at the chief's face, which was more careworn and drawn than he'd last seen it. He'd swear Little

Wolf had aged five years since their last meeting. "You're well?"

"We are well," Little Wolf replied, maintaining his grip on Zach's hand and returning his scrutiny. "You?"

"Fine." Swallow returned to Zach's side and he anchored him there with an arm around the boy's shoulders. "Glad to see you. Swallow is tired of riding shotgun, aren't you, son?"

Little Wolf's gaze moved between Zach and the boy, but Zach didn't move his arm. He wasn't ashamed of his affection for the boy and he planned to have some say in his future. Best to let Little Wolf know now where he stood.

"Come," Zach said, extending a hand toward camp. "I can smell Caroline's biscuits from here. Swallow, is there enough bird for everyone?"

"Woodenthigh!" Swallow gave a glad cry and ran to hug the young man with Little Wolf's deep, knowing eyes and his strong, compact body who was talking to Caroline.

"My son," Little Wolf said. The young man nodded to Zach, then turned back to Caroline. "He likes biscuits." Little Wolf smiled and Zach had the impression that it was not something the man did often.

As they ate, Little Wolf explained that his men would transfer the supplies from the wagon to the mules for transportation to their camp. Once empty, the wagon would be broken down for firewood, thus leaving no trace—no tracks and no trail for soldiers to follow. They would also be taking a circuitous route to the camp, backtracking, circling and covering their trail whenever possible. Zach offered to help, but Little Wolf insisted that Zach be blindfolded. Zach tried not to take offense, but was stung by the distrust. The man had trusted him with Caroline and the boy, but he didn't trust him with the location of his camp?

Little Wolf filled the blackened bowl of a well-used pipe, lit it and offered the smoke to the heavens, then the earth, then the four directions, and finally to Zach. "You cannot tell what you do not know, my friend," he said as he accepted the pipe back from Zach.

"True," Zach muttered, and gave Little Wolf a grudging nod. "Did any of your horses survive the burning at Punished Woman's Creek?"

"Yes," Little Wolf said. "A few. Why do you ask?"

"I noticed two thoroughbred mares—a blood bay and a roan—at the Arkansas River. They looked familiar. In fact, I'm pretty sure they were stolen from my wife when she was murdered."

Little Wolf nodded. "I know these horses. The animals you seek are now mine."

"How long have you had them?" Zach was surprised that Little Wolf owned the horses. Could the chief have had something to do with Patricia's death?

"A short time only," Little Wolf said with a smile. "When you saw these animals at the Arkansas, I see you look at them. I see that they look like your horse, not much like our ponies. Too high." He leaned his head back as if gazing up a sheer cliff face. Then he looked down.

Woodenthigh chuckled. "Long way down if you fall off."

Little Wolf nodded and shared a grimace with his son. "Women not like to ride so high in sky, and warriors ride stallions, not mares." Woodenthigh murmured his agreement.

"Pretty Walker, my daughter, likes to gamble. My son," he nodded at Woodenthigh, who grinned at Zach, "told brave who owned them that Pretty Walker admired the horses." Little Wolf shrugged. "Now they belong to me."

"You mean the brave let her win them, hoping that she'd take a fancy to him?" Zach asked, surprised at the subtlety involved. "And she gave them to you?"

"No, not give," Little Wolf shook his head. "We play. I cheat."

"You gamble?" Woodenthigh asked, bumping Zach's shoulder with his own and smiling.

"Oh, yes," Zach said. "Every day." Little Wolf and Woodenthigh caught his meaning and chuckled.

"You must understand," Little Wolf said, turning serious. "I do not know how these horses came to belong to my people. Because of my people's custom of giving horses as gifts, it will be difficult to learn who first brought them among us, but we will ask. For now, I am happy to return them to you, in thanks for your help with Caroline and Swallow.

"Who are you hunting?" Little Wolf asked, his gaze piercing. "And why do you seek this person among the Cheyenne?"

Zach's heart raced, but as he looked into Little Wolf's canny eyes, he knew he couldn't lie. He took a deep breath. "My wife was murdered and my son taken captive, along with their horses, several months ago. I'm trying to find my son."

"And you heard of Yellow Swallow living in our camp. My people were in Oklahoma at that time," Little Wolf said, showing no trace of surprise at Zach's revelation. "Yes, I knew that you seek a loved one." He smiled at Zach's shocked gasp. "And I did not see it in the smoke. My son and I will ask my people what they know of this."

"Thank you," Zach said, equally solemn. "Your help will be greatly appreciated."

He squinted through the smoke as they laughed and talked until the fire dwindled, his heart racing. He was closer to finding Luke. He could feel it.

Chapter Fourteen

"You have come at last!" Quiet Woman gave Caroline an enthusiastic squeeze, which was followed by a less-punishing hug from Feather On Head.

"You hear?" Feather asked, her sorrow evident in the deep circles around her eyes and the large hank of hair hacked off one side of her head.

"I saw the scaffold," Caroline said, knowing they were speaking of Short One, but out of respect, none of them would speak her name. Caroline gathered both women into another hug. They held onto each other, foreheads touching, no one speaking. When they finally separated, Caroline wasn't the only one wiping her eyes. "How did it happen?"

Feather couldn't speak and Quiet Woman's retelling of the events of that night was unusually brief. "Our husband very sad," Feather said. "He blames himself, but Morning Star, always pushing himself forward, caused her death. Still, better to lose one woman than four babies."

Caroline gaped at Feather. "Never have I heard you speak harshly of any *Tsitsitas*."

"I speak only the truth," Feather said with a glint in her eyes that Caroline had never seen before. Recent hardships had toughened Feather, made her more outspoken. If she put her feelings into action, Feather could be a force for good among her people. Caroline hoped she had gained the courage to step into Short One's shoes.

"The old fool!" Feather shook her head and sighed. "I wish them joy of him."

"He's gone?" Caroline looked about the camp as if she expected to see Morning Star come walking by.

"Yes," Quiet Woman said, bobbing her head and eagerly taking up Feather's story. "You should have seen him marching through the camp, hallooing like a bull moose in heat. He had words with our husband, then told everyone who wanted to come with him and be safe to gather their things and off they went. His poor family had not even bandaged their feet before he had them scurrying west. And now!"

When Quiet Woman paused to suck in a deep breath, Feather took over. "We heard that they were captured by soldiers the first day. But worse . . ."

"The agency has been moved!" Quiet Woman plunked her hands on her hips as if outraged. "It is now north and east of here. After all this running and fighting, the old fool has marched his family into the hands of the soldiers."

"No!" Caroline looked between the two women, horrified by their news. "Little Wolf must be sick at heart."

"Oh, yes," Feather said with a sad little nod. "We do our best to comfort him, but he spends much time alone. Bullet Proof, the one who speaks the *veho* tongue, returned today. He says the agency is now called Camp Robinson. Morning Star and his people are being taken there in wagons." She sighed. "At least they do not have to walk in the cold and the soldiers have given them food and blankets."

"But Bullet Proof says the soldiers talk about taking them back to the bad country, even though the people have said they will shoot themselves first." Quiet Woman scooped some stew into her large horn spoon and offered it to Caroline.

Caroline accepted the spoon with a grateful nod, even though she'd eaten earlier, and settled beside the fire. She would not offend her friends by refusing to share their meal. She drew her knife from its hidden sheath in her moccasin and speared a chunk of meat. She held up the meat and examined it before eating and turned to Quiet Woman with an eyebrow raised in question. She'd long ago learned to ask first, eat second. Some of the meats the *Tsitsitas* found acceptable didn't agree with her stomach, or her head.

"Elk," Quiet Woman said, her wide smile making the dimples flash in her cheeks. "I have missed you, my friend, and your cautious ways." She sighed. "It is good to have elk for the soup pot. Too many days have our pots— and our stomachs—been empty."

Caroline smiled. "I'm happy to share this bounty with my friends." She finished the chunk of meat in two bites and sipped some broth, then passed the spoon to Feather. She needed to ask about the young men, the ones the women in Kansas had told her about. She hoped most of them had gone with Dull Knife, that only a few remained in camp. If Little Wolf kept the young men busy hunting and scouting, she might not have to speak to them. She decided an indirect approach to the subject would be best.

"How are you liking this camp? There seems to be plenty of water and lots of game, good hunting."

"Yes," Quiet Woman said, spearing a large chunk of meat. "The men have been hunting every day." She stuffed the meat in her mouth, never one to be dainty.

"Did many of the young braves go with Morning Star?" Caroline asked, keeping her tone casual and fixing her gaze on a small chunk of meat.

Quiet Woman was still chomping, so Feather answered. "The young men stayed here, except for Morning Star's sons and Little Finger Nail, a few others. It is good. Morning Star can no longer control them. My husband does better. They were wild and unruly in that bad country where so much Cheyenne blood lay on the ground, but now they are again simple horse hunters. You have heard of the innocent ones killed in Kan-zas?"

"Yes," Caroline said and declined the horn spoon when Quiet Woman offered it again. Her throat had tightened and she was having trouble swallowing as she remembered the women she'd tried to help. So, the young men, the ones who'd raped and pillaged their way through Kansas, were now Little Wolf's men. She took a deep breath to quiet her queasy stomach.

"You are well?" Feather asked, watching her closely. She reached out and pressed her palm to Caroline's forehead. "You are pale and sweating. Better lie down."

"Good idea," Caroline said, rising slowly. "Where will I be staying?"

"Come!" Quiet Woman jumped up and took her arm. "We show you."

"Go slow," Feather warned her. "Look at her face, Woman."

Caroline walked as quickly as her friends would allow through the camp, ignoring the curious stares and whispered comments as they passed. When she realized that very few of the young men remained in camp, she relaxed and her stomach started to settle. She released her punishing grip on Feather's hand, not even aware that she'd been hanging on for dear life until Feather rubbed the red mark her fingers had left. She pressed her hand over the hilt of her knife through her buckskin skirt, feeling exposed, unprotected, as she moved among the people, and edgier than she had ever been among them. More nervous even than when Little Wolf first brought her to his wives.

"You have seen what was done?" Feather asked, watching Caroline's face. "It is bad?"

"Very bad." Caroline nodded. "Many women were hurt, even some children, and many men killed. These men were not soldiers or even cowboys or ranchers. They had no part in the bad things that were done to the *Tsitsitas* in that country." She looked at each woman, not wanting to alarm them, but feeling a need to alert them to the consequences of the raiding. "Many more soldiers will come now and their officers will not be ready to listen when Little Wolf asks to stay in the Powder River country. Your young men have caused great harm."

"We understand," Feather said and Quiet Woman nodded. "Little Wolf understands also, but his vow to forsake anger prevents him from taking action. It is a good thing for him to bear the Sacred Chief's Bundle, but his anger is like a growl trapped deep inside him, growing ever louder. One day it will burst out and he will not be able to stop his hand. That will be a very sad day for us."

"I pray that day will never come," Caroline said, clasping the hand of each woman. "But if it does, I promise you that I will always be your friend, and help you in any way I can."

"Hou!" Feather and Quiet Woman said. Then Quiet Woman pulled her forward, all bossy and officious. "That is for another day. Now, I show you where you and your man sleep."

Caroline balked, refusing to move. "He's not my man and I'm not going to share his furs. Please don't try to make a pair of us."

Feather giggled and patted Caroline on the back, gently pushing her to follow Quiet Woman. "Pair," she said, smiling as she trudged alongside Caroline, their feet dragging in the deep sand. "Like moccasins."

"Or leggings," Quiet Woman added. She held up one leg and pointed to it. "Caroline." She held up the other leg and Feather snorted. "*Veho* man." Quiet Woman glanced back at Caroline. "What his name?"

"Zachary McCallister," Caroline said, trying not to laugh at the other woman's antics. "Zach for short."

Quiet Woman held up the "*veho* man" leg again and pointed to it. "Zach-for-short."

"No," Caroline said, though she suspected her effort to correct her friend would be wasted. "Just Zach."

Quiet Woman again held up the leg. "Just Zach."

Caroline laughed and shook her head. She could never tell if Quiet Woman was teasing or serious. She shared a smile with Feather.

Feather led them down a winding line of sand hills where shelters had been cut deep into the hill. Armload-sized bundles of brush had been lashed together to form a wall of sorts at the front of each for privacy and to keep out the freezing wind, sleet and snow that would soon come. Small fires burned near the entrances, far enough into the shelter to provide light and warmth, but close enough to the entrance to allow the smoke to eventually slide up the ceiling and evaporate in the dark.

Clever, Caroline mused, amazed as always by the resourcefulness of these people. Here and there, the brush wall was pushed back to allow in the sweet, cool night air. Inside, she saw that the women had been busy making these crude holes warm and comfortable for their families. Busy hands had woven rush backrests. Those same rushes had been tied into sleeping mats and rugs that covered the floors. Antelope, deer and elk must be abundant in this area for she saw curing hides everywhere, and the few trees were strung with lines of drying jerky.

Feather drew to a stop beside two small shelters a bit away from the rest. Two holes had been dug into a large sand hill, close together, but not connecting, and situated on the rounded face of the sand hill so that their openings faced away from each other. Her friends had been busy, for the floors of both shelters were covered with closely woven rush mats and small fires burned cheerily at each entrance. At the nearest shelter, hanging from a tripod, a pot of soup sent fragrant steam circling upward and above it a string of jerky dangled. There was even a deer hide stretched to dry outside the shelter.

Caroline relaxed and gave her friends a grateful smile, feeling her tension evaporate. She'd been very anxious about their living arrangements, not knowing what to expect given the Cheyenne's straitened circumstances. Sharing a shelter with Zach, Little Wolf and her friends would have been incredibly awkward. As always, Feather and Quiet Woman had anticipated her needs with tact and generosity.

"For Zach?" she asked and pointed to the farther shelter.

"You here," Quiet Woman said. "See?" She demonstrated how to move the brush wall and secure it to a small post set in the ground at the shelter's entrance. "Wind blow this way, catch him, not you," she said with a wink. "Men strong. Have thick hide. You cook for him? Just Zach be . . . okay?"

"Very okay. Thank you, my friends," Caroline said and gave each woman a grateful hug. "We'll be very happy here."

As she eyed the other shelters over her friends' shoulders she couldn't help noticing how isolated her new home was, and how private. From inside, she wouldn't be able to see a single fire from the winding line of shelters to the east. She looked away from her neat rush bed heaped with blankets, and easily big enough for two, and kept her expression bland. Her friends were setting her up. She understood that they meant well and wanted her to be happy. In their culture a woman was incomplete without a man to hunt for her, to acquire the hides needed to create a home and the meat they would eat. In their minds, to be alone was to be cold and hungry.

However, with their matchmaking efforts focused on Zach, they wouldn't be pushing her to allow any of the young braves who might have participated in the raiding to court her. That would have been unthinkable. She forced her fears aside and threw herself into helping her friends add her own possessions to those already in the shelter, putting her own stamp on her new home.

When her friends left, finally satisfied with their efforts, Caroline pulled back the blankets on her bed and fell in face-first. She couldn't remember ever being so tired, and then she couldn't remember anything at all.

"Does this place have a name?" Zach asked by way of greeting the next morning.

Caroline snored in response.

Zach grimaced. This was the worst he'd ever seen her. Apparently, she'd fallen into bed fully dressed. Sometime during the night she'd tried to pull a blanket over her, but had only succeeded in covering her head and shoulders. Her legs were tangled in her skirt, which had hiked up to her knees. Another long snore made him smile.

Caroline and mornings were not good friends. He doubted she'd ever seen a sunrise, unless she'd stayed up all night. His stomach growled, reminding him that it was long past time for breakfast. "Come on, sleepyhead," he said, giving her shoulder a solid nudge.

"Go 'way," she mumbled from under her blanket. "S'not mor-nihn y't."

"What?" came a plaintive complaint from a few feet away. "No biscuits?"

"Go eat at som'un elsh's howsh."

"Well, that's not very neighborly." Zach put an arm

around Swallow's shoulders and led him away. "Shall we let Her Majesty sleep? Can you handle the fire?"

Swallow nodded and crouched beside the fire, where he stirred the smoldering ashes to life. "You make coffee?" he asked Zach, turning his head as far over his shoulder as it would go. "That wake her up plenty."

Zach tried to extricate her head and shoulders from the tangled blanket, but got slapped for his efforts. He stepped back, tipped his hat brim up and looked her over, shaking his head when she gave another loud, rumbling snore. She certainly knew how to sleep. He couldn't really blame her for being tired. They hadn't finished unloading the wagon and moving everything until the early morning hours. Although he and Little Wolf, and his son, Woodenthigh, had done most of the work, she'd had to direct the storing and distribution of the supplies, and separate their personal belongings. She deserved a little extra rest today. He lightly tossed another blanket over her legs, ignoring her contented rumble and provocative wiggle.

"Swallow, how about showin' me around camp this mornin'?" Zach had noticed that the boy seemed familiar with the area, and guessed that the Cheyenne must have camped there in the past.

"What you want see?" Swallow asked, watching Zach stir up some biscuits.

"I'd like to check my horse, make sure he's getting enough to eat." Zach kept his tone conversational, not wanting to let the boy know how important this visit to the horse herd was to him.

He and Swallow devoured breakfast, leaving a generous plate for Caroline—if she woke before mid-day. Zach worked as quietly as possible. Before leaving with Swallow, he made sure Caroline was well covered and that the low fire would provide enough warmth against the nip in the morning air.

He resisted the urge to crouch down beside her and stroke the stray hair off her face, to feel again the velvet

softness of her skin. He'd tried to ignore the pull between them, but it was becoming near impossible. And
now here they were, sleeping next door. With her cooking for him, as her two shy, smiling friends had explained
using broken English and lots of sign language, they
would be thrown together several times per day. Once
winter came, they'd be stuck in their—

He glanced around Caroline's shelter, which was dug
into the side of a hill. He couldn't even stand upright at
its highest point. What to call this place? It looked more
like a rabbit burrow than a cave. All burrows were good
for was sleeping and all the things that usually went along
with two people sleeping together, things that he and
Caroline had agreed never to do. What a shame. Her bed
looked wide enough for two, and a warm, willing woman
would make the cold nights more bearable. At the
thought of Caroline warm, willing and wrapped around
him, Zach straightened abruptly.

His hat hit the low ceiling and tumbled off his head.
He bobbled it a couple times before finally catching it,
which left his nerves jangling. He slapped it against his
thigh, unable to stick it back on his head.

Damn! It was going to be a very long winter.

"Swallow!" he called, and smiled when he saw the boy's
eager expression. "Let's see those horses."

Swallow led him to a small meadow, tall with golden,
heavy-headed grass that snapped and broke with a raspy
snick as they passed, catching at their clothes and slowing
their progress. The horses grazed near an arm of the lake
that snaked free of the main body of water. They were
preoccupied, too busy munching the tender shoots along
the water's edge to bother with humans. Speaking softly,
touching a flank here, a nose there, Zach walked among
the animals, until he found the two he sought. He
stroked the sleek neck of a roan mare he'd helped his father bring into the world and felt his world narrow into
sharp brilliance as the memories of a less-troubled time
filled his heart with peace. Over her neck he spotted a

bay mare, the horse that his father had believed would throw the best foals his farm had ever produced.

Zach's jaw tightened, but he continued crooning and stroking the sleek neck as reality plowed him in the gut: These animals had been stolen from his wife after her murder. They'd been used in his son's kidnapping. The fiend who had hurt his family was close, perhaps even watching him now. He felt it. He could smell the man's fear.

He would use it to make him pay, and make him talk.

Caroline walked quickly toward the lake, clutching her precious bar of soap, a towel and clean pantalets. Though the sun had climbed well into the eastern sky, making it close to noon, a low bank of fog clung to the chokecherry thicket on the other side of the lake and sent gnarled fingers crawling across the lake's surface. A shiver slithered up her spine. She glanced around but saw no one and kept walking. The sun would soon burn off the fog, allowing the full beauty of this lost valley to emerge. Already she felt its fertility; it was a miracle—alive, vigorous. A crane gave its distinctive cry and rose from the far side of the lake, followed by several of its fellows. A deer raised its head to peek over the fog at her, but quickly ducked below the vapor barrier to continue foraging. Beyond the chokecherry thicket, the ground rose into a hill that blocked the west end of the valley, crowned by a large stand of junipers. In the bitter months to come, it would turn away the worst of the winter winds. This verdant valley must feel like a blessing to the Cheyenne, direct from the hand of their gods, both above and below the earth.

As she bathed, Caroline focused on the hidden valley's tranquility, not her unease. Winter loomed, an ever-growing threat she could smell on the air, sense in the edgy bustle of the wildlife surrounding her, and feel deep in her bones. Though she felt safer here than she had in a long time, she also felt anxious, even afraid. Many of the men who had raped and pillaged their way through

Kansas now walked these same paths, drank the same water, shared the same camp. But she trusted the Cheyenne's strict laws and social order to protect her, and she also trusted Little Wolf. If circumstances had been truly perilous, if his people's feelings had been running high against the *veho*, he would not have brought them here.

Ignoring her misgivings, she sauntered back to her shelter. Before she got there, Zach came striding out of a patch of tall, golden grass that tugged at his pant legs as if determined to hold him back. One look into his eyes told her that nothing could deter him now. Heaven help the person at the receiving end of the fury radiating from him.

"You've found the horses?" she asked him, and realized as his gaze swung toward her that if she hadn't spoken, he would have walked by without seeing her.

"Yes." He stopped and she watched the rage slide from his face as his eyes focused on her. "The horses are Mc-Callister stock," he said, uttering each word as if it were bitter. "The man who murdered my wife and stole my son is here." He took her by the shoulders, his grip firm, almost punishing. "I'll find him, and when I do . . ."

"Are you sure? Whoever brought them could have traded for them, or even stolen them."

"I don't think so," Zach said, glancing around them. "Ever since we got here, I've felt someone watching me, someone who means to harm me."

Caroline didn't admit that she'd felt uncomfortable, too. Feelings, even combined with the horses, weren't enough. "I'll do everything I can to help you, but please keep an open mind, Zach. Don't jump to conclusions or make accusations you can't support."

Little Wolf drew long and deep from the pipe and passed it to Zach. He knew the man was impatient to speak, but he must learn that speech was not always needed. He was rigid, as stiff and unyielding as the rock in the moccasin that feels like a boulder.

"How can I help you find your son?" Little Wolf asked once Zach had a mouthful of smoke. He often waited to ask a question until a man could not answer; it gave the man more time to consider his words, not let them spill from his mouth in a tumbled rush. He saw that Zach understood and had paused before blowing out a long, smoky breath.

"I've seen the horses," he said, and Little Wolf waited as Zach again paused. "They belonged to my family." Little Wolf liked that the man searched for good words. It was not easy to tell a chief that one of his people had killed an innocent woman. It was harder still to ask a chief to allow that person to be punished by someone who was not one of his people. Because he liked this man and because the man had helped Caroline, Swallow and his people, Little Wolf set the pipe across his knees when Zach returned it to him. He nodded at Black Crane, who sat across the fire from him. The Crane rose without a word and left Little Wolf alone with Zach.

"You seek your wife's killer," he said, holding up a hand to keep Zach from speaking. "You think the man who stole your son and murdered your wife is the same who brought these horses to the Cheyenne."

Zach nodded and his body stiffened, but his thundercloud eyes remained fixed on Little Wolf's face. "I will find my son, alive or dead. I'd like your permission to move freely about the camp, be involved in the hunting, the council fires, the dances. I want to let people get to know me, to feel comfortable around me so that when I ask questions, they won't be afraid to answer."

Impressed, Little Wolf murmured a quiet, "Hmmph."

There was a small pause. "This will take longer than if I question them for you," Little Wolf warned him. "What about your son? Do you not fear for his safety?"

"Yes!" Zach said with so much emotion that Little Wolf felt a catch in his own heart. He asked himself if he would have this man's patience if his own child had been taken from him. He knew he would not. "These horses are my only lead. If I bungle it, I'll never find Luke. I have to handle this right. Because you're their chief, they may try to hide the truth from you out of fear of your punishment. I must earn their confidence to find my son."

Little Wolf picked up the pipe again and took another draw, then passed it to Zach. "I will tell my men you can come and go as you please and that no one is to harm or insult you." He passed the pipe to Zach, stem first.

Zach took it, but didn't smoke. "I have another question."

Ah! Little Wolf thought. *He will ask about Caroline. At last. My wives were right.* But he simply said, "Yes?"

Zach swallowed hard, then asked quickly, "What will happen to Caroline and Swallow once you reach the Powder River?"

"I bought Caroline from a Kiowa chief, White Bear, to keep her from being beaten to death. She was very near death already when I took her to my wives for doctoring. It took many moons, but her body healed. Her heart?" He shook his head and shrugged. "It may never heal."

"She, too, told me that she never shared your furs."

"It is not in her heart, and not in mine. She had the protection of my tipi, but not my furs." He spoke so low that Zach had to lean over the fire to hear his soft words. "Only my wives know that Caroline was never my wife.

"You have seen her scars." Little Wolf stated fact; he had seen it in the smoke.

Fury snapped Zach upright. He glared at Little Wolf over the fire. "You've said you were never her husband. How is it that you know about her scars?"

"For many suns after I brought her to my tent, my wives cared for her. At first, they could not cover her back. In some places, her back had been cut to the bone. My wives and Bridge worked great medicine for many moons before her back healed."

"Have you seen her ear?" Zach asked, his voice still challenging.

"Her ear is terrible, though not as badly scarred as her

heart, but we have no medicine to heal that," Little Wolf said and rose. Their smoke was over. He knew that he did not need to worry over Caroline again.

As Zach passed by, Little Wolf stopped him with a hand on his arm. "My friend, I hope you soon find your son. I will help in your search, if you need me. As for horses— do not gamble. Maybe you will lose."

"Thank you." Zach gripped Little Wolf's extended forearm, not surprised to find it rock hard. "I may need your help before this is over."

"You have it. But I cannot help you with Caroline. Only trust can mend her heart."

Little Wolf watched Zach stride away with a deep fear in his heart. If Zach found the killer among them, he could be killed also when he confronted the killer. Then who would help when the Cheyenne needed him? The sun rode the wind with sharp spurs, making the days pass too quickly. He must work fast.

Little Wolf returned to his fire, where he sat and smoked until he'd smoked the pipe dry. He was worried about his brother. He would send Bullet Proof to Camp Robinson. A Sioux friend lived not far from the fort. If he visited the Camp and kept quiet, no one would notice him. Once Little Wolf knew Morning Star and his family were safe, he would call in his wolves and let his brother walk the world alone.

Chapter Fifteen

"You come!" Quiet Woman called from the path below Caroline and Zach's shelters. Zach had barely finished tethering the three horses and glanced up to see Caroline step out of her shelter, her hair a bright cascade down her back and a warm shawl clutched around her shoulders against a cold wind.

"What's wrong?" she asked, pulling the shawl tight across her chest.

"Not wrong!" Quiet Woman said with a chuckle and shake of her head. "Elks give dance."

"I didn't hear any drums," Caroline said, frowning and looking east toward the other shelters.

"Little Wolf say no drums, only singing," Quiet Woman explained, obviously excited and anxious to get back to the dance. She kept taking little hopping steps sideways and her gestures were getting bigger, her voice louder. "You come!"

Zach smiled, watching the two women. Quiet Woman wasn't about to let Caroline beg off. His smile disappeared when her gaze narrowed on him. "You, too." She gestured again, a big windmilling swing of both arms that lifted her stout body onto its toes. "Come!"

"We'd love to come," Zach said, earning a displeased grimace from Caroline. "You go ahead. We'll find you."

"Hou!" Quiet Woman whooped, and with an unrestrained hop, flipped around and scurried off.

"Who are the Elks?" Zach asked when Caroline turned to glare at him.

"One of the warrior societies." She gave her hair an impatient toss and his gaze fixed on the long, thick waves. He wondered if it smelled as good as it looked and stuck his hands in his pockets to keep from snatching a lock and burying his nose in it to find out. "Little Wolf was chief of the Elk Soldiers before he became an Old Man Chief. Warrior chiefs give up their chieftanship when they become one of the four Old Man Chiefs. Little Wolf is the only man to hold both positions simultaneously. A great honor. Most of the men here are Elks."

"I know the Dog Soldiers are the rear guard when the people are on the move, but what are the Elk Soldiers known for? Their dancing?"

She laughed and tossed her hair back. Zach stared, mesmerized. He'd thought she was beautiful before, but here, with her hair streaming around her, gleaming in the moonlight, a smile lighting her face, she took his breath away. His heartbeat quickened and a flash of heat raced through him. He pulled his duster closed in front to hide his body's reaction. Despite her reluctant agreement to allow him to kiss her, she'd been aloof and skittish since their arrival in Lost Chokecherry Valley. He was not a man to force himself on an unwilling woman, but abstinence was wreaking hell on his nerves.

He needed a couple of nights alone in a town, and a warm, willing woman in his bed to slake his lust. But he didn't see that happening any time soon. If he left the camp now, Little Wolf would suspect him of contacting the Army. He'd have him followed and if he wasn't killed outright, how would he get back into the camp to find the man who'd destroyed his family?

The Cheyenne women had no use for a *veho* man; they'd rather spit on him than look at him, though some of the younger ones were warming up some. They'd sidle up when he was chatting with someone they felt safe with, like Woodenthigh, but they scurried away when he was alone. The only woman who ever smiled at him or called out their standard greeting, *"Hou, cola!"* was Pretty Walker, Little Wolf's daughter, whom he'd been told was a bit of a rebel. Though she was a beauty, he didn't want to stir things up right under Little Wolf's nose.

He stuck his left hand into his belt and offered his elbow to Caroline. "Shall we?"

"I really should do something with my hair," she said, lifting a nervous hand to the wave that lay over her left ear.

"You look beautiful," he told her, smiling broadly. He seldom got an opportunity to express his admiration. He meant to make the most of everything the night had to offer. He leaned in and whispered, "It's dark. No one will notice."

She patted her hair down, took a deep breath and then slipped her fingers into the crook of his elbow, blessing him with a bright smile. "Thank you, kind sir."

The dance was a very subdued affair. Little Wolf didn't allow any drums or flutes, just a small fire in a wide, level area where the sand had been packed hard under passing people's feet. Several young women danced around the fire, singing softly. Occasionally, one would flit out and choose a young brave to dance with them. Four young women circulated among the watchers, who were seated in a semicircle around the dancers, offering succulent roasted elk ribs and dripping slices of barely cooked, rare meat.

Zach escorted Caroline to a seat beside Feather, then stood behind them, watching the dancers. The steps seemed simple, but when he thought he understood it well enough to ask Caroline to dance with him, the dancers stopped.

Suddenly, Pretty Walker appeared before him, took his hand and led him to the fire. He glanced at Caroline, but she was engaged in a whispered conversation with her friends. The singing started again and Pretty Walker took his hands and showed him the steps. Zach concentrated on the steps, but the burn of hundreds of watching eyes made him stumble. She placed his hands on her hips, then put hers on his shoulders. Lifting onto her toes, she leaned close and sang in his ear, leading him with her voice and her body.

He glanced aside to where Caroline sat watching. Her eyes had grown enormous and she stared at him with an odd expression on her face. She suddenly rose in one graceful, fluid movement. He watched her approach, as did Pretty Walker, who gave him a tiny smile and wink. She dropped her hands and stepped back, letting Caroline take her place without a word.

"Let me show you," Caroline said, and stepped close, assuming a much closer position than Pretty Walker had dared. She took up the song, stepping in time to the rhythmic music, letting her body lead him when he missed a step.

He soon caught on, but when she tried to increase the

distance between them, he held her in place. "Stay close," he said, and felt a tremor pass through her.

She looked up at him, her eyes wide, her lips parted, and his body ignited.

"Careful, darlin'," he whispered, letting his cheek brush the silky hair at her brow. "If you keep lookin' at me like that, we'll be doin' more than dancin' tonight."

When she didn't answer, just cocked her head and considered him with a half-smile bowing her lips, he tensed. "Have you changed your mind? Do you want me in your bed?"

Her eyes flashed open and she stepped away from him, leaving his arms empty and his body aching. The singing stopped and the dancers dispersed to eat and visit. Caroline returned to her friends and Zach took a seat across the fire where he could watch her. Little Wolf sat beside her, but though the chief chatted with her, he never touched her, never looked into her eyes.

As the festivities continued, Zach often caught Caroline watching him. When he did, her gaze held his briefly, before skittering away again. He lost track of the conversation around him so many times that Woodenthigh slapped him on the back, causing several other men to laugh.

"Here," he told Zach and tossed a blanket into his lap. The other men around them nodded and smiled.

"What's this for?" Zach asked. He glanced up to see if Caroline had noticed Woodenthigh's action, but she was talking animatedly with Quiet Woman and Feather, who were motioning in his direction. Woodenthigh laughed as if he'd played some hilarious prank.

"Take the blanket," Woodenthigh explained and pointed to a couple, blanket in hand, leaving the firelit area. Once in the shadows, they stopped and wrapped the blanket around them, concealing themselves from head to ankle inside its folds.

"All right!" he heard Caroline say, then she marched over to stand in front of him. Flushed, obviously irritated, she looked down at him with her fists clenched in her skirts. He stared up at her, so surprised that he forgot to stand.

"Come with me," she said, not looking at him, her head bowed and lips pressed into a tight, disapproving line. "Bring the blanket."

He lurched to his feet. "You don't have to do this . . . we don't have to do this, if you'd rather not."

"No," she said. "I have to show them that I'm not afraid, that—"

"Caroline," he said, and stroked her arm to calm her. "You don't have to prove anything to anyone, but I'd be pleased to, uh, talk to you for a while." He gestured away from the other couples. "Over there?"

She leaned closer. "You don't understand. If we do this, it means that we're . . . that I'm your woman. That we're *lovers*."

"But we're—"

"Don't say it!" she whispered, her eyes going wide and flashing quickly from right to left. "If these men think I'm available . . ." She looked into his face and the fear in her eyes hit him like a blow to the sternum. The air rushed out of his chest, and his body went cold as a gun barrel in January. "Let me make sure I understand," he managed to say. "You want me to stake a claim that will keep these other men at bay."

"Yes!" she said. "They're the ones who . . . the ones that . . . I'm pretty sure some of them were at that house in Kansas." Her gaze darted from man to man and he saw true panic in her eyes. He winced as her fingers dug into his arm. She was afraid of these men and didn't want them to think they could court her, waylay her as she moved about the camp, pop in for dinner or do whatever Cheyenne men did to get their women to notice them. Hell, he didn't want them anywhere near her. Damn right he'd stake his claim.

Zach took her arm and practically carried her the few steps to the shadows outside the fire's light, but he paused before stepping into the dark; he wanted to be sure they'd be seen. He pulled her close and settled her against him, then flung the blanket around them, keeping it loose to allow them to breathe. With her body pressed to his, he felt the fine tremors racing through her, the shaking in her limbs.

"Put your arms around my neck," he told her, when her knees began to knock his shins. He helped her and when she'd locked her fingers around his neck, he picked her up, being careful to keep the blanket intact. A loud whoop came from the area where Woodenthigh and his friends sat watching. Slowly, she relaxed and started breathing normally again, not in the tight panicky gasps that had made her shaky. All the while, he simply held her, until she sighed and slid to her feet.

But she didn't move away. She remained pressed to him, her body supple now and responsive, following his every movement. Her breasts flattened against his chest, her nipples hardening and burning through his duster and his shirt, branding him. He groaned and pressed a kiss to her neck. He'd expected her to shove him away, but she angled her head to let him reach the curve where neck and shoulder met. His lips scorched the spot and she moaned.

Someone giggled. He listened but didn't hear any singing. The dance had ended.

He let the blanket slide off her shoulders, but they remained connected several heartbeats after it fell.

She stepped away and Zach looked up to find Little Wolf watching them, narrow eyed, lips pressed in a tight line. Zach returned his stare, then balled up the blanket and tossed it to Woodenthigh, who was no longer laughing, but glancing between Little Wolf and Zach.

"I'll walk you back," Zach said, and took Caroline's arm.

"No," she said, and pulled away from him. "I want to talk to Feather and Quiet Woman."

He glanced over at the women who stood waiting, their heads close together, talking fast and furiously as they watched Caroline.

She swallowed once, lifted her chin, then looked up at him and smiled. "I won't be long."

"I'll wait for you." She didn't seem to be trembling anymore, but he knew a brave front when he saw one.

"Please," she said, "go ahead. I'll be right behind you."

Zach finally nodded, after giving the two women a long, hard look, and enduring one from Little Wolf. Little Wolf might tell himself—and others—that he had no claim on Caroline, but his stern looks told a very different story. Zach sighed. It must be hard for the man not to interfere, after saving her life and watching out for her for months. He'd have to get used to Little Wolf's watchfulness until he proved himself to the man. But he wanted to take the chief's scheming wives out in the woods and talk to them, which wasn't going to happen because their English was bad and his Cheyenne nonexistent.

And after he'd talked to everyone else, he needed to talk to Caroline. He couldn't take many more of her long, hot looks without bursting into flames.

Zach rose early every day in answer to some biological clock that he couldn't explain—or ignore. This, his second full day of life among the Cheyenne, dawned no differently. Swallow had moved his bedroll into Zach's shelter without even asking. Though it amused him when he first became aware of the boy's intentions, Zach now realized he was glad Swallow had assumed he'd be welcome.

The boy never rose in the morning; he rolled out of his blankets, crawled and clawed his way to the "door" and stumbled outside to answer the call of nature. Sometimes, he even made it to the nearest bush. Luckily, bodily functions didn't require eyesight, for Swallow's eyes didn't completely open until his feet hit the freezing waters of the lake.

And that was another thing about the Cheyenne that amazed Zach. Every morning, no matter the weather, Cheyenne men headed for water—the colder the better, it seemed. They avoided the lake, preferring running water, where they stripped and bathed, some even wading into the ice-flecked waters and floating a while, letting their bodies chill. Once out of the water, though, they were men with a mission: food.

The exodus back to camp happened suddenly. As if a bugle had been blown to summon them, the men shook themselves dry—no towels among these stalwart fellows—and quick-stepped back to their warm shelters, hot meals and smiling women.

Not a bad life, Zach mused. A man could live with much less—and he often had.

Again as if in response to some unwritten schedule, the camp crier, Black Crane, made the rounds of the camp with the morning announcements, which Caroline translated for Zach. On this slightly overcast day, he informed the people in a low voice that Little Wolf wished them to keep cooking fires to a minimum. With the heavy clouds hanging over them, the fires were more likely to be spotted. Many manly groans accompanied this request, but the women smiled until Crane added that they were to see Feather On Head and Quiet Woman, who were helping Bridge replace medicines that would be needed during the winter.

Black Crane wasn't finished. He informed them that the young braves would be riding out one by one, heading in different directions to hunt deer, and reminded them to be as quiet as possible, for their camp lay very close to the main *veho* trail. They were to use knives and bows, no rifles.

Caroline had mentioned the people's complaints that the need for quiet meant a great deal more work, especially for the women. The older folks enjoyed new popularity; their skills and knowledge were in great demand to demonstrate the "old ways" of hunting, tanning and cooking that made less noise and less smell, but required more effort. Little Wolf had banned sweat lodges, smoking—unless in dire need—and gambling. The men grumbled loud and long over the last taboo.

Zach had to admit, Little Wolf was as much a genius at picking the site for a camp as he was in picking battle-grounds. The camp lay less than a hundred yards from the intersection of two well-traveled trails. Anyone who smelled food cooking or spotted a column of smoke ris-ing would think some traveler had made camp in the hills near the trail. The soldiers wouldn't think to look so close for their fugitives. They'd be combing the far reaches of the sand hills all winter, chasing their frostbit-ten tails, while the Cheyenne squatted here in relative comfort, ensconced in this paradise of wildlife, water and sheltering pines, right under their noses. Zach had to ap-plaud Little Wolf. The man was brilliant. Of course, Zach had learned from Woodenthigh, who was on his way out of camp earlier that morning, that small groups of Cheyenne warriors would be riding around the sand hills "allowing" themselves to be spotted in order to keep the soldiers searching well away from the camp.

"Finally," Black Crane said, reaching the end of his daily announcements, "the two *veho* camped at the west end will be living with us while the snow falls. Little Wolf asks that you welcome them. They have earned our grati-tude. Anyone speaking ill of them or mistreating them will answer to Little Wolf."

Zach grinned at Caroline, his translator. "I'll bet if you looked east right now, you'd see dozens of heads poking out of those sand hills. Does it remind you of anything we've seen?"

Caroline returned his smile and nodded, but Swallow giggled and said, *"Oskeso."*

"Swallow," Caroline admonished the boy sternly, "don't you dare tell your friends that Zach called them all prairie dogs."

Swallow frowned, looking belligerent. Clearly, he'd in-tended to do exactly that. Zach gripped the boy's shoulder and nodded toward the door. "Outside. We need to talk."

On the way out, Zach stumbled a little, just enough to give him reason to catch himself by clutching Caroline's waist. He bent over her from behind and whispered, "I'll be back soon. To talk to you." Her body stiffened under his hands and he mentally sighed. He shouldn't have let her distance herself from him over the past two weeks. If he wanted to convince her to go along with his plan, it would have helped if she'd been accustomed to his touch. By the time he returned, she'd be all tense and nervous. He wished he had time to soothe her, but he needed to talk to Swallow before the boy disappeared, which seemed to be one of his true skills.

Swallow waited beside the horses that Zach had tethered nearby—his stallion and the two mares Little Wolf had given him. "You know, Caroline and I enjoy having you here with us."

Swallow's head came up and his eyes widened in surprise. "You do?"

Zach smiled. "We do."

"I like to stay with you." Swallow considered Zach, his head tilted to one side, his expression distrustful. "What you want I do for you? I clean your guns, feed and water your horses, hunt for Caroline, wash dishes, carry water. I do whatever you say if you let me stay."

"Whoa, son," Zach said, surprised at the boy's skewed understanding of his place in their lives. "We don't expect you to do any of that by yourself, but you're welcome to help out if one of us is doing those things."

"I no work for you?" Swallow frowned and stuck his hands on his hips. "Not work hard enough?" His expression turned belligerent. "You feed me good. I strong now. Carry two waterbags and firewood." He gestured with open arms, indicating a load a grown man would have staggered under.

"Swallow, you're welcome to live with us because we care about you. Not because of what you can do for us." Zach's conscience pricked him, but he needed the boy's help. Not as a condition, but as a favor. He put an arm around the boy's shoulders and led him away from the shelter. "I need to know I can trust you, Swallow. I worry that someone might become angry with me, or with Caroline, and try to hurt us. I need you to tell me if you hear anyone say bad things about us." He stopped and squatted so he could look in the boy's face. "Can you do that? For me and for Caroline?"

Swallow nodded, his eyes wide and his expression determined. His fingers clenched into fists at his sides. "I tell you."

Zach patted him on the back, drew a deep breath and continued. "There's one more thing. I'll understand if you think this is somethin' you don't want to do. Understand?"

Swallow nodded, his boy's face appearing almost manly from his solemn demeanor.

"I need to find out how those two horses came to be among the Cheyenne. I need to know who first brought them. People are havin' trouble rememberin' who owned them first." There, it was said, asked. Zach hated using the boy in his investigation, but he needed answers quickly.

Woodenthigh had already struck out. The Cheyenne had given his horses so frequently, there was no way to trace them. The trail of owners, according to Woodenthigh, could wind all the way back to Oklahoma. Zach knew if he started asking about the horses, the culprit would cut and run, leaving him stuck here in the sand hills all winter, worrying about his son's well-being. He didn't know if he could endure the winter not knowing if the boy was dead or alive.

As investigators went, Woodenthigh also wasn't Zach's best option because of his relationship to Little Wolf. It was like having the chief himself poke his nose into your tipi. He'd decided Swallow was the perfect one to ask around. The questions of a young boy would be far less alarming, and likely to be dismissed as inconsequential by the culprit. Especially if Zach could keep the man's attention on himself, allowing Swallow to work in the background.

While he and Swallow were beating the bushes, Caroline would be gossiping with the women and gathering as much information as she could.

"I find out for you," Swallow said with a sly grin. "You let me take care of those two horses and I brag about it to friends. Then when I ask where they come from, people think I try to make myself bigger, bragging about *my* horses. Unner-stan?"

"Perfect," Zach said and tousled the boy's golden curls. "You'll take good care of them, feed them every morning and night, brush them, talk to them? Horses like conversation, you know."

"Oh, yes," Swallow assured him, looking very serious and important with his arms crossed over his chest. "You no be sorry."

"Very good," Zach said and turned with Swallow back to where the horses were still tethered beside his shelter. "Every night we'll tether them here so that they'll be close in case there's trouble. And every evening you and I and Caroline will share our discoveries over dinner."

Swallow nodded and began pelting Zach with questions about the animals' care and feeding. Zach answered automatically; his mind had snagged on the thought of evenings spent with Caroline after Swallow was tucked into his blankets. They'd be alone together with nothing between them but firelight.

First, he needed to have a talk with that woman. He had another offer for her, one he knew she wouldn't accept as willingly as Swallow had accepted his.

Zach grinned, feeling very . . . wolfish.

Chapter Sixteen

Caroline clutched her blanket tighter around her as she watched the brilliant sunset dwindle. If not for the crude accommodations, she'd be very content here in this sheltered valley. She had friends close by, and she knew that caring for Zach and Swallow would fill her days.

She watched them approach now with mixed feelings. Zach's arm lay around Swallow's shoulders as they walked, which forced Swallow to walk close beside him, occasionally catching hold of Zach's duster to steady himself. Zach shortened his stride and Swallow took bigger steps, though they were both too busy talking to notice their instinctive accommodation. A stranger watching them would believe they were father and son, they were so attuned to each other. Yet, she couldn't help wondering if Zach's ease and friendliness toward Swallow was a ploy to keep from thinking about his missing son. Was he using Swallow to alleviate the pain of not knowing what had happened to the boy? Worse, was he sliding Swallow into his son's place in his heart? She hoped not. It would make matters much harder for him if Swallow returned to the reservation in Oklahoma, especially if Zach couldn't find out what had happened to his son.

Swallow stumbled over a rock and Zach caught him before he fell, saying something that made Swallow look up and laugh. When they reached the horses, Zach rubbed each animal's neck while Swallow stroked its nose. When they'd finished feeding and tethering the horses, Swallow left with a laugh and a wave. Caroline ducked inside her shelter, her heart hammering.

She settled beside the fire and picked up her sewing basket. She'd been nervous and anxious all day, especially after spending time with Feather and Quiet Woman. It seemed that all the two women wanted to discuss lately was how to get Zach into Caroline's bed. They badgered her relentlessly, reminding her that she wasn't getting any younger—or any better-looking—and warned that many of the young, available women had expressed an interest in Zach, especially Pretty Walker, Little Wolf's very attractive daughter. Just the thought of Zach and Pretty Walker together made Caroline stab her awl into the hide she was sewing into moccasins for Swallow and straight into her thumb.

"Mercy!" she said and stuck her thumb into her mouth to suck on it.

Zach chuckled as he stepped through the open entrance. "Are you angry at that hide or tryin' to make a lastin' impression?"

"Mmmph!" Caroline mumbled around her thumb. "Fat lot you know about sewing hide." She scowled at her thumb; it hadn't stopped bleeding and was beginning to drip. "It isn't easy."

"Here, let me help. You're getting blood all over." Zach pulled off his bandanna and whipped it around her thumb, pulling it tight over the wound. He sat beside her, keeping a firm grip on her thumb. This close she could see underneath his hat brim. She could even see the dark gray ring around his irises, the crooked bump in the otherwise clean line of his nose, the black stubble shadowing his cheeks.

"See anything you like?" he asked, his voice whisper-soft.

Startled, she looked into his eyes, then quickly away, though her fingers itched to trace the laugh lines at their corners and maybe poke into the dimple that flashed in his cheek.

"Why do you always do that?" he asked, leaning closer and tucking her hand against his chest.

"Do what?" she asked, trying not to notice that the feel of his heart beating beneath her fingers made her own beat faster.

"Pull away whenever I get close." He tipped her chin up, turning her face so she had to look into his eyes.

"You know why," she said, so low that he had to lean closer to hear her. His breath warmed her cheek and she knew that if she were brave enough, all she'd have to do was turn her head and she'd be kissing him. Were Feather and Quiet Woman right? Was she wasting a precious chance to change her life? Could she let go of the fear that stifled her, trust him to teach her what her friends said she needed to know?

She could live without knowing how it felt to *make love*

with a man, but did she want to? Nothing could erase her memories of her time with White Bear, but could happier memories overshadow them, even replace them? And what about the heartache she'd suffer when Zach left? She knew he'd go, as soon as he learned where the horses came from, he'd be off in search of his son. Not even winter would stop him. The certainty left her feeling hollow, empty. Would loving him make their parting unbearable?

"Little Wolf watches you," Zach said matter-of-factly, renewing their conversation as if he hadn't noticed her withdrawal and long silence. He loosened the bandanna and examined her thumb, but didn't release her hand when he'd confirmed that the bleeding had stopped. "Even though he says you're free to take a man to your bed."

Caroline stared at him, her mouth hanging open. He gently shut it for her with a finger under her chin. "He worries about me," she said. "You know he was never my husband. There's nothing—like that—between us."

"We're livin' in his camp. Even though you were never his wife, you did live in his tipi, with him and his wives. You're an intimate, a family member, and he's right to take a proprietary interest in you. I don't want him gettin' angry at us if he thinks we're . . . close."

"Like we are now?" Caroline asked. His body seemed to surround her. She could feel every breath he took, hear every thought before he said a word.

"This isn't nearly close enough, darlin'," he said, his voice a low caress. His breath tickled her neck and she turned her head, instinctively inviting him closer. She knew what he wanted; he'd told her very plainly weeks ago, and she'd agreed to be more open to his advances.

Could she do it? Could she push her memories and her fear aside and allow him to touch her, to teach her how it could be between a man and a woman? When she was young, she'd thought a woman had to love a man before she could allow him to kiss her, touch her, hold her. She didn't love Zach. Did she? Could she make love with him, without loving him? She sighed.

Quit being such a coward! she chided herself. *You'll never find out if you don't take a chance. Try trusting him!*

"I've been thinking." The words were out before she realized she'd made the decision.

"Thinking's always good."

"My friends say I'm wasting away, that I need a man, and I'm thinking they may be right." At Zach's sharply indrawn breath, she hurried to finish her explanation. "I don't know if I can . . . *be* with a man, but I want to try, and you're the perfect man to teach me what I need to know, because you're leaving soon." His brows drew together and he looked annoyed, but she didn't stop to ask why. She couldn't stop now. If she did, she'd never again muster the courage to ask him.

"How many lessons do you think it will take?" She watched his face closely, saw surprise and pleasure come and go, followed by confusion.

"Lessons?" he asked, looking completely perplexed.

She huffed in exasperation. "I know I won't be able to learn it all in one night, so you'll have to take it slow and be patient with me. How many lessons?"

"Uh . . . three? Four?" Zach said, ticking off four fingers as if he was assigning a lesson to each digit. Eyes wide, he looked up at her and smiled the biggest, brightest smile she'd ever seen him smile. "Four ought to be just right."

"And you'll teach me everything?" she asked, determined to clearly outline her expectations at the start of this new agreement. "Not counting that stuff we did earlier."

"Yes, ma'am," he said, and she could tell he was trying not to laugh. He smiled and his gaze traced her features, as if he was trying to memorize her face. Why did he look sad all of a sudden? She'd given him what he wanted, hadn't she?

Still, he hadn't touched her. Why wasn't he touching her? Caroline wanted to feel his hands on her body—somewhere, anywhere—right now. She flipped his hat off and when he reached to run his hand through his hair, she stopped him. "No. Let me." She rose up on her knees, drove her fingers into the dark waves and pulled his face closer.

"Can we start now?" she asked, her voice a throaty ripple in the quiet surrounding them.

"Yes, ma'am," he purred and pulled her hard against his chest. He kissed her cheek, her jaw and nibbled his way to the sensitive curve between neck and shoulder, where he lingered to feast.

"Oh, wait!" she gasped and pushed away from him.

"No more waitin'," he growled, refusing to release her.

She braced both hands against his chest and searched his eyes. "What about Swallow?"

The steel band around her back loosened and he smiled at her, looking a little smug. "He's visitin' a friend who's invited him to spend the rest of the day with his family and sleep with them tonight."

"I see," Caroline said, disappointed that she'd spoiled the moment for no reason, but also annoyed. "You planned this?" She didn't want him to think she was a hussy, a loose woman. She also didn't like being predictable. Why, she'd waltzed into his plans—and his arms—without blinking.

"No, angel," he said and settled her back where she'd been. "But I wished it."

"Mmmm," she moaned as his lips reclaimed the sensitive spot on her neck. "I wouldn't want to spoil a wish." She turned her head aside, giving him better access and relishing the goose bumps that brought her whole body to a state of sensitized dizziness. While he nibbled, she stroked his sides, loving the hard, warm curve of muscle under her hands.

His fingers stole into her hair and he began pulling out hairpins, carefully collecting them and setting them aside. Gradually, the heavy mass unfurled down her back and he shook it loose, then ran his fingers through it, spreading it over her shoulders. Suddenly panicky as the hair lifted away from her scarred ear, she reached up to pat it back into place, but he caught her hand in his and kissed it.

"You are so beautiful," he whispered, kneeling before her, his gaze sweeping over her as if he couldn't see enough of her at once.

She shook her head and looked away, feeling heat flood her face. "No, I'm scarred . . ."

He caught her chin in his hand, made her look at him. "You are beautiful." Then he kissed her, gently at first, holding her shoulders, steadying her when she swayed under the onslaught of tenderness. She loved his gentleness, but she needed more. She needed warmth, and heat. She needed to touch him and be touched by him. She let her body settle against his and clutched his back, pressing her breasts into his chest. She couldn't get close enough.

He groaned and took the kiss deeper. His lips pressed more firmly and his tongue slid between her lips, along her teeth and she stiffened. She realized what he wanted, but she wasn't ready for him to enter her body, and his tongue, thrusting into her mouth, reminded her of the act she feared. Then she forgot everything as he kissed his way to her neck again.

"Open your mouth, Caroline," he whispered. "I want to taste you."

"Do I have any say in my lessons? If I don't like something, can I say so?" she asked, easing away from him.

"Of course," he said, his brows arching in surprise. "Don't you like me to use my tongue when I kiss you?"

"Sometimes," she admitted, finding the conversation awkward, but determined to have a voice in the learning process. "But when you thrust it into my mouth, it reminds me of . . . things I'm not ready to face yet."

"I understand," he said, shifting her so that she lay across his lap. "Less tongue," he murmured, then leaned over her and his lips covered hers again with more urgency than before. This time when his tongue slipped between her lips, she opened for him. She pushed back with her own tongue and he took it into his mouth. She giggled and pulled away. "I think I might have done something like this with a boy I once knew."

"What boy?" he asked with a mock growl as he pressed quick kisses to her cheeks, her forehead, the tip of her nose.

"Don't worry," she said with a coy laugh. "He's much too young for me now."

"Think you can tease me, huh?" He stared down at her. "I think it's time I finished this lesson."

"Must you?" she asked. "I'm enjoying kissing."

"Well," he drawled as he stood and swept her into his arms, "there's kissing and then there's *kissing*."

"Is there a big difference?"

He kicked aside the neatly folded blankets at the foot of her bed and laid her down. She tried to lie still while he stood staring down at her, but his intense gaze made her shiver. His broad shoulders blocked the light from the fire, leaving his face in shadow. The light made his body cast a huge shadow that threatened to swallow her. In the darkness, horrible memories lurked. Any minute now, he'd throw her onto her stomach, pull her up to her knees, shove her skirt up. Her breath froze in her chest, and she fumbled for the knife she'd hidden beneath the reeds that formed her bed.

"Don't go there," Zach said. "I'm not going to hurt you, darlin'." He caught her arm and moved it to her side, then he spread her hair around her and stretched out alongside her, his head propped on his elbow. "Stay here. Look at me."

He gazed down at her, his gray eyes warm and approving. "Do you know how many times I've imagined you like this—lyin' in your bed waitin' for me, your hair spread around you?" He kissed her cheek and stroked her arm, letting his fingers twine with hers. Gradually, her heartbeat slowed and she relaxed, feeling no threat. Finally, he lifted her hand to his shoulder and leaned over her. "Trust me, Caroline. I won't do anythin' that would cause you pain and I'll stop the minute you say the word."

Caroline lifted her hand to the back of his neck and pulled him closer. His body radiated heat everywhere it touched down the length of her body. She wanted him closer, wanted to feel him pressing over her. She didn't know everything she wanted, only knew that this wasn't enough.

"Show me, Zach." She lifted up, reaching for him and he met her. His lips settled over hers and his elbows came down on either side of her head as he slid his fingers into her hair. Her arms banded his back, pulling him closer and his leg slid over hers. Her whole body stilled, then came abruptly and suddenly to life. Heat swept through her, like a fire in her veins. She opened for him and his tongue slipped into her mouth, tangled briefly with her tongue, then traced her teeth, her lips, her mouth. She moaned and opened wider, and he turned his head, his mouth at a slant over hers as she savored him, learning his essence, a flavor she hadn't known she craved until now. A taste she knew she would never forget.

He groaned and eased more fully onto her. His lower body slid across hers, his heavy erection dragging across her warming center.

Her eyes snapped open and she cried out, struggling to free herself from his mouth. She turned her face away, avoiding glancing at his lower body, knowing what she'd see there and that it would bring on the frigid, sweating nightmares she hated. Like cold, creeping fingers, the fear swept away the warmth and heat she'd just begun to feel. She lurched out from under him, her knees jerking into a tight tuck, her back to him.

"I'm sorry, Caroline." He eased farther away from her, until finally he lay beside her, not touching. He might as well have been in another shelter, another camp, even another town.

"Why are you apologizing?" she cried, scooting further away from him. "I'm the freak!" She got her feet under her, intending to leave. She needed air that he hadn't breathed first. "I can't even let a man kiss me without . . . without . . ."

He caught her arm and pulled her back to the bed. "Don't run from me."

"I'm not running from you," she said, still unable to look at him. Her cheeks were on fire. Didn't he understand that she was running from herself, from her sorry inability to be a woman? "I'm sorry I asked you to do this."

Resting on one elbow again, he caught her chin and lifted it, meeting her gaze with a smile. "I'm not sorry, and I'm not letting you change your mind."

"I thought you'd be the perfect man to teach me," she said with a shrug. "You're only going to be here for a short time. You'll go on your way, back to Virginia or on to the Dakotas to search for your son, and I'll stay here with my rosy memories." She huffed a laugh. "How naive and stupid could I be?"

"Not at all." He sat up and pulled her into his arms, where he tucked her tight against his chest. She let her cheek rest over his heart and found the steady beat reassuring. She slipped her arms around his waist and sighed. "I could become accustomed to this."

"I hope you do," he said and his chuckle reverberated in his chest.

"You don't have to humor me, Zach," she said, lifting her head to look into his face. "We both know there is no future for us. Together, that is. Let's just forget I ever suggested lessons."

"A deal's a deal," he said, smiling as he gathered her into his arms. "And because of it, I get to do this whenever I want." With that, he kissed her, his lips warm, but not demanding, his tongue penetrating, but not plunging, and his hand slid down her side to her waist.

Caroline responded to the warmth, the caring in his kiss and when he pulled her tight against him, she settled there willingly.

"Four lessons," he whispered, his voice warm, confident. "I mean to hold you to it."

"Does this count?" she asked from her cozy spot beneath his chin.

"You bet," he said, then tucked his chin to look down at her. "Didn't you learn anythin'?"

"Just that I'm a sorry specimen of womanhood," she grumbled. "I don't know why you'd want to bother teaching me."

"Four lessons," he said firmly, pulling her up with him as he stood and moved to the shelter opening. "By then, you'll know what I know."

"What's that?" she asked, bewildered. Was he talking about kissing or making love, or something else entirely? Why did she have to wait until the last lesson to find out?

He shook his head at her, then kissed the tip of her nose and left.

"When shall we have our next lesson?" she called after him, but he kept walking.

Bullheaded, stubborn man! She huffed and stomped her foot. Why did he always have to keep her guessing?

He liked kissing Caroline awake, Zach decided. It was the high point of his day. And she didn't seem to mind it either. He smiled, watching her long dark-gold lashes flutter. Any second now . . . Her eyes opened. She blinked, and smiled. `

"Mmmm. I was dreaming of coffee and fresh biscuits," she whispered. "Was it just you?"

"Just me?" Pretending to be offended, he stood, then grabbed her hands and pulled her to her feet, catching her against his chest. "Daylight's wasting, darlin'. I brought you some fresh water." He nodded at the small barrel he'd set in the doorway. "Swallow and I are headed for the stream."

She'd already scooped a handful of water and splashed her face by the time he set the reed door back in place. "We'll be back for breakfast shortly."

She responded with a muffled, "Whmph!"

He grinned as he joined Swallow and tousled the boy's

hair as they started for the stream, joining the rest of the Cheyenne men heading in that direction. A couple of cranes lurched into the sky as they drew near the stream, croaking their distinctive cry as they flew. A breeze blew from the west, spreading the scent of the junipers from the western hill. Zach felt like beating his chest, but merely sucked in a deep draught of the crisp air. He glanced up at the sky. Cool, but clear. Another beautiful fall day. How odd, the comfort he found in the simple routine of this primitive camp.

Were his good feelings the result of the simplicity of life here, he wondered, or the fact that it had been seven days since Caroline's first lesson and he planned to surprise her with the second lesson tonight? He grinned and sucked in another deep breath, letting his lungs expand, his chest rise. He smiled, catching Swallow doing the same.

"Feels good, doesn't it?" he asked the boy, ruffling his hair. He wondered why Swallow never bothered to straighten it. Was it because he was a boy and boys didn't care how they looked, or because he knew Zach would mess it up again anyway?

"Yup," Swallow said, which was obviously all he could manage while holding his breath and puffing his chest out. Suddenly, the boy's chest deflated. "Beat you!" he shouted and darted ahead.

"Why, you little scamp," Zach shouted and joined the chase. He caught up several feet from the stream and hoisted Swallow under his arm. He carried him into the stream and dunked his head into the cold water, then set him on his feet. "That'll teach you to try to get the jump on me, young man."

Swallow didn't answer. Sputtering as he shoved dripping ringlets off his face, he stomped off to find a likely bush to water.

"You like boy."

Zach glanced behind him and found Little Wolf watching Swallow.

"Very much," Zach said. "He's smart, funny, and very wise for his age."

"He asks many questions about your horses," Little Wolf said as he bent and scooped water onto his chest. "Some people say he speaks your words."

Zach went still. He'd had no indication that the boy's questioning was causing him trouble. He'd been watching for the sidelong looks, whispered comments, heads rolling together as they walked through camp. "I asked him to talk to his friends only. What's he been doing?"

Little Wolf glanced over his shoulder to where Swallow's bright hair shone from beside a small bush. "My people look at the boy and see his father. They talk, say the boy brought you, he will bring soldiers, too. Now, his questions . . ." Little Wolf shrugged. "The questions make more talk."

"I'm sorry," Zach said, feeling like kicking himself. How could he have been so selfish? Nothing was worth risking Swallow's safety. Not even Luke. "I'll talk to him."

"No need," Little Wolf said. "I asked him to visit me and my wives, but he refused. He says he must tend your horses, that he lives with you and Caroline now."

"We've become pretty attached to him," Zach said, facing the wily old chief. Zach had learned that although Little Wolf never minced words, he sometimes took his time getting to his point. "Caroline would miss him if he stayed with you. So would I."

"Better for Swallow," Little Wolf said, dismissing Zach's assertion without so much as a shrug. He started walking back to the camp. "You learn more about those horses?"

Zach nodded, realizing that had been another reason for his good mood this morning. "Woodenthigh introduced me to Little Hawk yesterday."

"Good man," Little Wolf said with a sage nod. "Great warrior."

"He remembered that Little Finger Nail gave him the horses for his daughter's birthday. He said he was very sorry to give such good horses to Stays Behind, the baby who was born the first night you left Oklahoma, but the baby's mother needed them more than he did."

"This is true," Little Wolf said. "Stays Behind was born on the trail that night. His mother strapped him on her back, then ran hard to catch up." Little Wolf's comment seemed casual, but Zach could see his pride at the woman's courage in his face. "I told her to stay in Oklahoma, but she wants her child to live free and breathe the sweet air of home, so she come. She traded the horses for food, blankets. Good woman."

"I'm glad the horses helped her," Zach said, still marveling that the unexceptional-looking woman he'd met only the day before possessed incredible strength and virtue. His own wife had gone to bed weeks before his son was born and hadn't risen from it for weeks afterward. Some of the bright freshness left the morning as he thought of Patricia facing the hardships these women endured daily. She'd been a pampered, spoiled beauty, completely unprepared for life on the Great Plains.

He felt his face flush as guilt assailed him, as it always did when he faced his culpability in his relationship with Patricia. If he'd been more attentive, had made an effort to get home between assignments, she might not have been tempted to leave the farm with some no-account drifter. His son would still be safe with Josh and Abby. Instead, Patricia was dead and Luke was lost to him, somewhere out here in this vast wilderness. Zach prayed he was still alive, then realized that even his prayers were selfish. It was too late to do anything about Patricia, but if Luke lived he would have a chance to make amends for his selfishness. And he would make certain Swallow didn't suffer unnecessarily now.

Swallow ran up and stopped beside him. Zach tousled his hair and hesitated, let his hand settle on the boy's back. He glanced at Little Wolf, not surprised to find the man watching him. He crouched so that he'd be able to look into the boy's eyes.

"Swallow, Little Wolf and I have been talkin'." He waited while the boy glanced up at the chief. "His wives have asked him to invite you to visit for a while, and we think that's a great idea."

Swallow searched his face and gradually the happy, relaxed expression slipped away, replaced by the wary tension Zach had noticed when he first met the boy. "You no need me to take care of your horses no more?"

"I'll take over," Zach said, giving the boy's arm a gentle squeeze. "I don't know if I can do as well as you, but I'll try my best."

"Only horses," Swallow said with a shrug. He turned a shoulder to Zach and scuffed the toe of his new moccasin in the dirt.

"They're important to me," Zach said, taking hold of the boy's shoulders and turning him to face him. "And so are you. Understand?"

Swallow nodded and bit his bottom lip, which had begun to quiver. He blinked hard and looked up at Little Wolf. "We go now."

"Not yet," Zach said, blinking hard himself. "I've found out what I need to know about the horses, so you don't need to ask any more questions. You've been a big help. I wouldn't have learned so much without you."

Swallow nodded and two fat tears slid down his cheeks. Zach pulled the boy into his arms and held his small body tight against his chest. His heart felt like it was tearing apart and the boy's arms clutching his back ripped it asunder.

"I no want to go," Swallow muttered into Zach's chest.

"Little Wolf thinks it's best for now," Zach whispered, "but as soon as it's safe, I'll come for you."

Swallow pulled back and blinked up at him, knuckling away tears. "Yes?"

Zach nodded and tried to speak. It hurt like hell to talk around the rock stuck in his throat. "You can stop by to say 'Howdy!' now and then." He looked at Little Wolf, who nodded.

"I will," Swallow said, then asked solemnly, "You tell Caroline why I no tell her I go to visit chief?"

"I will." Zach hugged Swallow tight, then let him go and stood. "You'll watch out for him?" he asked Little Wolf, ignoring the fact that Little Wolf had acted out of concern for the boy. Although he and Caroline had thought they were helping him, they'd made things worse for Swallow.

"Go find Feather," Little Wolf told the boy, and they both watched him shuffle away with his head bowed, scuffing his toes in the dirt with every step. He turned to Zach. "He will be well."

"I know that," Zach said, his voice and words harsher than he'd intended. "We've become attached to him," he offered by way of explanation for his curtness.

"The boy cannot replace your son," Little Wolf said kindly. "And he will always be Cheyenne. His place is among his people."

"How can you say that?" Zach asked, his whole body rigid with outrage on the boy's behalf. "His *people* hate the sight of him. They treat him like a bad omen, they're suspicious of him, and so superstitious that he gets blamed for every bad thing that happens. How can he make a place for himself among people who treat him so poorly?"

"His blood is Cheyenne," Little Wolf said firmly. "He must learn our ways."

"His blood is white, too," Zach said, facing the man squarely. "His father is a hero among our people. He needs to learn about him, and your people despise the man's name.

"If you're so concerned for his safety, maybe I should take him and Caroline and find another place to spend the winter."

Little Wolf shrugged. "That is your choice. You are ready to care for them, keep them safe?"

Zach blanched. The man was right. He wasn't in any position to take on a woman and a child. He had to find his son. And what would he do with Luke, with all of them, when he found him? He couldn't drag a woman and two boys along on his government assignments, and he wouldn't dump them on Josh and Abby. Although he knew Abby would adore Swallow.

Little Wolf nodded, obviously reading Zach's answer in his face. "The boy stays with me. You stay, too." He looked up at the sky as he walked away. "Big snow coming. Not safe to leave now."

Zach looked up at the crystal-clear sky and shook his head. The man had to be clairvoyant. There wasn't a cloud in sight, unless you counted the big black one that had just unloaded on his head. He felt like he'd been hit by lightning, but he wasn't about to let it show or give Little Wolf the satisfaction.

And now he had to tell Caroline that because he'd jeopardized Swallow's safety, Little Wolf had taken the boy away.

He wondered how soon this big snowstorm was coming. Maybe he should delay telling Caroline, just in case they got snowed in. He couldn't imagine anything worse than being stuck in a hole in the ground with an angry woman.

Chapter Seventeen

"Where are we goin'?" Zach asked Swallow as he followed the boy out of camp.

"Quiet," Swallow hissed, motioning with a sharp cutting motion at his throat for Zach to stop talking. "Turkey hunt. Big medicine."

"Did you ask Little Wolf?" Zach asked, crouching lower in the little cover available and dropping his voice to a croak.

"His idea." Swallow cocked his head and listened, then added, "Him say you like hunt."

Zach heard a familiar, warbling call and a rush of adrenaline shot through him. He shook his head at himself. How could a grown man get such a kick out of hunting with a bunch of boys? The bushes parted beside him and a small, dirty boy crawled through, carrying a large knife with a curved blade. Zach recognized the boy: Black Coyote's son, the one who'd mistaken him for someone else the night he first met the Cheyenne. He stared at the huge blade. What was a boy doing with a knife like that?

The boy noticed him watching and crawled away. As he went, one of his leggings caught on a thorn and the tie came undone. The legging slipped off, revealing a huge black-and-blue bruise on the boy's thigh. Zach swore and scrambled after the boy, catching him by the ankle.

The boy kicked and squirmed, fighting to get free, all without uttering a sound. He used the knife, jabbing it into the ground and pulling on it, but Zach had a firm grip on his leg.

"What you do?" Swallow shouted. A ruckus ensued in the thicket ahead as the turkeys they'd been stalking fled. Several boys gave chase, but Zach hardly noticed. All his attention was on the boy's leg, which was covered in bruises—some fresh and deep purple, some yellow-green and healing. He caught glimpses of raised, bloody welts under the boy's tunic and breechcloth.

Zach clutched the boy's ankle, determined to examine the rest of him, but the boy rolled and a wild kick caught Zach in the throat. Zach's grip loosened and the boy kicked free, scrambled to his feet, and ran for the deepest part of the thicket.

"Catch him!" Swallow cried, then shouted something in Cheyenne and several boys sprinted after him.

"No!" Zach tried to shout, but his throat wasn't working. "Stop them, Swallow." He clutched a hand to his throbbing throat and waded into the lake, ignoring the damage to his boots, desperate to get some water down his throat. "We'll . . . find him . . . later."

Swallow called out to the boys in pursuit, who trotted back and watched Zach slosh out of the lake, then bend over, massaging his injured neck. "Mean . . . li'l . . . squirt," he croaked, shaking his head at his soggy boots. He'd never get them dry. "C'mon," he said, his voice a thready whisper. He gripped Swallow's shoulders. "Find . . . Little Wolf."

Little Wolf met them returning from the lake. "What happened?" he asked, his sharp gaze flicking from Zach to Swallow. "Who chased turkeys away?"

"My fault," Zach croaked. "That boy . . ." Zach gestured toward the chokecherry thicket where he'd last seen the boy, but couldn't say more. His lips moved, but nothing came out.

"Boy lives with Black Coyote," Swallow said, and the other boys nodded. "His leg, back bruised bad. He been whipped, too." Swallow swung his rump around and pointed, shaking his head as he talked. "Very bad. Leg all black, purple. Zach see bruises and try catch him, but boy kick Zach in throat and run away. Zach want to help, but boy scared." Swallow squeaked to a stop, his chest heaving. He propped his hands on his knees and looked to Zach, who nodded.

Little Wolf squinted at the sky, then frowned at Zach. "How long ago?"

"Fifteen minutes," Zach wheezed. "No more."

"Swallow, tell Crane I need searchers." He looked at the sky again. "Run."

Zach glanced up, too, and didn't like what he saw. The clouds, heavy and white earlier in the day, were now a dirty gray, hanging low and moving fast. The farmers in Kansas had warned him about the winter storms in this area. They'd all been caught flat-footed, out in a white-out, and they'd all lost a friend or family member to sudden, vicious blizzards.

"Got to . . . change," Zach croaked, and pointed to his shelter.

Little Wolf nodded. "Bring extra blankets."

Zach ran back to his shelter, changed out of his wet clothes and boots, grabbed a lantern and some blankets and left a note for Caroline. He kept an eye on the sky as he ran back to the thicket. The air had a distinct bite and the wind had picked up. If the temperature dropped much more, the boy—who wore nothing but a buckskin tunic and one legging—would be in serious trouble. He wouldn't last long, given his weakened state. The kid was a fighter, as Zach had learned firsthand, but they had to find him quickly.

By the time Zach returned, a dozen men and women had gathered at the spot where they'd last seen the boy. Little Wolf gave the orders, his voice low, his manner calm. Black Coyote joined the group as it spread out to begin the search, but Little Wolf pulled him aside. Zach didn't understand what Little Wolf said, but Black Coyote didn't say a word, just listened, then stomped back to camp. He scowled at Zach and paused as he passed, letting his hand settle on the hilt of his knife, clearly struggling to resist the desire to strike. Zach returned the man's stare, still outraged by the boy's condition, but at a sharp command from Little Wolf, Black Coyote left.

"I come with you," Swallow said, and started into the dense bushes.

"No," Zach said, looking to Little Wolf to support him. "It's about to start snowing. We don't need to be hunting for you, too."

"I stay close." Swallow had on his stubborn face, one that had become very familiar—and annoying. "I small, find good hiding places."

"He can help," Little Wolf said, and set the boy between them. Zach didn't agree, but there was no time to debate Little Wolf's decision. He kept Swallow in sight as they struggled through the dense brambles, flushing innumerable birds and rodents, but no boy. By the time they shoved through to the thicket's far side, they were at the foot of the huge hill at the west end of the valley, which was much higher and steeper up close than it appeared from the camp. The other men had fanned out and were now moving back toward the camp. Snow had begun falling—big, powdery flakes that stuck but didn't melt.

As he, Swallow and Little Wolf paused to get their bearings, the wind picked up and the snow fell faster. "Take Swallow back to camp," Little Wolf told him. He motioned up the hill to the deep stand of timber that grew over the crest. "The boy must be hiding in there. I will search there, then follow you."

Zach wrapped one of the extra blankets around Swallow, who was manfully trying to hide the fact that his shoulders were shaking. "Too dangerous to separate," Zach said, clenching his teeth to keep them from chattering. His throat had gone numb, whether from the cold or his injury he couldn't tell. "Safer to stick together."

Little Wolf nodded and they started up the hill with Swallow between them. Each of them grabbed one of Swallow's arms and hoisted him up the steep slope. The fresh snow slicked the ground under their feet, turning what should have been a short climb into an arduous scramble. Once they reached the junipers at the top, they struggled through the dense growth, but the snow was coming so fast they couldn't see more than ten feet ahead. The wind screeched through the timber, blowing the snow into their faces.

Little Wolf stopped, shaking his head as he stared around him at the dense trees. "We go back now. Boy would not come this far." He pulled his blanket tighter as he looked around, nodding. "He must have slipped past us down there."

Zach pulled Swallow in front of him, using his body to shelter him from the wind. If it knocked him over, he'd roll all the way back to camp. "You think the boy got around us and went home?"

Little Wolf glanced at Swallow, then looked at Zach. The bleak expression in his eyes confirmed the hollow feeling in Zach's chest. Little Wolf didn't want Swallow to hear that they'd never find the boy in this storm, and that if they wanted to save themselves, they had to head back now.

"You're right," Zach said, keeping his tone light. "He's probably already had his dinner and gone to sleep."

"Hah!" Swallow stuck his nose in the air. "He no brave like me."

"Not even close." Zach roughed up Swallow's hair and made sure his blanket was on good and tight. "You two go ahead," he said, pushing Swallow after Little Wolf. "I'll bring up the rear and make sure no one gets lost."

He watched Little Wolf and Swallow skid down the hill, then made one more wide circle, looking beneath the nearby trees, searching for small, dark lumpy contours. He wanted to search farther in, but knew that in this swirling, blinding whiteness, he'd get lost in no time. He needed to catch up with Little Wolf, but the thought that he might be leaving a child unprotected, certain to freeze to death in this blizzard, ate at his gut. What if it was his son who was lost and in danger? Wouldn't he want whoever was hunting for him to keep searching, even until he dropped over dead, if that's what it took?

A gust of wind rocked him back on his heels, forcing him to admit that Little Wolf was right. If they didn't head for camp, the Cheyenne would be searching for them tomorrow. He could hardly see Little Wolf at the bottom of the hill, staring up at him and he couldn't hear a word he was shouting. He took a step down the hill, then froze. Why was Little Wolf shouting? He squinted hard and stared. Not just shouting, but pointing, too.

Zach swung around and cupped his hands around his eyes, frantically searching, but saw nothing. Then he heard a weak cry and spotted a tiny white bump. It moved! Something rose out of the ground—a hand!— then fell again. But it was enough. Zach had seen it. His legs seemed to take forever to cover the ground between him and the small heap, but as he neared he could see the exhausted boy, almost completely covered in snow. He fell to his knees when he got to him, stripped off his duster and pressed it around him before his body heat could be whipped out of it by the wind. Then he wrapped the child in the last blanket, chafing his arms and legs, talking to him, telling him he was going to be fine. He was alive, but too exhausted to open his eyes. His chest barely rose as he breathed and his lips were blue. Zach picked him up, draped his arms over his shoulders and pulled his legs around his waist. He waved to Little Wolf.

He kept a tight grip on the boy, who hadn't moved since he'd lifted him. His body was too cold; it chilled Zach even through his shirt. And his heartbeat seemed faint and weak. He needed help. Fast.

Zach broke a large chunk of bark off some nearby deadfall, threw it down at the top of the slope, sat on it and braced his heels at the far end. He scooted a bit and the snow and steep slope did the rest, shooting him down the slippery hill as if the surface was ice and he was riding a skate. He used his weight to steer—leaning to one side, then the other—and one heel as a brake, then an anchor, when his sled hit a bump and threatened to take wing.

Swallow whooped his approval from where he and Little Wolf waited at the bottom of the hill, but the child in Zach's arms remained limp, unaware. Little Wolf said nothing when Zach spun to a stop at his feet, but he pulled the blanket back and examined the boy's legs while Zach held him. Zach glimpsed the injuries, which sent his temper soaring again. Little Wolf said nothing, but removed a small quirt from his belt. He walked back to camp beside Zach, helping to support Swallow, who'd run out of steam and was starting to drag. He snapped the quirt in the air beside him occasionally, as if to punctuate the angry thoughts growling inside him.

As they reached camp, Black Coyote stepped forward to take his son, but Zach refused to release him. Little Wolf spoke, very low and very angry. Black Coyote blanched, then followed Little Wolf away from the sand hill camp, but not before shooting a hate-filled look at Zach. Little Wolf snapped the quirt and Black Coyote followed him, glaring at the people who had crowded around to watch.

Old Bridge, the camp's medicine man, tried to lift the boy from Zach's arms, but he clung and cried out in his sleep. With Black Coyote's wife helping, Bridge gently extricated him. Zach watched them go. He wanted to follow and make sure the boy would recover, but the need to confront Black Coyote rode him. The brute liked to hit. Would he stand up to a target that could hit back?

As he hesitated, Woodenthigh thumped him on the back. "You do good. Boy be fine. Go." He nodded to where Caroline stood among the crowd, waiting for him.

Zach noticed Feather leading Swallow to Little Wolf's tent and shuddered as the wind blew a gust of snow swirling around them. "We'd all better get inside," he said and gave Woodenthigh an answering thump. His gaze lifted to Bridge, just stooping to enter his shelter. Seconds later, he shoved Black Coyote's wife out, his words and gestures harsh.

Zach felt like applauding, but only watched the woman walk to her shelter with her head high and her expression defiant. Seeing him watching, she picked up her pace and yanked the reed covering over the door. He started to follow Little Wolf and Black Coyote, but a hand settled on his arm.

"Let him deal with Black Coyote," Caroline said. "There's something going on there that you and I can't understand."

"I hope Little Wolf understands," Zach said, lumping his concern for the boy into the statement. "I should have checked up on the boy," he said, furious with himself for neglecting to follow up when he knew the boy was being hurt. "He's adopted, right? He should be given to someone else to raise. Someone who will love him and treat him well."

"You've done all you can," she said. "Let Little Wolf deal with it. That's why he's chief."

"You're right," he said and with a last, lingering look at

Bridge's shelter, he turned into the wind that now blew hard and steady from the west, flinging snow into their faces. He pulled Caroline to his side and together, heads down, they fought their way back to their shelters.

Caroline gathered another armload of firewood, while Zach checked the horses. He'd dug a shelter for them in the lee of a neighboring sand hill, but she knew he wouldn't be able to rest until he'd made sure they were protected.

She added a little more water to the stew she'd kept simmering for hours, then watched it cook while she rubbed her arms. Her shelter was fairly cozy since its door faced away from the blowing wind, but the temperature had dropped as the storm worsened. She shuddered and sent a silent prayer of thanks heavenward that the three most important men in her life had returned safely. She'd been so worried, she'd walked a trench in front of her sand hill.

Realizing what she'd just thought, she stilled, clutching her arms over her waist as chills chased up them. When had Zach and Swallow become so important to her? What if things had gone differently today and they had died in the storm? What would she have done? How would she have felt? She tried to imagine her life without them in it and couldn't. She'd worried about them, because she cared about them, loved them.

Her grip tightened and the chills hit again. She *loved* them? Both of them? Rubbing her arms, she started pacing beside the fire. Of course, she loved Swallow. Who wouldn't? The boy was sweet, precocious, mischievous—in short, a normal boy. Sometimes she wanted to grab him and squeeze him until he begged for mercy. But, of course, she'd never embarrass him that way, especially in front of his friends.

But Zach? Did she really love Zach? He was irritable, moody, handsome, bull-headed, bossy, kind . . . *kind?* She forced herself to think of an example and immediately remembered the day he'd discovered her bathing and seen her scars. Even after he knew the truth—well, most of it—he'd stayed with her. And he hadn't asked any nosy questions, or made snide remarks. Yes, without a doubt, the man was kind.

And there was no doubt he was handsome—to a fault. He knew it, too. That wicked, lopsided grin he always flashed at her when he knew he'd annoyed her, the dimple in his cheek, his beautiful gray eyes and the emotion that filled them—she loved them all. She even loved how his hair waved forward onto his forehead and his unconscious habit of shoving it back. He was capable and strong, too. His body thrilled her. She longed to see the muscles she'd felt rippling beneath her hands when he'd held her.

She knew he wanted her, too, physically, but that he didn't love her. He was a loner, a man who loved to roam and loved his freedom. Heavens! He'd had a beautiful wife, and even she hadn't been able to keep him close to home. How could a scarred, damaged woman, tainted by vicious experience, expect to succeed where his first wife had failed, and failed miserably? No, she'd take the precious gift he'd offered: the opportunity to replace her memories of rape and brutality with new, sweet memories.

He wanted to *make love* with her, not just bed her. Other men—men who had no other women available to them—would take her. Many had offered. Some might even be gentle, but none of them would give any thought to her needs.

She recognized Zach's uniqueness, his patience and caring, and couldn't help feeling that she didn't really deserve it, or him. She'd accepted his offer to teach her and she should listen to Feather and Quiet Woman and make the most of her time with him, savor the sweet memories they created together.

And if she was very lucky, he might have a few memories to cherish, too.

* * *

Zach sensed a change in Caroline as soon as he entered the shelter, fresh from washing up in his own shelter. The warmth from the softly glowing fire, the heavenly aroma of the plate of stew and biscuits she handed him with a sweet, welcoming smile put him on his guard. The tense, physically challenging day had exhausted him in every way possible, but Caroline's smile and sidelong look suggested that he'd better have some reserves. The gleam in her eyes told him the night wasn't over.

Later, he couldn't recall how the stew had tasted, even though he'd scorched his tongue, which was tender for days. He couldn't say if he asked for seconds, even though his stomach had begun growling long before he got there. He also didn't remember using his last bite of biscuit to scoop up every bit of stew, as he always did. However, he did remember Caroline bending to put the dirty plate in a bucket of water, and her answering smile when he told her to leave it 'til morning; that he'd never forget.

When she stepped into his arms and reached up to kiss him, he stopped thinking, forgot trying to remember anything but the sweet taste of her, the welcome weight of her body against his, the reassuring beat of her heart against his chest. He kissed her breathless, and she responded immediately when he traced her lips with his tongue. He teased her tongue with his, keeping the penetration shallow and was rewarded when she teased him back and tentatively explored his mouth in return. He groaned and pulled her closer, surprised by her responsiveness.

She pressed closer and her hip brushed his arousal. He sucked in a sharp breath and shifted her, hoping she wouldn't be startled. She slid her hands around his sides and stroked up his back, her fingertips tracing the ridges of muscle.

"Mmmm," she whispered. "You're so strong and your back is so wide. I can't get my arms around your chest."

"That's okay," he said, his words muffled as he kissed the tender spot at neck and shoulder. "Keep tryin'. I like it when you try."

She tried again to reach around his chest and he helped her by pulling her close and rubbing his chest against hers while leering down at her.

She laughed and returned the rub, then the smile faded. "Can I see your chest?"

He must have frowned because she looked away quickly, her cheeks turning pink. "I'm sorry. That was really forward of me."

He turned her face up to his. "You don't need to ask. If you want to see my chest—or any other part of me—help yourself. I'm here for the takin'."

Her eyebrows shot up and she searched his face. "All of you?"

"Oh, yeah," he said, his voice a low purr. "All of me. You'll find my little toes particularly interestin'. Ouch!" He rubbed his side where she'd pinched him. "That hurt!"

"You're making fun of me." She frowned up at him, her moist lips pulled down, her bottom lip jutting a bit.

He leaned down and caught her lip with his own lips and drew it into his mouth. When he let it go, her eyes had slipped shut, but they snapped open when he released her lip and it gave a little *pop*. "I have to warn you, darlin'," he drawled. "If you look at mine, I get to look at yours."

"My what?" Her eyebrows came together and her hands, which had been rubbing his back, stilled.

"You asked if you could look at my chest," he reminded her, and nudged her hands into motion again. "You're welcome to look at mine, but I demand the right to look at yours in return."

"You do, huh?" She frowned up at him. "But you've already seen mine."

"I have? When?" He'd never seen her chest. He wouldn't have forgotten something like that.

"That day. When I was bathing." She'd stopped rubbing again.

He sighed and nudged again, but she didn't respond. "When you were . . ." The whole event flashed through his mind in a rush. Yes, he'd seen her breasts, but he'd been focused on her back, and her breasts had been a blur of pink and alabaster. He hadn't *seen* them at all.

He pulled her into his arms and kissed the top of her head. "I don't remember much about that morning." His eyes closed when he felt the tension slip out of her. "Would you let me see them again? Here? Tonight? They'll be perfect, warmed by the firelight, gleaming all pink and rosy from my kisses."

She caught her breath and her arms tightened, but it was a moment before she replied. "I suppose."

"Then, go ahead." He reached for the bottom of his shirt, but she'd stepped back. Her hands lifted to the ties at her shoulders. With a quick jerk, she released the knots. His entire body tightened as her tunic slipped off her shoulders, only to catch on her nipples, where it dangled precariously. He kissed each gleaming shoulder and gave the tunic a tug, feeling it drop to her feet. Her breasts gave a little bounce and sprang back into place.

He was not a green boy, yet his heart drummed a throbbing beat as he lifted one perfect breast on each palm. They were firm and full, the nipples distended and shaped like plump raspberries, the deep rose aureolas puckered. He reached down and took a nipple into his mouth, first rolling it between his lips, then circling it with his tongue before drawing it fully into his mouth. He wanted to close his eyes, to not let anything distract him from the pleasure, but he watched her face for any sign of discomfort, or fear.

When Caroline gave a soft cry and rose on tiptoe, relief spread through him and he lifted her so that her breast was level with his mouth. She speared her fingers into his hair and pulled him close, forcing him to suckle stronger. He didn't know how long he feasted, but when he finally released her breast, she protested only to give a soft sigh when he merely switched his attention to her other breast.

He could have played with her breasts for hours, but he felt her growing restless and released her, setting her on her feet. Until his final breath left his body, he'd never forget the blush on her cheeks as she undid his belt and began unbuttoning his shirt. Time lurched to a halt, and he knew that every moment afterward would be chiseled into his memory.

He tried to speak, to ask what had happened to the tense, fearful woman he'd known, but he couldn't get a word past his suddenly tight throat. Instead, he let her undress him, button by button. After the third, she spread his shirt wide, rose on tiptoe and licked her lips, then pressed them to the patch of chest she'd exposed. His eyes rolled back in his head and he bit his lip to keep from moaning.

"Woman," he whispered, clenching his fists to keep his hands at his sides where they wouldn't be likely to scare her off, "you're killin' me here."

"No," she whispered against his skin, then trailed her tongue down to the next button. "I'm loving you."

His heart stuttered to a stop and this time he couldn't silence his groan. He sank his hungry fingers into her hair and started pulling out pins. When he'd found them all, she leaned back and shook her head, sending the sun-blessed mass tumbling down her back. Then, with a saucy smile, she yanked his shirt out of his pants, shoved it off his shoulders and stepped back to survey him.

"You're movin' a little fast for Lesson Two," he told her. He loved watching her. The tip of her tongue kept slipping out to moisten her upper lip. He wished she'd use it on his chest. As if he'd asked, she rose on tiptoe again and pressed her lips, then her tongue, to the hollow of his throat. He kept his hands on her shoulders and his eyes on the ceiling, until they rolled back in his head. He thought he heard someone moan, but he was so busy feeling, he couldn't think.

"Am I?" She reached out with both hands, placed them over his chest muscles and gave each a long, firm squeeze.

He was glad she couldn't see his body's response. At the very least, it would have startled her, if it didn't send her screaming into the blizzard. And when she leaned in and licked a nipple, he sucked in a sharp breath and shifted to accommodate his arousal.

Damnation! This was a first. Who was the teacher? He was so hot, if she touched him, Lesson Two would be all over.

"I've decided," she said, then paused to lick her lips and taste his other nipple.

"Whu?" he croaked, cleared his throat and tried again. "What?" He had to keep his head, just in case she lost her nerve. One of her cool hands slid down his stomach. Goose bumps erupted, making his chest ripple.

"Mmmm," she purred appreciatively, and smiled up at him. "You're the one who's beautiful."

"You've decided I'm beautiful." He chuckled, surprised that he could manage even that much. He lifted her and carried her the few feet to her bed, where he lay her down gently, being careful to lift her hair out from under her. Propped on his elbow, he fanned her hair out around her, stroked her arm, her side and down her leg to the slit in her skirt.

"Have you learned enough for one night, or do you want more?" He felt her tense when his hand settled on her thigh, just above her knee, but she quickly relaxed and smiled up at him.

"Kiss me again," she said, her gaze on his lips, and reached for him.

He obliged her, amazed that she had managed to keep her fear at bay for so long, awed that she trusted him so implicitly. Then he stopped thinking and sank into her arms, pulling her close, deepening the kiss until his tongue plundered the depths of her mouth. Once again, he scorched a trail down her neck but didn't pause at the sensitive hollow. He rolled onto his back, lifting her over him and pulling her down so that her breasts were accessible to his mouth and lips. No dessert could have been sweeter, and he partook until her arms shook. Then he rolled her onto her back and lay beside her again, plying her with gentle kisses as he fought the raging impulse to shove her skirt up and finish.

He stroked a hand up her thigh and smiled at the dampness he encountered. But when he neared the apex, she caught his hand. He kissed her breast, whispered, "Trust me."

She didn't relax her grip and he felt her body tensing.

"Have I done anything you didn't want?"

She shook her head, her eyes huge and fixed on his face.

"I won't hurt you, Caroline." He waited, watching her face and saw her decision an instant before she released his hand. However, her body didn't relax. He eased onto his side, leaving one leg crossed over hers at the calf. His body protested, but he knew that he couldn't rush her. A little patience now would reap tremendous rewards in the future. Impatience was not a luxury he could afford if he wanted to achieve his goal. He didn't simply want to leave Caroline with a few colorful, more pleasant memories. No, his plan was more ambitious. He intended to heal her heart. He planned to teach her to trust, and, hopefully, to love again.

So he quieted his clamoring body and began again. With light, nipping kisses, he cajoled her, sucking on her bottom lip, playing with her tongue, teasing and tantalizing her with bursts of passion, until she responded with abandon. She clutched his head close as he suckled her breast, arching her shoulders off the bed to give him more, and still more. Meanwhile, he stroked her thighs, flicking past the moist curls that tempted him until she stopped flinching every time he approached. When she opened her legs a mere whisper, fire rushed through his veins and he deepened his kisses, teasing her mouth with his tongue as he stroked her.

As he pressed the curls aside, he settled more fully onto her, until she bore more than half of his weight and was reaching for him, trying to get closer. Then he slid a finger between her nether lips and up to touch the sensitive bud in hiding there.

Her eyes flashed open and she clutched his arm. "What are you doing?" she gasped.

"Making love to you," he said and kissed her, once again plundering her mouth, letting his tongue teach her the rhythm, while he used his fingers to bring her to pleasure.

She ripped her mouth free, but didn't open her eyes. Her whole body moved as she rocked her pelvis against his hand, then she stiffened, her thighs slammed together and the first tremor shook her. "Don't . . . stop!" she pleaded, and wave after wave wracked her as she found release. "Zacha-riii-ah!"

He kissed her eyes, her cheeks, her limp fingers and collapsed beside her.

Finally, she turned to him, her eyes half-lidded and awestruck. "What was that?"

"Pleasure," he said, trying not to sound too smug. He rose from the bed a bit awkwardly due to his fierce arousal, pulled a blanket over her, threw his shirt over his shoulders and left quietly. Her snore followed him into the raging blizzard.

He staggered to the back of the sand hill, braced one hand against a spindly tree and ripped his pants open with the other. He struggled not to bellow like a bull moose, but a deep, guttural cry erupted as his body arched and clenched in release. Spent, he shuddered, and let his head hang.

A wolf howled as if in answer. Zach sighed and shoved his hair back. "You have no idea, mister." He righted his clothing and staggered back inside Caroline's shelter, where he laid several more small logs on the fire, stripped down to his pants and crawled into bed beside her.

He couldn't have made it any farther.

Chapter Eighteen

"Much noise at your end of camp last night," Quiet Woman said, glancing away from the meat she was roasting to give Caroline a shrewd glance. "You fine?"

Caroline fussed with the moccasin in her lap, cursing her fair skin and the heat that she felt glowing from her face. Quiet Woman giggled and Feather laughed.

"Okay!" She dropped the moccasin and pressed her hands to her cheeks, squeezing her eyes shut. "Does the whole camp know?"

"Oh, no," Feather said, "only . . ." She slid to a stop and grimaced at Caroline's disbelieving look. "Yes, everybody knows."

Caroline groaned and pressed a hand over her queasy stomach. How would she ever face them again? Everyone thought that she and Zach had made love. But they hadn't! And she wasn't about to tell anyone the truth. It was nobody's business but hers and Zach's.

Feather reached over and took her hand. "But everyone likes the idea."

Quiet Woman jerked around, her mouth hanging open. Caroline choked.

Now it was Feather's turn to blush. She hurried to add, "They like the idea of you and him. Together." She shrugged. "Good match." She pressed her lips together and continued patting Caroline's hand.

"So," Quiet Woman said, adopting her most nonchalant attitude, which alerted every nerve in Caroline's body. "How was it?"

Caroline shoved to her feet. "I can't believe you two. I'm not telling you anything. You're horrible gossips."

Feather rose, too, and gave Caroline a squeeze. "Was it as good as you thought it would be?"

Caroline glared at her friends. Quiet Woman had given up the nonchalance and now stood beside Feather, clutching her hand, as the two eagerly awaited Caroline's response. "Better," she said, and squeezed her eyes shut as her friends whooped their delight.

"We thought so," Feather said, dancing a little jig in her excitement. "How does he look?"

Caroline's eyes shut and she sank to her knees, clutching her thighs as sensations from the night before speared through her again. "Delicious."

The two women yanked her back to her feet and threw their arms around her. "See?" Quiet Woman crowed. "We were right. You look even more beautiful today. Like a fire has been lit inside."

Feather nodded. "We so happy you find a man to love."

Caroline's smile faded. How could she tell her friends that her wonderful night in Zach's arms was her first step toward the wrenching pain of losing him?

Quiet Woman and Feather quieted, watching her, waiting for her to explain.

"Yes, I love him," Caroline said simply. "But he doesn't love me, and probably never will." She started pacing in the small space, her arms tight across her stomach. "He's not the kind of man to settle down and stay in one place. He craves adventure, challenge. He won't let himself fall in love with me. And he shouldn't."

The two women exchanged a long glance, then gave Caroline a hug.

"We are sorry for your pain, little sister. He may leave you, but you will always have us."

Caroline chuckled and returned their hug.

"Winter is long and very cold." Quiet Woman nodded with her usual energy and enthusiasm. "Much can happen."

"Don't worry," Caroline said brightly, forcing herself to smile. "I'm not going to think about spring, when he'll have to leave to find his son. For now, I'm going to enjoy our time together, and not think about the future."

"Good," Feather said, and Quiet Woman kissed her cheek.

"Delicious?" Feather asked with a mischievous twinkle. "How you know this?"

"How do you think?" Caroline bent to pick up the fallen moccasin, hiding her blush.

Shouts from outside interrupted Feather's and Quiet Woman's laughter at her coy response. They all hurried outside and Caroline screamed.

Zach had fallen to one knee in front of Bridge's shelter and Black Coyote stood over him, his arm raised, a knife in his hand. As he brought it arcing toward Zach's back, Zach rolled. His leg swung out and he kicked the man's feet out from under him. Both men rolled down the sand hill.

"Hush!" Feather cautioned and put an arm around Caroline. "Do not distract him."

Caroline shoved the back of her hand against her mouth and watched in horror as Black Coyote leaped to his feet. The man was one of the Cheyenne's best warriors, the meanest and the dirtiest fighter. How could Zach beat him?

Damn! Zach cursed and sidestepped a vicious thrust, letting the other man's momentum carry him stumbling past him. Black Coyote fell to one knee but came up fast and flung a fistful of snow mixed with sand into Zach's face. The pleasure of planting a fist in the man's face wasn't worth this much trouble, but the boy needed someone to stand up for him.

Zach shook his head, but the sand clung, obscuring his vision. He jumped aside, trying to anticipate the direction of Black Coyote's next attack, but felt the knife catch him in the gut and slice across his abdomen, followed by hot, searing pain. He fell to his knees, clutching an arm over his stomach, bracing for a final blow to the back or neck.

Instantly, faces swam through his mind: Caroline, his son as an infant, Swallow, Little Wolf, Woodenthigh, Josh and Abby. *No! This can't happen yet!* his mind screamed in anguish. *I have things to do. People are counting on me. My son!*

He sensed Black Coyote beside him, gathering himself to deliver the blow, but something cracked in the air above them. A bloody knife fell into the sand a few feet away and Black Coyote cried out in pain.

Someone grabbed the knife. Not Black Coyote. He still stood at Zach's other side. Profound relief poured over Zach. Like a bucket of warm, soapy water, it washed away the fear. He wasn't going to die after all. Relief sapped his strength, making his legs tremble as he knelt. He shook the worst of the sand out of his eyes and blinked at Woodenthigh, who reached out and steadied him, holding Black Coyote's bloody knife poised as he glared at the man.

Little Wolf cracked his whip again and Zach grimaced as it sliced open Black Coyote's arm. He'd never seen a whip wielded like Little Wolf used his. Much more effective in close quarters than a bullwhip. He considered acquiring one of his own, but remembered Caroline's horrible scars and shuddered. He could never carry a quirt.

In some distant corner of his mind, he realized that he was mentally wandering, that his strength was failing. Then his strength gave out and the ground suddenly rose and slapped him in the face. As the lights went out, he heard a familiar scream.

Caroline. *Damnation!* He hadn't kissed her good-bye.

He dreamed that Black Coyote had him staked to the ground, arms and legs spread wide, while he heated a poker in a nearby blazing fire. Every few minutes, the fiend pulled the poker out of the fire and laid it across his belly, always in the same place, letting it sear the skin.

Here he came again! The poker hit his belly and Zach jerked awake, grabbing the fiend's arm. Only the fiend didn't have crow-black braids and a wicked smirk, it had blonde hair and determined blue eyes. And he wasn't staked, but Woodenthigh and Little Hawk were doing their best to hold him down. And Caroline wasn't holding a poker, just a bottle of whiskey.

"He strong," Woodenthigh muttered as he slammed Zach flat again. Little Hawk just grunted and did the same, shaking his head.

"He's awake," Caroline said. "Pour some of this whiskey down his throat. I still haven't got all the sand out of his wound."

Zach opened his mouth to tell the fools he'd had enough whiskey. The whole place was spinning. If he drank anymore, he'd be spewing it back at them. And he could tell them whiskey wasn't the best-smelling stuff the second time it hit air. But as soon as his mouth opened, whiskey flooded it and he had to swallow or drown. Instead, he spit the whiskey off to the side, being careful not to spew it in the direction of his wound.

Woodenthigh and the Hawk shouted something in Cheyenne, but they didn't let him loose. If Caroline hadn't been there, Zach would have shouted a few choice words himself.

"Let go of me," he said, using his best "command" voice, the one that made his men jump and run. Nobody moved. "I'll stay put," he said, trying cajolery.

Woodenthigh looked into his face. One eye was swollen and red, the skin around it beginning to turn purple. "You give me black eye already. You stay there." He nodded at Caroline.

Zach flinched as she tipped the whiskey bottle over his wound. "Damnation, woman! You trying to KILL ME? Aaagh!" he shouted as she poured the whiskey the full length of the wound.

Damn that slimy Coyote. Zach cursed after he caught his breath. Once he got away from these three hellions, he'd make the bastard pay for that cheap move. What the hell was wrong with him? He knew the guy was trouble. He should have been watching for a cheap move like that. He'd broken another one of his cardinal rules: Keep a cool head. Don't let emotion control you. He'd stomped up to Black Coyote and planted his fist in his face without even considering how the bastard would react. And now look at him. He deserved to be tortured. How ironic that the chief torturer just happened to be the woman he loved.

Loved? He shook his head, checking for flashes of light, black spots, spinning. Nothing. He was completely lucid and in love with Caroline. Now what the hell was he supposed to do?

The woman he loved chose that moment to douse his wound again. His body bowed off the bed and he couldn't keep from howling, then gasping as she probed the wound, cleaning it.

"You're lucky," she told him, shaking her head as she probed deeper with a wicked-looking pair of tweezers. "It's not that deep, but it's going to need stitches." She stopped probing long enough to look at him and smile. "Why don't you do us all a favor and go back to sleep?"

She renewed her probing and the next time she stuck him with her tweezers, his eyes rolled back in his head and he let the blessed blackness catch him as he fell.

Caroline sighed in relief as Zach's head rolled limply to one side. If only he hadn't passed out and fallen onto his wound. She'd been picking sand out of it for hours now. Her eyes burned from whiskey fumes and the strain of spotting the tiny kernels of sand and grit imbedded in the wound.

She poured some whiskey into a bowl and added her needle and the black catgut thread she'd be using to close the wound, making sure they were completely immersed.

"This will take a while," she told Woodenthigh and Little Hawk. "Take a break if you need it." Both men nodded and stepped out of the shelter, heading for the stream. Caroline wasn't surprised to find Old Bridge waiting for her.

"You removed the sand?" he asked, his rheumy brown eyes piercing.

"Yes," she said, rubbing her aching back. She'd been on her knees, leaning over Zach for hours and had at least one more to go. "I needed some fresh air before I start to sew."

Bridge nodded. "He not die, I think, but he be very sick. Many days. Close wound, then rest." He patted her back. "I make medicine to draw out poison."

She started to thank him, but for an old, bent fellow, he moved very quickly. She didn't always agree with his methods, some of which had no basis but superstition, but he accomplished miracles every day. If he could come up with one for Zach, she'd be forever grateful.

Swallow tugged on her sleeve. "Zach all right?"

She pulled him close and gave him a hug. "He's hurt bad, but he's going to be all right."

"You need anything—water, meat, wood for fire—you call me. I stay close."

Caroline smiled, well aware of the generosity of the boy's offer. "Thank you, but you're a young man now and you can't carry water and wood. The people would start calling you names. Zach wouldn't want that to happen. My friends, Feather and Quiet Woman, will help me, but if you could take care of Zach's horses, that would be a great help. Also, I will need meat for the soup pot."

Swallow puffed out his chest. "I no afraid of talk, but I watch horses and hunt. You want turkey? Rabbit?"

"Yes," she said, "both, if you can find them. I thought the turkeys were all scared away yesterday."

"Stupid birds. They come back. Fresh tracks in snow today." He stubbed a moccasined toe in the snow. "No more biscuits for a while?"

She chuckled and rumpled his hair. "Not for a while. But when I have time, I'll make a whole batch just for you."

His eyes went wide and he licked his lips anticipating the treat. "I go now. Find fat turkey."

"Don't go alone," she called after him as he hurried to Zach's shelter. He emerged seconds later with his boy-sized bow and flint-tipped arrows. "Take some friends with you."

He nodded and ran toward the camp—a boy with a mission. Clearly, he loved Zach, too. She sighed. At least they'd have each other when Zach left in the spring. Seeing Woodenthigh and Little Hawk returning, she headed for the bushes herself, then back to her shelter.

If she didn't get that wound sewed up, Zach wouldn't be going anywhere.

Caroline stepped out of the shelter and sucked in a deep breath of air so cold, it hurt to breathe it. She took another deep breath. The sun had set and purple shadows clung to the sand hills, reflecting her mood. For four days, Zach had run a high fever that showed no signs of breaking any time soon. The resulting delirium frightened her. At first she'd thought his rantings were mere hallucinations, but then she'd begun to recognize names like Lincoln and Booth. Her suspicion that Zach was a soldier had been confirmed, but he was like no soldier she'd ever heard of. It seemed his job was to track down conspirators like Booth, Lincoln's assassin, infiltrate their treasonous organizations and systematically destroy them. He belonged to a new organization created by the government for the sole purpose of spying on its citizens to protect government leaders. He'd been in Ford's Theater the night Lincoln was shot.

Once she'd made sense of his ramblings and rantings, she'd tried not to listen, but she was both intrigued and appalled by the things he'd had to do to fulfill his orders—up to and including torture, and even murder. His experiences had plagued him, tormenting his soul, despite his deep commitment to the government and the Army. He believed he had acted honorably, but the deaths he had brought about ate at him, and his agony was tearing her apart inside.

She kept remembering the leather-bound packet inside his saddlebags and the official-looking papers she'd glimpsed one day on the trail. She knew those papers were Zach's private, personal property. Heavens! She could be hung as a spy for even reading them—especially if they contained orders concerning the Cheyenne and she were to tell Little Wolf what she read—but she was becoming more and more worried about Zach with each hour that passed without the fever breaking.

She stuck her hands on her hips and began scraping the new snow away from the shelter door with the side of her moccasins while she weighed her decision. If he didn't survive, someone would want to know what happened to him. Who should she contact?

His brother, Josh, certainly. All she knew was that he lived on a horse farm somewhere in Virginia and had a wife named Abby. What about Zach's military contacts? Who was his superior officer? Would his orders tell her? And what if he wasn't here on military business, but was simply searching for his son, as he'd said?

She shrugged. If that were the case, she wouldn't reveal that she'd read the orders. No one would ever be the wiser.

Still, the idea seemed precipitate to her. She decided to wait one more day. If Zach hadn't improved, she'd ask Feather to watch him so that she could rest in his shelter, which would give her time to work up the courage.

"Shoot! Shoot him, damn you!" Zach cried from inside her shelter and something fell with a clang. Caroline hurried back inside to find that he'd tossed off his blankets and had knocked over the bowl of snow water she'd been using to cool his body. With a sigh, she began again.

By afternoon of the next day, she didn't need to use fatigue as an excuse. She really did need a break and some rest. Feather happily took over the task of trying to spoon venison broth down his throat.

Caroline stirred up the small fire she'd kept going in Zach's shelter to keep it habitable for Bridge, Feather and Quiet Woman to use while helping her nurse Zach. Swallow, too, occasionally took refuge here when Feather and Quiet Woman were busy elsewhere. She dragged Zach's heavy saddlebags to his bed and crawled under a blanket. She'd intended to search them first, but she fell asleep and when she awoke, it was dark outside.

Realizing Feather would be looking for her soon, she lit a candle and dug out the leather-bound packet of papers. She frowned. It was much worse than she'd feared. Zach's orders were to "infiltrate" the Cheyenne camp and convince the chiefs to surrender. If they broke their treaty and left the reservation, or in any way proved obstinate, he was to use "any means necessary" to facilitate their immediate return.

Mercy! The man had open orders. His superiors didn't care how he made it happen. All they cared about was the result: the Cheyenne were to be defeated and installed on the reservation.

Zach must be waiting to act until he found his son, but what would he do once he found him? Whatever he did, Caroline knew based on his rantings, would be done undercover, in the shadows, not out in the open. His work must always look accidental, or be untraceable.

Had his agreement with her been the "any means necessary" to infiltrate the camp? What about his personal interest in her? Was it a pretense intended to make her relax her guard enough to lead him to the Cheyenne? She flushed, embarrassed at how easily his plan had worked, how willingly she'd been duped.

She searched the orders looking for one more thing: Who did he answer to? His chain of command was very short: General Philip H. Sheridan; President Rutherford B. Hayes.

With shaking hands, Caroline replaced the orders in the saddlebag and hurried back to her shelter to relieve Feather.

After Feather left, happy for the reprieve from the backbreaking duty of nursing a thrashing, full-grown man, Caroline resumed her place beside Zach's bed with renewed vigor.

"Don't give up, Zach," she ordered, adopting a military tone as she stroked his flushed, hot skin with the cold water. "You've got to live so I can string you up from the nearest tree." Then she realized she couldn't do that without telling him that she'd snooped through his papers.

Mercy! What kind of mess had she gotten herself into now?

Old Bridge certainly knew his business, Caroline decided two days later. Zach's fever had broken during the night, and he'd finally slept, untroubled by delirium and nightmares. Feather and Quiet Woman, who'd helped with the nursing, could now bear personal witness to the man's physical beauty. But if Quiet Woman asked her one more time what she'd meant by "delicious," she would personally wipe the mischievous smirk off her face.

She'd found herself thanking God many times over the past week for her friends; for the snow that fell steadily, providing a ready coolant for Zach's fever-ridden body; for Swallow's cheerful smile and his never-ending string of poultry for her stew pot. She could go on and on, but most of all, she was thankful that she and Bridge had been blessed with another miracle.

Zach's fever had broken; he would live. He'd be weak for several weeks, Bridge said, and grouchy as a badger, but he'd live. She wished she could believe Bridge, but Zach still hadn't awakened from the deep sleep he'd slipped into when the fever broke. She worried, too, that there might be permanent damage to his mind when he did awaken because his fever had raged out of control for so long.

If only he'd stayed away from Black Coyote, but she understood his concern for the boy. In his feverish ramblings Zach had confused the boy he'd saved with his son. The boy was still in Bridge's custody. The old man refused to return him to Black Coyote, although he allowed his wife to check on him daily. As long as he didn't develop new bruises, Bridge said he'd continue to allow the visits, even though he knew the woman was threatening the child. After her visits, the boy was surly and difficult,

Bridge said. He wouldn't even look at him, and he never spoke. Bridge thought the boy might be unable to talk, might even be deaf.

Caroline crossed her arms over her stomach to quiet her nerves. If Zach awakened soon, as Bridge predicted, he would ask about the child. She wished she had better news for him.

She also wished she knew less about his personal business. How was she to resume their relationship without acting differently toward him? Would he even notice? Oh, yes, she breathed. He'd notice. That man noticed everything.

Little Wolf had stopped by twice in the last two days, twisting his quirt in his hands each time, a sure sign that he was worried about something. She'd promised to send Swallow to let him know when Zach awoke, but couldn't help wondering what had him so bothered. Was he anxious about Zach's health? Once the Cheyenne reached the Powder River valley, Little Wolf must face the authorities there and ask for a new reservation, which would be difficult because of the Cheyennes' depredations in Kansas. It wouldn't help his cause to have an injured white man living among them, especially one whose injuries were caused in a fight with a Cheyenne warrior. But Bridge expected Zach to recover fully, albeit with a nasty scar, and long before the Cheyenne reached the Powder River.

Could Little Wolf's anxiety be caused by the rumors floating around the camp that Dull Knife, or Morning Star, as the Cheyenne called him, was having some problems with the commander of Camp Robinson? She'd heard whispers that things were going badly, but hadn't been able to spare the time or attention to investigate. All her energy had been focused on Zach.

She returned to the shelter and settled on her knees beside him. Sweat beaded his brow and upper lip—what she could see of it through the black beard he'd grown. She wiped his face with a cool, wet cloth, lingering on his forehead, his lips. When his eyelids moved, she caught her breath and clutched his hand.

"Come on, Zach," she said, knowing she should let him sleep, but unable to restrain herself. "Wake up!"

He blinked and his eyes opened to mere slits. He licked his lips and croaked, "Water."

She dribbled a few drops on his lips, but he grabbed the cup from her hands and drained it, his whole body shaking with the effort of lifting his head. Once he'd emptied it, he let the cup fall and collapsed back on his bed. His eyes closed again and Caroline sighed, thinking he'd fallen asleep again. She pulled the covers up over his chest and started to stand, but he squeezed her hand.

"Leaving already?" he asked, and his eyes slowly opened again.

"I thought you were sleeping," she said, returning his squeeze.

"When did I get trampled?" His other hand lifted, then fell.

"Trampled?" She frowned at him. He sounded normal, but his mind must have been affected. "You weren't trampled."

"Oh, yeah, I was." He managed a slight nod. "A whole herd of horses has run over me. Twice."

"No horses," she said. "Just me and Bridge. Do you remember what happened?"

His eyes fell shut again and he took a deep breath, letting it out slowly. "Knife fight. He cheated. I lost." His eyes came fully open for the first time. "How's the boy?"

Relief flooded through her at his awareness, his acuity. She gave him the scant news, then sighed. "The people are calling him Swift Coyote, mainly because he got away from you."

Zach's eyes narrowed. "Not if I have anything to say about it. I don't think Coyote should be any part of his name."

"We can't keep calling him 'the boy,' like he's a pet dog or something."

"How about 'Swift Fox'?" Zach asked, shaking his head. "He not only outran me, he hid so well I never would have found him if he hadn't stuck a hand up."

"It might work. I'll suggest it to Swallow and ask him to tell his friends. Do you feel up to seeing Little Wolf?" she asked. Bridge had cautioned her to keep him quiet for a few days, but she didn't think he'd forbid it, and Little Wolf had been very worried. "He's been here a couple of times asking about you. He's got something on his mind."

"Sure," Zach said and tried to lift himself onto his elbow. He gave up and fell back with a gasp. "If he doesn't mind me lyin' here like a sack of meal, bring him on."

She started to leave, but he stopped her. "Before you do that, do you mind me askin' what you've been feedin' me lately? My stomach's so empty, it's gnawin' on my backbone."

"Mostly broth," she said with a smile, certain now that Zach had suffered no permanent ill effects from his fever.

"Well, no wonder." He grimaced and gingerly rubbed his stomach, keeping well away from his wound. "Got any of that stew today? The kind with the big chunks of meat in it?"

"Think you're ready for meat?" she asked, easing his hand away from the wound. "I suppose you'll want biscuits and coffee, too."

"I don't want to put you to any trouble," he said with his familiar easy grin and a very hopeful look in his eyes.

"Oh, you've already been that, and more," she told him, getting to her feet. She'd had a pot of stew simmering all morning, knowing he'd be hungry as a grizzly if he woke up. Now that he had, she couldn't believe she'd been afraid he never would. She was also glad she was able to talk to him as if nothing had happened, as if she didn't know his true identity. For now, she'd dance on this high wire, until the right moment came to reveal her knowledge. She'd decided it was much too dangerous to tell him she'd read his orders.

"I'll send Swallow to let Little Wolf know you're awake, then get you some food. That boy has worried himself sick about you." She paused and turned to smile at him. "We all have. I'm glad you're feeling better."

He rolled onto his elbow and lifted himself up, wobbly but obviously determined to be upright. "I have you to thank for that, don't I?"

She grinned at him, fiercely glad to have him back. "You certainly do."

"How can I ever repay you?" he asked, giving her a long, lazy look that started at her hair and slid all the way to her toes, leaving heat in its wake.

"I'll think of something," she said, trying to respond as she normally would.

"I can hardly wait," he whispered and flopped onto his back, his chest heaving.

Once she'd sent Swallow running for Little Wolf, she helped Zach eat, then dress and settle beside the fire, propped upright against a backrest cushioned with pelts.

He relaxed against the new backrest with a surprised smile. "When did you acquire the new furnishings?"

"That's yours, from Little Hawk and his wife."

"Why? All I did was punch Black Coyote in the nose and take a knife to the belly."

"They were worried about you."

"Little Wolf didn't *order* it, did he?"

"No, I did not," Little Wolf said with a chuckle as he stepped into the shelter. "My people know you try to help them. They do not like Black Coyote's way of showing gratitude."

"Hello," Zach said. "Caroline, have you got more of that stew or maybe some biscuits?"

"Coffee?" Little Wolf asked Caroline. As he settled onto the second backrest, she brought him a cup of heavily sweetened coffee, then left the two men to sort out the Cheyenne's problems, or whatever other dire dilemma was bothering Little Wolf. She hoped the problem wouldn't require Zach to do anything too strenuous before he'd had time to heal. And she prayed it wouldn't result in him needing to follow his orders.

Chapter Nineteen

Little Wolf drank his coffee down in one long gulp. He nodded, pleased that Caroline remembered he liked it sweet and not too hot. He looked over the *veho*, Zach McCallister, while he drank and did not like what he saw. The man's skin sagged from sickness. He was pale with black circles under his eyes. His hands shook as he lifted his coffee cup. Bridge and Caroline would make him strong again. But would it be soon enough?

It must be. Many lives depended on it. He would send Woodenthigh hunting this day for fresh meat. The *veho* was the only man who could help the Cheyenne now. And while his son hunted, Little Wolf would pray and smoke.

"You know the Little Father, Wessells, at this Camp Robinson?" Little Wolf waved to the northwest, the direction of the camp.

"Wessells?"

Little Wolf frowned. Why did the *veho* stare into his cup? He would not find Wessells's face there. Ah, at last the man looked at his face, but he had put on the empty face that told nothing. He must reach behind it and draw the man out.

"The boy you saved from death is well. His wounds are healing." Little Wolf smiled when Zach's mask slipped and a sharp, angry look came over his face.

"He's still with Bridge?"

Ah. Better and better, Little Wolf mused, as blood rushed into Zach's face. Yes, he would use the boy to manipulate the man, though he did not understand why this orphaned Sioux child stirred his heart.

"Yes," he answered, careful to keep his own face from revealing his thoughts. "I have sent a runner to the Sioux to find out if the boy has other relatives. Black Coyote's heart is cold. Not good father, I tell him. Him very angry. Not want to give up boy."

"Good." Zach pushed himself up in his seat. "When can I see the boy?"

Little Wolf shook his head, smiling to himself as he saw the man stretch higher, push his weak body. "Not good for you to see boy. Too much trouble."

"What do you mean? I'd like to talk to him, get to know him."

Little Wolf watched Zach's face. His mask had slipped away completely, leaving the real man exposed. Little Wolf liked what he saw in this face, in this man. He cared about the boy. Yet Zach's interest in the boy troubled him. Little Wolf decided he would follow the trail of the two McCallister horses through his people, not wait for Zach to do it. Something lay hidden and as chief he must find out what, and who, it was. But first, his people needed help.

"You must get strong fast," Little Wolf said, reaching for the coffeepot on the fire. "Morning Star has trouble."

"Morning Star? You mean Dull Knife, your brother? Is that why you asked if I knew Wessells?"

Little Wolf nodded at each question. The man's body might be weak, but his mind was strong. "You have heard that he and his people were captured and taken by soldiers to this Camp Robinson?" He continued when Zach nodded. "My brother thought he was leading his people to the Red Cloud Agency, but it has been moved. He walked his people into the arms of the enemy." He shook his head, still angry at Morning Star's decision. "And now, the soldiers want all their guns." He looked up from spooning sugar into his cup, saw Zach's smile and shrugged. "Too bitter without plenty sugar. You want more?"

"Black for me," Zach said, handing him his cup. "The blacker the better."

"You need sugar," Little Wolf said. "Make blood thicker. Make you strong faster."

"Why do I need to get strong faster?"

"I want you to go, talk to Wessells. Tell him let Morning Star go to Red Cloud, live with relatives." Little Wolf wouldn't tell him that Woodenthigh had returned two days before. He had escaped the soldiers, but the Cheyenne man he'd stayed with—a man who lived near the fort—had been taken by the soldiers. The man's wife and children were prisoners now also. Little Wolf hated to ask this *veho* to help turn the hearts of the soldiers, but his prayers told him much danger lay ahead for Morning Star. He saw screaming women and children in the smoke of his fire, and much blood on the snow.

"Aren't you afraid I'll tell him where to find you?"

"You not tell. Caroline, Swallow and boy stay behind. You know soldiers not care who they shoot." Little Wolf watched for Zach's reaction and smiled when Zach stared at him, his face still and hard.

"You'd hold them hostage?"

"You soldier," he said with a shrug. "Not trust soldier." He gulped the rest of his coffee and rose to leave. "Get strong fast. Morning Star have big trouble. Little Father, Wessells, lock them all up. No food, no fire, now no water. Children suffer. Women suffer. You hurry." He shook Zach's hand, pleased to have come to an understanding so quickly. This *veho* was very smart in some ways, but not so smart in others.

He was the only hostage.

Zach and Swallow stared up the slippery slope above the chokecherry thicket and groaned simultaneously. "Are we crazy, Swallow?" Zach asked. He crouched down beside the boy and examined the slope, looking for the easiest route to the tree-covered summit.

"Yes. Crazy." Swallow nodded vigorously. "Cold, too.

We hurry? I not unnerstan' why she want us to cut down tree. Crazy woman."

"It's a tradition, something most white people do every year at this time."

"Every white man do this?" Swallow shook his head. "Kill too many trees."

"Near the cities there are big farms where trees are grown so they can be cut for this special day. And there's a story that goes along with it. Caroline will tell you the legend tonight."

"She make biscuits?" Swallow looked uncertain, but hopeful.

"She's got something better planned," Zach said, and rumpled the boy's hair. "And the other boy is coming, too."

"Swift Coyote? He come, too?"

"Don't call him that," Zach said, starting up the slope, stepping sideways to keep from sliding back down the hill. He kept his footsteps close together so that Swallow could follow by stepping where he'd stepped. "I hate that name. What about the name I suggested, Swift Fox?"

"Not so good." Swallow frowned. "You have better name? No call him *Moksois*, 'Pot Belly,' like small boys. Swift Coyote got no belly."

"Maybe we should call him Black Swallow and give you a new name. How about Yellow Magpie?"

The boy huffed and concentrated on climbing. "Swallow my name. It good name. Swift Coyote good name for boy. He run very fast and hide good. We almost no find him."

"Let's call him Swift Fox," Zach said. "He'll like it, I'm sure." He didn't like to think about how close he'd come to not finding the boy that day. He couldn't bring himself to tell Swallow that he objected to the boy being named after the man who'd beaten him black and blue. Swallow didn't see the connection to the man, only the reference to the wily animal.

While Zach recovered, Little Wolf and Black Crane had kept him busy hunting with the older boys and training the green horses. He'd even spent some time making arrows—a skill he'd never use in the future, but interesting. He'd moved back into his own shelter and, though he still took his meals with Caroline, he'd been so tired every night that he fell asleep before his body hit the bed. He knew she was growing impatient for another lesson, but he wanted to be fresh, strong, to make it right for her. That meant he needed time to rebuild his strength. Though he'd been helpless as a newborn the first week, his strength was slowly returning.

For some reason, Woodenthigh or Little Hawk kept Caroline supplied with fresh meat and often stayed to eat and make sure that Zach ate well. He wished the two men had been as successful in tracking down the man who'd first brought his horses to the Cheyenne as they'd been with their hunting. Unfortunately, neither one had anything new to report. And Little Wolf had kept him too busy to get acquainted with the other men in the camp, let alone ask questions.

Now Little Wolf wanted him to ride to Camp Robinson to intervene on behalf of Dull Knife and the other Cheyenne. What did the man expect him to do? A Sioux warrior, sent by Red Cloud after his visit with Dull Knife, had told Little Wolf that Captain Wessells had the Cheyenne under guard and was withholding food, water and even heat from all of them, including the women, children and old ones, until they agreed to return to the reservation in Oklahoma. Wessells also wanted their guns, which the Cheyenne insisted they'd already given him.

Little Wolf thought Zach could break the stalemate, but Zach wasn't so sure. All he did know was that it was going to take some time, a precious commodity. When was he going to have time to search for his son? He'd hoped to be on his way to the Sioux by January if he hit a dead end here. Now it looked like he'd be with the Cheyenne to the bloody end—whatever, wherever, that might be.

He paused halfway up the hill to catch his breath and hauled Swallow up beside him.

"Caroline . . . no . . . crazy," Swallow said, catching a breath between each word. "*We* crazy." He faced his back trail and braced himself with his hands on his knees, letting his head hang.

"You like her biscuits, don't you?" Zach followed the boy's example and was surprised at how much easier he could breathe.

Swallow nodded.

"Well, you're goin' to love the cake she's makin'."

"You like this cake?"

"Oh, yeah. Our cook back home used to make it every Christmas."

"Okay. We cut tree." Swallow straightened and faced the hill. "If cake good, we give Little Wolf some, too."

"Why?" Zach resumed his careful ascent and watched to make sure Swallow was following.

"He let me come," Swallow said and smiled up at Zach. "I tell him much about you and Caroline every day. Wear him down."

"Very sneaky. Don't you think he figured out why you do it?"

"Oh, yes. He unnerstan' very well. That why you hunt with us."

"Remind me never to try to fool you. You're much too smart for me." Zach suspected Little Wolf kept him busy to keep him far away from Black Coyote and trouble, but he grinned at the boy, who beamed up at him.

When at last they reached the summit and found a tree Zach approved of, the sun was beginning to set.

"We'd better hurry," Zach said, once the tree was cut and he was rigging a rope around the bottom of the trunk so that he could drag it behind him. He looked around for Swallow, but couldn't see him anywhere. "Swallow!" he called. "Get back here." His own voice ricocheted back to him, but Swallow didn't answer. "Swallow!"

"Here!" Swallow backed into the clearing, dragging a

large, flat chunk of bark behind him. "Okay," he said straightening and dusting his hands together, a big smile on his face. "We go now."

"What's that for?" Had Caroline asked the boy to bring her some bark? What could she possibly need bark for?

"Go fast down hill," Swallow said, his smile dimming a little. "Like when you find Swift Coy—uh, Fox. You, me, ride down hill."

"Oh!" Zach grimaced, remembering the fear that had gripped him that day. Dire necessity had prompted his actions. He glanced at the purpling horizon and shrugged. A quick trip down would mean they didn't have to walk back in the dark.

"All right. We'll give it a try. I'm not sure we're heavy enough to drag the tree, but if it slows us down, I'll let it go. We may have to climb back up the hill to get it. Still want to try?"

"Yes!" Swallow dragged the bark sled to the crest of the hill and peered over the edge, his eyes widening. He backed away from the lip. "You hold me, no let me fall off?"

"Sure," Zach said, settling at the back of the makeshift sled. "You sit on the sled, up front there, and hold onto my legs." He grabbed the boy's waist with one hand, wrapped the rope that was secured to the tree around his right arm and started scooting, digging into the crusty snow with his heels. The sled slipped easily over the crest and hung poised to fly, suspended by the weight of the tree.

"Let me get this tree over . . . ," Zach said, tugging hard on the rope. The tree slid over the edge and bumped the back of the sled. Suddenly, they were flying. The tree's weight propelled them down the slope much faster than the last time he'd pulled this crazy stunt.

Swallow whooped in excitement, wrapping both arms around Zach's legs.

"Holy . . ." The wind choked him and he gripped Swallow tight with his legs and tried to get a grip on the bark. They started to turn sideways, but Zach leaned the opposite direction and kept them going straight. Faster and faster they slid until the wind made Zach's eyes water. As they got closer to the chokecherry thicket at the bottom, Zach used his feet and hands to slow them, but with the tree pushing the sled, he might as well have been waving in the wind.

He grabbed both sides of the bark sled and leaned hard to the left, using his elbow as a rudder. They swung sharply aside, sending snow spraying over the thicket, but the swerve didn't slow them. The sled took a small hill and shot Zach and Swallow high into the air, while the tree slid to a stop below. Screaming, they pierced the side of a deep snowdrift and stopped with a jarring thud. The drift caved in on top of them.

Zach spit snow and started clawing his way out. "Swallow! Swallow! Where are you?" His heart pounded in his chest as he dug upward. He'd never forgive himself if the boy had been hurt.

"Whoo-ee!" Swallow shouted, his head popping through the snow next to Zach. "Again! We go again?"

Zach shoved his way out of the drift, then finished digging Swallow out. The boy seemed to be having trouble moving. Zach's heart was still racing. He hadn't had a scare like that in a very long time. "That was enough excitement for me." When he pulled Swallow out at last, the boy's legs didn't seem steady. He kept bouncing.

"Stand still!" he told Swallow, checking him for injuries.

"I no hurt, Zach," he said, still shouting. "We go tomorrow?"

Zach gripped his shoulders and made him look at him. "No. Not tomorrow. Not ever. That was an accident. Do you understand? We could have been hurt, seriously injured."

"No danger," Swallow said, smiling at him. "I hold on tight like you say. You no let me get hurt."

"Let's get our tree and go home." They trudged back up the hill they'd sailed over and retrieved their tree.

Zach had expected some damage, but the tree had slid

butt-first, so, with the exception of a few lower branches, it had made the trip unscathed. He shook his head. Lady Luck had smiled on him today, but he wouldn't press her.

"Uh, Swallow? Let's keep that little ride between us, okay? Caroline doesn't need to know."

"Oh, no!" Swallow said, nodding sagely. "No room for her on sled."

"You've outdone yourself." Zach put an arm around Caroline's shoulders and squeezed.

Caroline gave their Christmas tree one more critical once-over and smiled up at him. The tree glowed in multicolored splendor at the foot of their sand hill where all the Cheyenne could see it. She'd been hoarding candle stubs and had made bows of calico scraps. Popcorn garland, dyed red and green and blue, crisscrossed the length and width of the full tree. She'd left her mother's collection of glass ornaments with Uncle James, but even without those precious mementos of past Christmases, the tree was splendid. The only thing lacking was an angel for the top, and the presence of Swift Fox, whose new name was beginning to take hold. Little Wolf refused to let him come, and though Zach had disagreed and argued, Little Wolf had refused to change his mind. She sighed, unwilling to let his decision spoil their celebration.

"It's a beautiful tree, isn't it?" She snuggled into Zach's side, letting Swallow monopolize his other side. "And so big and full. No wonder it took you two so long to get it down here."

"No take long," Swallow began, then he jerked and looked up at Zach. "Bee-yoo-tee-full," he said, smiling up at the tree, his expression awestruck.

Caroline smiled across Zach at the boy, who seemed more animated than usual tonight. He glanced up at Zach, then smiled back at the tree. She hadn't missed Zach's squeeze and quick nod. She knew two guys with a secret when she saw them. What were these two hiding? As if he sensed her disquiet, Zach's arm tightened around her shoulders. She decided she didn't need to know. Yet.

"We have cake now?" Swallow was all but dancing in place, his eyes wide and sparkling.

Caroline gasped in mock outrage, setting her hands on her hips. "Who told you we were having cake?"

"I, uh, might have mentioned it," Zach admitted. "Incentive for climbing hills," he whispered. She nodded. That's what was bothering her. Swallow had been dragging his heels about the tree all morning, and now you'd think it had been his idea.

"No cake until we open presents," she told Swallow, relishing the boy's excited reaction. She and Zach had planned this little party to introduce Swallow to Christmas. Now she wasn't sure it had been a good idea. After they were gone, there would be no more Christmas for Swallow.

As she and Zach followed the boy into the shelter, she pulled Zach aside. "Do you think we're doing the right thing?"

Zach frowned. "What? Christmas?" His gaze settled on Swallow, who was shaking boxes, looking like any other boy on Christmas Eve. "Perhaps not," he said. "But I'm hoping things will work out so that he has many more Christmases to celebrate."

"They don't celebrate Christmas on the reservation."

"Not yet, but they will."

Caroline's teeth snapped together. "You know, that's what I hate about the Christian do-gooder, that complacent attitude, that certainty that they know what's best for the savage Indian. They push ahead with their *noble* mission, destroying cultures that have existed for hundreds of years, telling the people who've lived those cultures that they're wrong, ignorant, even savage. You tell me, who's the savage?"

"Caroline," Zach said, his voice smooth, his nod directing her attention to Swallow, "there's a better time for this discussion."

She glared up at him, feeling her outrage evaporate in the chilly night air. Ever since she'd learned the truth about Zach, she'd had to keep a tight rein on her temper. She smiled, hoping Zach hadn't noticed her frequent irritability, or thought to question the cause. "There's never a good time for that discussion. That's the pity."

"Let's make it a pleasant night for the boy, and for ourselves," Zach urged. "You can shake out the dirty laundry another day and I'll be happy to discuss it with you. But tonight, let's enjoy Christmas together."

"All right," she said, feeling very Scrooge-ish as she mustered up a smile. "Let's play Christmas."

She threw herself into the occasion—opening presents, teaching Swallow carols and enjoying the plum pudding she'd made from ingredients she'd hoarded for months—but the sparkle had fizzled. Zach's frequent glances, his too bright laughter, told her the spark had died for him, too.

"Who is Christmas?" Swallow asked at last. He looked angelic—brown eyes shining, golden curls gleaming in the firelight—surrounded by his gifts: a new tunic and matching moccasins from Caroline; a new, larger bow and a quiver full of arrows from Zach. He rubbed his rounded stomach and yawned. "I like this holly-day."

Caroline ignored the question and busied herself straightening up. She'd hoped this question wouldn't come up, but realized now that Swallow was much too precocious to let it go unasked, or unanswered. Had Zach planned it this way?

"It's actually a birthday celebration," Zach explained, "for a special man. He started out a lot like you, you know."

"He have white father, too?" Swallow asked.

"You might say that. His mother and father were traveling the day he was born. They couldn't find a room to stay in and he was born in a stable."

"I born in tipi like all *Tsitsitas*." Swallow glared at Zach.

Caroline glanced at Zach over her shoulder. How was he going to extricate himself from this one?

"Exactly," Zach said, his manner nonchalant, as if they were talking about the man in the next tipi, not Jesus Christ. "He didn't have a big, fancy house and lots of money and horses, like white men. He was born poor and he remained poor all his life. And yet, people celebrate his birthday because he gave the world hope."

"What is 'hope'?" Swallow asked, sitting on the floor like Zach, with his knees bent to either side and his arms hanging over his legs. His gaze never left Zach's face.

Zach chuckled. "Now that's a tough question. Hope is believing that things will get better, that the sun will come up tomorrow and it won't snow, that a big turkey will waddle out in front of you, that the Cheyenne will make it to the Powder River and get to stay there. Hope makes you try harder."

Swallow smiled, nodding vigorously. "Like you hope you find your son." He turned to Caroline. "And you hope someone love you." He turned back to Zach, who was watching her. The boy's insight stunned her, left her naked in the dark, her gaping wound exposed. She clutched her arms over her waist and turned away to keep Swallow from seeing her pain. "Like I hope for family. I unnerstan'. Hope powerful medicine."

Tears sprang to Caroline's eyes, and she struggled to stop them. She didn't want Swallow to think he'd hurt her feelings. She glanced over her shoulder and saw that Zach's eyes were suspiciously shiny, too, but he hadn't turned away from the boy. Instead, he'd pulled him close beside him and was staring at her over the boy's head. He drew a deep breath and his eyes closed for a moment, then he said, "Yes, it's very powerful medicine. And we're lucky to have it. That's why we celebrate Christ's birthday every year."

"That why you cut down tree, too?" Swallow asked, pushing out of Zach's arms to look up at him. "Tree cutting down best part."

"It's a part of it, yes," Zach said, and whispered something to the boy as he glanced at Caroline. Swallow nodded and whispered back, then sent her a glowing smile. "You no need hope anymore, Car-o-line." He jumped to his feet and wrapped his arms about her waist. "I love you."

She gave up her struggle to stop the tears and let them fall as she returned his hug.

Swallow looked up and frowned. "Why you cry?"

"Because you make me happy." She pulled him back into her arms and hugged him hard. "Want some more cake?"

"No room here," he pressed a hand over his stomach.

Suddenly, there was a loud *whoosh* and a gust of hot air knocked the shelter's reed door into the fire. Zach jumped to pull it out and Swallow helped beat out the flames where it had caught fire. As they were setting it back in its place, Zach cursed under his breath.

"What?" Caroline asked, stepping up beside him, her hands still stinging from beating out the small flames that had popped up all over the shelter from flying sparks. She needed some snow to cool them off.

"Look," Zach pointed down the hill. Their Christmas tree had burst into flame. Caroline hurried down the hill, but before she reached it she knew it was hopeless to fight the fire. Flames engulfed the tree.

Zach bent and dabbed a finger in a scorched spot on the ground nearby and sniffed. "Kerosene," he said. He turned to Caroline. "We'd better check our supplies. This wasn't an accident."

Silently, they watched the tree burn, keeping well away from the shooting sparks of hot sap. The stench of burning kerosene stung Caroline's senses. She'd never light another lamp without remembering this sight.

Swallow stood beside Zach, tears streaming down his cheeks. Caroline's fists clenched. How could someone do something so petty, so mean? She knew the Cheyenne didn't like Swallow spending so much time with her and Zach. They felt he should be learning more about the Cheyenne and forget about his white blood. But when they treated him with such suspicion and outright revulsion, why would he want to be with them? If he didn't have her and Zach, and the Cheyenne didn't want him, what did that leave him?

"Somebody no want us to hope," Swallow said.

The boy's sagacity stunned Caroline. Of course. This wasn't the work of the Cheyenne people. It was malice; the spiteful work of one twisted, hate-filled heart. How much more misery would it cause before someone put a stop to it?

Zach grabbed her hand and squeezed. She found Swallow's and did the same.

"Whoever it was can burn our tree," Zach said, his voice ringing out over the crackle of the flames. "But he can't take our hope, Swallow. It's deep inside us. Here." He pressed Swallow's hand over his small chest. "Nobody can get to it unless we let them."

Chapter Twenty

Zach gave Demon one more scoop of grain. He knew he was delaying the inevitable confrontation with Caroline, but Demon required extra attention before the long ride in the bitter cold tomorrow. Woodenthigh had drawn him a map and assured him that Camp Robinson was only a half day's ride, but that was before last night's heavy snowfall. He didn't know this Wessells who was supposedly in command and harassing Dull Knife. His orders were almost eight months old. Would Wessells even see him, let alone listen to him? Zach wished he shared Little Wolf's optimism.

Zach tied Demon at the base of Caroline's sand hill and stroked the stallion's neck as he responded to nickers from the mares that were tethered near the stream. Zach had great hopes for the stud and those mares, and hoped this little jaunt into the wilderness wouldn't endanger the animal, and the future that centered around him. He'd finished his preparations and he would leave in the morning, but not before he talked to Caroline.

He stepped into the shelter, keenly aware of its rusticity as he mentally prepared himself for the rigid formality of a military installation. Though he saw the crudeness of it, he also felt the warmth of a bright fire, savored the aroma of food waiting for him, relished the presence of the woman who created this atmosphere of civility out of a wilderness hovel. It was her, more than anything she did, that made this shelter home. He loved her. He'd known it ever since Black Coyote sliced him open, but he hadn't told her because he still didn't know what he could do about it, or what he wanted to do about it. He believed that she loved him, too, even though she'd been a bit irritable and distant since his recovery. But he couldn't tell her how he felt; he had nothing to offer her.

Not that Caroline was another Patricia, who'd been more in love with his family's status and holdings than with him. But a man couldn't offer a woman an empty hand. What could he offer her? A seat on the horse beside him? The opportunity to grow old and tired before her time from exposure to the elements, from living on the road? Long bouts of loneliness and worry while he was away on assignment? That was no life for any woman, especially a woman like Caroline.

She deserved someone who'd be there to hold her, cherish her, make sure she knew she was beautiful, that she was loved. She deserved a home.

He couldn't give her any of that, but he wanted to, desperately. He'd finally found a woman who met him toe-to-toe, measure-for-measure, his match. But his life was a mess of scattered responsibilities—to his son, his brother, the government, her, Little Wolf. Somehow he had to bring some order to the chaos, resolve the obstacles confronting him. Then he might be able to find something that he could offer her.

The biggest surprise was that none of this scared him

the way he'd been scared when he considered offering for Patricia. He wanted to spend the rest of his life with Caroline. He couldn't see his future without her.

All he could offer her now was his love—not the declaration—but the execution. He'd show her how much she meant to him and hope she understood and forgave him when she learned the truth about him, as he knew she would. Too soon.

He watched her finish preparing their meal and helped when he could, taking the opportunity to touch her often. He wanted her accustomed to the feel of him near her, of his hands gliding over her. As the evening ritual continued, he found himself content to stretch out the moments before he must tell her he was leaving.

He'd decided to tell her after dinner. He didn't want her to accuse him of seducing her into agreeing, though he wouldn't do that tonight. Not that he was asking her permission. He intended to go, with or without her approval. But he'd rather have her approval.

Zach pulled her into his arms for a long, very satisfying kiss, the first they'd shared in weeks. "Where have you been?" he asked, nuzzling his way down her neck to his favorite spot. He nipped it gently, then kissed it better.

She shivered. "Right here. Busy. Like you."

He loved that he could make her breathless with one kiss. She was so incredibly responsive to his touch. If he kept this up, they'd end up in her bed, but it had been a long time since he'd taught her about pleasure and he wanted to savor his time with her. He hoped she'd give him the chance after she heard what he had to say.

"I've missed you," he whispered against the hair over her scarred ear. He was determined not to treat her as if she were damaged in any way, but he always respected the boundaries she set. He knew she would be uncomfortable with him lifting the hair away from her ear, or baring her back, so he did neither. In the past, he'd avoided stroking her back, but he looked forward to fondling her bottom at some point in the future. He sighed, kissing his way back up her neck and settling into another kiss.

"What's on your mind, Zach?" She leaned back and studied his face, keeping her arms between them.

"What makes you think something's on my mind?" He caught her hand, kissed the back of her fingers and put her hand on his shoulder.

"This," she said, and ran a fingernail through the crease between his brows. "And this," she said, moving down to the brackets pulling his lips straight. "I don't see enough of that dimple lately. What's on your mind? Are you still in pain from your wound? You haven't really been the same since that fever."

"That's not it," he said, stepping away and sitting beside the fire. He picked up a long stick and poked at the flames. He thought he'd done a better job of hiding his emotions. Foolish. He should have confided in her the day Little Wolf first approached him, the day he awoke from the fever. "Come here," he said, indicating she should sit beside him.

She settled beside the fire, watching the flames dance. "Tell me. Quit stalling."

"I'm leaving for Camp Robinson in the morning to try to sort out this mess with Dull Knife and the camp commander, a Captain Wessells. Little Wolf asked me to do it the day I came out of the fever, and he's been haranguing me about it daily since then."

"Why you?" she asked, sitting up abruptly. "Does he think Wessells will listen to you because you're a white man?"

Zach debated telling her everything, but couldn't bring himself to say the words: I'm a soldier. He wasn't ready to face that bullet. Instead, he said, "Yeah, something like that. I have to try. I wouldn't be able to live with myself if I didn't and somebody died."

Caroline watched him without saying a word for several long, tense seconds. Then she asked, "What aren't you telling me, Zach? There's more to this. Little Wolf wouldn't send you there just because you're white. He has to believe you can accomplish something. He's desperate."

"Exactly!" Zach snatched up the lifeline she'd thrown him, hoping he didn't sound too eager. "He's so desperate, he'd even send *me* to negotiate with Wessells."

She looked away from him, keeping her thoughts to herself. "What will you tell Wessells about Little Wolf, about the camp? He'll want to know where we're hiding."

"Nothing," Zach assured her, surprised by her agitation. "It probably won't even come up. He has no reason to suspect me."

"How can you avoid telling him?" She got to her feet and started pacing in the small shelter. "What if you refuse and he takes you prisoner, tries to force it out of you?"

"That's not going to happen," he told her, getting to his feet and stepping into her path to stop her pacing. "You're blowing this out of proportion."

He tried to pull her into his arms, but she pushed away. "No, I think you're trying to minimize it."

He gripped her shoulders and leaned down, looking into her face. "Nothing's going to happen to me. I'll be fine, and I'll only be gone for a week, maybe two."

She slipped from his grip and stepped out of his reach. "A lot can happen in two weeks, Zach. I'm not sure we're safe here. Since that tree was burned, things have been pretty tense. Black Coyote and his bunch are getting bolder every day."

"What have they been doing?" he demanded. If that thug had touched one hair of her head, he'd cut off his hand.

"It's not what they say, it's the way they look at me, and the way they treat Swallow. Bridge won't let Coyote near Swift Fox, but if you're gone, I'm afraid they'll try to take him."

Zach's gut twisted. He hadn't been allowed to see the boy since his injury. Little Wolf assured him that the boy was fine, healing well, getting stronger, growing, but he wanted to see for himself, not just take his word for it.

The thought that he could again be in danger chilled Zach. "Do you really think they'll try to take him?"

"Yes!" she said, then shrugged and shook her head. "No. I don't know. They're acting strange. Even Feather and Quiet Woman are worried."

Zach frowned. If Little Wolf's wives were worried, that meant Little Wolf was worried. "I'll talk to Little Wolf in the morning before I go. If he can't assure me that the boy will be protected, I won't leave. He'll have to find another way."

She glared at him, obviously not satisfied with his answers, but fresh out of arguments. "I still don't like it," she said, her arms clutched over her waist. "What aren't you telling me?"

"I'll be careful," he said, choosing his words cautiously, knowing he wasn't really addressing her concerns.

"See?" she said, defiant to the end. "You can't even say it, can you? You can't tell me you're not lying."

"I'm not lyin'." His conscience raked him, but he couldn't tell her everything and risk losing her. Especially when he wouldn't be close by to undo the damage once she'd cooled off. "I'm goin' to Camp Robinson. I'll be gone two weeks at the most, and I'll miss you every minute of every day." He reached for her, but she stepped aside.

"Oh, no, you don't. You're not about to sweet-talk me into nodding and kissing you good-bye with a smile on my face. And I don't understand why you're putting me through this when you've already made up your mind. It's risky, dangerous, and you don't know that you can help, unless there's some other argument for your going that you're not telling me about. I don't like it. When it blows up in your face, I'll be the first to say 'I told you so!' "

"Fine," he said. He shoved his hair back and stuck his hat on his head. "I'd thought maybe we could have another lesson in lovemaking tonight, but I can see you're not in the mood."

"Not in the mood?" He should have run, not walked, out of there when he heard the outrage in her voice. "Not in the mood!" A crock sailed out of the back of the shelter, thrown by one very strong, very angry woman. *Thwack!* It hit the ground and cracked in two.

"Woman! What do you think you're doin'?" He threw an arm up in front of his face and blocked the next bullet, a hairbrush. He picked it up and tossed it onto her bed. "That would've hurt!"

She grabbed it and threw it again, leaving him no choice but to tackle her to stop her attack. He caught her about the waist, picked her up and plunked her on her bed, then followed her down, holding her still with his body. She sputtered, hissed, kicked and fought like a cougar, but finally settled down. She stopped fighting so suddenly that he searched her face, afraid her old fears may have overcome her, but he saw only anger in her flashing eyes.

He couldn't smile at her if he expected to be able to ride tomorrow, but he could admire her. He loved her angry and tousled, her hair tangled around her face, her eyes spitting flame, her cheeks flushed and her lips . . . those lips were more than he could resist.

"Don't," he said, kissing her to punctuate the word.

"Ever," another kiss, a little longer.

"Do that," again he kissed her, letting his tongue slide along the tight seam of her lips.

"Again," he whispered. This time she moaned and opened for him. He plunged in, taking the kiss deep, exploring her mouth and searing her sweet taste into his mind, where he knew it would torment him every day he was gone.

"I have to go," he told her, gazing into her sky-blue eyes. He kissed the tip of her nose. "Will you keep an eye on Swallow and the boy while I'm gone?"

"Only if you get off me right now."

He rolled to his feet and stood smiling down at her, his hand extended to help her up.

"I'm fine right here, thank you."

He grinned at her, amused that she was trying so hard to stay mad, but failing miserably. "Come on," he urged.

She took his hand and let him pull her up and into his arms. He lifted her onto her toes and settled her against him. She fit as if they'd been cast out of the same mold, especially when she lifted her arms around his neck.

"Come back to me," she whispered and threaded her fingers into the hair above his collar. "I'm not through learning yet." She kissed him hesitantly, then with growing enthusiasm. His answering iron-hard erection strained against his pants. He wished he dared to press it against her and let her know how strongly she affected him, but he held back, not wanting to frighten her. She did have more to learn, but if he made love to her tonight, he wouldn't want to leave in the morning.

"I'll be back, darlin'," he told her, ending the kiss with a long nibble of her bottom lip, then ducked out of the shelter and walked straight into the nearest snowbank, which he greeted face-first.

The woman was killin' him.

"Come on, boy," Zach said to Demon, leaning low in the saddle and rubbing the exhausted horse's neck. Their half-day ride had taken a full day and half the night. They'd been slowed by snow driven by a strong northeasterly wind that still hadn't let up. He was afraid he had frostbite of the entire left side. If he could have ridden backwards, he would have. Even walking on the horse's right side hadn't helped. Then his feet froze, too.

The Great Plains in winter was the least hospitable place in the world and the distant lights of Camp Robinson looked very welcoming. He hoped it wasn't a snow mirage.

It seemed like hours later that Zach collapsed into a spare bunk, there being no officer accommodations available. He didn't care. At this point, a bed was a bed, or at least he thought so until reveille sounded at dawn and dozens of grumbling soldiers rolled out of their bunks. He rolled onto his back and stared at the ceiling.

He did not miss this. What a surprise! He'd thought the structure of the military gave his life purpose and him, identity. With sudden clarity, he realized he'd replaced the responsibility for making his own decisions about his life with Army regulations. No decisions to make, no choices, just listen to the bugle calls and follow orders. He'd needed—no, he'd craved—order and discipline in his life, and when he'd finally found it, he'd hidden behind it, used it to avoid responsibility.

Stunned, he lay unmoving on the bunk, a corpse with open eyes. How could he have been so blind? What had made him understand now? Had his love for Caroline, his desire to make a life with her, opened his eyes?

He jackknifed off the bed, enervated and anxious to make the changes this epiphany inspired. Why should he search the shadows for enemies, when they walked boldly in the daylight? Why let his "duty" to the Army, and the government that had done nothing but use him, keep him from having a life of his own? He pulled on his uniform, rushing to get on with this day. He had a task to finish.

He found Captain Henry Wessells too busy with his breakfast to see him. Though the snub from a junior officer rankled, Zach set out to observe the camp and assess the Cheyenne's situation firsthand. He didn't like what he saw.

The Cheyenne were confined to an unfinished barracks with armed guards at every window and corner. As a soldier guarding the perimeter approached one of the windows—all of which were boarded up from the inside—a warrior stuck a nail-studded piece of lumber out the window and swung it at the nearest guard. Wild laughter erupted from the men inside when the guard jumped, barely avoiding a painful injury.

"Crazy Injuns," the guard mumbled, settling his hat and jerking at his coat before continuing his patrol.

"Have they eaten yet?" Zach asked the guard at the door.

"No food, water or heat until they give up the rest of their guns and agree to return to Oklahoma peaceably," the guard replied.

"The women and children, too?" Zach demanded, stunned nearly speechless. He had lived among the Cheyenne for months now and found them a thoughtful, considerate people, slow to anger, though he could name a few exceptions. He'd never seen them do anything so rash as what he'd just witnessed. But he'd heard desperation in the warriors' laughter, and despair.

Screw Wessells and his breakfast. Zach wanted answers.

"What the hell is going on here? Why are these people being starved?" he demanded, refusing the seat Wessells offered him when he barged into the camp commander's office.

"What right do you have to force your way in here?" Wessells's temerity astounded Zach. The skinny runt was a good foot shorter than him, and outranked. He obviously didn't have the sense to be intimidated. He reminded Zach of a weasel, especially with that multicolored, bristling bush of a mustache disguising his small, thin-lipped mouth. Was he compensating for the sparse cover on top? He also blinked constantly, his washed-out blue gaze flicking about as if he expected a blow at any second.

This person couldn't begin to comprehend the dignity of a man like Dull Knife, let alone persuade him to give up his people, and his hope. This man was the walking, talking embodiment of everything that was wrong with the U.S. government's treatment of the Cheyenne. Zach wished he could march over to the barracks, release Dull Knife and his people and hurry them away from the feverish determination in Wessells's face, but anything less than the Cheyenne's complete surrender would precipitate a bloodbath.

Little Wolf's hopes for a compromise could never be realized. Zach vowed that whatever concessions he managed to wrangle out of this man for the beleaguered Cheyenne would not be bought with Little Wolf's surrender.

Zach took off his duster and hat and handed them to the orderly. "Coffee," he told him. "Black. And keep it comin'." Then he settled into a chair and looked up at Wessells's chair—practically a throne—behind the desk. The legs of his own chair had been shortened.

Wessells ascended his seat behind the massive desk and smiled. "There, now. Isn't that better? We can discuss this in a civilized manner. No need for hostility between officers."

"Orderly," Zach barked. "Bring me a different chair."

The orderly cleared his throat and glanced nervously at Wessells, who observed their exchange with a benign smirk. "They're all like that one," he whispered.

"Fine," Zach said, getting up, using the loud, firm tone he generally reserved for command. "I prefer to stand." He ignored Wessells's glare and charged into the fray. "What are your intentions for the Cheyenne?"

Zach listened to Wessells whine about the Cheyenne's stubbornness, their refusal to follow his orders, his certainty that they possessed more guns that they'd hidden on the persons of their women and children, his determination to force Dull Knife to agree to return to Oklahoma. It took hours.

He slapped his palms on the commandant's desk, leaned across and whispered, "You still expect them to surrender after you've withheld food and water for two weeks? They've had no heat for a week. You haven't even let them out of that pest hole to shit!

"*Damnation*, man! We treat dogs better than you've treated these people." Zach stared into the determined, twitching face before him and resisted a burning desire to choke the life from it. He'd killed men for less than this man had done to the Cheyenne. Unfortunately, he didn't have the authority to remove Wessells from command, nor assume it himself, and Camp Robinson wasn't yet connected to the telegraph lines. Sheridan was at least a week away by messenger. Well, Zach mused, he might not be able to keep the pot from boiling over, but he'd try to turn down the heat.

"Let me talk to Dull Knife alone," Zach said with a sigh and settled a hip on the corner of Wessells's desk, knocking over an inkwell in the process.

"No." Wessells reached toward the spreading mess, then planted his hand in his lap. "Not without me there."

"He won't *talk* with you there." Zach was finding it more and more difficult not to shout, but he refused to totally abandon decorum. He wanted to bellow in the man's face and lock him up in his own damn barracks. But he would restrain himself. Life was full of sacrifices.

Wessells shrugged. "No meeting without me present."

"We'll see," Zach said. "Bring him in."

When a trio of beefy soldiers escorted Dull Knife into the room, Zach snarled, outraged that the chief had been hobbled and his hands tied in front of him. A new bruise was purpling on his temple, but he smiled when he saw Zach and moved toward him, hands outstretched in greeting.

One of the soldiers stepped between them and struck Dull Knife in the chest with his rifle butt. Zach shoved the soldier away and caught Dull Knife, who crumpled and would have fallen. He cut off the ropes binding his hands and supported him until he could stand on his own.

"My brother?" Dull Knife whispered.

"Safe," Zach replied, then glared at the soldier. "Touch him again and you'll answer to me." The soldier gave a surly nod as he and the rest of the escort left the room.

Zach led Dull Knife around Wessells's desk and seated him on the throne, ignoring Wessells's sputtering protest as he removed the hobbling rope around the old man's ankles. Dull Knife needed food and water, not more discussion. His bones jutted from beneath the thin, paper-dry skin. He may have retained his dignity, but Dull Knife had clearly suffered from the recent ordeal.

Zach asked the orderly to bring something for the

chief to drink, but Dull Knife declined. "I will not drink while my people go thirsty." He glared at Wessells, who stood beside the desk clenching and unclenching his fists. "Why you bring me here? I not change my mind. My young men not let me. They will fight, and they will die, but not in Oklahoma. We choose to die here, in our hunting grounds. Our blood will stain your hands."

Wessells turned to Zach. "This is a waste of time." He gestured to his orderly. "Get them out of here."

"Wait," Zach said, and turned to Dull Knife. "If they return the three men they're holding for the crimes in Kansas, will you talk?"

"They not return them," Dull Knife said wearily. "I have begged and pleaded, as I pleaded for the lives of my people. Their ears are stopped. They no longer listen when Cheyenne speak, but we make them hear us one more time." He rose and gripped Zach's shoulder. "Thank you for speaking for us."

He shuffled out of the office followed by Zach, whose glare kept the soldiers from pushing him along with their rifle butts. He returned to Wessells determined to put an end to the standoff.

"Feed them," he demanded.

"Not until they surrender their weapons," Wessells said, wiping his chair with a pristine handkerchief.

"If they had weapons, don't you think they'd have used them by now?" Zach demanded. "Good God, man, Dull Knife can barely walk. What do you expect them to do even if by some chance they do still have weapons?"

"They can still breathe, can't they?" Wessells asked, settling himself on his chair and brushing at his desk. "They can breathe, they can shoot."

"And why do you need their agreement to return to Oklahoma? They're your prisoners. How can they prevent you from doing whatever you want with them?"

"If they're armed, they can overpower their guards and escape again. The Army has wasted enough time and money chasing them." Wessells continued cleaning his desk, his mouth tightly puckered beneath his bush of a mustache. "They will be returned to Oklahoma as soon as the weather clears. A division of the Third Cavalry arrived two days ago to escort them. The good citizens of Kansas want to talk to them."

"Ludicrous!" Zach said. "Whose brilliant idea was that? Do you plan to feed them before you start the march? Their clothes are little more than rags. They wouldn't make it to the Kansas border, let alone Oklahoma."

Wessells shrugged. "That is not my problem."

"Not your . . . !" Zach started around the desk. Court-martial be damned. He'd enjoy the feel of that scrawny neck snapping beneath his fingers.

"How did you come to be so familiar with this Cheyenne chief?" Wessells's beady stare settled on Zach. "You never said where you came here from, and your orders are almost a year old. Where have you been, and who have you been with?"

"I answer to Sheridan, not you, *Captain*," Zach answered with disdain, and headed for the door. Time to leave. He couldn't do anything for Dull Knife. Even Little Wolf and all his warriors couldn't get him out of this mess.

"As do I," Wessells said quietly.

Zach studied Wessells. Was he lying? He knew Sheridan, had served under him for years. His gut told him Sheridan may have given the orders, but he hadn't sanctioned the methods.

"You found Little Wolf and his band, didn't you?" Wessells's eyes turned an unholy blue as he continued to stare at Zach. He straightened in his massive chair and leaned forward, as if watching for his cornered rat to squirm. "You know where they're hiding."

Zach glared back. He didn't squirm for any man, let alone for weasels. "I'm wintering in Ogallala and will continue searching for Little Wolf when the weather clears, as you say. Don't worry. I won't be your *guest* long." Wessells could confirm his story with a messenger to Ogallala, but it would take days. Zach had to buy himself some time to escape the noose tightening around him and find a way to help Dull Knife and his people. Maybe if he could get to the agency at Pine Ridge, Red Cloud would intercede and send food and water. His voice, raised in outrage, could effect change.

It wasn't much of a plan, but right now it was all he could think to do.

"Do you miss him?" Feather asked, scooping up the ground root that was spilling out of the gourd in Caroline's hand.

"No!" Caroline said, startled. "What makes you think I miss him?"

"You have gas?" Quiet Woman asked.

Feather giggled.

"No, I don't have gas," Caroline said, blushing. Had she done something rude and not even noticed?

"You will," Quiet Woman said and winked. "You sigh all time now." She stared into the corner of the shelter and demonstrated, heaving a dramatic sigh.

Feather giggled again and covered her mouth with her hand.

Caroline's blush jumped from flicker to flame. "You're exaggerating," she accused Quiet Woman. "I don't miss him."

"Then why you sigh?" she asked. "You almost blow me over with last one." She rocked back on her wide bottom and Feather snickered.

"Not likely," Caroline said and they all laughed. "Yes, all right! I miss him. He should be there by now and I'm worried, that's all."

"He be fine," Feather said, patting Caroline on the back. "Little Wolf say he fix things. Be back soon."

"Little Wolf expects too much." Caroline screwed a hand-carved piece of wood into the gourd she'd almost spilled. "The tension has increased since he left and I'm nervous. Haven't you noticed?"

Her two friends looked at each other and shook their

heads. "No. Very quiet," Quiet Woman said, "except that Little Wolf take me to his furs last night and—"

"*Not* what I was asking," Caroline said, holding up a hand to stop her friend. She knew Quiet Woman was being silly, trying to distract her, but the last thing she needed to hear about was love play. A guilty flush rode her cheeks. Part of her tension was purely selfish concern for Zach's safety. How could he finish teaching her about lovemaking if he was hurt or killed? Would she ever see him again? They'd shared many sweet, memorable moments, but she wanted more. She wanted the chance to learn it all and to be with him fully, even if it was only once. Then, when he was gone, she'd have something to remember him by.

She heard a voice calling her name and stilled, listening.

"Swallow comes," Feather said, but she too had stopped her work to listen.

"Trouble," Quiet Woman said and they all hurried outside, wrapping blankets around their shoulders as they went.

"Come!" Swallow said, grabbing Caroline's hand and pulling her after him. "You too," he told Feather and Quiet Woman. "He try take boy!"

Caroline started running. Her blanket fell off, but she yanked her skirt up to her knees and caught up with Swallow, who was heading for Bridge's shelter. She should have been watching. She'd expected Coyote to make this move and had warned Little Wolf, but he hadn't believed Black Coyote would do something that stupid. With Little Wolf off hunting with the young braves, Black Coyote had seized the opportunity.

Knowing she'd been right didn't give her any sense of satisfaction. She took comfort from the feel of the knife tied around her leg as she ran, but knew she'd never be able to stop him. Hopefully, the three of them—she, Feather and Quiet Woman—could slow him down until Swallow could find one of the men.

She rounded the base of Bridge's sand hill and slid to a

stop. Black Coyote had reached the base, too, pulling the boy behind him. The boy had sunk his heels into the packed snow and was trying to slow Black Coyote down, but with one backhanded slap, Coyote knocked the boy senseless and threw him over his shoulder. No one could try to bring him down without hurting the boy, not that any of the Cheyenne would have tried. They'd been whispering for weeks that Little Wolf should release the boy and stop interfering in Black Coyote's family. That was not a chief's responsibility.

Caroline drew her knife as she slid to a stop. She didn't know what she'd do with it, but she wanted to be ready.

Black Crane stepped in front of Black Coyote. "You cannot take the boy."

"You cannot stop me, old man," the Coyote said, his grip tightening on the boy's legs. "This boy is mine."

"Give him to me," Black Crane said, his voice cool, level. "Little Wolf has said you are not to take him back. Let me have him before you hurt him more."

"Stand back, old man," the Coyote shouted. "He is mine, a child to fill the empty place beside my fire, to beat when the hatred rises, to teach the ways of the *Tsitsitas.* He will live beside me, and he will die beside me."

Black Crane glanced around him at the crowd of people watching. "Let us go inside." He placed a hand on Black Coyote's back to lead him back to Bridge's shelter. "Come. We will talk."

Black Coyote stepped away and drew his knife. "Touch me again and I will cut off your hand."

"Why do you raise your knife to a friend?" Little Wolf had arrived. He stepped out of the crowd with his quirt in his hand. Black Coyote watched the small whip nervously. He let go of the boy and shoved him off his shoulder, then faced Little Wolf and Black Crane, crouched and ready to fight. Bridge caught the boy and Feather helped him carry the boy back to his shelter.

"I will kill you both if you do not give me the boy,"

Black Coyote shouted. His eyes darted from Black Crane to Little Wolf and his knife was a gleaming blur as he tossed it from hand to hand.

Black Crane stepped forward, his hands extended, empty. "Come, let us talk about the boy."

Black Coyote, who had been watching Little Wolf, saw the Crane's move toward him and made a stabbing lunge. His knife sank deep into Black Crane's chest.

The watching crowd gasped as if with one voice as Black Crane fell to his knees, clutching the bubbling wound. Black Coyote stared as if he couldn't believe his eyes. Little Wolf caught Black Crane and gently lowered him to the ground. He held his hand over the Crane's mouth, but he wasn't breathing. He looked for Caroline and motioned her to come forward.

She sheathed her knife and felt for the Crane's heartbeat in his neck, but there was nothing. "I'm sorry," she said. "He's dead."

Black Coyote stepped off the dirty trail in the snow and stabbed his knife into a snowdrift to clean it, turning his back on everyone.

Little Wolf rose and shook his quirt free, letting it hang loose at his side. "Leave," he told Black Coyote. "Take your wife and anyone else who wishes to go. You are no longer Cheyenne."

Black Coyote said nothing, didn't even look at the chief, just turned toward Bridge's shelter.

Caroline had known Little Wolf would banish him. He had no choice, according to Cheyenne law. Suspecting he'd try to take the boy with him, she'd circled behind Black Coyote and now stepped between him and the shelter. She faced him, knife drawn. "You heard your chief. Leave."

"Not without the boy."

Black Coyote flipped the knife in his hand. Blade down, ready to kill again, he approached Caroline. Simultaneously, Little Wolf's whip cracked and an arrow hit Black Coyote squarely in the thigh.

On a rock a few feet away, Swallow notched another arrow into his bow.

Black Coyote's lip curled as he glared at Swallow, then Caroline, but he stepped back and sheathed his knife.

"Leave," Little Wolf told him again. "The boy stays with me. I will return him to his people."

Black Coyote broke off the arrow in his leg, threw it to the ground and glared at the people around him. His wife rode up, leading his horse and a mule already loaded with their belongings.

Relief rushed through Caroline as Black Coyote leaped onto his horse. Apparently, they had planned to take the boy, then run. Thank God Little Wolf had been close, had stopped them.

Screaming his loud, ululating war cry, Black Coyote galloped out of camp, nearly riding down an elderly woman as he went. Four men followed him.

Little Wolf nodded to a warrior, who mounted and followed more slowly. Little Hawk and several other warriors picked up Black Crane's body and carried it to his shelter, followed by his grieving family. Little Wolf wasted no time chastising Caroline.

"Never again do anything so foolish, woman! If Swallow had not shot him, I could not have stopped him from killing you."

She blanched at the anger radiating from him. "Did you think he would not do it because you are a woman? You are *veho!* White! His sworn enemy. If he had killed you I could not have punished him. You would have died for nothing. If you have no care for your life, remember others who do."

Caroline shook with the force of the emotion roiling through her. "I wanted to save the child," she said. "That's all I thought about. I knew I couldn't stop Black Coyote. I only wanted to slow him down, to give you a chance to save Bridge and the boy."

Swallow jumped down from the rock and slid down a

snowdrift to join them. He stepped up to Little Wolf, his expression solemn. "I do good?"

Little Wolf nodded and rumpled his hair. "Good bow. Where you get it?"

"Zach make it for me, for Chris-muss," Swallow said, giving it to him.

"You saved my life," Caroline said and hugged him tight.

"Of course," he said, smiling. "I love you, Caro-line."

"I love you, too, Swallow," she said. "Let's go check on the boy."

Little Wolf handed back the bow. "I will look at the boy. He needs quiet, rest."

Caroline and Swallow watched him climb the sand hill and duck into Bridge's shelter. She crossed her arms over her waist. Those two were hiding the boy, she realized. Now, why would they do that?

Chapter Twenty-one

Zach broke into a sweat. Gunshot! He'd heard a gunshot. He drew his weapon and charged up the stairs, propelled by women's screams and a man shouting for a doctor. He dashed into the theater box, but the assassin had jumped and there he stood onstage, pausing to shout something at the crowd. Booth. How had he gotten past him? Zach took aim, but Booth looked up, recognized him and ran.

Another shot, then a flurry of shots. Zach frowned. Something was wrong. There hadn't been more shots, just screaming, shouting, and more screaming.

Someone shook him awake. He stared up at the soldier above him, his gut knotted, his clothes plastered to his skin. Where was he?

"Wake up!" The man yanked up his braces. "They're makin' a break fer it! I'm gonna go shoot me some Injun!"

Zach reacted instinctively with a left jab, followed by a right cross. He shook his head to clear it, shaking free of the nightmare. He'd been dreaming, he realized, but this was no dream. He recognized the barracks finally and realized he was still at Camp Robinson. Given the increase in gunfire and the shouts and confusion of the men, he deduced the Cheyenne were making a run for it. He kicked the unconscious soldier off his boots. One less gun for the Cheyenne to dodge. He intended to aid the Cheyenne in their escape attempt. Though he was a sworn officer, he couldn't abide the way these people had been treated. As he hurriedly dressed, he vowed that if he had a clear shot at Wessells tonight, he'd take it. He'd be saving the Army the trouble and expense of court-martialing him.

The gunfire was steady now. Amid shouted orders, he heard the war chants of the Cheyenne men in jarring contrast to the screams and cries of the women and children.

He cautioned himself to be alert as he hindered the soldiers tonight. Wessells would certainly have warned his officers to keep a close eye on him, but Zach hoped that the confusion would give him the time he needed to outmaneuver them.

The light from a distant moon gleamed on old, crusty snow, casting just enough light to distort shadows. A cloudy or moonless night would have been better for the Cheyenne, but desperate men weren't known to be patient. Zach cursed the pale light that made him a walking target in his black duster. The Cheyenne would have to run for the nearby river channel and the bluffs on the far side. He circled behind the guardhouse where the Cheyenne had been held prisoner and moved up one side, sticking to the shadows. He passed one dead soldier, and found four dead Cheyenne men in front of the guardhouse. A bloody trail led to the other barracks. The boarded-up windows had been kicked out from inside and a couple of sections of wall had been loosened. The break had been well-planned, and executed late at night when the fewest sentries would be posted. Hearing voices inside, he returned to the back of the building, heading for the bridge across the river. After the stables, there was no cover, leaving him no choice but to crouch and run for it. With this light, and all the open ground between them and the bluffs, Zach didn't like the Cheyenne's chances.

As he'd expected, the Cheyenne had headed for the river, leaving a wide, bloody trail in the snow. Before he reached the river, he counted twenty dead: eight warriors, the rest women and children. Jaw clenched, he double-checked his load and ammunition. Keeping low, he hurried to catch up with the main body of soldiers. He couldn't start shooting from the rear; someone would notice men shot in the back while chasing Cheyenne. He had to find a parallel position. Once he slid into the river channel, he realized the Cheyenne had split up. Gunfire came from both directions.

He paused beside a dead soldier to take his weapon and ammunition, and decide which direction to take. Another soldier scouting the bank swung his gun around, but held when he saw that Zach wasn't Cheyenne. "You one of them ranchers?"

"Yeah," Zach said. "Where'd those savages run to?"

"They're hiding across the river, trying to climb up those bluffs," the man said, turning to look across the frozen water at the sheer rock face on the opposite side. Zach brought the butt of his Peacemaker down on his skull and the man dropped without a sound. Zach sighed. If he had many more encounters like this one, he'd have to make a run for it soon; they'd be looking for him. Better stay low, keep hidden and work fast.

Across the river, several Cheyenne stepped out of the shadows and began frantically climbing the rocks. The tall one raised a hand in greeting and Zach recognized Dull Knife. Zach tipped his hat, watched until Dull Knife disappeared into the dark, and whispered, "Good luck."

In the direction of the heaviest gunfire, he spotted a

group of civilians, all bunched up and shooting across
the river at running Cheyenne. Their targets were running shadows, indistinguishable as people, let alone men,
women and children.

Zach's blood ran cold. They didn't care! Man, woman
or child, it was all the same to them. He eased closer,
slipped behind a tree and opened fire on the civilians,
aiming low when he could, trying not to kill. He'd taken
out three or four when the group split up, some running
northwest toward the heaviest gunfire, others taking
cover and returning his fire.

As he neared the main body, he found the far bank of
the river, a steep and slippery slope, dotted with dead and
wounded Cheyenne. Too parched from thirst after two
weeks without water to keep running, many of the
women and children had paused to drink at the river's
edge. Others had fallen through the ice into the freezing
water, which left them too weak to run. The warriors who
had held back to aid the slower runners made easy targets against the pale snow.

For two hours, Zach shadowed the main body of
shooters—soldiers and civilians—staying as close as he
dared and shooting only from dense cover, the percus-
sion of gunfire broken only by Wessells's repeated orders
to "Shoot them! Shoot them all!" and the occasional
screams of the wounded.

When the shooting died down, the hunting began.
Soldiers combed the bluffs, above and below. At one
point, Zach watched, unable to help as a soldier faced
an armed warrior and demanded his surrender. The
warrior refused to drop his gun, instead taking quick
aim. The soldier's first shot didn't kill him immediately.
His second shot did. Many of the soldiers took the
women and children captive and sent them back to
camp for medical attention. Most didn't, and the civilians who had joined the hunt with such exuberance
were intent on taking trophies: pipes, knives, scalps,
guns, anything they could get their hands on.

Zach stepped behind a wagon carrying two men, joining the steady stream passing between the fort and the bluffs, hoping to escape notice. His plan appeared to be working, he thought, as a civilian rode by, heading for the river.

"Hey, Laughlin!" the wagon driver called. "You come to join the fun?"

"Got here too late for the shootin'," the rider answered cheerily, "but I kilt me a squaw." He waved a bloody trophy and rode on up the river, joining the cadre of men tracking the fugitives.

A soldier reined in beside the wagon and ordered the men to return to the fort. As they passed, he reached into the wagon and pulled a blanket off a stack. "Where'd you fellers get this?"

"We found it lyin' on the snow," the driver said. His passenger nodded. "Yup, jus' lyin' there. Don' know who it belonged to."

The soldier stared into each face, then tossed the blanket back into the wagon. "Get moving. And don't come back here tonight."

"Yassir," the driver said, and snapped the reins. "Damn bluecoats. Jus' hafta spoil our fun."

Zach kept his gaze on the pile of blankets in the back of the wagon as he trailed it back across the bridge. He stayed far enough back that he didn't make the driver suspicious. After the horrors of the night, the sight of those blankets made his blood boil. He'd seen them before, had a stack of them shoved under his nose the first night he'd met Caroline. He knew exactly where those men had *acquired* them. He'd last seen them wrapped around the waists of fleeing Cheyenne. Zach moved a little closer to the wagon.

As they neared the stables, he quickstepped up its side.

"You fellows interested in seein' my souvenir?" he asked, reaching into his duster and patting his chest. He gave them his best leer.

"Whatcha got?" the driver demanded.

Zach looked around, keeping his hand inside his coat. "Not out here." He jerked his head toward the deep shadows at the back of the stables. "Follow me."

"Cooo-eee!" the passenger whooped. "Ah cain't wait to see this! Whatcha think he's got in thar? Maybe some squaw's . . . umph!"

"Hush!" the driver said, his voice low, his quick glance around them wary. "You know you ain't supposed to say nuthin'."

"Pull up here," Zach said, once the wagon lurched into the dark. When the driver hopped to the ground, he stepped into Zach's fist, an uppercut to the jaw. He went down like a brick. Zach wanted to punish the second man, but quickly tired of his whimpering and knocked him out, too. He left the two lying in the snow, side by side.

He drove the wagon to the fort hospital and left it tied to the hitching post, hoping that some of the scavenged blankets—and whatever else the thieves had stolen—might make it back into Cheyenne hands.

After collecting his saddle and gear from the empty barracks, which was adjacent to the hospital, he cautiously made his way to the stables. He was relieved to find them deserted when he slipped inside. Demon whickered a greeting, tossing his head and prancing in his stall. He butted Zach's chest when he stepped into the stall to begin saddling him.

"Heard the shootin', didn't you, boy? Well, that's over for now, but we've got some ridin' to do tonight."

Zach headed northeast from the fort, aiming Demon's nose for the ranch of Little Wolf's friend, the one who'd been locked up for helping the Cheyenne. Zach needed to hide out for a while, but he wanted to be able to slip out to reconnoiter at night. He hoped that some of the Cheyenne had escaped and he wanted to be close if they needed help getting back to Little Wolf. Wessells would eventually send men out to hunt for him, but chasing down the rest of the Cheyenne would keep him preoccupied. Zach needed to warn Little Wolf, and let him know that Dull Knife had escaped, but not until Zach was certain he wasn't being followed.

He pulled his duster tighter around him. His nose was already a solid, unmovable lump on his face, his ears had gone numb, and his breath was forming icicles on his hat brim. Yet, despite the cold, he found himself praying for a good blizzard.

Little Wolf paced inside the brush circle at the center of the camp beside a small fire, waiting. Waiting. Too many days had passed since Zach had ridden to Camp Robinson. His wives sat beside the fire, and Caroline with them. They, too, were uneasy, their eyes often lifting to the east, watching for riders.

He could not tell them what he had seen in the smoke, what he saw even now on the dirty snow around him. Blood. Everywhere he looked. But when he looked again in the light of day, the snow gleamed pure and white. He feared for his brother and his people, for the people who trusted him to lead them. The spirits whispered in his dreams and sang songs of death and sorrow. Had he brought his people here only to be slaughtered like cattle? Had they run so far only to die in the snow?

What must he do now? Could he keep his people's blood from staining the snow?

A crow cawed twice and Little Wolf swung to face the east. A man was coming, someone the sentry knew. The crow cawed again, twice. Two men. Woodenthigh joined him at the fire, then Bridge. He watched for the men, his belly twisting. The first man stopped well out of shouting distance, his head covered and hanging.

Bad news. Why did the fool worry about old traditions now, when soldiers rode the snow-covered plains behind him? Little Wolf nodded to Feather, wanting her to leave, but she shook her head, as did Quiet Woman. Caroline watched for the second man.

"Tell him to come quickly," Little Wolf said and sent a man out to him with a horse.

Some of the women who had gathered began to wail. Little Wolf silenced them with a slash of his hand. "Silence! There will be time for mourning later."

The runner refused the horse and walked the rest of the way to Little Wolf. When he lowered the blanket he'd kept tight over his head, the women cried out, for half his face was ruined by a gunshot wound. Bridge shuffled away to get his medicine while Woodenthigh and Little Wolf helped the man sit down beside the fire. Feather offered him water to drink but the man wouldn't let her touch his face. "Speak . . . first," he said, his words slow and painful.

Caroline gave a shout and jumped to her feet, running east. Zach McCallister trotted toward them. He slid off his horse when she reached him, and would have fallen if she hadn't caught him. Woodenthigh ran to help her bring Zach to the fire. The wounded man shied away from Zach, but Feather, kneeling nearby, whispered to him and he sighed, nodding.

Woodenthigh settled Zach beside the fire, but both he and the wounded man pushed back from the now blazing fire. Their bodies could not tolerate the sudden heat.

"My horse," Zach said, and tried to get up. Woodenthigh pressed him back down and Little Wolf sent one of the young braves to tend the animal.

"Tell us," he said, and settled near the two men. Caroline translated for Zach as the wounded man told of the capture of Dull Knife's people, of the leaders taken prisoner and placed in irons, of the people's refusal to be taken south to the reservation. Angry murmurs rippled through the crowd as he told of the fasting, then the time with no heat and no water when no one was allowed to leave the prison barracks, but the women were taken to the bushes once a day by armed soldiers. Silence again fell when he told of the breakout and the running, of soldiers chasing and shooting, of women and children falling like bloody rags against the snow.

At last Zach spoke, when it was clear the wounded man

could say no more. "Over thirty dead," he said, his eyes
black hollows in his face as he stared into the fire. "More
than that wounded. For two weeks the soldiers hunted
the ones who escaped into the hills north of the river. Little Finger Nail led them. They finally threw up a breast-
work and made one last stand. And what a fight it was,"
he said, finally looking up. "They died fighting, every
man, and the Nail was last."

"Who escaped? What of Morning Star?" Little Wolf
feared the worst, but Zach smiled at him. "I think I saved
him. I knocked out a soldier who was shooting at a bunch
of Cheyenne and Dull Knife walked out from under the
bluff. I saw him climb out of there and no one has seen
him since. He may have found a safe place to hide." Zach
shrugged. "That's all I know."

"It is true," the wounded man said with a proud nod.
"Our chief escaped, but so many died." He started listing
the dead, softly speaking the names that would never
again be spoken, out of respect for the dead. If the *Tsitsitas* survived and found their way home to the Powder
River, the names of many of these brave ones would be
given to the children still to be born.

Little Wolf walked away from the camp and climbed a
far sand hill, whose crown had been scooped hollow by
the wind. He came here often to think and plan, and pray.

Soon he must decide what to do. The soldiers would be
busy for a time burying the dead and caring for the
wounded, but he must prepare his people to run again,
soon. These new deaths made him more determined
than ever to reach his goal to take his people home.

For now, he could do nothing but mourn the brave men
and women lost forever, and pray to the powers above and
below to spare the few *Tsitsitas* who remained.

Caroline sat in the dark watching Zach sleep. She'd given
him a tea for pain and put him to bed in her shelter
where her medicine bag was handy. Almost three weeks
he'd been gone, and most of that time he'd had no shel-

ter. He'd barely regained his strength from the knife
wound, and now . . .

He kicked off his blankets, tossing and moaning in the
throes of another nightmare. The man had few, if any, secrets left from her after his earlier delirium, and now
this. He had taken direct action against his orders by
helping the Cheyenne escape, and nearly got himself
killed in the process. She wasn't familiar with military law,
but she suspected he could be court-martialed for what
he'd done. All her assumptions about him went up in
smoke.

She didn't know what to think anymore, except that
she admired him. And she could no longer deny that
she'd fallen in love with him.

She hadn't spoken a word of this to Little Wolf, but she
believed he knew. Why else would he have sent Zach to
Camp Robinson? And if he knew, why wasn't he concerned about the enemy in his camp? Was he keeping
Zach close so that he could keep an eye on him? She'd
observed Little Wolf, especially his plans and maneuver-
ings, and she knew he did nothing without purpose. How
did he plan to use Zach? And where did she figure into
his plans? Little Wolf was very intuitive about people.
Had he realized that Zach would be a strong advocate
when the time came for him to plead for leniency from
the government? Did he hope that Zach would be able to
convince General Sheridan to allow the Cheyenne to remain in the north?

She sighed and rested her cheek on her upraised
knees. That was a huge responsibility for one man to
bear. Almost as much a burden as Little Wolf's. What
about Zach's goals, his search for his son? If Zach learned
that the boy was among the Sioux, would he leave the
Cheyenne and rush off to rescue him? How could Little
Wolf ensure that Zach stayed with the *Ohmeseheso* until
the end?

For a solid week, Caroline pondered these questions,
and debated confronting Little Wolf as she nursed Zach.

With good food and warm shelter, he recovered his strength quickly, but his recent experiences had left a deep impression. He was more withdrawn, more somber than ever before. He spent a great deal of time alone with Little Wolf, smoking, talking, walking. She watched and waited, dreading their coming confrontation, doing nothing to precipitate it.

The cold had deepened, making their flimsy shelters nearly untenable. How she longed for solid walls around her, for the warmth, comfort and protection of a real home. She began to hate the acrid stench of wood smoke that lingered on her skin, in her hair. It seemed to permeate her very being. She craved a bath, not the icy dash of freezing water against her shrinking skin. And then she felt guilty. At least she was alive, not dead, laid out in a row beside thirty of her friends on the banks of the White River.

She missed the closeness she and Zach had shared before the troubles of the Cheyenne had consumed his spirit. She felt him watching her, his eyes hungry. But when she smiled at him, he looked away. He'd kept to his own shelter after that first night, saying he didn't want to keep her awake. She let him go, let him take his secrets with him, but didn't tell him he needn't bother, that she already knew every one and loved him anyway. She didn't bother because she knew their relationship was doomed. Even if he fell in love with her and begged her to marry him—which she expected would happen the same day she reached up and plucked the moon out of the night sky—she could never marry him.

She still had one secret left, and she planned to keep it.

"Caroline!" Zach came running up the sand hill, calling her name.

"What's going on?" she asked as he reached the door. She looked past him and her heart started racing. Swallow wasn't far behind and he had his small bag of belongings slung over his shoulder, along with his bow and quiver. He tugged on the halters of two of her mules, hurrying them through camp, which was alive with people running and quietly gathering their belongings.

"We're leaving?" she asked, turning back to Zach.

"Yes, but we're not going with the Cheyenne," he said. "The wolves have spotted soldiers coming this way. They may not know we're here, but Little Wolf wants to get deeper into the sand hills and start moving north again. He's not taking Swallow or Swift Fox. There's been too much bad talk since the deaths at Camp Robinson. I've agreed to keep them and follow him to Fort Keogh, help him talk to the officers."

She nodded, her mind whirling and began loading her belongings. Luckily, there weren't many supplies left to pack. "Tell Little Wolf he can take three of the pack horses," she told Zach over her shoulder.

"I've given him four," Zach said.

"Four?" she said, facing him, hands on her hips. "Those are *my* mules. . . ."

"Darlin'," he said, leaning down to give her a quick kiss on the cheek. "There isn't time to argue. He needs them more than we do. Now, what can I do to help?"

The next hour passed in a blur as she and Zach loaded her meager belongings onto the backs of the two mules with Swallow's help. There was no time for more than a quick farewell hug with Feather and Quiet Woman, but Little Wolf brought Swift Fox to her shelter and pushed him toward her.

"I will send for you when the time comes." Little Wolf nodded at Swallow, Caroline and the boy. "They are yours now," he told Zach, as cryptic as always.

Caroline stilled, wondering how Zach would respond. When he didn't, she realized that he wouldn't look for deeper meaning in Little Wolf's comment. He was more worried about getting packed and away before soldiers arrived and found them in the camp.

Little Wolf gripped Zach's shoulder and looked into his eyes. "While you were at Camp Robinson, I learned that Black Coyote first brought your horses to us. He brought them with him when he came back from visiting the Sioux last summer. None of my men would tell me this while he lived among us, but once he was banished after killing Black Crane, many things were revealed to me." He released Zach's shoulder and stepped over to Swallow.

"Be strong," he told him. "Watch over Swift Fox. He is young and does not understand our ways."

Swallow nodded, his eyes filling with tears. He caught Caroline's hand and hung on tight.

For the first time since she'd known him, Little Wolf reached out and touched her face, and she realized he was saying farewell.

"Be careful," she said, love and gratitude for this man who had been like a father to her welling up inside her. "We'll look for you in the Powder River valley." Then she kissed his cheek.

He nodded and crouched in front of Swift Fox. "Be patient," he said, speaking in English.

To Caroline's surprise, the boy nodded and hugged Little Wolf. Without another word, Little Wolf left. Caroline watched him go with deep trepidation. Would this be the last time she saw him, and his wives, alive? Their fate loomed before them like a frightening specter. So many things could still go wrong. But she would welcome an end to the Cheyenne's desperate flight. She hoped that their final destination would justify their sacrifices.

Zach didn't let them watch the Cheyenne leave. He put her on one of his mares, Swallow on the other, and Swift Fox on her horse. Caroline stared in amazement. He rode as if he'd been born on horseback. She shouldn't have been surprised—after all, he was Sioux. Zach smiled broadly as the boy kicked the horse into motion, solemn and completely at home in the saddle. He leaned down and patted the horse's neck and its ears flicked forward as it moved into a trot. Swallow crowed in delight, startling his own mount.

"Well done," Zach said, beaming as if he'd taught Swift

Fox himself. He took the leading reins of one mule and tied the other mule's reins to Caroline's pommel, then led them out of Lost Chokecherry Valley, heading north and west of the trail Little Wolf and the Cheyenne had taken, out of the sand hills.

Caroline wasn't surprised at all to find herself teary-eyed as they left the valley behind. Though it had become a frail existence as winter dragged on, for a while it had felt like paradise.

"Get some rest now, boys," Zach said, settling them in the flimsy shelter he and Caroline had erected in a small grove of trees, where they hoped a fire would go unnoticed. Black Coyote and his friends were still at large, though Little Wolf's wolves had reported that they'd tracked the group heading north. Zach didn't trust the man not to double back and try to take Swift Fox, especially if he'd learned that Little Wolf hadn't taken him along. Black Coyote wasn't the only predator on the plains. Zach had made a few enemies at Camp Robinson, but he believed General Sheridan would listen first and shoot second. He didn't think any of the men he'd injured could identify him, but his sudden disappearance on that particular night would cast suspicion on him.

Tonight, he needed to discuss his plans with Caroline; tomorrow they'd begin executing them. Together, he hoped.

"Swift Fox," she began and shook her head as Zach joined her. They'd decided to tether the horses closer to their shelter after hearing several wolves howling. "He looks so wild. We've got to cut his hair, get him some different clothes." She sighed. "Even so, no one will mistake him for white. How are we going to keep him safe?"

"Well, bathing would help, don't you think?" Zach grinned down at her. How like her to fret over the safety of the child when her own safety was unsure.

Caroline nodded vigorously. "It's easy to see that two men have had charge of him. His skin is so dark, I don't know where the dirt stops and he starts. I'd love to get him in a real tub with a big bar of lye soap, but I'm afraid he wouldn't have much skin left when I got through with him. Do you think he'll miss those rags he's wearing if we burn them?"

Zach chuckled and pulled her into his arms. She laid her cheek on his chest, over his heart, and closed her eyes. As she settled against him, his worry subsided. "We'll get through this," he whispered against her hair. "Haven't we managed everythin' else we've come up against?"

"One way or another," she whispered. She angled her head back and smiled up at him. "But aren't you getting a little tired of having to manage? Don't you ever long for normal?"

"What's normal?" he asked, tweaking her hair. "It's all a matter of perspective. What's normal for you—livin' in a hole dug into the side of a sand hill and cookin' over a fire for months—would be some other woman's worst nightmare."

"You're right," she said, and her gaze slid to his lips. "But we've been so busy *managing,* we haven't had time for *enjoying,* or *learning.*" She reached up and kissed him. It was a quick, innocent brush of her lips, but it ignited a firestorm in his belly.

"Not because I didn't want you," he said, lifting her onto her toes. "And now," he said with a glance aside at the two sleeping boys, "we'll never be alone."

"We'll manage," she said and met his mouth with a fire of her own.

The kiss was hungry, feral, and quickly flared out of control. Zach forgot caution. His lips devoured hers. His tongue swept hers aside and claimed her mouth. He was ravenous and impatient, and she threw herself into the kiss exactly as he'd always dreamed she would. Her response was so passionate that he almost forgot who she was, what she'd been through. He felt her surrender, her acceptance of him and reveled in it. He'd waited so long to make her truly his. He didn't know if he could hold back, go slowly.

"Caroline, if you don't want this, tell me to stop now," he said, dragging his lips from her mouth and down her neck.

"Zach, I . . ."

A bloodcurdling scream ripped through the quiet. They froze in each other's arms and stared. Swift Fox lay rigid on his bed, his eyes closed, his mouth open wide in an unending cry of agony.

Zach forgot everything but getting to the boy. His scream tore at something primal inside him. He knelt beside Swift Fox and tried talking, but it didn't help. Zach hovered over him, unsure how to help him.

"Rub his arms," Caroline suggested. "He's not hearing your voice."

"But he hates to be touched," Zach said. "He's not going to hear anything I say, and I don't want to wake him up. He'd be frightened."

"Like this," Caroline said and knelt on the other side. "Hush now. Everything's all right. You're safe." She spoke firmly, soothingly and picked up the boy's hand. As she continued to speak, she rubbed his hand, then his arm and finally his shoulder. "Do it!" she told Zach when the screams continued.

"Shhh," Zach said, mimicking her tone and actions. "You're safe now. No one's going to hurt you." Swift Fox stopped screaming abruptly. His lashes flickered and Zach continued, hoping he was finally hearing him. He rubbed both arms from shoulder to wrist, aware that Caroline had moved away to reassure Swallow, who had awakened and was now sitting bolt upright in a pile of blankets.

Swallow stared at the sleeping boy, then rolled over and pulled his blanket over his head. When Zach looked back at Swift Fox, he had curled into a tight ball and was asleep again.

"Was he doing that back at camp?" Zach asked Caroline. "I don't remember hearing anyone screaming, and I would have noticed that sound."

"Not that I knew of," Caroline said, "but Bridge may have given him a sleeping draught. If his nightmares are this disruptive, I'll do that starting tomorrow night."

"I don't want him drugged," Zach said, sickened by the thought. The few times he'd been drugged, he'd awakened feeling like his head was stuffed with feathers, and he'd been groggy for hours. If they were going to keep up with the swift-moving Cheyenne, Swift Fox had to be alert. Also, he'd need his wits about him if they ran into any soldiers or unfriendly civilians.

Suddenly, Swift Fox started screaming again. Zach quieted him, but each time he got him calmed down, the boy would resume his ungodly shriek. Finally, Zach lay down beside him and held him. In seconds, Swift Fox relaxed and slipped into a deeper sleep. His breathing became slower and his eyes stopped jerking under his eyelids.

When Caroline brought Zach a rolled-up blanket to use as a pillow, he caught her hand and turned away from the boy to whisper, "We've got to bathe him tomorrow. And I think your sleeping draught might be a good idea—for all of us."

Chapter Twenty-two

Zach and Caroline gave up on bathing Swift Fox the second time he ran away and hid for the entire day. Every time she pulled out her scissors, he disappeared. Even demonstrating on Swallow's unruly locks didn't persuade him that she didn't mean to hurt him. Whenever they tried to bathe or in any way civilize him, he disappeared for hours. They'd fallen well behind the Cheyenne trying to deal with him.

Her heart ached at his skittish behavior, and Zach's patience with him amazed her. "He's been severely trauma-

tized, living with that bastard," he said as they searched
for him again, more than a week later. "Maybe he's afraid
of me. At the next trading post, I'll leave you and Swallow
with him while I purchase supplies, and some clothes for
all of us."

"And how do you plan to do that?" she asked. "I'm almost broke and I still haven't paid you. You should have
taken the money when I offered it to you back in Dodge
City."

He backed her up against a nearby tree and grinned
down at her. "It's not money I want from you, woman."

She shoved him away and glared at him, her hands on
her hips. "Are you saying you'll take my *favors* in lieu of
my money?" The surprise and dismay in his expression
told her he hadn't intended to insult her, but his careless
words stung. Also, the reminder that their time together
would soon be over left her feeling panicky. She had
lashed out before examining her reasons.

"I'll find the money to pay you, even if it takes years,
even if I have to sweep floors at a trading post or mercantile, if there is such a thing at Fort Keogh. But you'll
never touch me again, Zach McCallister. Not now. Not
ever."

Tears burned her eyes. Before they could fall and hu-
miliate her, she dashed away from him. "Hunt for the boy
yourself. I'll be back in camp."

The next instant the ground tilted and she was hoisted
upward by a pair of strong arms. Zach had lifted her as if
she weighed no more than a child.

"I'm touching you now and I'm going to keep touching
you until you shut up and listen." He held her high against
his chest, his eyes smoky and his face taut with anger.

"Put me down, you pistol-packing bully!" She squirmed
to get free, but his arms only tightened around her. "I am
not your *whore!*"

"That had better be the last time you say that word," he
said, his voice too flat, too calm. "Have I ever treated you
like a whore?"

"No." She bit out the word, holding very still. She wasn't about to put her arms around his neck, even though she feared he might drop her at any moment.

"You're the one who brought up money, not me. Have I ever asked you for it? Has our relationship ever been about money?"

"No," she said, "but it's come in very handy."

"To satisfy your needs, and to help the Cheyenne," he said, his gaze fixed on her face. "I've never asked you for money and I never will."

"All right," she said. "You've made your point. Put me down." She wedged her elbow against his chest and stared over his shoulder, avoiding his gaze.

"I'll put you down when I'm damn good and ready, woman." He gave her a sudden squeeze. Startled, her gaze flew to his. "Kiss me."

"What!" Outraged, she squirmed in his arms. "Of all the nerve," she shouted, then gasped as he suddenly released her legs. She caught his shirt in both fists to keep from falling.

"That's better," he said and yanked her to him so hard that she lost her breath as her breasts flattened against his chest. He wrapped both arms around her and lifted her completely off the ground. She had no choice but to hang onto his neck as he took his kiss.

She groaned, knowing she wouldn't be able to withstand his sensual onslaught, and then she lost the will to fight him. She wanted him to kiss her. *Heavens!* She'd been wishing he'd kiss her every night. The last time they'd been together, he'd given her such intense pleasure, she still couldn't believe it was possible, and was anxious to repeat the experience, mainly to find out if her body would respond like that again. The sand hills camp had been busy and their privacy disrupted constantly, and now tending to the needs of the two boys left them with no time for themselves. Here, alone in the woods, she let go of her anger and frustration, and threw herself into the kiss, answering each bold thrust of his tongue. Her fingers slid into the hair hanging over his collar and tangled there, though he seemed oblivious as he turned his head, slanting his mouth over hers.

She loved the feel of his arms around her, binding her to him. She tried to turn off her mind, but she couldn't. Though she loved kissing Zach and his caresses had brought her fulfillment such as she'd never believed possible, they still had not mated. He still hadn't put his hard male part into her, and she knew that when he did, it would hurt. It always hurt.

Could she relax enough to let him do *that* to her, when she'd vowed that no man would ever touch her that way again? If she couldn't, she'd never know if it was possible to find pleasure in the act of mating. She truly wanted to know why Feather and Quiet Woman always left Little Wolf's bed smiling. And to do that, she had to trust her body to this man, to whom she hadn't yet entrusted her heart.

She focused on the kiss, letting herself enjoy it, responding with more enthusiasm, and her body responded. She felt her woman's place turning warm and becoming damp, and she felt the need to be touched there. At the thought of Zach touching her there, her body spasmed, surprising her. She heard a whimper and was shocked to realize that it came from her.

Zach heard her and reacted immediately. Without breaking the kiss, he pulled her legs up his thighs, then higher until her ankles were crossed behind his hips. With her legs spread wide around him, she felt vulnerable. For warmth and comfort, she wore a cutoff pair of pantalets under her buckskin skirt, but there was no mistaking his rock-hard erection through the flimsy cloth. With his arms under her buttocks supporting her, he rocked her against his erection. She tried to slow the motion, but he slid his hands under her buttocks and pulled her flush against him. When he raised, then lowered her hips, the friction soon dampened her pantalets.

The hard ridge of his erection throbbed at her core,

pushing against the damp cloth, nudging between the sensitive lips, then it pressed that very sensitive spot above it. She groaned as ripples of sensation shot outward, then faded. There was no pain! She felt him there, poised to enter her body, prevented only by a wisp of cloth, and her body welcomed him. Her heart pounded in her chest as she hung suspended, on the brink of discovery.

Then Zach tossed his head back and sucked in a deep breath, his eyes squeezed shut as he took another, then another. He let her slide down his body, bracing her against him when her feet touched the ground.

"What's wrong?" she whispered against his sweat-dampened shirt. "Did I do it wrong?"

"You're wonderful," he said and pressed his forehead to hers. "Too wonderful." He leaned down and kissed her—a light press of his lips; a mere shadow of the kiss that had erupted into a maelstrom and left her shaken.

"When I make love to you, it won't be a quick romp in the woods." After one more huge breath, he took her hand and turned with her back to camp. "The boys are waiting at our camp."

She stared up at him. "They are? How do you know that?"

He put an arm around her shoulders and pulled her against his side. She slipped her arm around his waist and snuggled against him. "Swallow was here."

"What?" She braced her other hand against his waist and looked up at him, horrified. "Did he see us?"

Zach grinned down at her. "He didn't see much. He rubbed his stomach and motioned toward camp. The boy was with him. They're probably both hungry and tired."

Caroline pulled away from Zach and stopped. Mortified, she pressed her hands to her burning cheeks. "What should we say? We should have been hunting for the boy and instead, Swallow found us, like that . . ."

"Swallow wasn't embarrassed," Zach said, rubbing her arms at the shoulder. "In fact, he looked downright pleased. Gave me a big grin."

"Ooohhh," Caroline groaned. "How can I face him? Them?"

"You have nothing to be ashamed of. So they caught us kissing in the woods." He lifted her hand to his lips. As he pressed a kiss to the back of it, he stared into her eyes. "Feeling better? About this?" He gestured between the two of them. "Us?"

Briefly, she let herself imagine that there really was an "us," that she could trust Zach with her body *and* her heart. She wrapped her arms around him and sighed when he hugged her back. "For now," she said, "but I'm beginning to think we'll never get to that final lesson."

"We will," he assured her. "I promise."

Since those lessons were all she'd ever have of him, she meant to savor every one. She hoped, rather than believed, he'd have an opportunity to make good on his promise.

Little Wolf walked the line of the new breastworks finished only that night. *Hou,* he nodded, seeing the wood piled and ready, the water set aside, the guns and ammunition set where they could be easily reached if the *veho* soldiers came to fight. His people were tired, sick of running. They longed for peace, but they were ready to fight, and die, here at the mouth of the Powder River.

The last running from Lost Chokecherry Valley had been long and slow through the heavy cold that reached deep into a man's bones and slowed his very heart, to the blizzard that ended up only being enough snow to wet the ground. The people had smiled when the warm winds from the north blew into their faces, but then the ice began to break on the big rivers—the Yellowstone and the Powder—with a mighty noise, like the crack of giant guns. The ice split into great blocks that dammed the rivers and sent the icy waters flooding the lands around them and the people hurrying with them.

But the cold had kept the soldiers close to their warm fires and the noise of the melting rivers had hidden the people's passing. They had ridden through day and night, meeting few men desperate enough to travel in the deep cold. Now two Lakota scouts had come to visit their strong place and take word back to the *veho* soldiers who waited.

"We will not shoot first," Little Wolf said, watching the scouts take note of the breastworks built across the mouth of Hole in the Rock to give his men cover while they returned the soldiers' fire. "But we will fight if we have to."

The scouts nodded. "We will tell White Hat your words."

Little Wolf joined his people, making this last stronghold a safe place for them to fight, but hoping White Hat Clark, his *veho* friend among the soldiers, a man who had helped the Cheyenne before the long trip to Oklahoma, could help them find a home here in the north.

The scouts returned, whipping their horses. White Hat wanted to speak with him, wanted him to leave his strong place and come to his camp. Little Wolf searched the faces of the scouts and saw no treachery there. His heart told him he could trust this *veho* who had helped his people in the past, that he was a true and honest man, like Caroline's man, Zach McCallister. He knew he could trust these two good men, but they were not the Great Father in the east. They had little real power, but because they were good men, their words would be heard by the men who held the power.

He remembered the words of the Comanche shaman, the Great Spirit's messenger: . . . *you will be allowed to live where you wish.* Renewed hope filled his heart, his chest, and he knew what he must do.

"I will come to talk with my friend, White Hat." He gave up his weapons and followed the scouts out of his strong place, leaving his people behind.

"If I do not return, you know what you must do," he told Little Hawk, a good, strong warrior whom the people respected and would follow. Then, as if naked in the dark, he went alone to the *veho* camp.

* * *

Zach was relaxing by the fire, watching Caroline settle the boys into their beds that night, when he heard galloping hoofbeats approaching. Without a word of instruction, everyone sprang into action. Swift Fox grabbed his moccasins and drew his knife before he hid behind the shelter. Swallow took cover with an arrow already notched to his bow. Caroline snatched up a rifle, loaded it quickly and took cover among the horses. Each was in place in a matter of seconds. Zach checked the load in his rifle and stepped out of the firelight, aiming at the riders heading for his fire.

"Hello, the camp!" the first rider called as he slowed, then dismounted and walked closer. Two more soldiers rode into the firelight behind the first.

"Major Zachary McCallister?" the first man asked.

"I am," Zach acknowledged, well aware of Caroline's smothered gasp. The three men snapped a sharp salute, which he reluctantly returned.

"A message for you, sir, from Lieutenant William P. Clark, Fort Keogh." The soldier slapped a leather-bound missive into his hand.

"It's all right, everyone," Zach called to Caroline, Swallow and the boy. The soldiers' eyes widened as they each stepped out of hiding, armed and alert. "You can put your weapons away. Boys, back to bed. You have a long day tomorrow." He pointed to the beds and stepped closer to the fire, snapping open the portfolio and reading the papers inside.

"Gentlemen, you're welcome to bed down on the other side of the fire. Have you eaten tonight? You've had a long, cold ride." He introduced the three soldiers to Caroline by name and rank. They each gave her a polite nod, then looked to Zach for some clue as to what to do next. He smiled when she offered them the extra biscuits she'd saved for breakfast in the morning. They accepted her offer eagerly, along with some tinned apples. She didn't realize what a treat she'd given them, and they had no idea that the entire time she smiled and served them, she was shooting dagger-glances at Zach and fingering the hilt of her knife through her skirt. He sighed, wishing she hadn't found out this way.

"If you'll excuse us, I need to apprise Miss Whitley of my orders and make plans for tomorrow." He took Caroline's arm and led her away from the camp.

Once out of sight, she jerked her elbow away from him and faced him coolly. "Save your breath. I already know who you are. What I don't know is why you haven't told me."

"How did you . . . ?" he asked, incredulous. He'd worried himself sick, wondering how he'd tell her, only to find out she already knew! He stuck his own hands on his hips and leaned close so he could see her expression. "Why didn't you tell me that you knew?"

"How was I supposed to do that? You were being so secretive. I couldn't very well bring it up over dinner."

"How did you find out? Did you snoop through my saddlebags?"

"I beg your pardon!" she said, crossing her arms over her stomach and scowling at him. "I would never!"

"Did you?" he asked again.

"Only after five days of your feverish ramblings," she said, squaring her shoulders and staring him down. "I was worried. I didn't know if you would live. I needed to find out whom to contact in case you . . ."

He frowned and straightened. "I hadn't considered that."

"But don't think that lets you off the hook," she said, shaking her finger in his face. "You used me to get into the Cheyenne camp, and you've taken advantage of my . . . my . . . situation to lull me into trusting you, when you're nothing but a low-down sidewinder."

"Yes, I used you to get into the camp." He shrugged. "But that first night on the Arkansas, Little Wolf already knew I was a soldier. He said something about seeing me in the smoke." He still didn't understand that one, but there was a great deal about the Old Man Chief that didn't bear close scrutiny. He had a sneaking suspicion that Little Wolf had been using him from the first day, not the other way around.

And now, Lieutenant Clark, the man the Cheyenne called "White Hat" Clark, their friend, had sent a message asking him to come quickly. The Cheyenne needed him to speak on their behalf. How had his assignment gotten so turned around? His orders were to persuade Little Wolf and Dull Knife to take their people back to the reservation in Oklahoma. If they couldn't be persuaded, he had orders to "make it happen." He didn't relish telling Sheridan that if he wanted the two chiefs dead, he'd have to do the foul deed himself. It could cost him his commission; unless he resigned first.

"Did you read my orders?" he asked, watching her face. He'd know if she lied to him. Her outrage over the contents would be transparent.

"Yes," she admitted without hesitation. "You can't kill them," she said, again surprising him by pleading for the Cheyenne instead of lambasting him. "First of all, you haven't found your son yet. You barely found out that Black Coyote was the man who first brought your horses to camp. How you're going to question him, I'll never know, but I'm sure Little Wolf will be an important part of that. Dull Knife has disappeared, no one knows if he's still alive, let alone where he's hiding. And you've come to admire and respect Little Wolf. You could never kill him."

"So you're not angry with me?" Zach asked, feeling the tension that had been building inside him for months drain suddenly away.

"I couldn't be intimate with you if I was angry with you," she said, shaking her head at him. "But even though I let you kiss me, I don't trust you."

He stepped closer and pulled her into his arms. "Not completely, but you will, after you marry me."

"What?" She stared up at him, wide-eyed and puzzled.

He grinned, pleased that he'd surprised her. "I love you, and when all this is over, I want to marry you."

"No," she said, pushing out of his arms. "That's not possible."

Zach's heart jerked to a stop. "You don't love me?" he breathed, bracing for the stabbing pain that would change his life. He couldn't believe her. Everything she did told him otherwise.

"Yes, I love you," she said, and relief swept over him, leaving him weak-kneed and out of breath. "But it would never work," she said, avoiding his arms and stepping out of his reach.

"We're very different people. I crave a home and security, and you're a loner. Your work requires you to travel all over the country. You live in the shadows with danger lurking around every corner. That's no life for a man with a family."

"What if I gave all that up, settled down?" he asked, holding her waist, needing the feel of her beneath his hands to convince him this was really her, that she was here, refusing to marry him. How could she do this, say these things? "You love me! You just admitted it. We can make anything work as long as we love each other."

"I still can't marry you." She pushed out of his hold and he let her go. Regret plainly etched her face, but she held herself firmly, as rigid in stance as she was in her certainty that they could never be husband and wife. In this frame of mind, she wouldn't listen to his arguments, but there would be another day. He'd make sure of it.

"I warn you, Caroline, I won't stop trying to persuade you. And you know I can be very determined. Why do you refuse, when you've admitted you love me? What other objection do you have? Surely it's not because of your fear."

"No," she said, glancing quickly up at him. "After this afternoon, I began to believe that it was possible for me to find pleasure in the act."

He gave a dry laugh. "The act? You make it sound so

cold and unfeeling. Think back to this afternoon. Your body was hot and wet, and you begged me not to stop."

"Yes," she admitted, cutting him off. "I enjoyed this afternoon, and I'd hoped that someday you and I would . . . that you could . . . that we might be able to . . ."

"Make love?" he whispered against her hair. The shiver that ran through her was like salve on the open wound her refusal had left. She wasn't indifferent to him, and he would use her passion to bring her back into his arms to stay. "I will keep my promise, Caroline. No matter what happens, I will make love to you. You will be my wife. Get used to the idea."

She shook her head sadly, pushing away from him. "I can't."

"We'll see," he said, bracing for one last volley. "Tonight, while you sleep in your cold bed, remember this." He caught her up, lifting her high and catching her mouth with a hunger like nothing he'd ever before known. He wanted this woman. Here, like this, in his arms or beside him, for the rest of his life. Without her, his life would be empty, meaningless.

She didn't fight him, but there was a new reserve in her response, a kind of melancholy that he felt in her touch, heard in her sighs. Whatever her reason for refusing him, he knew that she believed it would drive him from her.

He chuckled deep in his throat, welcoming the challenge of proving her wrong.

Caroline watched Zach saddle his horse, preparing to ride out with one of the soldiers early the next morning. He seemed eager, even anxious, to leave. Was it a desire to flee before she could rethink her decision and change her mind about marrying him, or was he in a hurry to resolve matters with his orders and the Cheyenne so that he could continue searching for his son and get back to his own life?

"How long you be at Fort Keogh?" Swallow asked, chattering in his usual cheery manner as he helped Zach pack his horse.

"I'm not sure," Zach said, sending her a long, speaking glance.

She turned away, unable to hold his gaze, afraid that she'd succumb to the tears burning the back of her throat. This would be the last time she'd ever see him. She'd decided last night after his kiss nearly ripped her heart out. Being with him, seeing him again would destroy her. She must say farewell now.

He gripped Swallow's shoulder. "Take good care of them for me," he said, nodding toward Caroline and in the general direction they'd last seen Swift Fox take as he'd shied away from the soldiers.

He spoke quietly with the two soldiers who would be their escort to the fort, his words too low to make out, but his manner and attitude spoke clearly: The men would answer to him. Their sharp salutes when he finished, and his equally crisp salute in return, told her these men understood each other very well. Zach was a career soldier, a man who lived and breathed military order, discipline. Yet, he'd hidden this aspect of his character so well that, if she hadn't heard it from his own feverish lips, she wouldn't have believed it. Until now. Until seeing him in command. This man needed troops to direct, people to order about. She assured herself that she had made the right decision and must stick with it.

Still, when his gaze settled on her and she glimpsed the steely resolution in those gray eyes, she faltered, but briefly. "Good-bye," she said cheerfully, plastering on a big smile and extending a hand.

He took her hand but kept walking, lifting her off her feet and silencing her protest with a hungry kiss. He carried her several feet away from the soldiers, who chuckled, and Swallow, who gave an exasperated grumble.

She tried to resist, but she, too, was hungry. She relished this, her last taste of him, and met every thrust and sweep of his tongue. When at last he broke the kiss and let her slide down his body, he made it a long, slow glide and pressed her against his heavy arousal, which got even heavier when she didn't flinch away.

"Did that feel like 'good-bye?'" he asked, his voice a deep throb in his chest, his face taut with desire.

"It has to be," she said, determined to save herself more pain. "Thank you for asking me to marry you, especially since it's unlikely I'll ever receive another proposal. I appreciate it."

He grabbed her arms, his grip firm. "I *will* see you again, and you *will* be my wife. You can't hide from me, Caroline, so don't try. I'm a very determined, resourceful man."

"Oh," she said, blinking up at him innocently, knowing what she was about to say would hurt him, but hoping that someday he'd understand. "You'd hunt for me?" At his nod, she continued, "The way you've hunted for your son?"

He said nothing, but his jaw clenched and his expression dared her to continue. He rubbed her upper arms and shook his head, his gray gaze tender and wistful.

"I'll find Luke," he said, smiling at her, "and I won't let you chase me away so easily. When I return to Virginia, you'll come, too, as my wife and Luke's mother. Get used to the idea."

"I can't marry you, Zach," she reiterated, her fists clenched at her sides. "Please don't keep asking me."

"Can't," Zach said, cocking his head as he studied her face. "Not won't. Can't." He kissed her, his lips strong and firm against hers. Then he stepped back. "Let me know when you're ready to tell me why. I can't fix what I don't understand. I'll see you when you get to Fort Keogh."

"No, you won't," she insisted. "I never want to see you again, you mule-headed, obstinate man!"

"And you call me obstinate," he sighed and pushed his hat up his forehead. "I will see you again." He kissed her and with an arm around her shoulders led her back to where the soldiers and Swallow waited. As if to punctuate his words, he squeezed her bottom and whispered, "Don't forget, I owe you one more lesson."

Trembling with the force of her emotions, Caroline watched him ride away. As he passed over the lip of the hill that would take him out of view, he raised his hat in salute. Fuming, she stomped down to the small stream. He hadn't looked back once, but he'd known she was watching. *Arrogant, bullheaded, opinionated, stubborn, adorable man.* She'd done her best to push him away. Why wouldn't he let her go and spare himself the indignity of pursuing a woman who couldn't have him? Especially a woman nobody else would have?

At least her secret was safe. Her only regret in ending her relationship with Zach was that she'd never fully experience the pleasure of making love. All she'd ever have to remember him by were his kisses, the delight of personal ecstasy, and longing for more. And since no one like Zach was ever likely to cross her path again, she'd regret the lost possibility for the rest of her life. But it was better for him this way. It would be dishonest of her to make love with him now, without telling him, and that was something she couldn't do. The pain ran so deep, she didn't think she could say the words.

She bent beside the stream and broke the ice so she could scoop some of the cold water onto her face. It felt so good that she did it again and again, letting the coolness soothe her puffy eyelids and chase away the heat from their argument. At a tap on her shoulder, she jerked and almost fell into the creek.

She spun and shot to her feet, thinking she'd find one of the soldiers there. Instead, a small boy stood blinking up at her, soaking wet and shivering. He was completely naked, his dark hair slicked back from his face and his long, black lashes drooping. His pale skin was blotchy and red, as if it had just been vigorously scrubbed, and it had dark blotches, as if it had been painted or stained.

"I'm cold," he said, his lips blue, his teeth chattering. "Can I have my new clothes now?"

Caroline stared, goose bumps rising on her arms. She wasn't sure if it was from the cool water she'd splashed on her face, a sympathetic reaction to his shivering, or a premonition. "Who are you?"

He grinned, and her heart slammed against her ribs as a dimple flashed in his cheek. "Luke McCallister."

"You're Luke McCallister? Zach's son?" she gasped, grabbing his shoulders as he nodded. "You've been here, with us, all this time?" When he nodded, she shook him gently. "Why didn't you tell us? Why did you hide? Your father has been so worried about you." A guilty flush rushed over her as she remembered her words to Zach minutes before. If only she'd looked closer, had insisted on bathing the boy, or at the very least cut his hair. If only he'd smiled.

He started to answer, but his teeth were chattering too hard.

"Come on," she urged, taking his hand and hurrying him back to camp. "I have so many questions, but first let's get you dry and cut your hair, then you can dress."

Swallow took the news with a gleeful whoop and gave Luke a thump on the back. The soldiers stared at him in amazement. They'd seen him only briefly that morning, but neither man would have believed that the boy who scuttled away in fear at the mere sight of them was a white boy. But there was no denying his pale, blotchy skin and the direct stare from his dark brown eyes.

Caroline dried Luke gently with the square of linen she always used for her own baths. His scarred back tore at her heart, but she knew he could live with that, and most of the weals and cuts had healed. They would leave marks, but only one or two would leave deep gouges, like the ones crisscrossing her own back. His hair dripped something black, almost inky. A dye, she guessed, intended to make his dark hair black. His skin, she determined, had been stained so many times that the stain would have to wear off. She hoped the blotches on his face wouldn't be permanent.

As she set about cutting his hair, she smiled. "Finally," she said, leaning over his shoulder and giving him a hug. "I've been dying to do this for months!" At the first snip, he started talking, and by the time she finished, he'd explained how Black Coyote and his friends had murdered his mother's friend, then raped and murdered his mother. He had gotten away while they tortured the man, had hidden in the bushes nearby and tried not to hear his mother's screams. She'd cried out for him to run over and over, but he'd been too afraid. There were too many of them, and he knew they'd catch him. When she finally stopped screaming, he'd peeked out of the bushes and Black Coyote had seen him. He'd run, but Black Coyote had caught him, and he'd fought, which was why Black Coyote kept him, Luke said. He'd been impressed with his courage.

Black Coyote had taken him to their camp and given him to his wife, who couldn't have children. He was to be their son, and they made up the story about adopting him from the Sioux. All this was told to him by one of the warriors who could speak English. They dyed his hair, stained his skin, and Black Coyote's wife cut the buckskins off a dead Arapaho they came across on the prairie and cut them down to fit him. Black Coyote's friends wanted to trade the McCallister horses, but he'd never owned such fine horses. He refused to give them to some *veho* trader for a few beads or blankets.

After spending most of the hot months riding all over the prairie stealing from and murdering anyone they came across, Black Coyote and his friends finally returned to the reservation not long before Little Wolf and the Cheyenne escaped from the soldiers with the big guns. The McCallister horses had drawn too much attention, so Black Coyote gave them to one of his friends. His friends made sure the horses were passed around as gifts, so no one could trace them back to Black Coyote. He planned to get them back one day, but when Woodenthigh and Swallow started asking questions, he gave up that idea.

"Why didn't you say something to your father that night at the Arkansas River?" Caroline asked as she brushed the snippets of hair off Luke's bare shoulders.

"I didn't know he was my father," Luke said with a shrug. "He looked like Uncle Josh, so I ran to him."

Earning his son's love and trust would be a monumental task for Zach, Caroline realized, but one she hoped he would soon have the opportunity to begin. "Were you being beaten at that point?"

"Black Coyote beat me every day to make me work harder. It's part of a Cheyenne boy's training." Luke looked to Swallow, who shook his head. Luke sighed. "He lied to me a lot."

"Didn't his wife try to stop the beatings?" Caroline asked, outraged by the Coyote's brutal behavior. She sat beside Luke and squeezed his hand, knowing her gesture was small comfort for the horrors he'd endured.

"She hurt me most, to please him," Luke said, and shuddered. "When I hugged Father's leg, I knew he wasn't Uncle Josh, 'cause my Uncle Josh only has one leg. I wanted to cry. Uncle Josh loved me, and I hoped he and Aunt Abby would want me back. I wished that Father would come, but knew he wouldn't 'cause he doesn't like me much. But Black Coyote knew the man I hugged really was Father. He listened to Little Wolf and Caroline talking to him. He said if I told Father who I was, he would kill him." He looked up at Caroline, his eyes huge in his blotchy face. "I couldn't save Patricia, but if I was very good and did everything they said, I could save Father."

"Patricia?" Caroline asked. "Do you mean your mother?"

"She didn't like me to call her that. She liked it when I called her Patricia," Luke said, matter-of-factly. "Father didn't come to see us 'cause I was so ugly."

Caroline gasped at the appalling allegation as Patricia's personality crystallized in her mind. She'd discounted what Zach had said about his wife, certain he must be exaggerating out of anger at the woman for jeopardizing his son's safety. Now she understood that his comments had actually been kind. "Your father loves you, Luke. He's been so worried about you," she said and hugged him to her side. "You've been very brave. Your father will be so proud of you."

"I fooled Father," Luke said, shrugging as if he'd simply been engaged in a child's game. "When he started looking for me, Black Coyote tried to hide me and talked about killing me. But Little Wolf was watching and Black Coyote was afraid. Then I heard them talk about taking me to the lake, so I ran away.

"I wasn't hunting turkeys," he told Swallow, who sat cross-legged on the ground before Luke, listening in rapt amazement. "But Father saw my leg and . . ." He sighed. "I got away and then the snow started coming and it got so cold. When Father walked out of the snow, I thought he was a bear, but I was too cold to run anymore.

"When Old Bridge saw my back and legs, he wouldn't let Black Coyote come to see me anymore. Then he caught Black Coyote's wife putting more dark stuff on my legs and face. He took it away from her and made her leave. He told Little Wolf about it and they talked for a long time, then Old Bridge started putting it on me. Little Wolf asked me who I was and they kept me hidden. Little Wolf said it wasn't safe to let Father know. He said Black Coyote would try to kill us, or you," he said to Caroline. "But Little Wolf said first he needed Father to do something important, then he'd tell him about me.

"When he told me he was sending me away with you and Father, I cried."

"You cried?" Caroline asked, stunned. "Didn't you want to be with your father?"

Luke's gaze was clear and untroubled as he answered. "I was safe with Old Bridge. Nobody hurt me and I got to eat and not work all the time. I was afraid Father would be angry at me for running into the storm, and for not saving Patricia."

"Oh, Luke," Caroline said, shaking her head sadly, "your mother's death wasn't your fault. Even without knowing who you were, your father was afraid you would be hurt in that storm. Please believe me. He loves you very much and has been anxious to find you."

Even as she consoled Luke, Caroline reeled at Luke's explanation of Little Wolf's behavior. She couldn't question Luke's story. What possible reason did he have to lie? He could not have understood that Little Wolf and Bridge had used him, hidden his existence so that they could manipulate his father. Certainly, their motives were altruistic—they had the *Tsitsitas's* survival to ensure—but that didn't excuse their behavior.

"Little Wolf said I shouldn't tell Father or you until it was safe." he looked at the soldiers standing beside Swallow, listening to him. "Father will be safe at the fort, won't he? Black Coyote won't go there. And we're safe, too. Aren't we?"

"Yes, we're all safe now," she assured him. "You were right to do what Little Wolf told you," she said, and focused on helping him dress in his new clothes, not her desire to berate Little Wolf and Bridge. She'd let Zach have the honor, if she ever told him about it.

Luke's clothes fit perfectly, all but the shoes, which were snug but would have to serve until she could buy him another pair at Fort Keogh. The boy's transformation from Cheyenne orphan to young white boy stunned her.

"Ma'am," one of the soldiers said, approaching her after she'd settled the boy on a blanket with a plate of biscuits, bacon and gravy. "Would you like one of us to ride to Fort Keogh and tell the major you've found his son?"

"No, Sergeant," she said, after considering his offer for a moment. "I'll tell him myself."

She'd hoped to take the first stagecoach or train back to Dodge City once she turned the boys over to Little Wolf, but that would have to wait.

She'd have to see Zach McCallister one more time.

Chapter Twenty-three

The sun shone brightly the day Little Wolf and his people rode into Fort Keogh, their horses prancing to the music being played by the Second Cavalry band. People had gathered to watch and they clapped and cheered as the Cheyenne rode by. Zach and Lt. "White Hat" Clark rode beside Little Wolf, and behind them followed 33 warriors, 42 women and 35 children. Over 268 people had left the Darlington Agency with Little Wolf in September. Half of that number had taken the road to Camp Robinson with Morning Star and no counting had been made of them, but Little Wolf knew from the reports he had heard that over half of them had been killed or had died of their wounds. Like a storm cloud, grief over the needless loss of so many darkened the joyful day.

Now, riding before the column of men, women and children that he had brought safely home, Little Wolf thanked the powers above and below for their mercy. And he sent a prayer of thanks to the Great Spirit's messenger—wherever she might be—whose words had given him the courage to take the difficult path home when nothing but death surrounded him.

He did not let the noise and cheering fool him. The Cheyenne's future was still not secure. White Hat had made no promises to the Cheyenne people. Zach said he, Little Wolf, must speak to the *veho* chiefs and tell them why the people should be allowed to stay here on the lands they loved. This he would do, and with Zach and White Hat speaking for the Cheyenne also, he hoped the ears of the *veho* chiefs would be opened and that they would let them stay.

A loud *boom!* rang out. The women cried out in fear and drew the children into a tight circle, but the soldiers laughed and shouted, "Hurrah!" Another *boom*! came and Little Wolf followed the pointing fingers. The soldiers were firing the big cannons, but not at the Cheyenne. They were firing to make a loud noise of celebration that the Cheyenne had surrendered and they would not have to fight.

Little Wolf looked at Zach, who winked at him and shrugged, then rode back to calm the women and children.

As they reached the center of the fort, White Hat dismounted and motioned that the Cheyenne should also dismount and stand behind him. Then White Hat made a short talk to the white people, who cheered and laughed. Little Wolf heard little of what was said, until at the end of his talking, White Hat said, "And the Cheyenne surrendered without firing a shot. There were no deaths on either side."

Did White Hat not understand that his people had not fired because no soldiers had shot at the Cheyenne? They had never wanted to fight, only to live in peace, here where the water ran sweet and cold and the long grass made their ponies fat. But Little Wolf had not forgotten that Black Coyote had not surrendered. The hatred in his heart for all white people could destroy the hopes of the Cheyenne.

After the celebration, Little Wolf took his pipe to the tall hill where he stood on the crest and stared into the sunset, seeking guidance. There, in the changing light and growing shadow, he offered smoke to the powers above and below and to the four directions. Through the night, he prayed for peace with the whites, and for help from above for the *Tsitsitas*.

Three mornings after the Cheyenne's arrival at Fort Keogh, Zach rode with Lieutenant Clark at the head of a column of soldiers, his heart heavy with dread. His scouts had spotted a small camp of Cheyenne, six in all, four men and two women. From their descriptions, Zach recognized them as Black Coyote and two friends, Coyote's wife and a woman Zach had seen around the camp at Lost Chokecherry, and a child.

Without hesitation, he ordered his soldiers to encircle the camp, catching the culprits still sleeping. Black Coyote's defiance in the face of thirty loaded rifles in the hands of trigger-happy soldiers was pathetic. Didn't the man recognize his own doom staring him in the face?

"Put your hands in the air and stay where you are," Zach ordered the sullen warriors, training his Colt on Black Coyote's chest. Seeing movement to his right, he swung the pistol and fired a shot into the dirt at the feet of Coyote's wife who had been trying to slip away unnoticed. "You, too, ma'am," he said, and motioned with the gun for her to join her husband.

He gave the translator time to do his work, then ordered the six culprits bound and their goods searched. As Black Coyote glared, the soldiers discovered several damning items—the coat of the soldier shot while repairing the telegraph lines, as well as the horse, rifle and scalp of the soldier assisting him.

Zach and Lieutenant Clark chatted amiably on the ride back to town, letting the culprits run the fifty-plus miles at a sedate canter—all but the child, of course, who rode contentedly before a grizzled old soldier who snuck him bites of the peppermint stick he'd hidden in his pocket.

The sun had settled behind the western hills when White Hat and Zach came looking for Little Wolf, their faces long with with sorrow. Little Wolf welcomed them to his fire and lit the pipe. After they had all smoked, White hat nodded to Zach.

"We're sorry to bring bad news, Little Wolf," Zach said, and Little Wolf saw that he was weary, body and soul. He braced himself.

"Two soldiers have been killed," Zach said, and Little Wolf's whole body tensed. "We found the men responsible—Black Coyote and two friends. His wife was with them and another woman with a child. There is no

question that they did the killing. We found them with
the dead soldiers' clothing and other items, including
one man's scalp. They have all been locked up in the jail-
house, but we're worried." The two men shared a long
look, then Zach turned to him, his face grave and troubled. "This could destroy your chance of staying here at
Fort Keogh."

Anger seethed inside Little Wolf and his hand settled
on his quirt. He had feared that Black Coyote, riding free
on the prairie, not having a chief to stop him, could do
something like this. He would not care that his raiding
and killing could destroy the hopes of the men, women
and children who had suffered beside him on the long
trail from Oklahoma.

And what could he say, what could he do to stop this?
The *veho* fathers would not listen to the promises of a
chief who could not control his own men. He saw that
Zach watched him with a frown on his face and knew that
Zach understood his fear.

"We also feel your anger and share your worry," White
Hat said. "The Cheyenne must be seen as peace-loving
and willing to follow the white man's laws." He glanced at
Zach, who nodded. "We think that if you allow the guilty
parties to be judged by a military court, the commissioners will be satisfied."

"*Hou!*" Little Wolf nodded, quick to agree. "Take them!
Judge them in the way you think best, according to your
laws. They knew I had surrendered and they killed anyway. They are no longer Cheyenne."

Zach did as Little Wolf asked and General Miles,
pleased that Little Wolf had surrendered the men for
trial, told the commissioners sent to decide the fate of
the *Tsitsitas* that the three Cheyenne warriors were rene-
gades. Black Coyote and two of his friends were con-
victed and sentenced to hang without speaking a word
to defend themselves, their hearts and faces black with
hate as they faced the *veho* fathers.

Little Wolf listened to their trial and was glad to hear

the decision. If the chiefs had turned Black Coyote over to him, he would have been banished and there would have been more killings. Black Coyote's heart was rotten. He would continue killing until death stopped him. His wife and the other woman and child who had been with him were released. The commissioners agreed that the loss of their men, and consequently, their standing among the Cheyenne, would be punishment enough for the two women.

"You did the right thing," Zach said, shaking Little Wolf's hand after the trial.

Little Wolf nodded in agreement. "The Cheyenne will not miss Black Coyote."

"Are you ready to speak to General Miles and the others tomorrow?" Zach asked. "It's going to be tough. Representatives have arrived from Kansas, requesting that all your warriors be transferred there for trial."

"But only a few men were involved in the killing in Kansas, and many of them went with Morning Star and were killed at Camp Robinson," Little Wolf objected.

"Lieutenant Clark and I will argue that your men acted out of sorrow and a need to revenge the Cheyenne women and children who were massacred at Washita and Sappa Creek. Also, many people have protested the treatment of your brother and his people at Camp Robinson, and Captain Wessells is to be court-martialed. We believe the government will be lenient. The Army is tired of chasing the Cheyenne, and the newspapers back east have been writing about you. Public opinion is in your favor."

Little Wolf shook his head, not understanding what Zach was saying. "What does this mean for my people?"

"It means the people want you to stay here. That's a good thing."

"The Great Father listens to the people?" Little Wolf asked. When the Cheyenne first surrendered, he had been taken to see the great white house where the Great Father lived. He had been surprised by the people. Like the grasses on the prairie, they were too many to count.

Upon seeing them, he had known the Cheyenne must surrender and make peace with the whites. They could not fight so many. He touched the cross that hung around his neck, a gift from that time from the Great Father himself. "If the people have spoken to the Great Father, then my people will be safe."

"I think you may be right, my friend," Zach said, and clapped him on the back. "You may just get everything you wanted."

Little Wolf returned Zach's smile, knowing he was not the only one who would soon have everything he wanted. He had spoken to Caroline that morning and knew what she planned. "You, too, Zach McCallister. You, too."

Caroline knocked on the door to Zach's quarters, then wiped her sweating palms on her skirt. "Stay back, Luke," she whispered. "Give me a minute to talk to him first."

Luke nodded, his face pale, which made the remaining blotches of stain stand out in stark relief. His hair had been painstakingly combed, but it refused to lie flat. An unruly lock insisted on waving over his brow in a manner very reminiscent of his father. "Are you sure he wants to see me?"

She kissed his cheek and smiled when he immediately wiped the spot. "It's going to be fine," she told him. "He loves you. You'll see."

If Patricia weren't already dead, Caroline would have dearly loved to punish the hateful woman for sabotaging Luke's relationship with Zach. Her thoughts slid to a halt as Zach opened the door. Dressed in uniform, he took her breath away. The yellow stripe down the outside of his trouser leg made him seem even taller, and the uniform jacket fit his broad shoulders perfectly. The deep blue of his uniform turned his gray eyes a piercing gray-blue and made his tanned skin glow. His wide, welcoming smile made her heart stutter. Panic flicked through her when she realized she couldn't speak.

"Caroline!" he cried and whisked her into his arms.

"Were your quarters satisfactory? Did the quartermaster get you everything you needed? If he didn't, I'll—"

"Everything is fine, Zach," she said, thankful that her voice hadn't failed her. "The boys and I have been treated like visiting royalty, especially Swallow, who's eating it up."

Zach laughed. "That boy's more like his father than he knows. Where are my manners? Please, have a seat." He led her to a comfortable-looking leather chair, smiling down at her as she eased into it. "Can I offer you something to drink? A sherry, perhaps?"

Caroline shook her head, marveling at his civility. "Zach, what's happened—"

"Haven't you heard?" he asked, cutting her off in surprise. "The Cheyenne will be allowed to stay at Fort Keogh temporarily. It's not permanent, but it's a start. And if all goes well, Congress will allocate funds to establish a reservation here in the future. Dull Knife has turned up, too. He's been hidden all this time by his daughter, who married into the Lakotas. He'll be joining Little Wolf soon. Unfortunately, he lost his youngest son and daughter at Camp Robinson. His daughter was trying to save several children, but the soldiers killed her and the children. Dull Knife is taking the deaths pretty hard."

"Oh, I'm so sorry to hear that!" Caroline twisted her hands in her lap, keenly aware of Luke waiting outside. "You're probably wondering why I've come to see you today."

Zach turned from pouring sherry to stare at her. "Why would I wonder about that? The only wonder is that you haven't sent the duty sergeant after me for not visiting you and the boys. I apologize for not coming to see you as soon as you arrived, but my time hasn't been my own. The generals have wanted a full accounting of my time with the Cheyenne and I've been trying to resolve all the issues so that I can get on with my life."

"That's what I wanted to talk to you about," she said,

jumping at the opening he'd unwittingly tossed her. "The rest of your life." She felt awkward with him waiting on her in his dimly lit, well-appointed officer's quarters, his bed a distracting temptation in the background.

He smiled and started toward her, a glass of sherry in his hand. "You've changed your mind? You're ready to marry me?"

She shook her head, sending a hairpin flying. "No, I'm afraid I'm more convinced than ever that I've made the right decision. However, I've brought someone along that I'd like to introduce to you." She stood quickly and backed toward the door. "May I?"

"Certainly," he said, "but I warn you, I haven't given up. I'll convince you yet." He turned to set the sherry on his desk.

Caroline opened the door and beckoned Luke into the room ahead of her. Unfortunately, he had plastered himself against the wall and was frozen in place. His eyes were dark caverns in his pale face, and his lips were turning blue. She took his hand and began rubbing it. He gripped her hand so tightly she feared he'd leave a bruise, but she understood his trauma. "Breathe, Luke!"

He blinked at her, then sucked in a sharp breath.

"Another," she said, relieved to see color returning to his face. "Okay, here we go."

She led him into the room ahead of her as Zach turned to greet them. "Hello!" he said, crouching a little and smiling at Luke. "Who do you have here? One of Swallow's friends?"

"Yes, he's a friend of Swallow's. You probably remember him as 'the boy,' Swift Fox, or even 'Swift Coyote,' although you hated that name."

Luke grinned at her and the dimple in his cheek flashed. "I hated that name, too."

Caroline smiled at Zach, seeing his face pale as realization dawned. "May I present Lucas McCallister?"

Zach stood and stared at her in surprise, then joy lit his face. "All this time? He's been there, right under my nose?"

"Father?" Luke asked, taking a tentative step toward him. He got no farther. Zach fell to one knee and pulled Luke into his arms. While father and son clung to one another, Caroline told Zach briefly what had been done to his son. She wasn't surprised that tears glistened on Zach's cheeks, nor that his fists clenched and unclenched behind Luke's back, and that the two of them still hadn't moved when she finished. But she didn't feel a tear looming anywhere nearby. In fact, she felt like celebrating.

Quietly, she left, turning at the door to sear the image of father and son into her mind forever.

"I love you both," she whispered, and left them alone to discover one another.

Several hours later, a sentry pounded on Zach's door, breathless with the news that the Cheyenne prisoners had committed suicide. Zach listened to the details in silence. The men had hung themselves, all of them with the same leather strap. Black Coyote had died last. He'd had to wait while his friends strangled to death, then remove the strap from his last friend's dead body before he could hang himself.

Zach dismissed the sentry with a wave. When the door closed, he slammed back a double shot of whiskey, savored the pungent burn, then tucked the covers tight around his sleeping son.

A few days later, Zach paused outside the mercantile at the far end of the fort, keeping the boys out of the way of customers bustling in and out of the store. He checked his pocket watch. Only mid-morning, but he felt like he'd been working horses all day. After muscling Luke and Swallow into their fancy new clothes, bought especially for this occasion, he needed another bath and a stiff drink.

"Your feet cold?" Swallow asked, pulling at his new celluloid collar.

"No," Zach said, fixing the collar. "I don't have cold feet."

Swallow shook his head, obviously trying to be more understanding. "Very hard thing, man ask woman to share his furs. What we do if she say 'No!'?"

"Thanks for making this easier for me," Zach said, wondering why he'd brought the boys with him in the first place. Caroline had already refused him, more than once. He was gambling on the boys, certain that once she heard his plan, she wouldn't be able to refuse. She'd never turn down the boys.

He hoped.

"Come on, Father," Luke said, elbowing Swallow. "She said she loves you."

"Yes, she did," Zach said, trying not to let his nerves make him irritable. "But a woman doesn't always say what she means, or mean what she says." He shook his head. *Damnation!* He was confusing himself.

He opened the door and let the boys precede him. They headed straight for the candy jars on the gleaming counter. "Not yet," he told them, under his breath. "After we've talked to her and have something to celebrate."

"Sir," he said to the man smiling at them from behind the counter. "We've come to speak with Miss Caroline Whitley. Is she working today?"

The gentleman beamed at the boys and winked at Zach. "She certainly is, Major McCallister. You'll find her back in yard goods." He pointed to the opposite end of the store. After so many years of guarding his identity, Zach found it unnerving for strangers to address him by name, but he merely nodded politely.

Halfway there, Zach halted and turned to the boys. "Let me talk to her first," he said, "then you can join me."

"Father," Luke said, shaking his head, "she told you she loves us. She'll marry us, too. You don't want her to change her mind when she finds out, do you?"

"He right," Swallow said, nodding at Luke. "I with him." He slung his arm over Luke's shoulders. "We together."

Zach rolled his eyes. This was likely to go down in the record books as the most ridiculous marriage proposal in the history of the West. But he couldn't argue with Luke's logic. The boy had a good head on his shoulders. He'd been very pleased to discover that his son was so much like him.

Before he could get them moving again, Caroline swung around the corner, heading straight for them. She stopped, blinked at them, and smiled. "Don't you look fine? How nice of you to visit me." A small crease formed between her brows, a crease that meant she was thinking and she didn't like what she was thinking, which meant that he wouldn't like it either. "Why are you all dressed up? You look like you're going to a wedding. Or a funeral."

She caught her breath, and looked up at Zach. "Has someone died?"

"No," Zach said, hurrying to reassure her and spare her any concern. "Everyone's fine. We're—"

"We're going to a wed-... *umph!*" Swallow glared at Luke, who'd elbowed him in the ribs, then Zach, who'd thumped him on the back.

"Not yet!" Luke said in a very loud whisper.

Zach rolled his eyes.

Caroline covered her smile.

"Well, it true!" Swallow said, irrepressible as ever. He dodged Luke and Zach and caught Caroline's hands, staring up at her. "Zach found Luke, so he out of the Army, but he no go back to Vir-jin-yuh. He buy big land here, raise horses. And us. You be his woman?"

"What?" Caroline asked, again looking to Zach. "You've left the Army?"

"Yes," Zach said with a laugh. He pulled Swallow to his side, hoping he'd stay put—and be quiet. "I've retired from the Army and I bought a few acres nearby where I can raise horses and cattle. And kids. These two, in particular," he said, putting an arm around each boy and smiling at them. "And I've a yen for a little girl with blonde curls like her momma's."

He held his breath, waiting for her to answer. His heart was in his throat, pounding like hooves drumming a hard-packed track. The boys waited, too, their bodies tense with excitement.

Swallow jiggled in place, his eyes bright and his cheeks flushed. "Kiss him quick. Preacher man waiting at hotel and train leave without us!"

Zach sighed, feeling the blood rush out of his head. His heart slowed and his whole body slumped and went cold. He vowed to put Swallow on bread and water for two weeks.

Caroline cocked her head and looked up at Zach. "There's a preacher waiting for us—all of us—at the hotel?" Her foot started tapping as she waited for his answer. Not a good sign.

Zach smiled sheepishly as both boys nodded eagerly. The bright shine of pleasure in Luke's eyes warmed his heart, but he knew that, if not for the boys, she'd have slapped his face by now. He should have talked to her alone. The boys' enthusiasm had derailed his proposal.

"Boys," she said, her oh-so-pleasant tone making his gut clench, "run up to the front of the store and tell Mr. Lambert that I said to give you three licorice whips. Each."

The boys' eyes widened and they dashed out of sight. When they were gone, she turned to Zach and crooked her finger. "Come with me," she said and spun on her heel. It was an order he didn't dare disobey.

She gestured to Lambert to let him know she'd be in the back room. He nodded and handed each boy another piece of licorice, sliding Zach a sympathetic glance. Zach grimaced.

As soon as the door shut behind him, she rounded on him. "How dare you use those boys in such an infamous manner?" Hands clenched into fists, she paced back and forth in the small room, which was lined with floor-to-ceiling, overflowing shelves and crammed full of crates and barrels. The dilapidated desk shoved into a corner seemed an afterthought. There was barely room for her to turn around and when she did, her skirts lashed his ankles, reminding him uncomfortably of Little Wolf's quirt.

He caught her by the arms the next time she turned and stopped her. The fury in her eyes kept him from embracing her. "Why are you so angry? The boys were excited, they wanted to be here when I told you my plans." He sighed, rubbed her arms once and let his hands fall to his sides. "I've told you I want to marry you. I love you and you said you love me. What's to prevent us from marrying? Is it the boys? Do you not wish to raise someone else's children?"

"Of course not," she cried. "I love both of them, and you, too."

Hope burst into his heart and he reached for her, but she held up a hand.

"I can't marry you."

"Why not?" he bellowed, not even trying to control his voice.

"Because I love you," she said, and turned away to whisper, "and you deserve better."

"That's ridiculous," he said, again reaching for her and making her face him. "You're the best, the only woman for me. You're daring and brave and courageous, and you make me want to be a better man. And, as if that weren't enough for any man, you're damn beautiful to boot. The boys love you, too. There is no one better."

Her cheeks flushed a deep rose, but she shook her head. "I can't marry you. You deserve someone who can give you what you want, what you deserve. And I can't." She turned away, her shoulders hunching as if bracing for a blow. "I—I can't have children," she whispered in a choked voice.

He blinked, not understanding her at first. Then her words penetrated and he stilled. "You're barren?"

"No," she said, still unable to face him. She held her head high, and kept her gaze fixed on the cluttered desk, but her voice shook. "I'm . . . damaged. I became pregnant by White Bear. I didn't tell him, but one of the old women caught me vomiting one morning and guessed my secret. That night he beat me. He stomped my belly until I miscarried the child. I bled for weeks, then never again. A doctor in Dodge City said I'd never be able to have a child." She looked over her shoulder and he recoiled from the pain in her eyes. "I've never told anyone. I didn't want to tell you, but you push and push! Why couldn't you simply accept my answer?"

A red haze of rage enveloped Zach, but he wasn't angry with Caroline, unless it was for believing that he couldn't love her unless she was perfect. His anger was for the beast who'd hurt her, who'd left her believing that she was "damaged," of no value or worth to any man because one man had been unable to love her. Zach knew he could talk for hours, even swear on a stack of Bibles that he loved her heart, her courage, her determination to survive when faced with hopelessness and despair. In her present frame of mind, she wouldn't believe him. She'd think he pitied her, and he couldn't build the rest of his life on that basis. He must convince her to take a chance, to open herself to the possibilities that love could bring. Loving her had changed him forever, and he knew that only love could heal her.

He thought he knew how to reach her, and though his idea could backfire on him—as his ideas had a tendency to do—he had to persuade her to give their love a chance. If he could persuade her to trust him with her body, could he convince her to trust him with her heart?

"Is that your final decision?" he asked.

She nodded and clutched her arms over her waist, as if she'd fly apart if she let go. When she finally turned to face him, she had schooled her features into a mask of resignation.

"I understand," he said, pretending to accept her decision, though every particle of his being screamed against it. "The boys will be disappointed, but not half as much as me."

"What will you tell them?" She swallowed hard, but kept a tight grip on her emotions.

"I'll think of something." He leaned toward her slowly,

giving her time to back away, inhaling her unique scent, savoring the heat and closeness he might never know again, the supple give of her waist beneath his fingers, and kissed her cheek. "Good-bye, Caroline."

"Good-bye."

Those few feet from the cramped and cluttered back room of the mercantile to the street where the boys waited were the longest he had ever walked, but he took them quickly. He'd have to work fast if he didn't want to lose the woman he loved.

Chapter Twenty-four

By day's end, Caroline felt numb. She'd smiled and chatted with the many customers in the busy mercantile, but she couldn't recall a word that had been said, except: "Good-bye."

She'd known that moment with Zach would be difficult, but she hadn't expected it to cause physical pain. Ever since he'd left her in the stuffy storeroom, she'd felt a piercing pain in her chest, over her heart. The pain, combined with the walnut-sized lump lodged in her throat, made breathing difficult. But she'd held herself together and ignored Mr. Lambert's concerned glances.

She'd done the right thing, hard as it was, but it gave her no satisfaction. Instead, she felt alone, wandering the dark, windswept prairie with no destination, no purpose. No hope. She blinked back tears of self-pity, to which she wasn't entitled. She'd made this decision and acted on it. To have accepted Zach's—and the boys'—proposal would have been dishonest. She couldn't have lived with herself, knowing she'd misled him because she was too weak to tell him the truth.

Her throat tightened and she picked up her pace, feeling her composure slipping. She needed to get back to the boardinghouse, where she could fall apart in private.

"Miss Whitley?" The broom was gently taken from her and she glanced up in surprise to find Mr. Lambert standing beside her. "There's a gentleman here to see you. He's asked to walk you home."

Caroline shot a startled glance at the front of the store. Even with most of the lamps out and the building dark, she recognized Zach, once again dressed in black, gripping his hat before him. "I—I can't," she whispered, panic seizing her by the throat. "Please send him away."

"I tried that, ma'am, but he's not an easy man to dissuade." Mr. Lambert glanced uneasily at Zach. "He insists on talking to you. I'll finish here. You've had a difficult day. Please take tomorrow to—to—uh, recover your spirits," he concluded awkwardly and patted her on the back.

Caroline gathered her shawl and reticule from the back room, moving quickly to avoid the echoes of their earlier discussion that lingered in the room. She allowed Zach to hold the door for her, thankful that he didn't comment on her lack of independence.

Once in the street, she faced him squarely, though her stomach was knotted and her voice shook. "I can't do this, Zach. I have nothing more to say to you."

He smiled down at her and spread his hands. "All I want to do is take you for a walk. No talking, I promise."

She searched his face, but found nothing there that alarmed her. "Where are the boys?"

"They're staying with Feather and Quiet Woman tonight. Little Wolf is taking them riding bright and early tomorrow." He turned her away from the lights and noise of the fort, in the direction of a small stream just outside town. "I wanted one last chance to be with you, without the noise and confusion. Will you walk with me?"

She nodded and reluctantly fell into step beside him. Zach took her hand and tucked it into the crook of his arm. She tried to pull away, but he pressed his other hand over her fingers and his elbow close to his body.

Silence hung over them like a damp blanket. How had their relationship come to this? No matter what happened or how angry he made her, they'd always been able to talk about it. She swallowed hard and tried to think of something to say.

"Uh, did I understand you correctly earlier? You're going to be raising Luke and Swallow?"

Zach nodded. "Little Wolf agreed, but he wants Swallow to spend time with the Cheyenne as well. He wants him to understand the Cheyenne people, not just the white. Since I've decided to live here, it's not a problem."

"Swallow seemed very happy, and he and Luke appear to be getting along well." The lump in her throat became more manageable with every word, and the pain in her chest had also eased. "Swallow said you were leaving on a train. Did you miss it?"

Zach nodded. "I had hoped . . ." His fingers tightened over her hand briefly. "We won't talk about what I'd hoped."

"Thank you," she murmured, as her heart, which had slammed against her ribs, resumed its normal pace.

"I'm plannin' to return to Virginia to let Josh and Abby see Luke for themselves. They need to know the boy is happy with me, and that I'll be a good father to him now. Also, I want to purchase more breedin' stock and perhaps another stallion to get my ranch established."

"You're really going to stay here and ranch?" she asked, incredulous. "Why?"

"I'm tired of chasin' vermin all over the country. I want to settle down and build somethin' of my own, raise a family. Lieutenant Clark has been transferred to Arizona territory, and the Cheyenne need someone here to speak for them when the time comes to establish their reservation."

"Do you really believe it will happen?" she asked, airing her skepticism to avoid his comment about raising a family. "The government hasn't kept any of its promises to the Cheyenne yet. What makes you think they'll start now?"

"Little Wolf impressed the commission, and so did the Cheyenne's determination and grit. As long as things stay quiet here, which I think they will now that Black Coyote's gone, I believe the Cheyenne have a very good chance."

They walked a few more paces in silence, Caroline contemplating the joy a northern reservation would bring the Cheyenne. Their journey had been long and difficult. She hoped it would come to pass, that the result would justify their sacrifice.

Ahead, on the far side of the stream in a grove of junipers, Caroline noticed a lone campfire. Just beyond it, a tipi glowed softly, lit by a fire from within.

"It's a gift from the Cheyenne," Zach said, watching her face. "Feather and Quiet Woman helped me set it up."

"For me?" Caroline asked, overwhelmed by the generosity of the gift. On several occasions she'd helped flesh the twenty-one buffalo hides required for just the tipi cover and knew first hand the amount of backbreaking work involved in the preparation, construction and decoration of a tipi. And these days, buffalo hides were precious and few.

"For us," Zach said and turned her to face him, holding her hands.

Suddenly, his simple request for a walk seemed deceptive and her friends' gesture meddlesome. Caroline backed away, shaking her head, but even her body betrayed her, flushing with heat at the thought of what would happen in that tipi, if she let it. The thought stuck in her brain, lodged there by her body's reaction, and her body continued responding as she remembered another night and the incredible ecstasy she'd discovered in his arms.

"I can't!" she gasped, pulling her hands free. "I'd never be able to walk away if we . . ."

"I made you a promise," Zach said, "and I'm willing to fulfill it, if you want me to. In the morning, if you still feel the same, I'll let you go without recriminations."

She backed away, one more step, but couldn't resist a longing glance at the tipi and all it represented. Then Zach circled behind her, his body a burning brand against hers, his breath hot on her neck, his hands scorching her shoulders through her clothes.

How could she even think of agreeing to this? She shivered and pressed her hands flat against her thighs. Her body was already as hot as the fire crackling outside the tipi. Before she could think of a coherent protest, Zach lifted her into his arms and strode across the shallow stream. When he set her down, he turned her to face him.

"Don't think," he whispered, his lips trailing down her neck to the sensitive curve of her neck. "Just feel."

"Zach, please," she objected and strained away from him.

"That's what I'm trying to do. Please you. And me." But he stopped and cupped her face in his palms. "Let me love you. Just once. Then we'll both have a memory to keep us warm on the long winter nights ahead."

Still she hesitated, but Zach wasn't through with her yet.

"Where's the fiery, spirited woman I first met? The one who walked alone into a busy saloon and waved a pouch of gold in the faces of vultures? Where's the woman who withstood capture, enslavement and torture to once again be free? That's the woman I love. The one who isn't afraid to reach out and take what she wants, who knows that life is one huge risk and who isn't afraid to take chances. Where has she gone? When did she start hiding behind her fear, her insecurity, making excuses for who she is, and what she's not?

"What do you have to lose, Caroline? I stand before you, a man who loves you and who wants to be with you, even if one night is all you have in you to give me. If you turn me away now, you'll spend the rest of your life wondering what could have been, and you'll wither and dry up like a seed that never gets planted. Reach out! Take a chance."

His impassioned plea stole her breath and made her

see that she had been hiding behind her fear. Well, no more, she vowed.

"Show me," she said, her voice a mere whisper that echoed through her head and heart. "I want to know." She reached for him, but he was already there, his arms lifting her to him, his lips hungry as they captured her mouth. His need rocked her, jarring that pain in her chest again and bringing the sting of tears to her eyes. He was voracious in his need, his lips demanding, his hands roaming over every curve. Her own needs matched his, driven by the heat growing inside her, fired by the desire to be truly his, at last.

When he pulled free of her mouth and looked into her eyes, she glimpsed depths she'd never imagined, an emotion that transcended earthly planes and humbled her. "I've missed you," he said and led her to the tipi. He lifted the flap and she ducked in ahead of him.

Feather and Quiet Woman had outdone themselves. A deep pile of fresh hides and blankets beckoned from the far end of the tipi. The spicy scent of the dried prairie roses hanging from each lodge pole sweetened the air. There were even two beaded willow backrests near the bed, fresh water and food; no detail, no matter how small, had been missed.

Zach had given her a few minutes to survey their bower, but the heat from his body close behind her kept her own temperature rising, and as she looked over the tipi, she'd begun unbuttoning the front of her high-necked dress.

She turned to Zach as she loosed the last button, below her waist. Seeing his face in the warm glow of the tipi's small, central fire, she gasped. He seemed to have aged in the hours since she'd seen him. His face seemed leaner and his features more defined. The bones in his cheeks and jaw stood out prominently and his eyes seemed deeper and darker, due to the circles under them. His brow had a new crease in the center and his eyebrows appeared thicker and drew together, shadowing his eyes.

"Have you been ill?" she asked and cupped his cheek. She noted with surprise that he'd recently shaved. His cheeks and jaw were smooth and taut, free of the heavy stubble that usually shadowed his rugged features by evening.

He caught her hand and kissed her palm. "Not ill, just worried."

"I understand," she said. "It's been a difficult time for the Cheyenne."

"Not about the Cheyenne," he said, his gaze roaming her face as if wanted to memorize every feature. "About you! It's been weeks since I've been able to see you, spend time with you. I've felt you slipping away and didn't know how to stop it, how to keep you mine. And now I've failed." His eyes closed briefly. "But we're here tonight. You're in my arms and that's enough for now."

Guilt washed over her. She'd neglected her Cheyenne friends and the boys, avoiding places where she thought he might be. She'd had no idea that her selfishness had caused him any grief, let alone heartache. "I'm so sorry, Zach. I never meant to hurt you."

"Hush," he said and pushed his hands into her open dress. She shivered as his hands spanned her waist, then slid up her sides. She sighed, loving the rough-tender caress. Her eyes closed as he lifted her breasts on his palms. When he bent and kissed each one, she speared her fingers through the thick waves of his hair and sighed again.

How wonderful his lips felt against her skin! Even the roughness of his fingers stirred her deep inside. Dear God, she loved this man. Not just what he made her feel when he touched her, but what he made her feel when he looked into her eyes. She didn't want to give him up, let some other woman enjoy his touch, his kiss, his hard, unyielding body. He was hers! And he'd offered himself to her, body and soul. Why couldn't she take him? He thought she was good enough for him. But she knew she wasn't.

That realization made each touch, each caress,

poignant, a moment to be savored and remembered, captured in vivid vignettes that she could pull out and relish again and again in the long, lonely years ahead.

His lips on her breasts had turned hungry and he bent her over his arm, drawing her entire nipple into his mouth, suckling deeply. She felt the pull deep between her thighs and groaned, clutching his head closer, urging him to take more. As if he felt her need, he rubbed against her, but her dress and petticoats denied her the relief she craved.

She burned to touch him, to feel the heat from his skin. Quickly, she released his shirt buttons and yanked the tails out of his pants. It was his turn to groan as she explored the supple, muscular planes of his chest. He lifted her, carried her to the bed of furs and laid her down gently, then shed his shirt and came down on top of her. He took her other breast in his mouth and began drawing deeply on it. She felt a pulling ache at her center and her legs fell slack. He pressed one thigh high between her legs and she moaned as it pressed against her.

"Easy, darlin'," he whispered, releasing her breast with one last pull on the nipple. "Slow and easy." He lifted her out of her dress, shoving it down her hips, leaving her wearing only her camisole from the waist down. Then he removed that, too. He lingered beside her, his eyes roaming her naked body.

"You're so tiny here," he said, stroking her waist. "So beautiful." He stroked down her side, from her waist to the curve of her hip, then down her thigh. "And when you blush, you blush everywhere," he said as her skin flushed a deep rose in response to his perusal.

"You're embarrassing me," she said, then her eyes slid shut as he stroked up the inside of her thigh. But they opened quickly when his fingers brushed through the nest of curls at the top of her thighs.

And when he leaned down and nuzzled them, she gasped his name and tugged on his hair. "Zach! What are you doing?"

"Memorizing," he said, that brooding look that tugged at her heartstrings back on his face. "I'm going to smell you, taste you, lick you, feel you . . ."

"Taste me?" She wasn't sure she liked that idea.

"I've already tasted your lips, your neck, your wonderful breasts, and soon I'll taste you everywhere."

"Everywhere?" Her voice sounded a little thin and nervous. What else was left to taste? "Surely you don't mean to . . ."

"Don't ask silly questions," he said, pulling the pins out of her hair and shaking it loose around her head. "There, that's better. Just relax and feel."

"Feel," she echoed, a little breathlessly, for he'd straddled her body and pressed his bare chest against hers. The light pelt of hair that adorned his chest tickled her skin. She grinned and arched up to rub against it. "I like the way you feel."

"Minx," he said. "I love the way you taste." He nipped at her nipples, pressing her breasts together until the nipples were close and he could switch quickly from one to the other. Then he released them and kissed his way to her navel, where he traced circles with his tongue while waggling his eyebrows at her. "Having fun?"

"Fun?" she asked, her smile fading. "If someone had told me this could be fun, I never would have believed them."

He rose above her, his arms rigid and captured her mouth in a deep kiss. "You're thinking too much," he said, between nips and nibbles and thrusts of his tongue. He settled over her, his weight pressing her into the pile of furs, his hips nudging her thighs wider. His tongue slipped into her mouth and she parried.

She loved the feel of him on top of her. His weight forced her to spread her legs to let him settle more comfortably, which he did with a deep groan. His erection slid lower, nudging at the layers of cloth between them and the moist opening between her legs. She lay beneath him, completely naked and wide open to him, but he still wore his pants.

She caressed his back, thrilling at the bunch and slide of muscle as he cocked his hips. His erection pressed her through his pants, nudging her swollen, weeping lips.

She stiffened. His penis felt big and blunt. "It's going to hurt, isn't it?"

"It shouldn't," he said, "but I'll take it slow and get you ready."

"Very slow," she said. "Take off your pants. I want to see you. I want to touch you here." She squeezed his buttocks and he rose to his knees. With quick, jerky motions he stripped off his pants and the drawers he wore under them.

She got only a brief glimpse of his erection, but it was enough to steal her breath. He was so big! White Bear hadn't been half that size and he'd nearly torn her apart every time. "Are you sure you'll fit?" she asked, and he chuckled and gave her a peck of a kiss. "Oh, yes. But I promise, you won't even think about that when the time comes."

She frowned at him. "Not think about it? How can you keep me from thinking about it?"

"Trust me," he said, and renewed his onslaught of her senses with increased vigor, as if the removal of his pants had heightened his senses. It certainly had heightened hers.

While his tongue ravaged her mouth, he straddled her thigh and pressed his own thigh high against her, causing her breath to hitch at a tingling burst of sensation. He kissed down the length of her throat, over her shoulder to her collarbone—with a detour to the tiny indentation at the base of her neck—then on to her breasts, which he suckled long and deep, leaving her shaking with an aching need that she knew he could fulfill if he'd only touch her down there, between her wet lower lips.

He kissed his way to her navel and while his tongue delved there, his fingers slipped into her damp curls. He stroked and tugged and when he started kissing his way into the curls, she bucked upward, surprised. She burned! She needed to be touched, there at that secret place, as he had the night he'd given her that first taste of pleasure.

As he slid lower, anticipation made her muscles flex and she felt moisture gathering. She flinched when he stroked up the inside of her thigh, but he didn't reach for that spot, that aching button. Instead, his fingers parted her and exposed her woman's place. He leaned down and kissed her. There!

"Zach!" she cried, then she couldn't say another word. He'd caught the sensitive bud between his lips and was nibbling it, then he kissed her lower and her eyes rolled back in her head. "Oh, please," she cried, knowing what she was begging for, certain she'd die if he didn't give it to her soon. "Please!"

He kissed her again and slipped a finger between the swollen lips, pushing them open wider and sliding his finger deeper. Then he kissed her just above his finger and sent his tongue probing. His kiss shocked her, but the sensations were mesmerizing. She couldn't open her eyes, could only feel. When she did finally look, the sight of his dark head between her legs intensified the growing ache. The ripples she'd felt before twanged through her and Zach lifted up to look at her.

The look on his face mirrored her feelings. His eyes were a deep, storm-tossed gray, his lips wet and deep rose. As she stared at him, he licked them and smiled. It wasn't a smile of humor. It was satisfaction, as purely male as any look he'd ever given her. Then she realized that he had risen over her and settled his hips between her thighs. He lifted her legs, nudging her knees wide and his penis probed at the center of that throbbing ache. She moaned as he slid inside her, feeling her body stretch to accommodate his size and length.

She gripped his arms, her fingers wrapping around the corded, straining muscles, and was surprised to find them trembling. She watched his face as he slid into her, inch by inch, until at last his abdomen met hers. He was fully sheathed, completely imbedded inside her and she felt wonderful. Very full, but wonderful, and a bit edgy. He eased her knees a little wider and smiled at her surprised gasp when he slid even deeper.

"Are you okay?" he asked, his features taut, his body tense. Sweat beaded his brow. He settled over her, an elbow on either side of her chest, and kissed her. He rocked his hips and made his penis dance inside her as his tongue tangled with hers.

"You were right," she whispered. "It doesn't hurt. Are you finished?" She hoped he wasn't. Her body pulsed around his cock, and she felt his every movement inside. He chuckled and she felt the vibrations deep inside. A sharp burst of light shot through her, making her eyes close and her heart race.

"We're just gettin' started, darlin'." He smiled at her and withdrew, then slid all the way in again and she drew a sharp breath as his movement created more lightning bursts.

"Do that again," she breathed, and this time when he withdrew, she lifted her hips to welcome him back.

He gave a low growl and pressed his forehead to hers and began to slowly pump his hips, making her keenly aware of his body moving, always moving, deep inside her.

It doesn't hurt at all! she realized, her heart pounding in wonder. She arched her back and raised herself to meet his slow, deep thrusts. "Zach!" she cried, trying to match his slow, controlled rhythm, but hers was much faster, almost frantic.

"Slow and easy, love," he said, and adjusted her so that her feet were flat on the bed beside her hips, then showed her how to brace herself and match his pace. She lifted her hips to meet his downward thrust and when his body ground against the bone at the apex of her thighs, a wave of sensation ripped through her and a kaleidoscope of light glowed beneath her eyelids. She met him again, then again and again, and each time the sensation grew. His pace increased and he slid a hand beneath her buttocks, lifting her to meet his thrusts, which came faster and faster, until with a joyous cry, she convulsed around him, and together they were flung into the light.

He collapsed on top of her, breathing hard, his body limp. "I love you, Caroline," he gasped, and kissed her.

Caroline lay beneath him, relishing the weight of his spent body upon hers, her arms tight around him, her heartbeat a thundering echo in her head.

Dear God! What a fool she'd been!

Zach woke suddenly, one minute oblivious, the next completely alert. At first he thought he was alone in his bed, that he'd been dreaming of making love with Caroline. It had been the most vivid dream of his life and had left him physically spent. Then he felt her breath tickling the hair on his chest, and saw her bright hair tumbled around them. They were both naked.

He hadn't been dreaming! It had happened! He stared at Caroline sleeping in his arms and felt sure his heart would burst out of his chest. He wanted to clutch her to him, to refuse to let her go, but he'd promised. And he always kept his promises.

If only he knew how to tell her that love like theirs didn't come along every day. He'd never felt this way about another person, not even his son, whom he loved so much it hurt to think about it. She was the core of his soul. He couldn't imagine life without her.

For tonight, he didn't have to. But, by God, if he had to give her up come morning, he wasn't going to waste a minute of the night. Gently, he rolled her onto her stomach and smiled when she snuggled into the furs. He knelt beside her and gathered her hair into his hands, letting it sift through his fingers like liquid gold. Then he pushed it aside and kissed her cheek, her lashes, her nose and finally, the curve of her neck. She wriggled and her hips rose, then fell. He kissed her again, and the same thing happened. Then he straddled her, letting his cock ride the cleft in her bottom as he kissed her neck again and enjoyed her answering wiggle.

She woke with a start and squealed, struggling to get out from under him. Zach rolled off her and she flipped herself off the furs, where she crouched, her hair a wild cloud around her body, her chest heaving and her eyes wide and fearful. He watched her with a sinking heart, afraid that he'd undone any good that might have come from their earlier lovemaking. Gradually, her breathing slowed and she sank onto her knees in the furs, then she surprised him and crawled into his lap.

"I'm sorry," she whispered, her breath hitching a little as if she'd just run a long distance. "White Bear always took me from behind. Sometimes he'd wake me up by . . ." She shuddered and couldn't say more.

"Do you trust me?" Zach asked, determined to rid her of the ghost of that bastard one brutal memory at a time. At her shaky nod, he said, "Lie down on your stomach."

She stared at him a moment, then did what he asked, her body stiff, her fists clenched at her sides.

"Close your eyes," he said, hating the fear he saw there, determined to rid her of it. He stroked his fingers through her hair, loosening the tangles, then spread it over her back.

Her hands relaxed at her sides.

He rubbed her shoulders, moving slowly down her arms, giving her hands equal attention. Then he shifted to her toes and up to her feet, her calves and thighs and, finally, her firm, beautifully rounded bottom. He couldn't resist finishing off with a nibbling kiss on each full cheek. He didn't think, he just enjoyed the smooth glide of her skin beneath his hands.

She sighed and her lashes fell closed, until he moved her hair off her back. She shoved upward and twisted away from him, but he eased her back with soothing words. He didn't let himself think of the pain she'd suffered or the fact that she'd almost died. Instead, he began kissing the scars, each one sending a stabbing pain through his heart as his lips caressed it. She collapsed on the bed. When he looked up, her lashes were wet.

When he lifted the hair off her scarred ear, she raised up again, protesting, but he pushed her back down, kissed her poor ear and gently covered it.

He sat in the middle of the furs, lifted her into his arms and held her. When tears started leaking from her eyes, he rocked her, certain it was a luxury she'd never allowed herself and fiercely glad to have given it to her.

When she finally calmed, he stroked her hair off her hot face, kissed her flushed, damp cheeks and whispered, "If I could, I'd kiss all of your scars, especially the ones inside, every day for the rest of your life. But since I can't, and since this will be my only chance to show you how much I love you, I'll just have to make love to you again."

"Are you going away?" Caroline asked, looking into his eyes with a puzzled frown and a smile twitching at the corners of her lips. "Can't I come with you?"

Zach stared at her, until comprehension hit him. "No!" he said. "I'm not going anywhere. Not without you, that is." Had she meant what he thought she meant?

She smiled, a glorious, wide, beautiful smile that lit the entire tipi. For a moment, he was certain he heard a flute trilling madly.

"You've changed your mind?" he asked, not trusting his ears. "You have to marry me."

She cocked an eyebrow at him. "That's hardly romantic."

"You will, won't you?" he said, knowing he was babbling, but so thrilled he didn't care. "I don't think I could survive without you. You're my heart, my soul—without you nothing's exciting or interesting, not even Luke and Swallow."

"Can you forgive me, Zach?" She wrapped her arms around his neck and kissed him, then straddled his lap. "I was so afraid, but you've shown me there's nothing left to fear. I love you more than I can say. It fills me so full, it hurts here." She pressed a hand over her left breast. "I didn't dare hope, or believe that anyone would ever want me, let alone someone wonderful, like you.

"I love your heart, your determination, your sense of duty, your eyes, your smile, your dimple . . ." She reached up and shoved his wayward lock of hair off his face. "Even your stubborn hair. I can't bear the thought of another day alone. Please, forgive me for being afraid, for not trusting you?"

"You're forgiven," he said, and kissed her, long and hard and deep. His arms slid from around her waist to band her hips, then he grasped her bottom and squeezed.

"And to prove it . . ." He reached between her legs, stroked her, inserted a finger and made her wet and hungry all over again. When she clutched his shoulders and moaned his name, he positioned her over his straining erection and showed her his sincerity.

Chapter Twenty-five

Morning arrived late the next day. In fact, for Zach and Caroline it didn't truly arrive until the following day. Caroline basked in Zach's love, relishing the opportunity to explore his body and learn more about him in between short naps.

At one very intimate moment, they paused, hearing Feather and Quiet Woman whispering outside the tipi. Later, Caroline followed her nose to the wonderful aromas outside and found a roast rabbit and a basket of biscuits, which Zach used to teach her creative ways to eat and make love at the same time.

She'd never imagined loving a man could be so liberating and invigorating at the same time. Zach made lovemaking fun and so enjoyable that her fears rarely raised their ugly heads. And if they did, he immediately set about replacing the old, bitter memory with a new one filled with joy. She felt like laughing, like running naked through the stream, but most of all she felt like making love. So they did.

By the second day, she agreed with Zach's suggestion that a break would be a good thing, and when she once again heard her friends whispering outside, she was delighted to discover a pot of salve. Thankfully, this one wasn't made of bear fat.

She had just the place for it, and, surprisingly enough, so did Zach.

They emerged from the tipi around noon on the second day, feeling a bit sheepish. Well, she felt sheepish. Zach's self-satisfied grin couldn't be measured. She suggested separating, with her going to let Mr. Lambert know he'd have to find another clerk, and Zach speaking to the preacher, but they agreed that the first thing they needed to do was tell the boys the good news.

They found them with Feather and Quiet Woman, and discovered that they didn't have to say anything. The boys attacked them, buoyant and excited, jumping and hugging and laughing exuberantly. Little Wolf arrived along with Woodenthigh and most of the Cheyenne. During all the back-pounding, teasing and laughter that followed, Zach kept his arm around Caroline, not letting her stray far from his side.

"We go on train now?" Swallow asked, when the first rush of excitement had passed.

"Soon," Zach said. He smiled at Caroline. "First, we're going to make it official."

"You'll be my mother now?" Luke asked, standing quietly before her.

Caroline bent to look into his eyes. "I know I can never replace your real mother, Luke, but I'll do my best."

Luke gave her a fierce hug. "I love you more already."

Caroline returned his hug, blinking back tears. "And I love you."

When she rose, one arm around Luke, the other

around Zach's waist, Little Wolf stood before her. "It is good that you marry this man, forget your past. My heart is glad to see you happy and well." He pressed a fist over his heart and nodded.

Caroline smiled and kissed his cheek, love and gratitude making her eyes tear. "Thank you, Little Wolf, for everything. You saved my life and I will never forget it."

Little Wolf returned her smile and motioned for Quiet Woman to come to him. Feather stepped up on his other side. "My wives are happy that you will live close," he said. He put an arm around Quiet Woman's shoulder. "This one has much advice to give you on how to please your man."

Quiet Woman bobbed her head and started to speak, but Little Wolf hushed her with a look. "But Feather has much knowledge of how to please a man, too, in *quiet* ways."

Caroline laughed with the women, marveling at the trust between them that enabled them to live in harmony with one husband. She glanced at Zach and knew that she'd find it difficult to live with another woman, knowing she'd shared intimate moments with him, too. Her new experiences gave her a deeper understanding of the demands of the Cheyenne lifestyle, and a greater appreciation for her friends.

Finally, she found a quiet moment with Feather and Quiet Woman. "Thank you both for the beautiful tipi, and everything you did to help Zach prepare it for me." Heat swept into her face as she recalled all that had happened within that tipi.

"Do not be shy," Feather said, patting Caroline's hot cheek. "We understand. We have been new wives, too. Though it has been a long time for some of us." She shot a teasing look at Quiet Woman.

"Humph!" Quiet Woman snorted, as always swiftly rising to Feather's bait. "She forgets she is older than me, even if she is second wife."

"Wait!" Caroline cried, interrupting their good-natured banter. "That discussion could take all day and I don't want to be away from my men that long. I came to tell you that you were right. I should have listened to you and not let my fear control me. How can I thank you?"

Quiet Woman stepped close, casting a wary glance at the men milling around. "You can tell us. Is he still . . . what was that word?"

Caroline grinned and leaned down, pulling them both down, too, with an arm around their necks. "Delicious," she whispered. "The man is absolutely yummy."

Quiet Woman and Feather sighed in unison and Quiet Woman murmured, "*Hou!*" All three women popped up as the sweet notes of a flute rang sharply among them.

"Did you hear that?" Caroline asked, glancing between the two women, then around them, but no one nearby held a flute.

Quiet Woman's eyes had gone wide, but Feather smiled. "A happy song. It is good, yes?"

Caroline shrugged, returned to Zach's arms and gave him a short, but meaningful kiss.

Swallow groaned and muttered, "No more kissing!" then, "*umph*," as Luke's elbow dug into his side.

Zach and Caroline were married a week later in a double ceremony—by a preacher and a Cheyenne shaman. The groom wore unrelieved black: boots, pants, shirt, leather vest and hat. The bride wore buckskins, tanned to a pale cream color and supple as the finest silk. Luke dressed in black to match his father, except for a pristine white shirt and bright red bolo tie. Swallow wore buckskins, but sported a new cowboy hat with a large turkey feather. Little Wolf gave the bride away. Feather and Quiet Woman attended the bride and the boys attended the groom. The entire fort attended both the ceremony and the party afterward. By twilight, Zach's hand felt like a well-wrung rag and Caroline's cheeks were beginning to chap. With the help of Woodenthigh and his buddies, they prepared to make their escape on horseback.

Woodenthigh thundered into the fort on Zach's horse, whooping and hollering and exciting the soldiers into reaching for guns on their bare thighs. Hysterical at the sight, he slid off the horse and handed Zach the reins.

Zach picked up Caroline and stepped into the stirrup, lifting her up with him.

"Very smooth, sir," Caroline exclaimed, releasing the breath she'd been holding and the tight grip she'd had on his neck.

"You liked that?" Zach said, leering down at her. "I've got lots more where that came from."

"That's what I'm hoping." Caroline snuggled into his lap as he kneed the horse, and they waved to the crowd. The boys ran alongside for a bit, then returned to Feather and Quiet Woman with their arms slung over each other's shoulders. It had been over a week since she and Zach been together and she was surprised to realize she was hungry for more lovemaking.

"I've got something to show you," Zach said and pulled a folded yellow sheet of paper out of a vest pocket.

"I can't read it in this light," Caroline said, squinting at it and frowning.

"That's okay. I've got it memorized. It's from Josh and it says:

Congratulations on marriage. STOP Knew you would find Luke. STOP Look forward to meeting Caroline next month. STOP Have adopted a son and daughter. STOP Love, Josh"

"Oh, Zach," Caroline said, smiling up at him. "I'm so glad they've adopted. I've been feeling guilty, thinking we might be taking Luke from Josh and Abby."

Zach hugged her. "Me, too. They'll miss Luke, but now they'll have their own children to raise and won't have any regrets."

"I can't wait to meet them and to see your home." She laid her cheek against his chest and hugged his waist. "I'm very close to completely happy."

"Close?" he asked, his voice a deep rumble beneath her ear. She shifted, letting her hip nudge the firm ridge growing beneath her, and smiled when Zach's heartbeat quickened.

"I'll let you know when I get there." She wiggled her bottom and paused as if considering her answer. "There's one more thing I'd like." She reached up and whispered her answer in his ear.

"Hi-yah!" Zach kicked the horse into a gallop and had it tethered beside their tipi—which they hadn't seen for a week—and her in bed, naked, in mere moments.

His clothes seemed a stubborn hindrance to both of them, but in a few more moments, he joined her and when she pushed him onto his back and took control of their lovemaking, she delighted in his agonized groan.

Much later, she turned to him, hair tousled, skin damp from her exertions, feeling dreamy and contented. "Now," she said, and settled her cheek on his shoulder.

"Now?" he echoed, sounding slightly alarmed, but holding her close as they recovered.

"Now, I'm completely happy."

Her heart swelled as she gazed into his clear gray eyes. He brushed the sweat-damp hair off her brow and kissed her. "So am I."

And in the distance, a solitary flute trilled in delight.

Author's Note

The perilous trek of the Northern Cheyenne eventually concluded happily, but Little Wolf's trepidation as he entered Fort Keogh was prophetic. Although Little Wolf and the 114 people who survived were allowed to remain in the Powder River country they loved, it was not until 1900 that the Northern Cheyenne Indian Reservation was confirmed by presidential order. It remains a living testament to the courage and determination of Little Wolf and his people.

Dull Knife eventually joined the Northern Cheyenne at the Powder River, where he died in 1883. Due to the massacre at Camp Robinson, Dull Knife has become more familiar to the general public than his brother, even though his leadership resulted in the deaths of nearly half of the 268 people who originally fled the Darlington Agency, including all but two of his own children.

In February of 1879, seven Northern Cheyenne men from both Little Wolf's and Dull Knife's bands were extradited to Kansas to face charges for the devastation wreaked in Kansas. Finally, in October, due to changes in venue and difficulty obtaining witnesses, the prosecution dropped all charges and no further action was taken.

Among the military, retribution was swift, but not always sure: several military officers found themselves facing a military court, among them Captains Rendlebrock and Wessells. Upon court-martial Capt. Rendlebrock was sentenced to dismissal from the service, though he was due to retire shortly. The sentence was later remitted by President Rutherford B. Hayes.

In all fairness, the actions of the military at the battles of Turkey Springs and at Punished Woman's Fork cannot be compared to the atrocities committed at Camp Robinson under the sanction of Capt. Wessells, particularly the execution of women and children. Public outcry at the news of the Camp Robinson massacre compelled the Army to convene an immediate investigation, wherein it was decided that while the methods applied by Wessells smacked of torture for the purpose of gaining information, dire methods were excusable under the circumstances. Capt. Wessells's military career continued its advance through the Spanish-American War, wherein he earned the Silver Star for bravery as a member of Teddy Roosevelt's "Rough Riders." He retired at the rank of Brigadier General.

Little Wolf lived until 1904. Unfortunately, his later years were not happy ones. He suffered from depression and often sought relief in the white man's whiskey. One day, depressed and inebriated, he shot and killed a fellow Northern Cheyenne, Starving Elk, a man who had been a thorn in his side for many years. Little Wolf exiled himself from his tribe, only returning to council shortly before his death to surrender the sacred Chief's Bundle and name his successor. Due to this event, Little Wolf has not been remembered with respect among the Northern Cheyenne.

Fortunately, before his death Little Wolf developed a close friendship with George B. Grinnell, whose extensive writings on the Northern Cheyenne have kept Little Wolf's story from being forgotten forever. Only lately have the Northern Cheyenne people begun to remember the deeds that made Little Wolf one of their greatest chiefs.